W9-BRB-989
3 6402 10046513 3

MOTH

MOTH

JAMES SALLIS

Carroll & Graf Publishers, Inc.
New York

First Carroll & Graf edition 1993

Carroll & Graf Publishers, Inc.
260 Fifth Avenue
New York, NY 10001

Library of Congress Cataloging-in-Publication Data

Sallis, James, 1944–
Moth / James Sallis. — 1st Carroll & Graf ed.
p. cm.
ISBN 0-88184-945-6 : $18.95
1. Runaway children—Southern States—Fiction. I. Title.
PS3569.A462M6 1993
813′.54—dc20 93-24739
CIP

Manufactured in the United States of America

To the memory of
Chester Himes

Father, the dark moths
Crouch at the sills of the earth, waiting.

—James Wright

1

It was midnight, it was raining.

I scrubbed at the sink as instructed, and went on in. The second set of double doors led into a corridor at the end of which, to the left, a woman sat at a U-shaped desk behind an improvised levee of computers, phones, stacks of paperwork and racks of bound files. She was on the phone, trying simultaneously to talk into it and respond to the youngish man in soiled Nikes and lab coat who stood beside her asking about results of lab tests. Every few moments the phone purred and a new light started blinking on it. The woman herself was not young, forty to fifty, with thinning hair in a teased style out of fashion for at least twenty years. A tag on her yellow polyester jacket read Jo Ellen Heslip. Names are important.

To the right I walked past closetlike rooms filled with steel racks of supplies, an X-ray viewer, satellite pharmacy, long conference tables. Then into the intensive-care nursery, the NICU, itself—like coming out onto a plain. It was half the size of a football field, broken into semidiscrete sections by four-foot tile walls topped with open shelving. (Pods, I'd later learn to call them.) Light flooded in from windows along three walls. The windows were double, sealed: thick outer glass, an enclosed area in which lint and construction debris had settled, inner pane. Pigeons strutted on the sill outside. Down in the street buses slowed at, then passed, a covered stop. Someone in a hospital gown, impossible to say what sex or age, slept therein on a bench advertising Doctor's Bookstore, getting up from time to time to rummage in the trash barrel alongside, pulling out cans with a swallow or two remaining, a bag of Zapp's chips, a smashed carton from Popeye's.

I found Pod 1 by trial and error and made my way through the grid of incubators, open cribs, radiant warmers: terms I'd come to know in weeks ahead. Looking down at pink and blue tags affixed to these containers.

Baby Girl McTell lay in an incubator in a corner beneath the window. The respirator reared up beside her on its pole like a silver sentinel, whispering: *shhhh, shhhh, shhhh.* LED displays wavered and changed on its face. With each *shhhh,* Baby Girl McTell's tiny body puffed up, and a rack of screens mounted above her to the right also updated: readouts of heart rate, respiration and various internal pressures on a Hewlett-Packard monitor, oxygen saturation on a Nellcor pulse oximeter, levels of CO_2 and O_2 from transcutaneous monitors.

Baby Girl McTell
Born 9/15
Weight 1 lb 5 oz
Mother Alouette

I could hold her in the palm of my hand, easily, I thought. Or could have, if not for this battleship of machinery keeping her afloat, keeping her alive.

The nurse at bedside looked up. Papers lay scattered about on the bedside stand. She was copying from them onto another, larger sheet. She was left-handed, her wrist a winglike curve above the pen.

"Good morning. Would you be the father, by any chance?"

Reddish-blond hair cut short. Wearing scrubs, as they all were. Bright green eyes and a British accent like clear, pure water, sending a stab of pain and longing and loss through me as I thought of Vicky: red hair floating above me when I woke with DT's in Touro Infirmary, Vicky with her Scottish *r*'s, Vicky who had helped me retrieve my life and then gone away.

Teresa Hunt, according to her nametag. But did I really look like an eighteen-year-old's romantic other?

Or maybe she meant the *girl*'s father?

I shook my head. "A family friend."

"Well, I had wondered." Words at a level, unaccented. "No one's seen anything of him, as far as I know."

"From what little *I* know, I don't expect you will."

"I see. Well, we are rather accustomed to that, I suppose. Some of the mothers themselves stop coming after a time."

She shuffled papers together and capped her pen, which hung on a cord around her neck. There was print on the side of it: advertising of some sort, drugs probably. Like the notepad Vicky wrote her name and phone number on when I found her at Hotel Dieu.

Tucking everything beneath an oversized clipboard, Teresa Hunt squared it on the stand.

"Look, I'm terribly sorry," she said. "Someone should have explained this to you, but only parents and grandparents are allowed—oh, never mind all that. Bugger the rules. What difference can it possibly make? Is this your first time to see her?"

I nodded.

"And it's the mother you know?"

"Grandmother, really. The baby's mother's mother. We . . . were friends. For a long time."

"I see." She probably did. "And the girl's mother recently died, according to the chart. A stroke, wasn't it?"

"It was."

There was no way I could tell her or anyone else what LaVerne had meant, had been, to me. We were both little more than kids when we met; Verne was a hooker then. Years later she married her doctor and I didn't see her for a while. When he cut her loose, she started as a volunteer at a rape-crisis center and went on to a psychology degree and full-time counseling. It was a lonely life, I guess, at both ends. And when finally she met a guy named Chip Landrieu and married him, even as I began to realize what I had lost, I was happy for her. For both of them.

"Did she know Alouette was pregnant?"

I shook my head. "Their lives had gone separate ways many years back." So separate that I hadn't even known about Alouette. "She—" Say it, Lew. Go ahead and say her name. Names are important. "LaVerne had been trying to get back in touch, to find Alouette."

She looked away for a moment. "What's happened to us?" And in my own head I heard Vicky again, many years ago: What's w*r*ong with this count*r*y, Lew? "Well, never mind all that. Not much we can do about it, is there? Do you understand what's happening here?" Her nod took in the ventilator, monitors, bags of IV medication hanging upside down like transparent bats from silver poles, Baby Girl McTell's impossible ark; perhaps the whole world.

"Not really." Does anyone, I wanted to add.

"Alouette is an habitual drug user. Crack, mainly, according to our H&P and the social worker's notes, but there's a history of drug and alcohol abuse involving many controlled substances, more or less whatever was available, it seems. She makes no attempt to deny this. And because of it, Alouette's baby was profoundly compromised *in utero*. She never developed, and though Alouette did manage to carry her as far as the seventh month, what you're looking at here in the incubator is something more on the order of a five-month embryo. You can see there's almost nothing to her. The eyes are fused, her skin breaks down wherever it's touched, there aren't any lungs to speak of. She's receiving medication which paralyzes her own respiratory efforts, and the machine, the ventilator, does all her breathing. We have her on high pressures and a high rate, and nine hours out of ten we're having to give her hundred-percent oxygen. *Two* hours out of ten, maybe, we're holding our own."

"You're telling me she's going to die."

"I am. Though of course I'm not supposed to."

"Then why are we doing all this?"

"Because we can. Because we know how. There are sixty available beds in this unit. On any given day, six to ten of those beds will be filled with crack babies like Alouette's. At least ten others are just as sick, for whatever reasons—other kinds of drug and alcohol abuse, congenital disease, poor nutrition, lack of prenatal care. The numbers are climbing every day. When I first came here, there'd be, oh, five to ten babies in this unit. Now there're never fewer than thirty. And there've been times we've had to stack cribs in the hallway out there."

"Are you always this blunt?"

"No. No, I'm not, not really. But we look on all this a bit differently in Britain, you understand. And I think that I may be answering something I see in your face, as well."

"Thank you." I held out a hand. She took it without hesitation or deference, as American women seldom can. "My name is Griffin. Lew."

"Teresa, as you can see. And since Hunt is the name on my nursing license, I use it here. But in real life, *away* from here, I mostly use my maiden name, McKinney. If there's ever anything I can do, Mr. Griffin, please let me know. This can be terribly hard on a person."

She removed vials from a drawer beneath the incubator, checked them against her lists, drew up portions into three separate syringes and injected these one at a time, and slowly, into crooks (called heplocks) in Baby Girl McTell's IV tubing. There were four IV sites, swaddled in tape. Almost every day one or another of them had to be restarted elsewhere, in her scalp, behind an ankle, wherever they could find a vein that wouldn't blow.

She dropped the syringes into the mouth of a red plastic Sharps container, pulled a sheet of paper from beneath the clipboard and, glancing at a clock on the wall nearby, made several notations.

"I don't know at all why I'm telling you this, Mr. Griffin, but I had a child myself, a son. He was three months early, weighed almost two pounds and lived just over eight days. I was sixteen at the time. And afterwards, because of an infection, I became quite sterile. But it was because of him that I first began thinking about becoming a nurse."

"Call me Lew. Please."

"I don't think the head nurse would care much for that, if she were to hear about it. She's a bit stuffy and proper, you understand."

"But what can one more rule matter? Since, as you say, we've already started breaking them."

"Yes, well, we have done that truly, haven't we, Lew. Do you think you'd be wanting to speak with one of the doctors? They should be along in just a bit. Or I could try paging one of them."

"Is there anything they can tell me that you can't?"

"Not really, no."

"Then I don't see any reason for bothering them. I'm sure they have plenty to do."

"That they have. Well, I'll just step out for a few minutes and leave the two of you to get acquainted. If you should need anything, Debbie will be watching over my children while I'm gone."

She nodded toward a nurse who sat in a rocking chair across the pod, bottle-feeding one of the babies.

"That's Andrew. He's been with us almost a year now, and we all spoil him just awfully, I'm afraid."

"A year? When will he leave?"

"There's nowhere for him to go. Most of his bowel had to be removed just after birth, and he'll always be needing a lot of care. Feedings every hour, a colostomy to manage. His parents came to see him when the mother was in hospital, but once she was discharged, we stopped hearing from them. The police went out to the address we had for them after a bit, but they were long gone. Eventually I suppose he'll be moved upstairs to pediatrics. And somewhere farther along they'll find a nursing home that will take him, perhaps."

I looked from Andrew back to Baby Girl McTell as Teresa walked away. Names are important. Things are what we call them. By naming, we understand. But what name do we have for a baby who's never quite made it into life, who goes on clawing after it, all the while slipping further away, with a focus, a hunger, we can scarcely imagine? What can we call the battles going on here? And how can we ever understand them?

Through the shelves I watched people gather over an Isolette in the next pod. First the baby's own nurse, then another from the pod; next, when one of them went off to get her, a nurse who appeared to be in charge; finally, moments later, the young man in lab coat and Nikes who'd earlier been standing at the desk in front. Various alarms had begun sounding—buzzers, bells, blats—as the young man looked up at the monitors one last time, reached for a transparent green bag at bedside, and said loudly: "Call it." Overhead, a page started: *Stat to neonatal intensive care, all attendings.* He put a part of the bag over the baby's face and began squeezing it rapidly.

Then I could see no more as workers surrounded the Isolette.

"Sir, I'm afraid I'll have to ask you to step out," Debbie said. She stood and placed Andrew back in his open crib. The child's eyes followed her as she walked away. He didn't cry.

I filed out alongside skittish new fathers, smiling grandparents, a couple of mothers still in hospital gowns and moving slowly, hands pressed flat against their stomachs. An X-ray machine bore down on us through the double doors and lumbered along the hallway, banging walls and scattering linen hampers, trashcans, supply carts. Where's this one? the tech asked. Pod 2, Mrs. Heslip told him.

Most of the others, abuzz with rumor, clustered just outside the doors. Some decided to call it a night and went on to the elevators across the hall, where I knew from experience they'd wait a while. I found stairs at the end of a seemingly deserted hall and went down them (they smelled of stale cigarettes and urine) into the kind of cool, gentle rain we rarely see back in New Orleans. There, when it comes, it comes hard and fast, making sidewalks steam, beating down banana trees and shucking leaves off magnolias, pouring over the edges of roofs and out of gutters that can't handle the sudden deluge.

I turned up the collar of my old tan sportcoat as I stepped out of the hospital doorway just in time to get splashed by a pickup that swerved toward the puddle when it saw me. I heard cackling laughter from inside.

Earlier I had noticed a small café on the corner a few blocks over.

Nick's, Rick's, something like that, the whole front of it plate glass, with handwritten ads for specials taped to the glass and an old-style diner's counter. I decided to give it a try and headed that way. Moving through the streets of the rural South I'd fled a long time ago. Bessie Smith had died not too far from here, over around Clarksdale, when the white hospital wouldn't treat her following a car accident and she bled to death on the way to the colored one.

At age sixteen, I had fled. Fled my father's docility and sudden rages, fled old black men saying "mister" to ten-year-old white kids, fled the fields and the tire factory pouring thick black smoke out onto the whole town like a syrup, fled all those faces gouged out and baked hard and dry like the land itself. I had gone to the city, to New Orleans, and made a life of my own, not a life I was especially proud of, but mine nonetheless, and I'd always avoided going back. I'd avoided a lot of things. And now they were all waiting for me.

2

A few weeks before that, at nine in the morning, I'd just finished putting a friend's son on the bus to send him home. He'd kind of got himself lost in New Orleans, and I'd kind of found him, and I think finally we were all kind of glad, parent, child and myself, that I could still do the work. It was a beautiful morning, unseasonably cool, and I decided to walk home. So I left the Greyhound Terminal and started up Simon Bolivar, with downtown New Orleans (what they're now calling the CBD, for Central Business District) looming at my back like so many cliffs.

I never have figured out just how a street in this part of the city got named for a South American liberator, but that's New Orleans. Some of the streets down here actually have double signs, a regular-size one and a smaller one riding piggyback, with different names. Further up, where it becomes La Salle, Simon Bolivar has one of those.

I walked past the projects. Newer ones of slab and plastic looking like cheap college dorms from the fifties, older brick-and-cement ones like World War II institutional housing, most of them with sagging porches, window frames and entryways, air conditioners propped on long boards, spray-painted lovers' names or exhortations to *Try Jesus* on the walls. Then, crossing Martin Luther King, I passed the old Leidenheimer Bakery and a lengthy stretch of weathered Creole cottages and doubles, storefront churches, windowless corner foodstores. Every couple of blocks there were clusters of chairs and crates beneath trees on the neutral ground where the community's social life is carried on. Lots of boarded-up buildings with signs on them. *Do Not Enter, No Admittance, Property Pelican Management.* There were even signs on the Dumpsters outside the projects: *Prop. of HANO.* Signs on everything. The ones we read, and the ones we just know are there. We learn.

I went on up to Louisiana, turned left, looked in the window at Brown Sugar Records and across at the Sandpiper's sign over the door, a two-foot-high martini glass complete with stirrer and olive and a rainbow arcing into the glass. It's supposed to be lit up, of course, probably all greens and blues, but the lights haven't worked in twenty years at least. These great old signs still turn up all over the city. Things are slow to change here, or don't change at all.

I went on across St. Charles to Prytania, stopped at the Bluebird for coffee, and stepped through my front door just as the rain began. First a few scattered drops—then a downpour so hard you could see and hear little else.

Fifteen minutes later, the sun was struggling back out.

I poured an Abita into an oversized glass and settled down by the window to look over notes on Camus and Claude Simon. It was my semester to teach Modern French Novel, something that rotated "irregularly" among our three full-time professors (who got benefits) and four part-time instructors (no benefits: administration would be ecstatic if *everyone* were part-time), and it had been a while. My last couple of books had done well, and I hadn't been teaching much. But then I started missing it. Also, I couldn't seem to get started on a new book. I'd begun two or three, but they kept sounding more like me—*my* ideas, the way *I* see things—than like whatever character I supposedly was writing about.

Aujourd'hui, maman est morte.

That great opening line of the novel I probably admire more than any other I've read. And I thought again how much blunter, how much more matter-of-fact and drained of passion the phrase is in French than it ever could be in our own language. How well it introduces this voice without past or future, without history or anticipation, with only a kind of eternal, changeless present; how Meursault, and finally the novel itself, becomes a witness upon whom only detail (sunlight, sand, random clusters of events) registers. Telling in the calmest way possible this astonishing story of a man sentenced to death because he failed to cry at his mother's funeral.

I remembered, as I always did now, reading this, the telegrams Mother had sent, one before, one after, when my father was dying.

Afloat in reverie, I'd been distractedly watching a man make his way over the buckling sidewalk beneath an ancient oak tree opposite, and when now he turned to cross the street, I took notice.

Moments later, my doorbell chirred.

In the stories, Sherlock Holmes is forever watching people approach (and often hesitate) in the street below, and by the time they're at the door ringing for Mrs. Hudson he has already deduced from carriage, dress and general appearance just who they are and pretty much why they've come.

I, on the other hand, had absolutely no idea why this man was here.

"Mr. Griffin," he said when I opened the door. Still wearing, or wearing again, the suit he'd had on last week. It hadn't looked too good then. The tie was gone, though. "I hope I'm not interrupting anything, and I apologize for coming into your home like this. I'm—"

"I know who you are."

At his look of surprise, I said: "Hey. I'm a detective."

"Oh." As if that, indeed, explained it.

"And of course, as a writer, an inveterate snoop as well."

That was true enough. Sometimes sitting in restaurants or bars I'd become so engrossed in eavesdropping that I'd completely lose track of what my companion was saying. LaVerne had always just sat quietly, waiting for me to come back.

"Oh." A perfunctory smile.

"Actually, I saw you two out together a few times. The Camellia, Commander's, like that." Only a partial lie.

"Then you should've come over, said hello."

I shook my head.

"I know what she meant to you, Griffin. What you meant to one another."

He didn't. But he was a hell of a man for coming here to tell me that.

"You want a drink? Coffee or something?"

"Whatever you're having."

"Well, I tell you. What I've been having is this fine beer made out of hominy grits or somesuch right here in Governor Edwards's own state. But what I'd really like is a cup of *café au lait.* One so muddy and dark you think there've got to be catfish down in there somewhere. You in a hurry?"

"Not really."

"Then I'll make us a pot. What the hell."

He followed me out to the kitchen, staring with fascination at shelves of canned food and two-year-old coupons stuck under magnets on the refrigerator door, rifling the pages of surreptitious cookbooks, fingering the unholy contents of a spice rack.

"I don't know why I'm here," he told me when the coffee was ready and we were back by the window, he in a beat-up old wingback, me in my usual white wood rocker. "I mean, I *know;* but I don't know how to *tell* you."

He sipped coffee. From his expression it was, in miniature, everything he had hoped for from life.

"You and LaVerne, you were together a long time."

He looked at me. After a moment I nodded.

"We weren't." He looked down. I thought of a Sonny Boy Williamson song: *Been gone so long, the carpet's half faded on the floor.* Or possibly it was *carpets have faded*—hard to tell. Though mine were hardwood. "What I mean is," he said.

And we sat there.

"Yeah," I said finally. I got up and put on more milk to heat, poured us both refills when it was steaming, settled back. My rocker creaked on the floorboards.

"I don't know," he said. "We got together pretty far along in life. I sure didn't think there was anyone like LaVerne out there for me, not anymore. All that stuff about candlelight and the perfect mate and little bells going off, that's what you believe when you're nineteen or twenty maybe, some of us anyway. Then you get a few years on you and you realize that's not the way the world is at all, that's just not how it goes about its business. But still, one day there she was."

He looked up at me and his eyes were unguarded, open. "I hardly knew her, Lew. Less than a year. I loved her so much. Sure, I know an awful lot's gone under the bridge, for both of us, but I still think we'll have some time, you know? Then one day I look around and she just isn't there anymore. Like I'm halfway into this terribly important sentence I've waited a long time to say and I suddenly realize no one is listening. I don't know. Maybe I've been hoping somehow I'd be able to see LaVerne through your eyes, have more time with her, find out more about her, that way. Stupid, right?"

"No. Not stupid at all. That's what people are all about. That's something we can do for one another. We always get together to bury our dead. And then to bring them back, to remember what their lives were like, afterwards. Though Verne's life wasn't one either you or I can easily know or imagine."

He nodded.

"Good. You have to know that before you can know anything else. But I just don't see what you want me to tell you. That she loved you? She must have, and you must know it. That it's terrible how she was taken from you? Hell, of course it is, man. Join the fucking club."

"You think—" he started, then took another draw of coffee. "I'm sorry. I haven't made myself at all clear. I didn't come here for assurances, however much I could use them just now. And yes, I know LaVerne loved me." He looked up from his cup. "Just as she did you, Lew."

Something grabbed my throat and wouldn't let go. I swallowed coffee. It didn't help much.

"There have to be a lot of reasons why I came here. Maybe there'll be a time to sort them all out later. But primarily I came here to hire you."

"Hire me?" I said. It sounded more like *hrm*.

"I need a detective, Lew. A good one."

"I don't do that anymore. Hell, I never did it very much. I sat in bars and drank, and eventually guys I was looking for would stumble by and trip over my feet. I'm a teacher now."

"And a writer."

"Yeah, well, that too. Once you've lost your pride, it gets easier, you know: you'll do almost any damned thing. You start off small, a piece for the local paper, or maybe this tiny little story about growing up, something like that. That's how they hook you. Then before you know it, you're writing a series for them."

"Yeah. Yeah, LaVerne told me a thing or two about your pride."

"Which in my particular case went *after* a fall."

"And I read your books, Lew. All of them."

"Then you must be one hell of a man for sure. Don't know if *I* could do it."

"Yeah," he said, placing cup and saucer on the floor beside him and waving off my tacit offer of more. Some people still know how to let a good thing be. "You wanta stop pushing me away here, Lew? 'S'not much about this whole thing that's funny. You know?"

I shook my head. Not disputing him: agreeing. The invisible something eased off on my throat and went back to its dark corner.

"I'm listening," I said.

"Good." He took a cream-colored envelope out of his inside breast pocket and held it, edge-down like a blade, against one thigh. "You know anything about LaVerne having a kid?"

"She never had any. Always told me she couldn't."

"Not only could, it seems, but also did. Back when she was married to Horace Guidry—"

"Her doctor."

He nodded. "Went on fertility drugs or something, I guess, when he kept insisting. Then when they split, I guess he got full custody, no visitation. Even a restraining order."

"In consideration of the respondent's unwholesome past, no doubt."

"And of the petitioner's large sums of money and standing in the community, right. You got it."

"Why would she never have said anything?"

"I asked her that once, when she first told me. She couldn't say. But I think maybe it was kind of like she shut that door completely—like she had to, just to keep on getting by. Know what I mean?"

I did. I also knew that winds have a way of coming out of nowhere and blowing those doors open again.

We sat there silently a moment and he said, "Yeah, I guess we don't ever know anybody as well as we think we do, huh?"

"I'm beginning to think we don't ever know anyone at all."

"Yeah. Well anyway, we're sitting in Burger King one night, we'd been together seven or eight months by then, and LaVerne looks across at me between bites and she says: I've got a kid, you know. Talk about getting hit by a semi. And she proceeds to tell me all about it, right there and then, with these teenage kids blowing wrappers off straws at each other in the next booth. So what you think I should do about it? she asks me afterward. What you wanta do? I say. And she goes: I think maybe I have to try and talk to her, Chip. I think I want my daughter to know who her mother was. Cause of course she'd be like eighteen now, able to make her own decisions about things like this. And the stuff LaVerne saw every day at that shelter she was working at, it had to make her think about all that. Parents and children, husbands and wives, all the things they can do to one another. About being all alone, too."

"You find her?"

"We started looking. Retained a lawyer to contact the father—"

"Anything there?"

"Damn little. Lots of fast footwork from *his* lawyers. Including, as I understand it, a brief admonitory call from a judge."

"I take it, then, that the girl—what's her name?"

"Alouette. We're not sure what last name she's using."

"I take it she's not with the father. With Guidry."

"Apparently not for some time. And short of a court order, which wasn't about to happen, that's pretty much all we could get out of the good doctor's lawyers. Then finally our own lawyer suggested we might want to get in touch with a PI out in Metairie, a guy who specializes in finding people—"

"Who was that?"

"A. C. Boudleaux."

"Achille. I know him. He come up with anything? If he didn't, you might as well hang it on the line, 'cause nobody else will either. He's good."

"Here's his report." He handed over the envelope. "It's not much, but he was only on it for a couple weeks. Then LaVerne. . . . Well, you know what happened. And that kind of ate up most of the money I had left. Don't ever let anybody tell you medical insurance is good for shit, cause it ain't, not when the time comes you need it. Besides, nothing else much seemed to matter then but her. Not that I could really do anything for her."

"So now you're trying to do exactly that."

"Do something for her, you mean. Yeah. I guess. What the hell else is there? If it's money you're thinking about, how I'm gonna pay you, don't worry. I'll get it. I always manage."

I'd been looking through the contents of the envelope as he spoke. There wasn't much, but it proved enough to wash this reluctant Sinbad up, days later, on the foreign shores of the Mississippi. Nigger Lew looking around, and no raft or Huck anywhere in sight.

"I don't want your money," I told him.

"What, then?"

"How about a sandwich and a beer or two, for a start. On me."

"You drive a hard bargain, Griffin."

"Okay, I'm flexible. *You* buy."

3

The novel's true protagonist, I tell my students, is always time. With the years, it's gotten somewhat easier to say things like that without immediately looking over my shoulder or down at the floor. And *then,* of course, you go on and talk about the flow of time in Proust, about Faulkner's sequestrations of history, about the abrogation of time *and* history in Beckett.

So by commodious vicus (you all know the tune: feel free to sing along) we arrive now at a point one week before Chip Landrieu showed up like an orphan at my doorstep, this being *three* weeks before I stood watching someone repast on chips and cola from a trashcan in Mississippi.

Everybody with me so far?

Nine in the morning, then. I was sitting in that same white rocker with a bottle of Courvoisier on the floor alongside and an espresso cup in hand. I'd gone from beer to scotch to the strongest thing I had. I hadn't been able to find anything like a proper glass but figured the cup would do.

Some people have aquariums, into which they stare for hours. Here in New Orleans, we have patios. And in those patios, likely as not, we have banana trees. Lots of banana trees if we're not careful, because they grow almost while you watch. The parts you see are shoots off the real tree underground, and there's not much to them: just an awful lot of water bound in honeycombs of thin tissue, topped by enormous leaves the wind shreds to green fringe. They'll go down with a single hard swipe from a machete (looking in cross section much like celery stalks), but a week later there'll be two more already shooting up, two or three feet high.

Squirrels here seem virtually to live off these trees. They hang upside down like bats (or, for that matter, like the fruit itself) and dine from bunches of ripe bananas; then when those are gone, smaller, green ones; and finally the bright red blooms. Littering the patio floor with a continuous fall of shredded banana, peel, leaf, bloom. The squirrels are scrawny gray ones with tattered, sketchy tails, not at all like the plume-tailed red squirrels of my Arkansas childhood.

Life's not anything here if it's not adaptable. And relentless. A year or so after I first came to New Orleans, I took a snapshot of the old camelback shotgun on Dryades where I was living with four or five other guys and a couple of families, and was surprised to see how green everything was. Not just trees and grass, but wooden stairs, the edges of beveled glass in doors and windows, cracks in painted walls, balcony railings, sidewalks where air conditioners dripped—as though a fine film of green had settled over the entire world. And I had gotten so used to it that I didn't see it anymore, until that snapshot saw it again for me.

I was still sitting there sipping Courvoisier, thinking about life's adaptability and musing further upon the fact that "seeing again" is finally what art's all about, when my doorbell chirred. Almost before it stopped, there was a pounding at the door. And then before I could get to it, the door opened.

"Lock your fucking door, Lew," Walsh said, closing it behind him. "Where the hell you think you live?"

I sat back down. "Don't you have criminals you ought to be out there catching or something?"

"They'll still be there. Always have been. So's the goddamn paperwork. You got any coffee?"

"I can make you some."

"Don't bother. Probably had too much already."

He went out to the kitchen for a Diet Coke, came back and sank into the wingback's tired embrace, looking for a hard moment at the bottle on the floor, the cup in my hand.

"Goddamn it, Lew, what the fuck are you doing here, anyway? You oughta be at the church already. You got people up there waiting for you. You just sitting here getting drunk, that it? Business as usual?"

"Nope. He's definitely not getting drunk, Don old friend. Not that he hasn't tried. Valiantly."

"So, what then? You're just gonna pretend it didn't happen? You gonna just blow off the whole thing, after all she meant to you? And after all the crap she put up with from you for all those years? Cause you didn't give her shit when she was alive, man, you know? You know that, I know you do. And it's damn little enough you can do now."

He leaned back, breathed deeply. Held up his empty can in a mock *salut*. "I'm sorry. I coulda said that better, I guess. Most things I could, these days."

"You scored the point, Don. It's okay."

He shook his head, looked out to the patio. "I don't know, Lew. Ever since Josie and the girls left, everything looks different. I don't know; I'm one hell of a guy to be giving advice. But sometimes it seems to me like you spend half your life doing everything you can to avoid things and the rest trying to make up for it. I have trouble understanding that. Always have."

"So you got another point to make?"

"Well, I got this point that you better get up off your butt and haul that same sorry thing on over to Verne's goddamn funeral. That's the only other point I got. For now, anyway."

"I'm not going, Don. I can't."

"Lew." He sat back again, exhaled deeply. "Listen to me. I swear it, Lew: you're going. If I have to get a squad down here and have 'em help me drag you into that church, you're going. You hear what I'm telling you?"

"Such devotion and friendship's a rare thing."

"Yeah, Lew, it is. It sure as hell is. But what the fuck would you know about that?"

I looked at him then and felt tears force their way out onto my face.

Stones in my passway, as Robert Johnson said. And my road seem dark as night.

Surely the funeral could not have been conducted in silence—surely (to whatever recondite end) I've invented this—but in memory that is how I always see it: several dozen people sitting straight as fences on the hardwood pews, not a sound anywhere, even traffic sounds from outside curiously hushed and transformed as though broadcast from somewhere else, from another world or time, and people moving, when at last they began to do so, as though that silence were substantial, something that resisted, something they had to push through, slowing and drawing out their movements. As though we all had slipped unaware into some timeless deep.

I remembered James Baldwin's funeral a few years back. The solemn slow progress of cross and chasuble, and then, breaking over it, tearing that long European sentence apart, the sudden leap and skitter of African drums.

And that was just how the world came back, sudden, staccato, as Don and I stood on the steps outside the church.

"Where can I drop you, Lew?"

"I think I'll walk back. Maybe swing by the school."

"C'mon. It's five, six miles at least."

"I'll be fine, Don."

"No you won't. You haven't been fine more than ten minutes in all the years I've known you. But if you're saying you'll get through this, yeah, I guess you will. You always do. Take care, friend. Buy you dinner some night?"

"Sounds good. I'll call you."

"No you won't, Lew. You'll mean to, but you won't do it. And then eventually I'll just come on over there and pry you out of the house and haul you off somewhere. Just like always."

He started away, shaking his head.

"Don . . ."

"Yeah?" Turning back. I had never noticed before this just how deeply the web of fine lines had sunk everywhere into his face, or that flesh now hung slack beneath chin and cheekbones. Even his eyes had a grayish cast to them.

"Thanks."

"Hey, don't embarrass me in front of Verne's friends. I hate it when you get all teary-eyed, I ever tell you that?"

"I mean it."

"Yeah. I know you do. I know that."

"You hear much from Josie?"

"Not so long as the checks keep coming. Shit, I don't mean that. She sends me pictures of the kids every few months. She's real good about doing that."

"She still loves you, Don."

"Yeah. Well. Guess I better go shut down a few crack houses, huh? Got a few hours left in the day. You sure you don't want a ride?"

"I'm sure."

He climbed into the Regal, his own, that he'd been driving at least ten years, waved to me in the rearview and hauled it into a lumbering U back toward downtown. The department kept offering him new official cars and he kept telling them his was fine, he was used to it.

I walked down State to Freret and turned right. Kids on bicycles heading to and from classes at Tulane or Loyola shot past me. I hadn't had a car since Vicky left. At first I'd planned to buy one, but I kept putting it off for one reason or another, and after a while it just stopped being important. I'd got used to walking and liked it, and if I had to get somewhere I couldn't walk, well, cabs in New Orleans are plentiful as roaches.

I crossed Napoleon and, one street over, turned onto General Pershing. Blackjack Pershing, they called him. Most of his mounted troops were "buffalo soldiers." Black men. They performed so well that Pershing suggested only blacks should be taken into the armed services. Except for officers, of course.

Squirrels ran along power lines with blue jays screaming and swooping about them. It was garbage pickup day for this part of town; emptied plastic bins sat inverted or on their sides before most houses. This stretch was pure New Orleans, a jumble of wrought iron, balconies, leaded glass, gingerbread, Corinthian columns. Grand old homes well preserved, decaying ones once every bit as grand and now carved into multiple dwellings, simple raised cottages and bungalows.

I walked along thinking hard about Verne, and about something I'd read in an art journal, unable to sleep, at two or three that morning. The lives we lead, it said, the art or artifacts we produce, all these are but scrims, one layer over countless other layers, some that reveal, some that conceal.

Twenty-six years ago I killed a man. I was playing detective in those days, and I was pretty crazy back then too, so I guess I must have been trying on some half-imagined role as avenging angel. Like other roles I've tried, before and since, it didn't fit.

The thing is, I rarely think about it. Though from time to time, walking these shabby streets (especially at night, it seems), I'll glance into a stranger's face and something there, in his eye, takes me back. Dostoevski said that we're all guilty of everything. And while I never could bring myself to accept Christian notions of sin and atonement, there's definitely something to karma. The things we do pile up on us, weigh us down. Or hold us in place, at very least.

4

I tried to call Boudleaux after reading through the report, but his machine told me he was in Lafayette on business and would be away "indeterminately." I could have tried motels up there, but he was almost certainly staying with family. And that spread it pretty thin, since one way or another he seemed to be related to just about everyone in Lafayette *and* Evangeline parishes.

Six months old now, the report was, like all his reports, thorough, concise and poorly spelled, typed on a Royal portable he'd had since college and to every appearance never once cleaned in all that time, *e*'s and *o*'s indistinguishable, *a*'s little blobs of ink atop frail curved spines. And valuable, like most documents, as much for what it did not say as for what it did.

The map is not the territory. The limits of your language are the limits of your world. Catchphrases from the fifties and from circa 1921.

Apparently Alouette, as Boudleaux discovered (hard upon stone-walling from Guidry and a pride of lawyers, and a call from that same judge, who casually inquired concerning the status of his PI license), had not been in her father's home for some time.

Early spring of last year, one of her teachers, Mr. Sacher, homeroom and American history, began reporting her as nonattendant. Per procedure, he notified his supervisor and principal and attempted, on his own, to reach Alouette or her parents at the phone number listed in school files. Repeatedly, there was no answer at this number. Nor does any record of administrative response exist, though the principal is certain that he and Mr. Sacher "discussed the matter."

Parents were listed in Alouette's file as Horace and L. Guidry, and above *Occupation* (the forms were filled out by the students themselves) was entered *Fuzzician.* Sacher checked the phone book and found no home number (assuming it was unlisted) but in the yellow pages a *Horace Guidry, Internist,* with offices in the Touro area. When he called and finally talked his way past the receptionist and a nurse, Dr. Guidry listened a moment and told him he would have to get back to him. And when, later that afternoon, he did, it was by way of a conference call, their two phones looped into an intercom phone at the downtown offices of Bordelon, Bordelon and Schmidt.

Stating his concern, Sacher was informed by one of the lawyers that Alouette had upon her own volition and without notice, some weeks previously, departed her father's board and care. Her present whereabouts were unknown, though efforts were still under way to locate her.

Had there been family difficulties? Sacher asked. Was Alouette under any unusual pressures?

You are her teacher, am I correct? a third voice inquired. And upon Sacher's assent, went on: Then I'm afraid I see no compelling or appropriate reason for us to answer such inquiry.

Boudleaux had found his way to Mr. Sacher within three hours of being engaged by Chip Landrieu. As it happened, he had a couple of cousins who worked in the mailroom at Bordelon, Bordelon and Schmidt. And so, not long after closing that same day, a Friday, Boudleaux knew what there was in B, B&S's file concerning Alouette. Which wasn't much.

Following a couple of practice runs, absences of two or three days the first time, then several weeks, from both of which she returned properly sorrowful and acquiescent, one Tuesday morning she headed off to school and to all appearances fell through a rabbit hole. Police were properly notified. Friends interviewed. Malls, clubs and other teenage water holes scouted. All to no avail.

The Guidrys had themselves engaged a local agency, South-East Investigations, to conduct a search for the girl. Clyde South and Michelle East were married, and Boudleaux knew them both. They were running into stone walls too.

To his report Boudleaux had appended a list of others he'd interviewed and (before being taken off the case) planned to.

On second or third reading, one of the attributions caught my eye. *Counselor,* it gave as occupation, then: *Foucher Women's Shelter.* Where Verne had been working the last few years. The name above was *Juan Garces.*

I called to be sure he was in, then walked over to Tchoupitoulas and grabbed a White Fleet cab. An elderly woman behind a minuscule desk in the lobby (it had once been the foyer where residents had mailboxes, and I hope there weren't too many of them) directed me upstairs.

He was sitting before a computer monitor and swiveled partway around, hands staying on the keys, when, in the absence of a door, I knocked at the frame. He swung back to the keyboard, hit Save and Exit, came all the way back and got up. We shook hands.

"Sorry," he said. "But you have to do what they want you to. You must be Mr. Griffin." He waved me into a chair.

Uneven stacks of folders and stapled papers all but covered the table space around keyboard and computer. To the right at shoulder level, beside a narrow window, a plastic board was lined with yellow Post-It notes in a tiny blue script. Garces reached over and peeled off the top one, dropped it into the trashcan under the desk. The other wall was taken over, above, by a reproduction of Matisse's *Blue Frog/ Yellow Nude* (or is it the other way around? I can never remember) and, below, by a shelf of books running to Robert Pirsig, Genet,

Laing and Szasz. I took note of Delany's *Dhalgren* and *The Motion of Light in Water.*

Garces was fair-skinned with light blue eyes, and somehow gave the impression of being short and gangly at the same time. His dark hair was close-cropped. He wore a black T-shirt, pressed slacks, a linen sportcoat with the sleeves turned up a couple of times, cordovan loafers without socks. Fortyish.

"So what is it that I can help you with, Mr. Griffin? Something to do with a friend, you said on the phone."

"LaVerne Landrieu."

"Of course," he said after a moment. "You're Lewis: *that* Griffin. I didn't connect, when you gave me your name earlier. I'm sorry, Mr. Griffin—"

"Lew."

"Lew. It's a loss to us all, you know. She made a difference in a lot of lives around here. But you must know that."

"No. I don't."

"Oh. But whenever she spoke of you . . . You two haven't been in touch, then?"

I shook my head.

"I'm sorry. I didn't know. Do you mind my asking if there was any particular reason for that?"

"What I keep telling myself is that I didn't think her marriage needed ghosts like me showing up on the stairs."

"Did you meet Chip Landrieu?"

"Afterwards, yes."

He nodded. "Things so often happen in the wrong order in our lives."

"How well did you know Verne, Mr. Garces?"

"Richard."

I pointed inquiringly back toward the doorframe, the name plaque beside it.

"No one outside my family ever calls me Juan. And no one, period, calls me Mr. Garces. But I'm afraid I don't understand."

"I mean, did the two of you ever talk? About personal things."

He shook his head. "I'm sorry. Once I found out who you were, I naturally assumed . . . We really should start this whole encounter again from scratch, I think. I assumed you knew LaVerne and I were close. That this was why you came here."

The phone buzzed. He excused himself, picked it up, listened for a moment, then responded in Spanish that was far too rapid for me to follow. He hung up and penned a note that he added to the board.

"Over the years LaVerne and I became good friends, yes. It happened slowly, very slowly, and without either of us planning or even expecting it. People have always come to me to talk, that's kind of how I got into all this. But that's as far as it ever goes. And LaVerne was one to keep her distance; you knew that when you first talked to her. We were both private people. Never mixed much socially with those we work with. Try to keep it professional."

"But you and Verne. . . ."

"Yeah, and it was funny. *I'd* always been the one to listen. But after a while—we'd go out for coffee after work, or sometimes later on we'd meet for breakfast in the morning—I found myself babbling on and on about *my* problems, *my* previous or current live-in. Or my relationship with my parents, for God's sake. That had never happened before, and I've been doing this work for a long time. Then one morning when the plates have been cleared and we're sitting there over a final cup of coffee she says to me: I want to tell you about my life, I want someone to know all this."

"People here didn't know?"

"What they knew was that this woman had paid her dues at one of the country's toughest rape centers, and then on her own she had gone back to school and got a degree in psychology and now here she was, twelve or fourteen hours a day sometimes. That's all they had to know."

He looked briefly out the window. A jay screamed as it swept across the pane and out of sight.

"I listen, sometimes all day and part of the night, to people's problems. I know what it's like out there, and how little I can do. One of my clients, last month her boyfriend fucked their year-old daughter and then slammed her headfirst against the wall 'so she wouldn't tell.' I've got pregnant mothers trying to live out of Dumpsters and a shopping cart. And husbands or parents swooping in all the time with their lawyers and threats trying to take my clients' kids away, always with this same attitude, like if I just'll listen to them, I'll know what's right. I don't know what's right, Lew."

He looked back at me. "I'm sorry. A little off track there. But there are days, and this is one of them, when I have to wonder what my place really is in all this."

"I understand."

"Yeah. You pretty much lived it, LaVerne said."

"Not anymore."

"Well. Maybe not. Not on the surface, anyway."

I thought of a review of my third novel, published in a small magazine specializing in mysteries. I've had dozens of bad reviews, most of them justified, I'm sure, but that was the only one I ever felt unfair. Cadging personal details from my publisher and a common acquaintance, the reviewer proceeded to ignore my novel and instead to review me, claiming that *Black Hornet* was nothing more than a record, a document, of my personal failures.

Maybe that reviewer was right. And maybe Richard Garces was right, too. Who knows what evil . . . ? Well, the Shadow do. Or he be sposed to, at any rate.

"Over the next months," Garces went on, "LaVerne told me what I guess must be her whole life story. Even for me, I have to say, it was something of a revelation. And then, to think that she could come through all that and arrive where she did."

"She was rather an amazing woman."

"I don't think any of us ever quite realized *how* amazing."

"We don't, usually. Not till afterwards. Things happening in the wrong order, like you say."

"Yeah." We were both quiet a moment. "She told me one night how she waited for you for over two hours outside, what was it, a bus station? Your friend from Paris—"

"Vicky."

"—had just gotten on the plane to go back, and I guess this was a little after LaVerne and Guidry split up, when she'd already been working rape-crisis for a while. You hadn't seen each other, I guess, for a long time by then, and she went down there without any idea what to expect, how you'd react. Or even how she felt about it all herself."

" 'Whatever works. You wait and see.' "

"Right. And she told me that that was maybe the hardest thing she'd ever done in her life. That she'd never been more afraid than she was that night, and the next few days. I don't know. But that story has really stayed with me. Whenever I think about making decisions, really hard ones, I still think about that."

"She ever talk much about when she and Guidry were together?"

He shook his head. "That whole period was kind of walled off. She did once tell me that the whole time she was married to Dr. Guidry she felt she was masked, as for Mardi Gras, and that no one would ever be able to see who she really was, however closely they looked. I remember thinking it was something like the way people remember war experiences: these brief, incredibly concentrated periods of time that become central to their lives and all-consuming, but then that time's gone and the experiences are essentially meaningless in the everyday practical world around them, and they let them go. Except in a way I guess LaVerne was talking about a period of peace, surrounded by war."

"You sure of that?"

"Which part?"

"The peace part."

"You mean, was the period as tranquil as it appeared?"

"Right."

"Few periods are, really—even after our memory's got to work on them. But I more or less felt she wanted somehow to preserve that time, keep it apart. Pure, in a manner of speaking."

"Maybe so. But she and Guidry split, not at all too peacefully from what little I know. So what happened? Did they get along? Were there problems between them, even early on?"

Garces shrugged. "The book's closed."

"So maybe we'll have to go see the movie."

I stood and thanked him for his time and help. Then in a time-honored tradition stretching back from Columbo at least to Porfiry

Petrovich, I thought of one more thing. "So why do you think LaVerne wouldn't talk about that period with you, when she talked about everything else?"

"I really don't know any more than I've told you."

"Was there something different about it? Not just that she was chasing the American Dream and it almost caught her. But something—I don't know—traumatic, maybe?"

He hesitated, but when he glanced at me then, we both knew.

"You mean her daughter."

I nodded. He exhaled.

"I'm sorry, I wasn't trying to mislead you. Hell, of course I was; nothing else I can call it. But LaVerne had told me you didn't know about Alouette. She didn't talk about her very much herself. I guess things hadn't gone well for a long time."

"And then they didn't go at all."

"Yeah, that's pretty much it."

"Did you know LaVerne had tried to get in touch with her daughter? To see her?"

"No, she never told me that. I know there were court orders involved, at one time. Those would no longer apply, of course. But LaVerne always said she wouldn't contact her daughter, that it would be easier on Alouette that way."

"She changed her mind. You know anything about what the problems might have been between Verne and the good doctor?"

"No, I'm sorry. Though I'm not certain I'd tell you even if I did. If I thought I did, that is. There's a kind of professional reflex at work here."

I thanked him again. I'd got almost out the door when he said behind me: "You're trying to find Alouette, is that it?"

I turned back. "Chip Landrieu asked me to. I figure it's little enough."

"Yeah. Well, I could probably help you with that."

5

One of the first things I fell in love with in New Orleans was its cemeteries. The house I lived in on Dryades when I first came here had one nearby, a block of gravesites smack in the middle of street after street of houses and apartments, with a low brick wall and, just beyond, a border of the tiers of vaults here called ovens—all of it white and dazzling in the sunlight. There was at the same time such gravity and such lightness to it; and ever since, when things crowd too closely in upon me, I tend to head to the cemeteries for a strange solace I find nowhere else.

The largest (though really it's a blur of many smaller, distinct ones) is at Canal and City Park, a wilderness of tombs stretching far into the distance, a sprawling city of the dead. Many older crypts have sunk almost completely into the ground. And above them, as though reaching for sky, loom thickets of crosses, angels, statues large and small, figures of women shrouded in grief.

The oldest is on Basin Street, St. Louis Cemetery No. 1, at what was long ago the edge of town and later the edge of Storyville. Marie Laveau, Paul Morphy and the city's first mayor dwell there now. Occupying but a single square block, it's pure chaos: a riot of twisted pathways that end as often as not in cul-de-sacs. Tombs sit askew, at every conceivable angle and tilt, the lower corners of many of them wrenched free of the ground.

My personal favorite is on Washington. It fills two or three blocks in a well-decayed part of town, chockful of gravesites in a bewildering jumble of styles, size and age, cut through by narrow, corridor-like paths, yet in its own way rigidly symmetrical: disorder's cur brought to heel. Whenever I'm down that way, I make a point of going by.

Which I did that afternoon on the way home, wandering its pathways for half an hour or more, reading off names at random. Intimate stories began unfurling. Then I moved on to the next, or the one after.

Finally I left and ambled along Washington. Stopped off at a corner grocery for a quick po-boy and beer. Took the beer with me to finish as I walked up La Salle, jagging from sidewalk (where there was one) to street (where there wasn't, or where, from blockage or a quakelike upheaval of tree roots, it proved impassable).

A couple of blocks up, I turned into an alley between shoulder-to-shoulder doubles to trash the Dixie bottle. Most of the places along here seemed to be occupied—presumptive Christmas decorations hung on some abbreviated porches, leftover Halloween skeletons on one—but the houses either side of this particular alley, for whatever reasons, had been scuttled. One, to the left, once lime-green, had all windows and doors boarded over; its yellowish neighbor lacked windows and doors entirely and was heaped with refuse ranging from rotting lumber and linoleum to remains of impromptu parties (fast-food bags, bottles, candles) and grocery sacks of garbage, perhaps from adjoining quarters.

I lifted the lid of one of the bins, *La Salle* painted on in red, and saw just beyond, at the back of the alley against the latticework wall, a body. A woman's, I confirmed, stepping closer. She lay face-down, skirt thrown up over back and head. Pale, bloody rump in open air.

Twentyish, I decided, after turning her over. And dead. Possibly from a blow to the head: temples were spongy, eyes pushed forward and swollen. Possibly from a knife held against the neck as they butt-raped her, nicking a carotid.

Not that it mattered.

I knocked on the nearest occupied door, pushed my way in before the woman who answered could protest or ask questions, and dialed 911.

"Walsh," I told them.

"We'll have to get your name, number and location," the guy said.

"Walsh—or I hang up. There's a body. *You* decide."

Two minutes later, Don was on the line.

I spent an hour or so answering the usual array of police-type questions to at least three different groups of people, then went home. Later that night I sat with a glass of gin, neat, one of my own books face-down, unheeded, against my thigh, open to a particularly violent scene. I didn't need to read it, I knew it—by heart, as they used to say.

For years now, sequestered in this house, the one Vicky and I lived in together, the one Verne often visited, I had written book after book about street life, crime, about violence both random and purposeful, about frustration and despair and, occasionally, vengeance. But what I wrote, all those supposed "realistic" scenes, were only a kind of nostalgia, a romancification, sheerest dissembling; I could never portray what it was really like out there.

It wasn't that, in the years of my retreat, violence and pain had grown; but that I myself, believing I understood, believing I was saying important things, huddled down there, had steadily grown smaller.

I did not and do not understand. I will never understand.

6

They never really knew what happened to Clare Fellman.

One morning in late October she'd been conjugating the verb *parler* for her first-period students and suddenly, between first- and second-person *présent du subjonctif,* she was on the floor, unconscious, all sensation and control (as she would discover, three days later, upon waking) gone from her body's right side. Because they didn't know what else to call it, after sending her off on numerous day trips through CAT scanners and MRI's and the like, the doctors at Oschner called it a CVA.

She was twenty-two at the time. Now she was thirty-six.

Nothing much ever came back to that right side. Over the next year, first at Oschner, then at a rehab hospital near Covington, she had painstakingly learned again to reach and pick up things and hold on to them, to guide a spoon from lift-off to touchdown through the uncertain space between planets of bowl and mouth, to negotiate the fall between chair and bed and wheelchair and toilet, and finally to walk. Life had become all new conjunctions for her, she told me:

impossible joinings and connections others took for granted. She still wears braces at knee and ankle, canvas with Velcro these days, and a slight drag in her gait shows the extra focus required whenever that side is called on. It reminds me, oddly enough, of the way a jazz player, confronted with straight eighth notes, instinctively drags them out into dotted eighths and sixteenths.

Her speech, too, bears the mark of having been relearned. She speaks slowly, carefully, as though each word carries in its wake its own small period, filling the spaces with quick smiles and, often, with laughter that seems as much at her own halting progress as at anything else.

We'd met a year or so back at an Alliance Française event, a special showing of a film version of *L'Étranger* and buffet dinner after, to which I'd gone with Tony (Antoine, but don't dare use it) Roppolo, one of our English Department adjuncts. Absolutely guarantee you the stinkiest cheeses imaginable, Tony told me. And how could a guy pass up a thing like that?

Moments before the film began, Clare sank into the aisle seat beside me; Tony leaned forward for a quick hello and brief introduction. She held out her left hand and I took it, somewhat awkwardly, with my right. Afterwards we all sat at one of the long folding tables shuffling morsels of Cheshire, Brie and Camembert in among careful mouthsful of wine. By the time we'd switched from nouveau Beaujolais to a dark, ripe cabernet (Kool-Aid! she had exclaimed with her first sip of the Beaujolais) and Tony had washed out to sea (where periodically we caught sight of him bobbing here and there among bodies) Clare and I were well on our way to becoming (as she put it) new best friends.

For a time then, things moved pretty quickly, certainly far more quickly than made any kind of decent good sense. We were both old enough and, I'm sure, in our own ways damaged enough to know better. Nor did either of us, I think, really anticipate or intend what happened.

Then over the last couple of months, breathless and blinking, and with no clearer resolve or culpability than that with which we began, we'd found ourselves pulling back from one another. Too many unasked questions between us, maybe; too many wartime raids and too little faith in the cease-fire. Sometimes sitting beside Clare I felt as though unsaid things were growing like vines all around us, filling the room.

Of course, I felt that way with most of the people close to me.

And I was surprised, returning home from the Foucher shelter and my cemetery stroll, to find a message from her on my machine.

It's Clare, Lew. The spaces between her words were chinked with the tape's quiet hissing, anonymous background sounds. *Yeah, me. I'm sorry to bother you. I know about LaVerne, and I'm so sorry. If there's anything I can do, just let me know. But I have a friend who's got a problem, and I thought you might be able to help.* A pause. *Could you call me when you get a chance? Please?*

She answered, breathing hard, after six or seven rings.

"Lew. Thanks for calling back. Give me a minute, okay? I was doing my rehab stuff."

Threaded on the phone's fine silver nerve, we hung there. I listened as her breathing slowed.

"Okay, thanks. I know this is a bad time."

"Something about a friend, you said."

"Sheryl Silva. She works in dietary at the school and usually takes her break when I do, right before lunchtime. For her it's a little island of peace between preparation and storm. And after three straight periods, the last one my honors group, I'm pretty desperate. I try to stay away from the teachers' lounge, which is mostly bitching and conversations about children or new refrigerators, neither of which I have or expect to. So there'd just be the two of us there in the lunchroom, and after a while we fell into the habit of sitting together. Though a lot of the time we wouldn't say much of anything. Just sit there sipping iced tea, smiling vaguely at one another and looking out a window. Then last week she asks me if I'm 'married or anything.' I mean, we know absolutely nothing about one another. And when I tell her no, she asks me if I ever had a man beat me, or try to hurt me. Says she has, when I tell her no, but she thought that was all over."

"And it isn't."

"I think it's just threats, so far, from what she tells me."

"Husband?"

"I don't know. She wasn't too clear about that. They lived together, at any rate."

"Lived. You sure we're talking past tense here? *Le passé simple?*"

For a moment I was flooded with a sense of unreality, as though lights had dimmed and now I could see the stage set around me for the insubstantial, trumped-up thing it was, and knew the actors very soon must exit to stage-left lives of lunch meat, arrogant children, cars needing tires and new batteries. A cue card flipped up in the back of my mind; or a prompter whispered beyond the footlights. *This is none of your business, Griffin, none of your business at all.* But I had a longtime habit of ignoring scripted lines and improvising.

"Not for a while. I asked her what he'd done and she just looked at me. And then, after a minute, she said: Well, he put these dead chickens in my mailbox. And on the back porch. Just kind of hung them out there, like a string of peppers or garlic."

"She black or white?"

"Latin."

"Too bad. She be black, she know zackly what to do: *fry* them suckers."

"Very funny, Lew. Maybe I should hang up and call Dr. Ruth instead. She probably knows a few tricks you can do with chickens."

"Might read you her favorite salivious, I mean lascivious, passages from Frank Harris. Salacious? Man had a way with geese, as I recall."

"Look, this is the thing: You can talk to him, make him see he's heading for real trouble if this goes on."

"Man to man, hm?"

"Yeah, kind of."

"Well, Clare, I tell you. While it's true I used to do that sort of thing once in a while, it's also true that at the time I was twenty years younger and hadn't been riding my buns and a desk for six years straight. Be like all those almost hairless guys from the sixties trying to make their comeback as rock and rollers. I.e., ludicrous. Besides, all my tie-dye's at the cleaners."

"Please, Lew. As a favor to me? How can you turn down a poor little crippled girl?"

"Oh. Well, since you put it like that."

"Then you'll do it?"

"I'll talk to the guy, Clare. Politely. And that's all. He says boo, I'm a ghost."

"You're a jewel."

But when I looked in the mirror afterwards it wasn't sparkle I saw, more like a dullness that drew everything else to it. I remembered how old and used-up Walsh had looked to me the day of Verne's funeral. I couldn't be looking much better, and probably looked a hell of a lot worse. But enough of such reverie, I thought: there were things in the world that needed doing. Missions to be undertaken, wrongs to right, rights to champion.

Lew the Giant Killer.

7

So at midnight or thereabouts, here I am, with a list of this guy's habitats and less sense than your average lemming, prowling bars along Louisiana and Dryades looking for the chicken man.

Just like the good old days. Shut away from the world, the heady smell of piss and beer and barely contained fury all around me. And threading through it all, like a Wagnerian leitmotif, the quiet refrain: This is none of your business, Griffin, none at all.

I remembered a history professor back at LSUNO talking about the Russians' propensity for throwing themselves beneath tanks just to slow things down; saying that such irrational ferocities made them fearsome fighters.

But I was just going to talk to this guy, of course.

The Ave. Social & Pleasure Club was my tenth or twelfth try. I'd started at Henry's Soul Food and Pie Shop over on Claiborne and worked my way here.

It was a cinderblock affair, the butt half of a grocery whose painted-over windows advertised *Big Bo' Po-Boys* and *Fresh Seafood,* with an unbelievably crude painting of a crab holding a po-boy in its claws and (who would have thought it possible?) leering. The club, alas, didn't get such star treatment: only its name and a long arrow pointing to the single door.

Several underfed light bulbs hung here and there from the ceiling as though waiting for their mothers to come take them home. Most of the light came from two pool tables in back. I shuffled to the bar against the right wall, which looked to have been cobbled together from scraps of cabinet wood and countertopping, and ordered a beer. Archaeological layers of odor here: raw whiskey, stale beer, urine and sweat; the edgy smell of fish, rotting greens and sour milk from next door; under it all, mildew and mold, a fusty smell that seems to be everywhere in New Orleans.

Most of the activity, like most of the light, was concentrated around the pool tables. A man and woman barely old enough to be in here legally sat nearby at one of a number of battered, unmatched tables. The man drained his malt liquor can, reached for the woman's and said, "Now baby you *know* where I stays." There were a couple more guys at the bar perched on wobbly stiltlike stools.

"Do me a beer, man?" one of them said, turning his whole upper body to look at me. "I'm hurtin'."

He got his beer.

"Here's to Truth, Justice and the American Way," he said, lifting his glass in a toast. "All those wunful things we fought for." He belched. " 'Long with career politics, of course."

One of the players in back made a tough shot and for a while everybody kept busy walking around the tables doing high fives, slapping palms, exchanging money.

"You in here a lot?" I said.

He thought about it. "I ain't here, Luther don't bother opening up."

"Know a guy named T.C.? Regular, they tell me. Tall dude—"

He grinned. Not a good sign.

"—hair cut short, wears one earring. Light skin."

"Man, I tell you, these beers be disappearing in a hurry on a day like this one here. You notice that?"

I put another five on the bar in front of him.

"Well, then. He be coming out of the bathroom back there just about any time now, I 'spect," he said after ordering and sampling a new beer. "What you want with T.C. anyway? He ain't much."

"Friend asked me to talk to him."

"Ain't much for talk, either."

And at that, as if on cue, the man himself stepped into the penumbra of light behind the pool players, six-four or -five and at least two-fifty, all of it muscle except maybe the earring, followed a moment later by two guys in sportcoats and jeans who hurried on out of the bar.

He watched me approach without registering anything at all: alarm, suspicion, caution, interest. Or humanity, for that matter.

"Buy you a drink?" I asked.

"Why th' hell not?" And after we'd bellied up to the bar over my beer and his double Teacher's rocks, he said: "So what is it you're needing, my man? How much and when. And a name, somewhere along the way."

Faint tatters of an accent drifted to the surface, Cuban maybe.

"I'm throwing a chicken fry for my friends," I said. "Someone told me you were the man to see."

He looked at the bridge of my nose for a minute or so. No sign of alarm, suspicion, etc. (See above.)

"I get it," he said. "You're crazy, right? Like ol' Banghead Terence over there. Hey: you been buttin' down any walls lately, boy?"

"No *sir,*" Terence said. My informant.

"Nigger got his head scrambled right good back there in Nam, so now every few days we'll find him in some alley somewhere and he'll be running headfirst into the wall over and over again till he falls down and can't get up no more. Wall just sits there."

He finished his drink, rolled ice around the bottom of the glass.

"Figure something like that must of happened to you. Ain't no other *possible* reason you be comin' here this way, rubbing up against me like this. You got to be crazy too. Now you tell me: am I right?"

I smiled, ordered a couple more drinks for us, and started telling him why I was there. That Sheryl wanted me to talk to him, explain why he had to leave her alone.

"So you just run on out and do whatever any pussy tell you. That it, man?"

I started over. Clare was a friend of Sheryl's and—

"So you be fucking them both at the same time? Or they do each other while you watch."

I tried once more. I really did intend, or at least had convinced myself that I intended, just to talk to him. But intentions are slippery things.

When the gun came over the table's edge, suddenly, at the exact moment he switched his eyes toward the door and lifted his face as though in greeting, I slammed my glass down as hard as possible on that hand. The glass shattered, but I didn't feel it then. I did feel bones give way under the glass. My other hand was already moving toward him with a heavy ashtray, and that connected just above his left eye.

"Righteous," Terence said from the bar.

T.C. went back out of the chair, toppling it, but sprang almost at once to his feet and made a grab for my shirtfront. Suckered, I leaned back with the top half of my body—and he swept my feet out from under me.

"Moves," Terence said. " 'Member that shit."

Things looked quite different from down there. It was absolutely amazing, for instance, how much bigger T.C. had gotten. Or how many cockroaches there were skittering about under chairs and things. At one point when T.C. was sitting on top of me kind of boxing my head from side to side playfully, I saw by a table leg what I'm certain was a severed, dried-up ear.

Then I watched two fingers jam up hard into his nose and heard cartilage give way there. When he lifted his hands to pull mine away, I struck him full force in the throat and he fell off me, gasping. I kicked him in the ribs, then a couple of times in the head before I noticed he was lying still and turning blue. No one made any move toward us; they simply watched.

"Better call the paramedics," I told the bartender, staggering over to him. It sounded like: *Btr. Kawl. Thpur. Medix.*

He looked about the room, timing it.

"Man does comedy too," he said.

There was skittery laughter.

But he also said, to me: "You better get on out of here. We'll just 'low Mr. T.C. to sleep it off a while. But come closing I 'spect I'll notice him there. Don't see no way 'round that. And then the Man's gonna want to know things."

I started out.

"That be two-ninety for the last round," the bartender said.

8

I rang the bell and then just kind of leaned there against the sill to wait. I didn't know what time it was. After one, maybe closer to two. Lights still burned in many of the houses. Streetlights, moon and windows all had a red haze about them. I'd wrapped a handkerchief around my hand, but it was soaked through now, and periodically thick gobbets of blood would squeeze their way out and fall like slugs.

After a while I heard her coming to the door, duh-DA, duh-DA, duh-DA, in perfect iambs. She wore a short, sky-blue, kimonolike robe.

"Don't tell me," she said. "You wanted to beat the rest of the kids to the candied apples and other treats."

"Already been tricked," I said. Then: "You should see the other guy."

"Who won?"

"I did."

"Then I don't think I want to see the other guy. Aren't you getting a little old for this?"

"Tried to tell you that. Damn glad now I *didn't* wear my tie-dye."

"Sheryl's ex-live-in?"

"The chicken man himself."

"Oh Lew. I'm so sorry."

"Sorry enough to let me come in?"

"What? Oh, sorry. Sure. You really do look like shit, by the way." She turned and stepped away from the door. I took a step forward. Nations disappeared, new suns appeared in the sky, planets formed around them. I took another step.

"Are you okay?" she asked.

"Just a little damaged in transit, as they say at the post office. Then, of course, they hand you this thing that's taped back together three ways from Sunday and whatever was inside is crushed beyond recognition."

"Are you?"

"Crushed? Absolutely. Many times over. But it always springs back. Well, these days I guess it's more like it *seeps* back."

"Stronger than before?"

"Not that I've noticed. You?"

She shook her head. "Be nice if it were true, though. Like a lot of things."

I eased myself onto the couch.

"Tell Sheryl T.C. won't be bothering her anymore. Actually, I'm not sure he'll be bothering *anyone* anymore."

"Must have been one hell of a talk."

"*I* won't forget it soon. You got anything to drink?"

"Might be some scotch under the cabinet from when my parents were here. Want me to look?"

"Oh yes."

There were a couple of inches left in the bottle she put on the coffee table before me. Ignoring the glass, I tilted the bottle up. Seemed easier that way: less movement, less pain. I remembered O'Carolan asking for Irish whiskey on his deathbed, saying it would be a terrible thing if two such friends should part without a final, farewell kiss. I tilted the bottle again.

"I feel like I just blinked and twenty years went by—backwards," I said. "Definitely an old TV science fiction show. Can't be real life." I looked at her. "Sorry. It's late."

"It's okay, Lew. Really."

"Tell you what. I'm going into that bathroom down there at the end of the hall to face up to some hot water and soap. Pay no attention to screams, and if I'm not out in ten minutes, you can decide on your own whether to call paramedics or the funeral home. *I* sure as hell don't know which, even now."

"Need any help?"

"Me? Look at what I've already accomplished, all by myself."

"I'll make coffee, then. Once I'm up, that's usually it for the night."

I stepped carefully down the hall. Must be heavy winds and a storm coming up: the ship listed badly both to port and starboard.

Ablution accomplished, nerve ends singing like power lines in a hurricane, I came back and sat as Clare poured something yellow into the cuts, smeared on antibiotic salve and bound my hand tightly in gauze.

"That's going to need stitches. Lucky you didn't cut a tendon or an artery."

"It's not bleeding anymore. It'll be okay."

"Lew, don't you think you've worn your balls as a hat long enough for one night? Jesus!"

"Okay, okay. You're right."

"You'll go to the ER?"

"Tomorrow."

"Promise?"

I nodded and she went out to the kitchen, brought back a lacquered wooden tray with coffee in one of those thermal pitchers, two mugs, packets of sugar and sweetener, an unopened pint of Half & Half.

She poured for both of us and we sat there like some ancient married couple, sipping coffee together in the middle of the night without speaking. The moon hung full and bright in the sky outside, and after a while Clare got up and turned off the room's lights. Then, after sitting again, finishing her coffee, pouring anew for us both, she said quietly, "I don't understand what happened between us, Lew."

I said nothing, and finally she laughed. "Guess I'll put that on the list with quantum mechanics, the national debt and the meaning of life, huh?"

I looked at her.

"I'd come over there and sit at your feet now if I could, Lew. Just lean back against you and forget everything else. That's what I'd do if I could. But I can't. Probably fall, if I tried. Coffee okay? You want a sandwich or anything?"

"The coffee's wonderful, Clare. *You're* wonderful. And I'm sorry."

A silence. Then: "You have things you'd do, too—if you could?"

I nodded. Oh yes.

Another, longer silence. "Think maybe you'd consider spending the night in this wonderful coffee maker's bed?"

"I'm not in very good shape."

She laughed, suddenly, richly. "Hey, that's *my* line."

Later as we lay there with moonlight washing over us and the ceiling fan thwacking gently to and fro, I mused that pain was every bit as wayward, as slippery and inconsistent, as intentions.

"Half in love with easeful death," Clare said, striking her right side forcibly with the opposite hand and laughing. "Little did he know. But what's left is for you, sailor."

Human voices didn't wake us, and we did not drown.

9

It was not a human voice at all to which I woke, in fact, but a cat's. Said cat was sitting on my chest, looking disinterested, when I opened my eyes. Its own eyes were golden, with that same color somewhere deep in a coat that otherwise would have been plain tabby. *Mowr,* it said again, inflection rising: closer to a pigeon's warble than anything else.

"You didn't tell me there was a new man in your life," I said when Clare came in with coffee moments later.

"Yeah, and just like all the rest, too: only way I can keep him is to lock him in at night. Lew, meet Bat."

She put a mug of *café au lait* on the table by me and held on to the other, which I knew would be only half filled, to allay spillage.

"I was in the kitchen one morning, bleary-eyed as usual, nose in my coffee. Glasses fogging over since I hadn't put my contacts in yet. I heard a sound and looked up and there he was on the screen. Just hanging there, like a moth. I shooed him down but a minute later he jumped back up. That went on a while, till I finally just said what the hell and let him in. From the look of it, he hadn't eaten for a long time.

"He was just a kitten then. There wasn't much to him but these huge ears sticking straight up—that's how he got the name. I asked around the neighborhood, but no one knew anything. So now we're roomies. He's shy."

"I can tell." I wanted the coffee bad, but the cat didn't seem to understand that.

"No, really. I bet he spent all night behind the stove, just because he didn't know you."

"Help?" I made clawing motions toward the coffee mug.

"What? Oh sure." She scooped the cat up in an arm (it hung there limper, surely, than anything alive can possibly be) and dropped it onto the floor (where it grew suddenly solid and bounded away into the next room). "Hungry?"

"Yes, but it's my treat. What time is it, anyway?"

"Eight-thirty."

"Aren't you late?"

"I called in."

"Not feeling good, huh?"

"*Au contraire,* believe me."

"Okay. So we can make the Camellia when it opens. Before the crowd hits. If that's all right."

"That's great."

We splashed water on faces, brushed teeth (unbelievably, she still had a toothbrush of mine there), dressed (as well as clothes to replace encrusted ones from the night before), and took her car uptown. Since the car was specially outfitted, there was never any question who would drive. She parked by an elementary school on the far side of the neutral ground and we walked across Carrollton, dodging a streetcar that lugged its way toward St. Charles beneath towering palms, bell aclang. She was wearing sneakers, jeans and an old sweatshirt from the rehab hospital that read *Do It—Again.*

Lester told us how good it was to see us after so long, wiped quickly at the counter, set out tableware rolled into crisp white napkins. Without asking, he brought coffees with cream, and within minutes was also sliding our breakfasts onto the counter before us, pecan waffle for Clare, chili omelette for me.

We ate pretty much in silence, smiling a lot, then walked over to Lenny's so she could get a *New York Times*.

"What now, Lew?"

"Maybe you could drop me off at Touro's ER."

"Would you mind too much if I stayed with you? It'll probably be a long wait, and you never know how you might be feeling afterward."

"You don't have to do that, Clare."

"I know I don't."

So she did.

At the triage desk I gave my name and other information to the clerk, answered that no I had no medical insurance but would be paying by check for services rendered, and earned for that a lingering, weighty glance, as though it were now moot whether I was the worst sort of social outcast and deadbeat, or someone important who perhaps should be catered to.

"Please wait over there, Mr. Griffin," he said, pointing to row upon row of joined plastic chairs I always think of as discount-store pews. "A doctor will see you shortly."

Shortly turned out to be just under three hours.

The place was more like a bus station than anything else. That same sense of being cut off from real time, much the same squalor and spread. Everything stank of cigarette smoke, stale ash and bodies. Stains on the chairs, floor, most walls. Steady streams of people in and out. Some of them picnicking alone or in groups from fast-food bags and home-packed grocery sacks, a few to every appearance (with their belongings piled alongside) homesteaded here.

Periodically police or paramedics pushed through the automatic doors with drunks, trauma victims, vacuum-eyed young people, sexless street folk wound in layers of rags, rapists and rapees, resuscitations-in-progress, slowly cooling bodies. Every quarter hour or so a name would boom over the intercom and that person would vanish into the leviathan interior. None of them ever seemed to emerge.

Nurses and other personnel strolled past regularly on their way outdoors to smoke.

A young woman from Audubon Zoo came in with the hawk she'd been feeding attached to her by the talons it had sunk into her left cheek.

A detective from Kenner arrived to inquire after a body that had been dumped on the ER ramp earlier that morning allegedly by a funeral home that claimed the next of kin refused to pay them.

An elderly woman inched her way in and across to the desk to ask please could anyone tell her if her husband had been brought here following a heart attack last night, she couldn't remember where they said they were bringing him and had tried several other hospitals already and didn't have any more money for cab fare.

Clare, it turned out, was right on several counts. Once the whale finally got around to swallowing me, I emerged with a dozen or so stitches. I emerged also, barely able to walk, on wobbly legs, demonstrably in poor condition to attempt wending my way home unaided.

To her credit, she made only one comment as she watched me wobble toward her in the waiting room: "Well, *here's* my big strong man." Then she took me home.

I woke to bleating traffic and looked at the clock on my bedside table. Four fifty-eight. From the living room I could hear, though the volume was low, Noah Adams on NPR, interviewing a man who had constructed a scale model of the solar system in his barn.

Clare sat in the wingback reading, a glass of wine beside her.

"I know it would be far, far too much to hope that, anticipating this second, unexpected morning of mine, you might have coffee waiting."

"*Fresh* coffee, as a matter of fact." She glanced at the wall clock. Time—thief of life and all good intentions. "Well, an hour ago, anyway."

It was wonderful.

I drank the first cup almost at a gulp, poured bourbon into the next and nursed it deliciously. We sat listening to traffic sounds from Prytania, a block or so away, and to an update on Somalia relief efforts.

"I ever tell you about my father?" Clare asked.

"Some. I know he died of alcoholism when you were still pretty young. And you told me he was a championship runner in college."

"Leaves a lot of in-between, doesn't it?"

"That's what life mostly is, all the in-between stuff."

"Yeah. Yeah, I guess so." She crossed her leg and leaned toward me, wine washing up the side of her glass in a brief tide. "I don't remember a lot, myself. Mostly I have these snapshots, these few moments that come back again and again, vividly. So vividly that I recall even the smells, or the way sun felt on my skin."

A woman walked down the middle of the street pushing a shopping cart piled with trash bags. White ones, brown ones, black ones, gray ones. An orange one with a jack-o'-lantern face.

"I remember once I'm sitting in his lap and he's telling me about the war. That's what he always calls it, just 'the war.' And he says, every time: a terrible thing, terrible. And I can smell liquor on his breath and the sweat that's steeped into his clothes from the roofing job he's been on all day over near Tucson.

"You know about code-talkers, Lew? Well, he was one of them. The Japanese had managed to break just about every code we came up with, I guess, and finally someone had this idea to use Indians. There were about four hundred of them before it was all done, all of them Navajo, and they passed critical information over the radio in their own language, substituting natural words for manmade things. Grenades were potatoes, bombs were eggs, America was *nihima:* our mother.

"They were all kids. My father had gone directly from the reservation up near Ganado into the Marines. He was seventeen or eighteen at the time. And when he came back, three years later, to Phoenix, he couldn't find work there. He wandered up into Canada—some sort of pipeline job or something, I'm not sure—and he met Mama there. The sophisticated Frenchwoman. The *Québecoise.* Who devoted the rest of her life, near as I can tell—though who can say: perhaps misery was locked inescapably into his genes—to making the rest of *his* life miserable.

"By the time he died he'd become this heavy dark bag my mother and the rest of us had to drag behind us everywhere we went. What I felt when he died, what my mother must have felt, was, first of all, an overwhelming sense of relief.

"I think about that still, from time to time. The feelings don't change, and it seems somehow important to me that I don't lose them, but it does keep flooding back. Like givens that are supposed to lead you on to a new hypothesis. . . . You have any idea at all what I'm talking about?"

"Not much."

"Neither do I. But I *almost* had it, just for a moment there."

" 'Keep trying.' "

"Tolstoy dying—right?"

"Scratched it with a finger on his sheet, yes."

"What would *you* scratch out, Lew?"

"Something from a poem I read a while back, I think: 'find beauty, try to understand, survive.' "

Moments later: "You ready for bed?"

"Hey, I just got up."

"So? What's your point?"

Mozart replaced Noah Adams, traffic sounds relented, the old house creaked and wheezed. We got up a couple of hours later and walked over to Popeye's for chicken, biscuits, red beans and rice.

10

I got home midmorning and was walking toward the answering machine with its blinking light when the phone itself rang.

"Lew," Achille Boudleaux said. "You look'n 'roun' for me, I hear." He could speak perfectly proper, unaccented English if he wanted, but rarely bothered without good reason, and never among friends.

I said there was absolutely no way he could know that.

"Why I so damn good. What you wan'?"

I filled him in, including my tracking down Garces at the shelter.

"Is there anything else, A.C.? Something you may have left out of the report? However tenuous it might seem."

"Hol' on. I done pull out the notebook cause I know what you wan' me for."

Virtual silence on the line. A match striking in Metairie and a long pull on his cigarette. A cough that died aborning, rattling deep in his chest like suppressed memories. Car alarm somewhere down the street. Police siren racing up Prytania.

"Ain' much here, Lew. One t'ing I din't put in, but issa long shot, pro'ly don' lead nowhere. Miss Alouette, she bin keepin' comp'ny wit' a guy call hi'self Roach, some say. Make goo' money, that boy, but he don' seem to work at anythin', you know? He from up 'roun' Tup'lo."

"You have any idea how long they'd been a number?"

"Don' know they were, rilly."

"Any address for this Roach?"

"You bin off the street too long, Lew. Roaches don' have no 'dress, you know that. You wan' him, you just get on downtown and ax 'roun.'"

"Okay. *Bien merci,* Achille."

"Rien."

I cradled the phone and hit *Message.* After a brief pause, a momentary shush of tape past pinions, Richard Garces identified himself, saying: "Give me a call when you can. I think I have a couple of leads on Alouette."

I dialed, got a busy signal three times in a row, at last got through and was put on hold. "You're So Vain" fluted into my defenseless ear and I found myself thinking about Carly Simon's lips. Something I was pretty sure Richard Garces never did.

"Mr. Griffin," he said. "Sorry to keep you waiting. Something of an emergency with one of my girls."

"Lew—remember? And no problem."

"Super. Okay, here's the thing. I'm a hacker, or at least I was a while back, and there was a time there when a lot of us kind of stumbled into one another over the years on various bulletin boards. We were all doing social work, that's what brought us together. Some like myself in small shelters or support services scattered throughout the country, some in institutions, most in public health —MHMR or other government services. Those early contacts developed into a loose network, a place we could go for information we didn't otherwise have access to, a kind of information underground."

"Right." The country—whatever your special interest: law, liberal politics, magazine sales, white supremacy—was rife with such networks, electronic and otherwise. Often I imagined they might represent this skewed nation's only true intelligence, skein after skein of fragile webs piling one atop another until a rudimentary nervous system came into being.

"Well, I hadn't logged on to the network in quite a while. My work here at Foucher's pretty circumscribed. But after you left the other day, after I'd thought about it a while, I got on-line. And after half an hour or so of 'Good to see your number come up' and 'How's it been going' and 'Where the hell you been, man'—I guess the economy's gotten so bad that these guys don't have much else to do but sit home, stroke and get stroked by electronic friends—I started asking about an eighteen-year-old who might give New Orleans as a prior address, might be reluctant to say more and is probably in trouble.

"That's what the network's about, after all. Alouette doesn't have any resources, any skills. Wherever she winds up, sooner or later she's going to have to hook into one of the available programs."

"And you can track her that way."

"Ordinarily, no. Well, I guess you *could,* but it would take forever. There's no official channel. No central data bank or clearinghouse. The network itself is sketchy, but we've got people scattered all through the country, at all levels, and every one of us is facing the same problems day in and day out, a lot of them basically insoluble. So sometimes we're able to help one another. Provide information or a way around this or that obstacle, maybe cut a corner or two."

Okay, so it reeked of J. Edgar Hoover-style rationalization. And sure, you had to wonder to what use those less scrupulous might put such information, were it available to them. But I had no reason to believe that Richard Garces was any less liberal in reflex or thought than myself: he'd doubtless covered this same ground many times over.

"You have any indication Alouette was pregnant?" he asked suddenly.

"Not really. Did you?"

"It's a possibility. You have a pen and paper?"

"Yeah." I always kept early drafts and aborted pages, folding them in half to make a rough tablet that stayed there by the phone.

"Okay. Out of a couple dozen maybes, I boiled it down to three. These may all be way off base, you understand. Wrong tree—even wrong forest, for all we know. But age, accent and physical description are all good matches."

"I understand."

"The first one showed up in Dallas a few months back, brought into Parkland when she was raped by some guys who were looking through the Dumpster she lived in for leftover hamburgers and found her instead. It was behind a Burger King. Right now she's in the Diagnostic Center. That's around the corner from Parkland, up on Harry Hines. She'll be there another few days, then she'll be farmed out to whatever treatment center or hospital has a bed open up. Gives her name as Delores, and says no next of kin. Right age and general physical appearance."

"Have a number for the place?"

He gave it to me and said, "I don't know how much good this will do you. Phones there tend to be answered by untrained attendants who have little comprehension of what they're up against, even less of any moral and constitutional limits to their protectorship."

I knew just what he meant, recalling sojourns in psychiatric hospitals and alcohol-treatment centers where constitutional rights, legal principle and simple human dignity were violated unthinkingly and as a matter of course.

"Second is over at Mandeville, the state hospital. Listed as Jane Doe, since all she'll say is 'God listens, the angels hear.' Her social worker's name is Fran Brown." He read off a number and extension.

"Third's up in Mississippi. This is the pregnant one. *Was* pregnant, anyhow: she delivered last week. Way premature. The baby's in NICU, barely a pound. And barely hanging on, as I understand. As you'd expect. Her case worker is Miss Siler." He spelled it. "That's all I could get: Miss Siler. No first name, credentials, job title. Girl gave *her* name as McTell. No record of social dependence—as we put it—in Mississippi. No medical coverage or prenatal care, and no father of record entered."

Again, he read off a number.

"Got it. Thanks, Richard. You ever want to get into a new line of work, you'd make one hell of a detective."

"Yeah, well. Once in a while we do something that really helps, you know. I hope this is one of those times. A favor?"

"You got it."

"Let me know?"

"Absolutely."

So then I had to go find Roach, of course.

Bars, taverns, street corners. The Hummingbird Grill, the Y at Lee Circle, Please U Restaurant, a group of men seated as usual on the low wall before a parking lot. One establishment had as identification only a piece of cardboard with *Circle View Tavern* hand-lettered on it; it was taped to the window among campaign posters (*Dr. Betty Brown, School Board, Third Ward: Your Children Need Her*) and long-out-of-date showbills (*Catch Some Soul at Fat Eddie's*).

I asked at Canal and Royal, again at Carondelet and Poydras, around Jackson Square, along Decatur, Esplanade and into the Faubourg Marigny. When New Orleans's founding Creoles overflowed the Quarter, they spilled into the Marigny—years before Irish, British and other Anglo settlers began moving into the regions above Canal. When I first came to New Orleans, the Quarter itself was crumbling and everything below Esplanade was strictly no-man's-land. Then, gradually, those buildings were reclaimed; and in recent years the Marigny's become a cozy residential area where alternative bookstores, lesbian theaters, small clubs and flea markets thrive.

One small corner bookstore there has, packed in with Baldwin, Kathy Acker, Virginia Woolf, Gore Vidal and a wall of books on sexuality, what must be the definitive collection of a genre few know exists: lesbian private-eye novels. I counted once, and there were fourteen different titles; whenever I'm in the Marigny I drop by to check for new ones. This time when I stepped in off the sidewalk a face turned up to me and its owner carefully set back on a shelf the book he'd been paging through.

"Lew," he said.

It was Richard Garces. "What are you doing here?" seemed a pretty stupid question, but I asked it anyway.

"I live here. Buy you a drink?"

"Why not?"

We walked down to Snug Harbor and settled in at a table by the window. Women in cotton dresses and army boots went by. Men with ponytails and expensive Italian suitcoats worn over ragged T-shirts and jeans. Richard and I decided on two Heinekens.

"I've been down here almost since it started," he told me. "Had a store myself for a while, sold prints and original photographs, a lot of it friends' work. Paid someone else to run it, of course. I still do a turn now and again at the Theater Marigny, and I work weekends on the AIDS hot line."

"A pillar of the community."

"My community, yes. Actually I am."

A middle-aged couple came in and stopped by our table to say hello to Richard before moving on to a table of their own. It was obvious from their ease with one another that they'd been together a long time. Both were black, introduced by Garces as Jonesy and Rainer (not René: he spelled it). A youngish woman came and peered into the window, hands curved around her eyes like binoculars, before stomping away. She wore a taffeta party dress, Eisenhower jacket and old high-top black basketball shoes.

"I had no idea you were gay, Lew," Richard said. "Not often I miss the call, after all these years."

"You still haven't missed it."

"Oh?"

"Oh."

"Hear that a lot."

"I bet."

"And you're not even going to tell me some of your best friends are gay?"

"No, but just between the two of us, one or two of them are black."

He laughed, and finished off his beer. "Well, I'm sorry to hear that. The first thing, I mean. And I have to tell you, there's a certain sense of loss involved here. You want another beer?"

Our waiter glided new bottles soundlessly into the shadow of former ones. Richard leaned across the table and poured anew into my glass.

"I guess you're sure about that," he said.

"For the moment, anyhow."

"So: what? You're just down here slumming? Looking for Fiesta Ware to complete your set, maybe? Soaking up local color for a new book?"

"Something like that."

"Yeah, well." He drank most of his beer at a gulp. "So now I just say good to see you and go on home alone, huh?"

"Way things are."

He killed it. "Okay. That's cool." He extended a hand across the table and we shook. "Take care, Lew."

"And you."

After he was gone I asked for coffee, got something that had been sitting on the back burner since about 1964 and drank it anyway. Thinking now of many things. Walking thick woods in predawn mists beside my father, the smell of oil from his shotgun at once earthy and sharp in my nose. Vicky and I on our first, awkward dates. LaVerne twenty-six years old in a white suit across the table from me at Port of Call. My son's last postcard, and the taped silences from my answering machine that I somehow always knew were from him and still kept in a desk drawer.

Ceaselessly into the past. Kierkegaard was right: we understand our lives (to the extent that we understand them at all) only backwards.

Backwards was the way I caught up with Roach, too, as it turned out.

Like many city dwellers, I try to carry a kind of bubble of awareness around me always, alert to whatever happens within that radius. And now as I stepped off a curb, without knowing how or where, I sensed the zone had been violated—just seconds before I was seized from behind, arm at my neck, and slammed against a wall.

"Say you been asking all over for the Roach and don't no one know you."

He was close to my size and at least ten years younger. Hair cut in what these days they're calling a fade. Black T-shirt, baggy brown cargo pants, British Knight sneakers the size of tugboats. A most impressive scar along almost the full length of the arm pressed against my windpipe. One dainty ceramic earring.

"Gmmph," I said.

He patted me down quickly with the other hand. "You cool?"

I said "Gmmph" again.

"Now it's jus' too damn hot for running. I have to run after you, that's gonna make me mad."

The tugboats backed out a step or two. Air shuddered into my lungs.

"Howyou . . . findme?" I said when I could.

"Shit, man. You weren't doing any good at finding *me,* so I figured I'd best come find *you.* How many old black farts you think we see down here asking for the Roach, anyhow? And wearing a sportcoat?"

"I'm not a cop."

"Even cops ain't stupid as that. Not most of them, anyway."

He paused to stare at a group coming toward us. They had been looking on inquisitively, but now hurried to cross the street.

"My name's Lew Griffin. I—"

"I be damn. Lew Griffin. You don't remember me, do you? Course not. No reason you should. I was in a house down here same time as you, man, must be eight, nine years ago. People wondered about you, talked some. You roomed with a guy named Jimmie later got hisself killed. Heard you did something about that."

I hadn't—not the way he meant, anyway—but I let it pass. Never dispute a man who thinks you're a badass.

"So how you been, man?"

"Just about every way there is to be, one time or another," I told him. "Right now I'm good."

"You know it." He stepped back, as though suddenly noticing me crowded there against the wall. "So what you want with the Roach,

Griffin? You're a drinker, as I recall—and memory's my *other* thing that always works fierce. Not behind pills and powder."

"I'm looking for a girl named Alouette. Guidry, but I don't know she'd be using that name. You know her?"

"Might. She family?"

I shook my head. "Favor for a friend."

"Then I know her. Did, anyway. Stone fox, the way these light women get all of a sudden they're thirteen, fourteen."

"Alouette's eighteen."

"You know, I found that out. Had to cut her loose, too, but that wudn't the reason. Sorry to have to do it, I tell you that."

"What *was* the reason?"

"She carrying around some heavy shit, Griffin, you know what I mean? Now I'll do a line same as the next man, I won't hold that against no one. But Lou, you let *her* do a few lines, even get a few drinks and a toke or two in her, and it'd be like this big hairy thing had climbed out of a cage somewhere. She was doing a lot of crack there toward the end, too, and there ain't nobody don't go crazy on *that* shit."

"When did you last see her?"

"Must be four, five months ago, at least."

"Was she pregnant?"

"Never said so. Didn't look like it."

"You know where she was living?"

"Not right then. She'd been staying with a friend of mine over by Constantinople. But then he had some *new* friends move in, you know? She got to talking about 'going home' along about then, I remember, and one day I said to her, 'Lou, you don't *have* a home.' She slapped me. Not real hard, and not the first time. But it was going to be the last."

"You didn't see her again?"

"Took her to the bus station that night. She ax me to."

"Any idea where she was going?"

"Probably wherever twenty dollars'd get her. Cause that's what I gave her."

"Greyhound station?"

He nodded and started away.

"Hey, thanks for the help," I called after him. "You have a name?"

"Well," he said, half turning back, "I used to be Robert McTell, I guess. But I ain't no more."

11

Two days later at six in the morning, behind the wheel of a car for the first time in at least six years, I tooled nervously out I-10 through Metairie and onto the elevated highway stilting over bayou and swampland, past *Whiskey Bay, Grosse Tête,* looking at walls of tall cypress, standing water carpeted green, pelicans aflight, fishing boats. *This is the forest primeval*—remember? You're definitely in the presence of something primordial here, something that underlies everything we are or presume; nor can you escape a sense of the transitory nature of the roadway you're on, perched over these bayous like Yeats's long-legged fly on the stream of time. With emergency telephones every mile or so.

Spanish moss everywhere. Gathering it used to be full-time employment hereabouts; before synthetics, it was stuffing for mattresses, furniture, car seats.

I was being borne back into the past in more ways than one. The rental car was a Mazda very close in design, color and general appearance, even after these several years, to Vicky's. (In all the wisdom of her own twenty years the agent hedged at turning it over, balking at my lack of a major credit card, but finally accepted a cash deposit.) And my destination, a red umbilicus on the map, was I-55, snaking like a trainer's car alongside the Mississippi up past river towns like Vicksburg and Helena, with their Confederate cemeteries, tar-paper shacks and antebellum mansions, toward Memphis. Pure delta South. Where the blues and I were born. Since leaving at age sixteen, I had been back just twice.

First, though—before all this history could begin reiterating—I was called upon to support my local police lieutenant.

The call came around midnight. I'd climbed, that night, back up out of the Marigny to Canal, tried for the streetcar at St. Charles and then at Carondelet and, encountering veritable prides of conventioneers at both locations, hoofed on up to Poydras and flagged a cab, an independent with *Jerusalem Cab* stenciled on the side and its owner's name (something with a disproportionate number of consonants) on front fenders. We miraculously avoided serial collisions as the driver filled me in on the Saints and chewed at a falafel sandwich. Car and karma held, and on half a wing and muttered prayer at last we touched down, at last I was delivered, disgorged, cast up, *chez moi.*

I put together a plate of cheese and French bread and opened a bottle of cabernet. It was Brazilian, simply wonderful, and two ninety-five a bottle from the Superstore. It was also only a matter of time before other people discovered it.

Had dinner and most of the wine by the window, sunk like Archimedes, displacing my own weight, into *L'Étranger,* life for the duration of that book, as every time I read it, a quiet, constant eureka.

Then I woke half between worlds, knowing it was the phone I heard, knowing in dreams I'd transformed it to the whine of a plane, trying to hold on, impossibly, to both realities.

I finally picked the thing up and grunted into it.

"This the fucking zoo, or what?" Walsh said on the other end.

"I didn't do it."

"Didn't do what?"

"Whatever I'm suspected of. Though I feel I have to mention that back in the good old days when you were just a little younger and a lot more interested in doing your job you actually went out and *found* the suspects and didn't just call and tell them to get their butts down to the station. Course, I guess that's one of the benefits of a reputation. Bad guys hear the phone ring, know it's you, and start writing out confessions before they even answer."

"I told you to fuck yourself lately?" He was slurring his words terribly. I'm a man who knows a lot about slurring words. And not a little about terrible.

"Only last week. I tried. The chiropractor thinks he'll be able to help me."

"So what's up?"

"Well, a lot of people are sleeping, for one thing—for lack of anything better to do, you understand."

"Hey. Lew: woke you up. Sorry."

"No problem. But look, I've got to pee and drink something. Give me a minute, okay?"

"Want me to call back?"

"No. Once is enough. Just hang on, okay?" A morselike bleat on the line. "Whoa, another call. Look. I lose you, you call me back, okay?"

That other person wanted Sears, but why at this time of night I couldn't imagine. Maybe they'd sent him the wrong size cardigan.

I went out to the kitchen and put the kettle on. Had a couple of glasses of water from the tap (glass there by the sink looked okay), then stomped upstairs to the bathroom. Listened to pipes bang and groan behind the walls on the way back down.

"You still there?"

"Yeah, I'm here." Throat clearing. "You got anything else you need to do first? Run out to the corner for a paper? Go grab a burger at the King? Whack off, maybe?"

"Let me think about it. What can I do for you, in the meanwhile?"

Outside, a banana-tree leaf long ago frayed by high winds now fluttered in a gentle one in the moonlight, spilling mysterious, ever-changing shapes against the window.

"Tell you what, Lew. I came home tonight about eight, and ever since, I've been sitting here at the kitchen table with a bottle of K&B's best on the table, a pizza I picked up on the way home and now can't bear the thought of even opening up, much less eating, and my Police Special. Not the Colt. That's put away by the bed the way it always is when I get home. This's the one the department gave me, I first made detective. It stays wrapped in oilcloth in the closet, you know? But tonight I went and got it."

The French call what I felt just then a *frisson.*

This too, what was happening with Walsh, was something I knew a lot about.

"Don. What's going on, man?"

"New reports came in today. Homicides down to thirty-one for this quarter. Petty crime and misdemeanors down almost twenty percent. Surprised you hadn't heard. NOPD's doing a helluva job. You be sure and write Mayor Barthelemy and the chief and tell them, as a citizen, how much you appreciate that. They're waiting to hear from you. Operators are standing by."

I heard ice clink against a glass, a swallow, then what could have been a low sob.

"She's married this guy she met, Lew. Owns some fancy-ass sporting goods store, Florida somewhere. Pogoland. Now how the fuck'd she ever meet someone like that, what's she need with that kind of shit? But she's already moved down there with him. I finally went around to see the kids—it'd been a while and she'd been dodging me whenever I called, so I was determined, and primed for a fight—and the house was empty, doors wide open, nothing in there but some empty beer cans and paper bags and a rubber or two. So I lean on a neighbor finally and find out she moved out a couple of weeks before. Then the next day, registered mail, I get papers that this guy's putting in to adopt the kids."

Ice against glass again. Don's breath catching there at the other end. A car engine clattering outside.

"I called you because you're the only one I know who's been as fucked up as I am right now, Lew. Somehow you always get through it. And you've always been a good friend."

"No I haven't, not to anyone; we both know that. But *you* have been. Look, I'm on my way, okay? We'll talk about it."

"Yeah, what the hell. You always did talk good, Lew. You gonna want some pizza when you get here?"

"Ten minutes."

"Tinmins. Right."

My neighbor three doors down owns his own cab, a bright-green, shopworn but ever-presentable DeVille. Since it spends evenings against the curb in front of his house and rarely goes back out, I guess he does all right.

Lights were on there, and a kid about twelve answered my knock and said "Yeah."

"Your father home?"

"Yeah."

After a moment I said, "Think I might speak to him?"

"Don't see why not."

After another moment: "So: what? We're just going to wait till he has to go somewhere and notices me here in the door?"

"You some kind of smartass."

"Just asking."

"Old man don't like smartasses."

This could easily have gone on all night, but the boy's father appeared behind him, peering out. He wore baggy nylon pants, a loose zipped sweatshirt, a shower cap. I'd wondered what a kid that age was doing up this time of night, but it seemed the whole family lived counterclockwise, as it were.

"Hi, we've never met, but I live a few houses down."

"I know who you are. Raymond, you get on about your business now."

"Who is it, honey?" came a feminine voice from deeper in the house.

"Neighbor, Cal."

"I'm sorry to bother you, but—"

He held out a hand. Muscles bunched along the forearm as we shook. "Norm Marcus. Call me Norm or Marc, whichever comes easier to you. You want to come on in, have a beer or something?"

"I'd love to, but a friend of mine just called and things don't sound so good over there. Since I don't drive I wondered if—"

"You need a ride, right?"

"I'll make it worth your while."

"Worth my while, huh?" He half turned, called into the house "Be right back, Cal" and stepped out, pulling the door shut. "It's already worth my while, Lew. Man can't help a neighbor, why's he bother living anywhere—know what I mean? Where we headed?"

I got in beside him and told him the address. He punched in a tape of Freddie King, hit the lights, and swung out toward St. Charles.

I tried to pay him when we pulled up at Don's place, but he said don't insult him. "You want me to wait?"

I thanked him again and said no, and that we had to get together for that beer soon.

"Absolutely. Or you just come on by for dinner, any night. Eat about nine, usually."

The front door was locked, but like mine Don's house is an old one whose frame and foundation have shifted time and again, and whose wood alternately swells with humidity and shrivels from heat. I pushed hard at the door and it opened.

He was still there all right, in the kitchen, head down on the table, facing away from me. An inch or so of bourbon remained in the bottle. The pizza, out of the box now, lay upside down on the floor, Police Special nearby.

I quickly checked a carotid pulse. Strong and steady.

He bobbed to the surface, without moving or opening his eyes.

"You, Lew?"

"Yeah. Let's get to bed, old friend."

"I tell you my wife was fucking Wally Gator?"

I hauled him more or less to his feet and we caromed from wall to wall down the narrow hall to his bedroom. I let him go slack by the bed, went around and pulled him fully aboard. Took off his shoes and loosened belt, trousers, tie.

I was almost to the bedroom door when he said: "Lew?"

"Here."

"You're a good man. Don't ever let anybody tell you different."

I sat there in his kitchen the rest of the night, though at this point there wasn't a lot of *rest* left, fully understanding that I wasn't a good man, had never been, probably never would be. The world outside faded slowly into being, like prints in a developing tray. And when magnolia leaves swam into focus against cottony sky, I put my thoughts aside, finished the bourbon and got coffee started. Not long after that, Don's alarm buzzed into life. I walked in with two cups of *café au lait,* looked at him, and shut the damned thing off.

12

The dead walked at last, or more accurately stumbled, at nine or so, into the kitchen where it looked at the clock, looked at me, back at the clock, mumbled *shit* most unexpletively, and slumped into a chair.

I poured coffee and put it down before him. He sat looking at it, estimating his chances. Gulfs loomed up everywhere. Washington and the Delaware. Napoleon crossing to Elba. Raft of the Medusa. Immigrants headed for Ellis Island, shedding history and culture like old clothes. Boats packed with new slaves, low in the water, nosing into compounds at Point Marigny across the river from what was now downtown New Orleans.

Finally he launched a hand into that gulf. It wavered but connected, and he drank the ransomed coffee almost at a gulp.

"I talk much last night?" he said partway into a second cup.

"Some."

"Before you came over here, on the phone? Or after."

"Before, mostly."

"Then I told you about Josie."

I nodded.

"And I was thinking about doing something stupid. I really don't remember too much else."

"You weren't thinking at all: you were feeling. But yes, it did look for a while like maybe you were going to stop being stupid for good."

"Yeah, well." He looked around the room, down at the floor. "Anyhow, the moment's passed. You eat my pizza? Stuff's great for breakfast, cold, you know."

"Sorry. It was crawling across the rug, making for the door. I had to shoot it."

He shook his head. "You're a sick man, Lew."

We finished the pot and he called in while I scrambled eggs. We ate, then sat over a second pot of coffee. Heading back to bed finally, he paused in the doorway. Looked off down the hall.

"Thanks, man. I won't forget this."

"I owe you a few."

"Not anymore you don't."

I found nongeneric scotch in the pantry beside five cans of stewed tomatoes, a stack of ramen noodles and two depleted jars of peanut butter, poured some into a coffee cup webbed with fine cracks beneath the surface, and dialed Clare's number. When her machine told me what to do and beeped at me, I said:

"This is your sailor, m'am. Who'd like to buy you dinner tonight, if you're free. Garces okay? Call me."

Garces is a small Cuban restaurant, tucked away in a decaying residential area a few blocks off Carrollton, as close to a special place as Clare and I had. Family-owned and -run, it started out years back as a grocery store and serves daily specials astonishingly simple and good, including a paella you'd kill for, cooked while you wait, one hour. Paella's where jambalaya came from, word and recipe freely translated.

I walked six or eight blocks and grabbed a bus on Magazine. Got home, rummaged through mail, listened to messages. Someone I didn't know wanted me to call right away. The English Department secretary needed to speak with me at my convenience. And Clare said: "Lew, I dodged home for lunch and found your message. Wish you'd gotten to me earlier, now I've already made plans. How're the sea legs? Talk to you later."

I stretched out on the couch for a nap and thought about Don, how he'd been looking lately, his long slow fall last night, this morning. Probably the steadiest man I ever knew. But you stand there peering off the edge long enough, whoever you are, things start shifting on you. You start seeing shapes down there that change your life.

The phone had been ringing a while, I realized. In my dreams I'd turned it into a distant train whistle.

The tape clicked on just as I answered, and I stabbed more or less randomly at buttons, *Answer, Hold,* trying to stop it. Taped message and entreaties to "Wait a minute, I'm here, hang on" overlapped, waves colliding into a feedback that made the room sound strangely hollow and cavernous.

"Can a girl change her mind?" Clare said when the tape had run its course.

"Why not? Always another ship coming into port somewhere."

"Okay. So I'll cancel this other thing and see you at Garces at, what? Six be okay? Want me to pick you up?"

"I'm not sure where I'll be before then. I'll meet you there."

"Then maybe I can take you home, at least."

"Just how do you mean that, lady?"

"Hmmmm . . ."

Where I was before then, as it turned out, was right there on that couch, though I did rouse a couple of times, first to answer the door and tell a private-school girl still in uniform (white shirt, blue tie, checked skirt, black flats) that I didn't need candy or wrapping paper, later to explain to an elderly Latin man that I *liked* the grass kind of high there in my patio-size front yard.

Around five I roused more definitively, showered and shaved, and called a cab.

Clare, a Corona, salsa and chips were waiting for me. A speaker set into the ceiling over our table spooled out the news in rolling, robust

Spanish. We ordered—rice and black beans, shredded meat stewed with onions and peppers, a Cuban coffee for me; nachos, empanadas and croquetas for Clare—and filled in recent blanks like the old friends we were. I told her about my lead on Alouette and said I'd be out of town for a few days. She told me that Bat had claimed squatter's rights atop the refrigerator and passed along new revelations from a course in Flemish art she was taking at Tulane.

Somewhere along in there, with half or more of my beans and rice gone, I said something about knowing we'd been kind of backing away from one another these last months, and noticed she was looking into her plate a lot.

"Lew," she said when I stopped to order another coffee, "I have no idea what the hell you're talking about. You know that? I haven't been backing away. *You* have. All I've done is just keep trying, every way I know, to keep myself from taking that necessary step or two toward you. To close the distance. When the whole time that's all in the world I wanted."

My coffee came, dark and heavy and sweet as summer nights, in its stainless-steel demitasse cup and saucer.

"*I'll* tell you how you can tell the dancer from the dance," she said. "Sooner or later the dancer always has to talk about why he's doing what he does. The dance just happens." She laughed. "Yeats: what the hell did he know, anyway? Impotent most of his life. Writing all that romantic, then all that mystical, stuff. And a child again, himself, there at the end."

I pushed beans onto my fork with a chip, doused the chip in salsa and then in chopped peppers from a tiny side dish.

"So. Guess this means you're not going to take me home, huh?"

"No," she said, eyes meeting mine. "No, it doesn't mean that at all, Lew. I don't know what it means. Maybe it doesn't mean anything. Maybe meaning doesn't have anything to do with any of this."

She folded her napkin and laid it on the table.

"Coming with?" she said.

Oh yes.

I have been so very long at sea.

13

Before the old man finally gave up on it—before he finally gave up on just about everything—he used to haul me out hunting with him the first few times he went out each season. Something was supposed to happen out there in the woods, I guess, with just the two of us, a father and his son, men of a different size observing these ancient rituals together, but it never did. I'd already learned to shoot, with bottles heeled into a hillside out behind our house, and that was the part I was interested in. So I'd just walk alongside Dad with my old single-shot .410 cradled in the crook of an arm and carefully pointing to the ground as he'd taught me, in early years daydreaming about friends and would-be friends in the neighborhood and next weekend's get-togethers, later about the things I'd begun discovering in books, with the twin plumes of our breath reaching out into the chill morning and reeling back, Dad every so often (it seemed always a continuous action) shouldering his .12-gauge, firing, and tucking dove, quail or squirrel into the game pocket of his scratchy canvas coat. After a couple of hours we'd stop, find a tree stump and have coffee from his thermos, wrapping hands around nesting plastic cups for warmth. On extremely cold days he brought along a hand warmer the size of a whiskey flask; you filled it with alcohol, lit the wick, slid on a cover and felt sleeve, and it smoldered there in your pocket. We'd pass it back and forth the way men pass around bottles of Jim Beam at deer camp, like athletes toasting a victory. But neither of us was an athlete. And neither of us would know many victories in his life.

I remembered all this, something I hadn't thought of in many years, as I drove up I-55 through mile after mile of unfenced farmland stretching to the horizon, past refurbished plantations, crop duster airfields and country stores selling everything a man could need, *Gas, Food, Beer*: this long sigh of the forever postcolonial South. I pulled off for coffee at truckers' roadside stops and Mini Marts where people seemed uneasy, even now, at my presence, despite (or just as easily because of) my dark suit, chambray shirt and silk tie. Attendants at gas stations watched me closely from their glassed-in pilothouses. When I stopped for a meal at The Finer Diner near Greenville, two state policemen, bent over roast beef specials in a booth by the door, repeatedly swiveled heads my direction, conferring.

Paranoia? You better believe it. My birthright.

In the town where I grew up, there was one main street, called Cherry in my little rubber-stamp town, Main or Sumpter or Grand in a hundred others like it. At one end of this street was a café, Nick's, where my father and I in stone darkness Saturday mornings heading out to hunt would order breakfast on paper plates through a "colored" window leading directly into the kitchen (the only time I recall anyone in the family ever eating out), and at the other, ten blocks distant, a bronze statue of a World War I soldier, rifle with bayonet at ready, which everyone called simply the Doughboy.

For a period of several months when I was thirteen or so, every Saturday night, like clockwork, someone managed—no simple task, with city hall and the police station right there on the circle—to paint the Doughboy's face and hands black with shoe polish. You'd go by every Sunday morning and see one of the black trustees from the county jail up there with a bucket and rags, scrubbing it down.

Then, just as suddenly as it had started, it stopped. Some said because the smartass nigger responsible had graduated from high school and, good riddance, gone up North to college. Some said because Chief Winfield and his boys had caught him in the act and done what was only right.

And my father, from whom I never before remember hearing a racial complaint, this man who called the children of white men he worked for *Mistah Jim* and *Miz Joan,* said: "Lewis, you see how it is. Here we raise his children for him, cook for him, bring up his crops, butcher his hogs—even fight his wars for him—and he still won't acknowledge our existence."

We were sitting on the steps of the railroad roundhouse across from Nick's eating our breakfasts one of those lightless early mornings, maybe the last before I stopped going along. Steam rose off eggs and grits in the cold air; our paper plates were translucent with grease.

"You know those Dracula movies you watch every chance you get, Lewis? How he can never see himself in mirrors? Well, that's you, son—that's all of us. We trip across this earth, work and love and raise families and fight for what we think's right, and the whole time we're absolutely invisible. When we're gone, there's no record we were ever even here."

For years I thought of that as the day my father began shrinking.

Now, years later, I remember it as one time among many that he was able momentarily to rise out of the drudge of his own life and offer an example—to give me sanction, as it were—that in my own something more might be possible.

It's a terrible thing, that I could ever have forgotten these moments, or failed to understand them.

Oddly connected in my thoughts with all this as I Mazdaed into pure Faulknerland, *Oxford, Tupelo,* was a night Clare and I met, early on in our friendship, at a Maple Street pizzeria and went on to the Maple Leaf for klezmer music, impossibly joyful in its minor keys, clarinet beseeching and shrieking, stolid bass and accordion plodding on, half East Europe's jews dying in its choruses.

Here's what I think in higher flights of fancy. Once there existed beings, a race, a species (call it what you will) who truly belonged to this world. Then at some point, for whatever reason, they moved on, and *we* moved into their places. We go on trying to occupy those places, day after endless day. But we'll always remain strangers here, all of us. And for all our efforts, whatever dissimulations we attempt, we'll never quite fit.

14

Lights came up behind me not too far outside Greenville—for all I know, the two young men who'd been enjoying their roast beef specials at The Finer Diner.

They, the lights, winked into being far back in my mirror, pinned in the distance at first, believably neons or traffic lights, or one of those blinking roadside barriers. But then they rushed in to close the gap, like something falling out of the sky, and suddenly were there behind me, filling mirror and road.

I pulled over and watched the one in shotgun position climb out and make his careful, by-the-book way toward me. Once years ago I'd made the mistake of stepping out of my car to meet a state policeman halfway and found myself suddenly face-down on the asphalt shoulder with a knee in my back. So now I sat very still, not even reaching for my wallet, watching him come toward me in the rearview, walk out of it, reappear in the wing mirror, then at the window.

He had to be midtwenties at least but looked all of sixteen, with a close-trimmed mustache, discount-store mirror shades, black goat-ropers. Coming abreast and bending down, he removed the glasses in a quick left-to-right sweep, releasing startling green eyes.

"License and registration, sir? Proof of insurance?"

I probably imagined the slight pause and emphasis on *sir*.

I reached slowly into the glove compartment for the car's papers, handed him those (in a leatherette wallet) along with my license and rental agreement. He studied them all carefully, looking from the picture on my license up to me and down again. Walked behind the car to check plates against the numbers listed.

"Would you excuse me for a moment, Mr. Griffin?"

He went back to the squad and passed documents across the sill. Waited. Exchanged a few words, straightened, came back toward me: rearview, side mirror, window.

"We apologize for holding you up, sir. You know a Lieutenant Walsh? NOPD?"

I nodded.

"He says thanks. Called headquarters here and asked us to stop you and tell you that. Said you'd be coming through in a Sears rental, gave us the plate number. Said just to tell you thanks, he wouldn't forget it—you'd know what he meant."

I smiled. Years ago when things were at their worst, Don was the one who stuck by me. First he, then Vicky, had made it possible for me to go on, helped me find long-lost Lew in brambles of remorse and inaction.

And Verne. How much of what I've become owes to Verne? I was never able to tell her what she meant to me; never really knew, until it was too late. And yet, somehow in all those years we circled and closed on one another like binary stars, all those departures and partial returns, somehow, in some indefinable manner, we had held one another up, had been able to climb together (even when apart) out of the wastes of our pasts.

How could I not have known that?

"Mr. Griffin?"

"Sorry. A sudden attack of memory."

"Right." He looked at me curiously. "Lieutenant Walsh also said we were to tell you to call if you need him. For anything, he said—anything at all."

I nodded, thanked him again.

"Drive safely, Mr. Griffin."

He tipped a brief salute against his hat brim and headed back to his squad.

An hour and spare change later I stood in my newly rented cabin at the Magnolia Branch Motel drinking the cream of a newly cracked fifth of Teacher's from one of those squat tumblers you never see anywhere else. I'd even had to unwrap the glass, like a Christmas gift, from crinkly, twisted paper. There was a strip of paper across the toilet seat. Rubber flower appliqués on the floor of the tub. The bed was equipped with Magic Fingers, but two quarters didn't persuade them to do anything.

Missagoula, Mississippi, was like a hundred other towns scattered through the South. The interstate zipped by only a few miles away but may as well have been in China. Remnants of an old town square hosted two gas stations (one of which doubled as post office), a café and steakhouse, a combined town library and meeting hall, a doughnut shop, a junk store or two, and an insurance office. For two or three blocks around that hub there were a scatter of paint and hardware stores, utility companies, used-clothing or -furniture shops. Then everything opened back up to farmland, trees and sky. I'd counted four churches, so far.

The Magnolia Branch squatted at the border of town and not-town. I can't imagine who would ever stay there, in a town like that, but rates were cheap and rooms immaculate. They still weren't very used to having blacks drop in, I'd guess. My request for a room occasioned considerable discussion behind the wall before the clerk (and owner, as I'd later discover) returned to push across a key and take two nights in advance. I asked about the possibility of getting a drink and was told I could get beer down at the café but if I wanted anything else I'd have to go over to Nathan's.

Nathan's turned out to be the gas station that didn't double as post office. I dropped off luggage at cabin six, walked back into town and, saying I understood liquor was for sale here, got ushered into a shed out back of the station. Bottles were set out on cheap steel shelving before which the attendant hovered impatiently. I pointed to the Teacher's and paid him. He followed me out, locked the door carefully behind us.

So now I stood there in my Magnolia Branch Motel doorway lapping at the first few most welcome sips of scotch and looking away (Dixieland!) into dusty Delta distances. News unrolled on the TV behind me. A coup attempt somewhere in Latin America, Philadelphia man's citizen's award revoked when it was discovered the recipient routinely molested the adolescents his Care House harbored, Housing Authority of New Orleans under investigation by feds.

Immediately upon returning to the motel I'd phoned Clare. Her recording had come on, and I'd started telling her where I was, how she could reach me. I'd got as far as the Missagoula part when she picked up.

"I'm here, Lew. *Where* did you say you were?"

I spelled it for her. I may even have got it right.

"And the girl's supposed to be there?"

"She gave it as an address at the hospital, finally, Richard said. Claimed she lived here with a relative. I'm pulling out in just a minute to try and find the place."

"Good luck, then."

"Thanks. I'll call again tomorrow."

"Lucky, lucky me!"

I finished my drink, rinsed the glass and put it face-down on a towel. I'd just pulled the door shut behind me when the phone started ringing. I unlocked the door and went back in.

"Lew," Clare said, "remember when you said that about another man?"

"What?"

"You were talking about my cat. Joking that there was a new man in my life."

"Oh, right."

"Well, there is."

"There is what?"

"A new man in my life."

I didn't say anything, and after a while she said, "You there, Lew?"

"I'm here."

"I didn't know how to tell you. I kept waiting for the right time, and it never came. Then you left, and the more I thought about it, the worse I felt. After I hung up just now, I knew I had to tell you, that I couldn't wait anymore."

"It's all right, Clare."

"It wouldn't matter if I didn't really care about you. I do, you know. I don't know what's going to happen, but I know I don't want to lose you."

We both fell silent, listening together to choruses of ghostlike voices far back in the wires, at the very edge of intelligibility.

"Oh Lew, are we going to be able to do this?"

"We've both been through a lot worse."

"Indeed we have, sailor. Indeed we have."

Silent again for a moment, we listened, but the voices, too, now were silent. Listening to *us,* perhaps.

"You'll call and let me know how it's going?"

"I will." Though as it turned out, I didn't.

"Bye, Lew. Love you."

And she was gone.

15

I stopped at Nathan's to ask directions and, following a consultation between the surly black man chewing on cold pizza behind the counter and a mechanic with grease worked into the lines of his face so profoundly that it looked like some primitive mask, headed out of town away from the interstate, leaving pavement behind after a few miles, tires clawing for safe ground among gullylike ruts, the little Mazda sashaying and hip-heavy.

Houses were infrequent and set back off the road, simple wood structures built a foot or two off the ground, most of them long unpainted and patched with odd scraps of lumber, corrugated tin, tar paper, heavy cardboard. Many had cluttered front porches and neatly laid-out vegetable gardens alongside. Small stands of trees surrounded house and yard; beyond that, flat farmland unrolled to every side.

I pulled in, as I'd been told back at Nathan's, by a yellowish house on the right, first one I came to after crossing railroad tracks and going through two crossroads. An old woman in a faded sundress scattered grain for chickens at the side of the house. She was oddly colorless, pulpy like wood long left outdoors, collapsing into herself with the years. She looked at me with all the interest a tree stump might display.

"Hello, m'am. Sorry to bother you, but I'm looking for Alouette."

Nothing showed on her face. "Not bothering me," she said. Then she turned and walked away, to a rough shed nailed onto the back of the house at one end, open at the other. I followed a few steps behind. She dumped grain back into a burlap bag and folded the top over. Hung the pail from a nail just above.

"Could you tell me if she's around?"

"Have to ask what your business with her might be."

"I promised a friend I'd look her up."

She grunted. It was more like the creak of a gate than any grunt I'd ever heard. "Name's Adams. Where you from, boy?"

"New Orleans."

"Mmm. Thought so." She looked to see how the chickens were doing. They seemed more interested in pecking one another than the food. "I was up to Memphis once. You been there?"

"Yes m'am, I have." Memphis was where my father died, though I wasn't there then.

"You care much for it?"

"Not particularly. It's like just about any other town you see around here, only a lot bigger."

She groaned—it couldn't have been a laugh—and said that was God's truth. Then she looked at me for a while before saying: "Well then, I guess I know who you must be. That Griffin fellow LaVerne took up with. Don't much like you, from what I know. Don't expect me to."

"You knew LaVerne, then?"

Again that long, affectless regard.

"Mother gen'rally knows her only daughter."

"I'm sorry, Mrs. Adams," I said shortly. "I didn't know. I had no idea Verne's parents were still alive."

"Just the one. But neither did she, boy, that you'd notice. Not that her daddy and I ever wanted things any different, you understand.

Vernie had her life down there in New Orleans, and she was welcome to it, but *we* didn't want any part of it. Wrote once or twice."

"LaVerne really turned things around, later on. She helped a lot of other people get their lives together, too. You both could have put all that behind you."

"Maybe we could have. Maybe not." She eyed the chickens again, looked up at the sky. Darkness had begun working its way in at day's edge. "Things had changed here too."

"So Alouette came here because you're her grandmother?"

"You have the kind of troubles that girl had, you just naturally go to a woman. From what I know about down there where you-all are, there wasn't much of anybody she *could* go to."

"Her mother was trying to get in touch with her, before she died. That's why I'm here now."

"Girl didn't know that. Didn't say much about her mother ever. Not that I cared to listen."

"How did Alouette find you here? Or even know about you, for that matter?"

"Long time ago, right after Vernie had her, I sent that girl a book of stories I came across in the back of a cabinet, something that was Vernie's when she was little. Thought she might make some use of it. Envelope had the address, and she says her mother cut that out and pasted it in the front of the book. Never sent another thing to that girl. But I ain't moved, of course. And she still had it."

"Where's Alouette now, Mrs. Adams?"

"Couldn't tell you that, I'm afraid."

"But she is here? With you?"

Her eyes were as lifeless as locust husks abandoned on a tree. "Stayed here a few days. Then when it looked to be some trouble, I had Mr. Simpson drive that girl over to the Clarksville hospital. I did midwifing back in the old times. You don't forget what birthing trouble looks like."

"Did you visit her at the hospital? Did anyone?"

"Haven't seen her since the day Mr. Simpson came by to get her."

"Didn't you wonder how she was doing? Think she might need you?"

"Don't waste much time worrying and thinking. I figure the girl found me once. If she wants to, she can do it again. She'd be welcome enough."

"You know about her baby?"

"Mr. Simpson told me it's still alive."

"Mrs. Adams, I have to ask you something. Please don't take this wrong. Was your granddaughter using drugs when she was here?"

She thought for a moment. "Wouldn't know how to tell you. She wasn't normal. Laid around half asleep most of the time, didn't have any appetite. All that could be what was going wrong inside her."

"You don't have any idea where she might have gone, then, after leaving the hospital?"

"Didn't know she left."

"Well, I'll be getting on, then. Thank you for giving me so much of your time."

"Didn't give it. You helped yourself."

"You're right, but thanks all the same. When I find Alouette, I'll be sure to let you know."

I started back around the house to the car.

"Boy?"

"Yes, m'am?"

"You be heading over to Clarksville now by any chance?"

"Yes, m'am."

"Going to see that baby."

"Yes, m'am. And to ask more questions."

"You figure you might have room to give an old lady a ride over there? Sounds like that baby's going to be needing someone."

"Yes, m'am. It does sound that way. And I'd be glad to take you."

"You wait right there."

She went into the house and came immediately back out with a Sunday-best purse, probably the only one she had. It was covered with tiny red, blue and green beads.

"Let's go, boy," she said. "Dark's coming on fast."

It always is.

16

So, midnight, raining, miles to go, I arrived at the berth bearing Baby Girl McTell to whatever ports awaited her.

In the car on the way Mrs. Adams asked me to tell her about Verne's last years, offering no comment when I was through. We passed the remainder of the trip, just over an hour, in silence, watching the storm build: a certain heaviness at the horizon, rumbles of thunder in unseen bellies of clouds, lightning crouched and stuttering behind the dark pane.

Mrs. Adams had me drop her off on the highway outside town, at a cinderblock church (*Zion Redemption Baptist*) where, she said, her sister lived, adding "pastor's wife," her toneless voice (it seemed to me) implying equally scorn and acknowledgment of status. She would go on to the hospital first thing in the morning.

Closer in, I stopped at one of those gargantuan installations that look like battleships and seem to carry everything from gas and drinks and snacks to novelty T-shirts, athletic shoes and the occasional Thanksgiving turkey. You could probably pick up a TV or computer system at some of these places. I pushed a dollar over the counter toward a teenage girl wearing a truly impressive quantity of denim—shirt, pants, boots, jacket, even earrings—and poured my own coffee from a carafe squatting on the hot plate (*One Refill Only, Please*) beside display cards of Slim Jims, snuff and lip balm. Then I pulled the car to the edge of the lot and sat there breathing in the coffee's dark, earthy smell, feeling its heat and steam on my face, sipping at it from time to time. New Orleans coffee makes most others seem generic, but I was at this moment far, far from home, a wanderer, and could make do. Besides, for the true believer coffee's a lot like what Woody Allen says about sex: the worst he ever had was wonderful.

Back at the hospital years ago, later at AA meetings, coffee would disappear by the gallon, as though it were getting poured down floor drains. These people were *serious* coffee drinkers. Someone or another was pretty much always at work making a new pot, draining the urn to re-up it, dumping out filters the size of automobile carburetors or measuring out dark-roast-with-chicory by the half pound. Antlike streams of porters to back doors, fifty-pound sacks saddling their shoulders. They should have just pulled up tanker trucks outside, run a hose in.

So the mind, weary from the day's travel, released for a time even from purposeful activity, wanders.

To a dayroom where a youngish man sits staring fixedly at reruns of *Hazel, Maverick, I Dream of Jeannie, Jeopardy,* swathed in the dead, false calm of drugs, mind all the while sparking and phosphorescing like the screen's own invisible dots.

To a still younger man waking against a heap of garbage bins, loose trash, half a burned-out mattress, on a New Orleans street, shotgun houses hardly wider than their entry doors in dominolike rows as far as he can see looking up from the pavement there, wondering how last night bled over into this bleary, pain-filled morning, how he shipwrecked here, wherever here is, finding what little money he had left, of course, gone.

To a teenage boy then, spine bent in a question mark above Baldwin or *Notes from the Underground* as flies buzz the screen and morning nibbles dark away from the window, a boy just beginning to sense with fear and elation how very large the world is and to believe that, turning these pages, naming things in these mirrors, he'll discover secret doors and passageways few other of the castle's inhabitants suspect.

Forward suddenly to a man in his forties as he sits over a drink and the final pages, proofing them, of a novel titled *The Old Man,* wondering if he'll ever be able to do what he has just, amazingly, done, to create so vivid and reflective a world, ever again.

Two young black men pulled in by one of the pumps. They were driving a Ford that looked as though it had been badly burned then skin-grafted with pot metal; a plywood wall of speakers replaced the backseat. Even at that remove the heavy bass, all I could really make out, tugged hard at my viscera. I swallowed the last half mouthful of cold coffee, started the engine, and pulled back out onto the highway. A mile or so further along, a sign reading *Clarksville* pointed off to the right. I turned onto a two-way highway surprisingly populous with late-model cars, pickups, and several awkward, unwieldy pieces of farm machinery, like dinosaurs strayed from their own slow time, confused and lost in the furious rush of modern life.

The hospital sat on what passed for a hill in this part of Mississippi, on the far side of a city whose business district comprised maybe ten square blocks, a preponderance of its commercial space appearing to be given over to wholesale food concerns, beauty supplies and auto-parts shops. *Clarksville Regional Hospital.* An automatic ticket dispenser stood sentry at the parking lot, but the gate was up. I drove in, parked and started for the building just as the rain let go.

Even inside, in the lobby, I could hear it slamming down. Windows ran with water, closing off the outer world, and when lights blinked briefly off and back on I had the momentary, terrifying sensation of being enclosed in an aquarium. I reached out and touched the wall to steady myself.

"You all right, sir?"

A young man stepped through one of the doors, two older women close behind. They were all black, all in whites and carrying coats.

"If you're looking for the emergency room, it's down this hallway to your right. I can call for help if you'd like. Or I'll walk you down myself, since it doesn't look like I'll be going anywhere soon."

I told him I was fine, just tired, that I'd been driving all day from New Orleans. Other personnel began gathering out of various hallways and doors, looking out at the downpour with irritation and anger. But even as they watched, the rain abated, settled into a soothing, slow rhythm. Most sprinted toward cars, coats or newspapers held over their heads. I asked the young man to direct me to the newborn intensive-care unit.

Then, following his instructions, I took a nearby elevator to the second floor to meet Baby Girl McTell.

17

For a long time, meaning that I rarely woke without memory of the previous night's events, and never in hospitals or jails anymore, I'd had my drinking under control.

I knew it wasn't that simple, of course. What is?

One of the distinctions of this addiction, because only true alcoholics have them, are blackouts. We go on moving through the physical world, driving cars, carrying on conversations and cooking meals, with whole banks of relays and higher functions closed down, unwitting passengers in our own bodies.

I was by this time a veritable quagmire of information on addiction. I could draw you diagrams, cite percentages, talk to you about noradrenaline and dopamine and receptor sites. I knew the alcoholic's body for some reason doesn't metabolize intoxicants the same way other people's do. That the addiction lodges itself where reality curves gently away from appearance, and thrives there, pushing them ever further apart. That all his life, whatever he does, a physical, psychological, ontological dialogue will be going on inside the alcoholic, and that as long as he continues to drink, however controlled it appears, sooner or later, a day, ten years, or twenty, he'll wake up once again with the world quivering terribly behind the thinnest of membranes, thoughts bending slowly, unstoppably away from one another in the terrible gravity of alcohol's black sun.

The membrane was there for me when I woke the next afternoon. As though I were almost, but not quite, within the world; almost, but not quite, real. And as though the slightest misstep, the slightest tear at the membrane, might bring the waters of some endless night crashing down upon me from the other side.

Starting off for food after leaving the hospital, I'd changed my mind on the way and instead driven back to Missagoula, to my room at the Magnolia Branch and the Teacher's. I remembered switching on the TV, part of a talk show, a *Columbo* rerun, and a movie about aliens (it's possible that I don't have this quite right) who had learned to survive and indeed flourish by disguising themselves as Coke machines. Obviously I'd drunk the entire bottle in short order. I didn't want to think too much about what else I might have done. There was a crumpled bag in the trash, and remnants of some kind of sandwich under that, so at some point I'd gone out for food, I had no idea where.

Using what volition I had left, I showered and shaved, dressed, straightened the room, carried bags to the car and went to the office to check out. I stopped for breakfast on the highway, biscuits and gravy and lots of coffee, then drove back into Clarksville and took a room at Dee's-Lux Inn. Pale pine furniture and kidney-shaped tables from older days when motels were tourist courts and their neon signs advertised *Climate Controlled*.

I unloaded my suitcase into the top drawer of the low bureau, set my Dopp case out by the sink, and over the following days my routine varied little. I was in and out of NICU constantly, but went mostly at night, after Mrs. Adams, who kept vigil all day, sitting stiff-backed at bedside, departed, and while the British nurse, Teresa Hunt, was on duty. When I wasn't at the hospital, or trying to catch a few hours' sleep, I was scrambling after leads on Alouette.

I learned the monitors, what they were for and their various sounds; learned about blood gases and hematocrits, interstitial edemas, fibrosis, fluid overload, lipids and hyperalimentation, surfactant. I got to know several of the nurses and doctors by name, and never missed the fatigue and sadness in their eyes as they answered my questions or told me that all was pretty much as before. I spent hour after hour sitting on metal stools or in rocking chairs by Baby Girl McTell's incubator, staring in at her and speaking softly (once, not knowing what else to say, I recited "The Raven" and much of the prologue to *The Canterbury Tales*), helping Teresa or other nurses whenever I could with small tasks of caring for her.

On the streets by contrast, as I asked after Alouette, shooting pool with young hawks in satiny sweats, going into busy barbershops and sitting there as if waiting my turn for a cut while I talked to others, handing out cigarettes to elderly men clustered in scrubby street-side parks or around bars and convenience stores, I learned nothing.

Teresa and I had dinner a couple of nights, collecting surreptitious looks and the occasional outright glare at Denny's and a barbeque place, then one morning as we were leaving the hospital together, to no one's particular surprise, I think, went on to breakfast and to her house on Biscoe Street. It never happened again; there was never much question it would, really; and Teresa and I remained close.

Hospital records, as I anticipated, were of no help at all. None of the usual places a footloose young woman might alight briefly—shelters, Clarksville's only (church-run) soup kitchen, a strip of music clubs near the heart of the city—bore any visible trace of Alouette's passage. I showed her picture at malls, game arcades, on streets around what passed here for pricey downtown hotels, always prime panhandling territory.

Finally, after a couple of calls had passed back and forth between Don and myself, I met a Sergeant Travis for coffee and had him fill me in on local drug action. Much of it, he said, took place around schools and downtown bars; nothing new there. And a lot of it was small potatoes, ten or twelve hopheads carting pills, grass and cocaine, scrambling to pay for their own monkey.

I asked him about crack.

That too, he said, though it wasn't near as big here as in larger cities. Not yet, anyway.

And once you got past those ten or twelve user-friendlies?

He waited till the waitress poured more coffee and moved away. "You do realize this is an ongoing investigation?"

"I'm not a cop or a fed. I won't step on anyone's toes. Or on my own dick."

"Yeah, well. I'm only here as a favor to NOPD. We really don't know *what* you are."

So, briefly, I told him.

He sat quietly a moment, afterwards.

"Guy calls himself Camaro's probably the one you'd want to see."

"I need to guess what he drives?"

"Prob'ly not. Around here, if he didn't sell it, he knows who did. Got tentacles running out everywhere."

"Everywhere, huh."

"I won't lie to you: there's been a couple times we were able to do one another a favor. More than a couple. You know how it is."

"You get a bust, he gets the competition offed."

"That old sweet song."

"Where's Camaro likely to be this time of day?"

"He's not at the Chick'n Shack up on Jefferson, then he's at the Broadway, a bar—and grill, the sign says, though I never saw anybody ever cook, or for that matter eat anything there—corner of Lee and Twelfth."

"Can I say you sent me?"

"You can say whatever you want. He's only going to hear what he wants to, regardless."

I stood and thanked him, shook hands.

"No problem," he told me. "May want to call in the favor someday, who knows?"

I found the eponymous pusher sitting at a booth in the Broadway, near a front window where he could keep an eye on his chariot. It was truly a splendid vehicle, beetle green with strips of chrome highlighting windows, doors, hood and trunk. A filigree of silver paint running down each side. His, their, name in silver script at one edge of the front left fender.

Camaro wore a beige suit, mostly cotton from the look of it, with a blue shirt and rust-colored tie tugged loose at the neck. The clothes set off the deep coffee color of his skin. As he lifted his drink, I caught a glimpse of gold watch and signet ring. He looked for all the world like a successful C.P.A. decompressing after a day at the computer.

He watched me walk over and sit across from him in the booth. The waitress was there instantly, dropping one of those stiff little napkins on the table in front of me. I ordered a scotch, water by. Sat drinking it, smiling over at him.

"Hope I ain't bothering you too much, sitting here like this," he said after a while.

I shook my head, smiled some more.

"I mean, you got friends or the rest of your band coming or something, you just let me know and I'll be glad to make room, okay?"

He took a long pull off his drink, pretty much killing it. Held up a hand to signal the waitress.

"You about ready for another one, too, friend?"

I laid a ten on the table. "My round."

"Whatever you say."

I introduced myself and over that drink and another, we talked as freely as two black men with secrets, rank strangers to one another, ever can. Camaro's mind was orderly and sharp; his world was a kind of pool or glade where the edges of discrete bodies of information glided by one another, sometimes catching. When I told him about Baby Girl McTell, he said he'd had a kid years ago, when he wasn't much more than one himself, that it had lived three weeks in an incubator, shriveling up the whole time till it looked like a piece of dried fruit, and then died.

I said I was looking for the baby's mother. Explained that she'd left the hospital and not gone back to her grandmother's, had dropped out of sight.

"And she's a user," he said, at my sudden glance adding: "Only reason you'd be here. That what messed the baby up?"

I nodded.

"Shit does that. People ought to know it. Course, people ought to know a lot of things." He held up his glass, looked through its amber to the light outside. I knew from long experience just how that warms the world and softens it. "You want another one?"

"Better not. Still a lot to do. We square with the tab?"

"It's cool." He looked at his watch. "Well, I've got an appointment myself. Tell you what." He slid out of the booth and stood. Bent to pick up, yes, a briefcase. "I'll ask around, see what I can come up with. You have a picture of this girl?"

I took out my wallet and gave him one of the copies. Also one of my cards, scribbling the motel's phone number on the back, then, after a second's thought, the NICU number and *Teresa.*

"If you can't get me, leave a message for her. And thanks, man."

He shrugged. I sat and watched as he climbed into the Camaro, buckled up, started the engine, hit his turn signal and eased out into traffic, sunlight lancing off the chrome.

18

My second week in Clarksville, on a Tuesday, I got back to the motel midmorning, having left the hospital at five or so and been on the streets since (with a stopover at Mama's Homestyle for a kickass breakfast), and found two messages waiting. I didn't look at the second one till later. But Teresa had called to say they were "having some trouble" with Baby Girl McTell and she thought I might want to be there.

A nurse I hadn't met before, Kristi Scarborough, brought me up to date. Around six that morning, sats had dropped into the seventies and hovered there; ABG's confirmed a low PO_2 and steadily increasing PCO_2. It could, of course, be a number of things: cardiac problems, a sign that the lungs were stiffening beyond our capacity to inflate them, infection, pulmonary edema. The baby was back on 100 percent oxygen, and ventilator pressures had been raised. Gases were slowly improving. I stood before an X-ray viewer staring at loops of white in Baby Girl McTell's belly. Like those ancient maps where the round, unknown world has been cleft in half and laid out flat. Necrosis of the bowel, Nurse Scarborough told me; a further complication. It almost always happens with these tiny ones. But for now she's holding her own.

Kristi used to work the unit full-time, she told me, but last year had married one of the residents and now put in only the hours necessary to keep her license, a day or two every other week, while husband John oversaw an emergency room just across the Tennessee line, broken bones, agricultural accidents and trauma from the regional penitentiary mostly (once, a hatchet buried in a head), and "they" tried as best they could to "get pregnant."

I left at three or four, finally, once Baby Girl McTell seemed to be out of immediate danger, and over a cheeseburger and fries at Mama's looked at the second message.

Call me. Clare.

I went back to my room and did just that. She answered on the third ring, breathing hard.

"Greetings from the great state of Mississippi."

"Lew! I've been worried about you."

I told her about Baby Girl McTell.

"Hospitals are tough. You haven't found Alouette yet, I take it?"

"She's as gone as gone gets. But I will."

"I know. I've missed you, Lew. Any idea when you'll be back in town?"

"Not really. I don't know what I'm into here, or how long it may take. I'll give you a call."

Outside, a fire truck and police car went screaming by.

"I spent about half of my teenage years waiting for people to call who said they would, Lew."

"I'm sorry," I said after a moment.

"I know. You really are—that's what makes it so difficult." I listened to the sirens fade. Wondered if she could hear them, all those miles away. "But it *is* good to hear your voice."

The door slammed in the room next to mine and a woman stalked toward her car, a pearl-gray Tempo. She got in and started it, then sat there with the engine running. A man came out of the room and leaned down to the window, holding his hands palm up.

"You're very important to me, Clare."

"I know, Lew. I know I am."

The man walked around the car and got in. They drove away.

"When I get back—if it's possible, and if you want to, that is—I'd like for us to spend some time together. A lot of time."

She was silent a moment, then said, "I'd like that too, Lew."

"Good. I guess I'd better try to get some sleep now."

"Take care."

I hung up and watched my neighbors pull the Tempo back into its slot, get out together and go back into their room.

An hour later I got up and, sitting naked on the side of the bed, improvising abbreviations in my rush to get it all down, scribbled ten pages of notes.

In a featureless gray room with light slanting in through windows set high in the wall a man says good-bye to a group of men we slowly realize are his fellow prisoners, the community he's lived among for almost ten years. He is being released because another man has confessed to the murder for which he was convicted, and which he in fact committed. He distributes his few possessions: half a carton of cigarettes, a transistor radio, a badly pilled cardigan. No one says much of anything. He turns and walks to the door, where a guard joins him to escort him out. "Don't do nothing I wouldn't do," Bad Billy says behind him, but he can't imagine anything Bad Billy would not do—or hasn't done, for that matter. He will go out into the world and find that he is absolutely alone and hopelessly unsuited for the narrow life available to him. And so he will invent a life, a thing that makes a virtue of his apartness, cobbled together from routine, false memories, old movies, half-read books. Until one day a woman will come suddenly, unexpectedly ("like a nail into cork") into his life's ellipsis to disrupt it; and, as he struggles up out of his aloneness, as he fights against his own instincts and the circumstances of his life just to make this single human connection, his careful, wrought life collapses. When he steps out into sunlight now, it blinds him.

Those ten pages, virtually word for word as I scribbled them in the motel room that night, became the first chapter, and the very heart, of *Mole,* a book unlike anything else I had written, purely fiction in that every character, every scene was invented, purely true in that it is in purest form the story of all our lives.

19

The desk clerk and I obviously were not destined to become close friends. He wasn't accustomed to taking messages for guests and didn't like it much, and as I came in from the hospital the next morning, he motioned at me through the front glass (a hand held high, opening and closing twice, as though waving good-bye to himself) then wordlessly shoved a couple of slips of paper over to me.

Of course, one had to take into account that he seemed to work around the clock—whenever my erratic *va et vient* took me by the office, day or night, I'd look in and see him here—which is enough to make even one of Rilke's angels growl.

Teresa had called to let me know that, minutes after I left the unit that morning, someone had tried to reach me. I flipped over to the second slip of paper, which just read *Camaro,* then back to the first. *Said you might want to check out a house in Moon Point. No direct connection that he knows, but things happen there. Hope this makes sense to you, Lew.* And an address, of sorts.

They grow their boys tough out there by the catfish channels, I want you to know, and they ain't *about* to bend over for no big-city dude in a coat and tie.

I always forget how very much alike rural and inner-city attitudes are.

Asking at the motel office, a gas station nearby, another on the highway and, finally, a postman I drove by a couple of times on a dirt road six or eight miles outside Clarksville, I found the house, a two-story frame, white many years ago. A jeep and a '55 Chevy rusted away on blocks in the front yard. There were some appliances, including a vintage avocado refrigerator, sitting at precarious angles at the side of the house. A tractor covered in vines at the back. Two Mustangs and a BMW in the circular front drive.

I knocked at the door and politely inquired after Alouette to the young man in a beige silk suit and black T-shirt who eventually answered. A relative, I told him.

"Ain't here," he said after a moment.

"Thank you. But allow me to make an assumption, possibly unwarranted, from that. To wit: that she has, at some unspecified point in the past, been here, though she is not presently."

"Say what?"

Another youngish man, unseen, joined him at the door: "What's up, Clutch?"

"Nigger looking for his squeeze."

"Yeah? He think we run some kind of dating service here? Tell him to get missing."

"You heard the man," Silky said.

"What man? All I heard's your boy hiding back there behind the door."

Silky sighed, and said door flew open. I have to tell you he was one ugly black man. Someone had been really creative with a knife or razor down both sides of his face and in one long jagged pull across his neck. The nose had spent as much time taped as not. He would have struck terror in all hearts, save for his stature: he was well under five feet tall. His body looked to be normal size, but everything else seemed oddly foreshortened. Neck, arms, legs, fingers. Temper.

"*I* got your assumption, motherfucker. Right here."

"Excuse me," I said, looking straight ahead, "I hear something, but I don't see anyone."

Which was how I got the shit beat out of me again. Or how it started, anyway. I'd never make it as a standup comic, I guess.

The first guy went low, tumbling me over, as his dwarfish buddy scrambled up my back like a chimp and started hammering temples and kicking kidneys with considerable fervor. The taller one was trying valiantly to get a knee into my groin. I reached down and grabbed his nuts, crushing them together in my fist, bringing him up off the floor like an epileptic.

At the same time, holding on, I reached out and snagged in my left hand a thick wedge of wood used in warmer days to hold the door ajar. Slammed it hard into the dwarf's mouth, as teeth caught at it and sinews, possibly the mandible, gave. Lodged it there.

I had a dim, peripheral perception of others standing just inside the door, watching.

I got up onto my knees. Blood ran down my face. I tossed my head to clear it out of my eyes. My lower back throbbed with pain and for days, whenever I peed, the water in the bowl went red.

"Where's Alouette?"

"Man, if we knew, we'd tell you."

This was from the tall guy, kind of grunting it out, hugging his nuts with both hands.

"Go on."

"She be here a coupla times. Been a while."

"How long?"

No response. I set the heel of my hand against the wedge and drove it in deeper. This time the mandible gave for sure.

"Jesus, man," Silky said. "I don't know. A week, maybe two."

"Mrff, gdfftm, lfft," the dwarf said. Blood bubbled up out of his nose when he breathed.

"You didn't have to do that," Silky said.

Probably not.

I stopped off at the Clarksville Regional ER for stitches and X rays. Nothing was broken, but everything hurt like hell. What else was new? I declined Tylenol 3, went back to my room, swallowed half a handful of aspirin and poured three fingers of scotch into the plastic cup. Watched part of a movie about child abuse. Poured another drink. Fell asleep there in the chair.

Then someone was pounding at my door.

I opened it. Sergeant Travis had two quart-size styrofoam containers of coffee balanced piggyback in one hand, a paper bag of doughnuts in the other.

"Thought you might could use this."

He held out the cups so I could take one and came on in. Put the bag on the dresser. The TV was still on and he sat watching a Tom and Jerry cartoon and sipping at coffee. I did the same.

"Your name kind of came up, Griffin."

"Names have a way of doing that."

"Made me wonder enough that I called your friend on the force in New Orleans, Walsh, and talked to him about you. He told me if he sent you out to the corner for a paper, chances would be about fifty-fifty of his actually getting one, but that he'd trust you with his life. One of your stranger character references."

"Two of your stranger characters."

He finished his coffee and dropped the cup into the trashcan. "You guys go back a ways, huh?"

"There's history, yes."

"You want one of these?" He'd snagged the bag of doughnuts and pulled one out. Chewed on it a moment and dropped it into the trashcan too. "Damn things always *look* so good. But they taste like sugared cardboard and turn into fists in your gut somewhere. Thing is, we had a report of probable assault from the hospital—"

"I made no such complaint."

"Didn't have to. We like to stay on top of things around here, Griffin. Man comes into ER all beat to hell, the staff's just naturally going to let me know about it."

"They're not big fans of legal fine points such as patient confidentiality, I take it."

"Well you know, city people are the ones that seem always to be worried about protecting their anonymity. Maybe that has something to do with *why* they're city people. Town this size, everybody tends to know everybody else's business anyway. This has to be one of the new ones," he said, nodding toward the TV. "The old ones were rough as a cob—jerky and poorly drawn, violent—but they had a magic to them somehow."

He shook his head sadly for all lost things.

"So I hear about this apparent assault and I have to wonder if there might be a connection between that and an incident out on county road one-seventeen a little earlier. Because someone big and black swooped in there like some kind of avenging angel—avenging what, no one knows—and beat the bejesus out of a couple of our self-employed businessmen. One of them's having his jaw wired about now, gonna be getting tired of liquids pretty soon. People who were watching said this guy just walked up and took them down, just like that, no reason or anything."

"There was probably reason."

"Yeah." His eyes hadn't left the TV, where a cat, chasing a mouse, crossed offscreen right to offscreen left and moments later came fleeing back across, pursued by the mouse. "Probably so. Look: Walsh tells me you're okay, I'm willing to go along with that, at least until I see different. But if you're going to be running around busting jaws, I need to know now."

"Things got a little out of hand."

"Things have a way of doing just that. What I want is for you to tell me you're going to be able to keep that hand closed, so things don't get out of it anymore."

I nodded.

"I'll bust you quick as I will anyone else, if it comes to that, friends or no friends. And whether I personally want to or not. The point could come. You understand that, don't you?"

"Yes."

"So I'm trusting you to walk carefully, and watch your back. Especially watch your back. Camaro didn't have any way of knowing you were going to go in there and John Wayne those boys all to shit, or he wouldn't have sent you out there. But those boys have a lot of business associates."

"Also self-employed."

"Yeah, well, it does tend to be an at-home kind of industry. But I'm saying they might take it personally, some of the others. Especially if they find you getting in their faces again."

"I understand."

"Take care then, Griffin. You get in too deep, you give me a call."

"So you can lead a cavalry charge?"

He laughed. "Hell no. So I can step back out of the way."

20

Whenever things begin to look absolutely, unremittingly impossible and I find myself sinking into despair for myself and the human race, I read Thomas Bernhard. It always cheers me up. No one is more bitter, no one has ever lived in a bleaker world than Thomas Bernhard.

The only contender is Jonathan Swift, whose epitaph might do as well for Bernhard: "He has gone where fierce indignation can lacerate his heart no more."

All Bernhard's work is visible struggle: invectives against his Austrian homeland, combats occurring solely within the human mind and imagination, blustery dialogues that finally surrender pretense and paragraphs to become clotted, hundred-page soliloquies. And beneath it all, his certainty that language above all embodies humanity's refusal to accept the world as it is, that it is a machinery of essential falsehoods and fabrications.

Unable to get back to sleep following Sergeant Travis's visit that afternoon, having no Thomas Bernhard at hand and little prospect of finding any there in the hinterestlands, I did the next-best thing. I made a cemetery run.

Confederate cemeteries are scattered throughout the South, some with only a half-dozen or dozen gravesites, others sprawling over the equivalent of a city block. They're often grand places, with elaborate headstones and inscriptions, generally well-kept and -visited. And one of the most celebrated, I knew, was not far from Clarksville.

It was almost dark when I got there. You turned off the highway just past Faith Baptist Church (I stopped twice along the way to ask), drove down a narrow asphalt road (pulling to the shoulder whenever vehicles appeared on the other side) and onto a wider dirt one, then through a modern graveyard of low headstones and bright green grass into a copse where half-lifesize statues of soldiers reared up among the trees. Still farther along lay a separate Negro graveyard with wooden markers.

The trees were mostly magnolias, mostly dormant now. Clusters of leaves, still green but curiously unalive, hung as though holding their breath, waiting.

Marble and cement soldiers, horses, angels, beloved dogs, pylons, pinnacles, sad women.

A squat obelisk of veined marble bearing the figure of a child, though he wore an officer's uniform: *Let Us Remember That After Midnight Cometh Morn.*

A casket-shaped headstone with a central spire of wrought iron: *Honor. Family. Faith.*

And on a small, simple marker hand-carved to resemble a scroll, far more appropriate to New Orleans (where it would have indicated the young man died in a duel, not war): *Mort sur le champ d'honneur.*

Poor ol' Tom Jefferson with his slave mistress Sally Hemings and his two hundred slaves at Monticello and his denouncements of slavery as a great political and moral evil, knowing all the time he would suffer economic ruin if his own slaves were freed. And that the neighbors would talk something awful.

Life, Mr. Jefferson, is an unqualified, neo-Marxist bitch.

Everything comes down to simple economics, however fine-spirited we are.

Looking up, I saw that a white boy of twelve or so stood off at the side of the field with a shotgun cradled in his arms, watching me.

I nodded his way.

He nodded back and kept watching.

As Robert Johnson said: Sun goin' down, boy, dark gon' catch me here.

Maybe not a good idea, even this late in the American game. So I mounted my Mazda and rode into the sunset, leaving the dead, those dead, forever behind.

21

Baby Girl McTell died on November 19th, on a starless, overcast morning, a little after 2:00 A.M.

The phone in my motel room dredged me from sleep. Topmost levels of my mind came instantly awake; I waited as others drifted up to join them. Lights from a car in the lot outside made a shadow screen of my wall, everything outsize and tipped at odd angles as in old German Expressionist films. The car's idle was set too low; every few seconds it began sputtering out and the driver had to tap the gas pedal.

"Yeah?" I said.

"Mr. Griffin?"

I said yes, and Doctor Arellano told me they had done all they could.

I thanked him, said I'd be in later to see to arrangements, and hung up. There was nothing to drink, or I would have drunk it. Outside, a car door slammed and a woman shouted, as the car pulled away, Damn you! You hear me? God damn you!

I splashed water on my face and sat for a while staring out into the darkness with late-night radio blathering behind me. Then I turned on water in the shower to give it time to warm while I shaved. I was climbing in when the phone rang again.

"Lew? Teresa. Becky Walden just called. The nurse who was taking care of our girl tonight. She knew I'd want to know. I'm so sorry, Lew."

I watched dampness spread slowly over the carpet at my feet.

"Lew, are you okay?"

"Fine." Clearing my throat, I said it again.

"Listen, it's my night off. Would you like me to come over? Maybe it's not a good idea for you to be alone tonight. I'm up anyway—I can't ever sleep like a normal person, even on my nights off—and watching old movies. I could be right there, provided you don't mind stay-at-home old clothes and aboriginal hair. There's no sense in your going in to the hospital till morning, anyway. None of the administrators are there before nine."

"I'd like you here," I said after a moment.

"Then I'm on my way."

Her stay-at-home old clothes turned out to be designer, French and recently pressed. The aboriginal hair looked pretty much the way it always did.

Myself, I'd barely managed a dash through the shower, jeans and a T-shirt.

"Lew," she said when I opened the door, "I'd like you to meet Beth Ann, the only reason I'm still here in the States. I hope you don't mind my bringing her along."

Her companion was a stunning, tall woman with light brown skin, golden eyes and elaborate Old South manners. She took my hand and seemed for a moment on the verge of curtsying.

"Beth Ann's from Charleston. She's never been able to quite get over it."

"Now that I've seen her, I'd be surprised if Charleston ever got over *her.*"

"What did I tell you?" Teresa said to Beth Ann.

"You told me he was a good-looking charmer. And you were at least half right."

"Does the word coquettish come to mind?" Teresa asked me.

"Among others," I said. Mutual admiration was flowing thick in there. Pretty soon we'd have to hack our way through it with machetes.

"I'm sorry about the little girl, Mr. Griffin."

"Lew. And thank you. Though I guess it's what we all had to expect."

"That doesn't make it any easier."

"No. No, it doesn't."

Teresa lowered a paper bag onto the dresser and reached in, pulling out three mugs, each fitted with its own lid. She handed one to each of us, kept one herself. Mine was so hot I could hardly hold on to it.

"Mistake," Teresa said. "Trade. This is coffee: yours. B.A. and I have tea."

"Tea's wonderful. Split it with me?"

"Of course. But I didn't know you were a tea drinker. You've always had coffee."

"When in Rome," I said.

"Quite."

I had never told her about Vicky. Now I did.

"You loved her," Teresa said when I finished.

"Oh yes."

"And you let her go."

"The way one lets the wind blow, or the sun come up. She made her own choices, her own decisions. There wasn't much I could do."

"There are always things we can do, Lew. You could have gone back with her. She asked."

I shook my head, much as I had done all those years ago. I handed Teresa the mug. She drank and passed it back.

"Do you hear from her?"

"I did, for a while. Less and less as time went on. She had a family, a son, a busy husband doing important things, a new daughter. And her own career, of course. Ties loosen. Memories get hung on walls or put away in the corners of drawers and life goes on."

Teresa held out the almost-empty mug and, when I shook my head, drank off the last swig of tea herself. Then she pried the lid off the coffee, sipped, passed it on to me. We were all sitting on a long plastic-covered couch under the picture window with its theater-curtain drape, looking at cinderblock painted green and light from the bathroom spilling out over brown carpeting.

"You miss her," Teresa said.

"I miss a lot of things—"

"She wasn't a thing, Lew."

"—but the train keeps moving on."

"When I was ten," Beth Ann said, "my sister, the one who raised me after my folks died, put me on a train to Chicago, to see my grandparents. I'd never been out of Charleston, never been much of anywhere but home and the Catholic school I attended. I was scared to death. I didn't even know there were bathrooms on the train. And I was starved. I'd left home at six in the morning without breakfast and everybody around me now was eating chicken or sandwiches out of bags and boxes. I hadn't moved this whole time. I was just sitting there, half a step from peeing my pants, when a conductor walked up. I'll never forget him. A white man, in his thirties I guess, though he seemed horribly old at the time. And he just said: Come with me, girl. Took me back to the club car, showed me where the bathroom was, the one he and the other employees used. And the rest of that trip he kept bringing me ham sandwiches. Just a slice of ham, two pieces of white bread and mayonnaise, but they tasted better than anything else I'd ever had in my life."

We'd long ago finished the coffee, but had kept passing the mug back and forth in one of those spontaneous, unspoken inspirations that occasionally arise. Whoever held the mug (we now realized, all at once) had to speak.

Teresa: "Many women have loved you, Lew."

Beth Ann: "Life could be worthwhile without Terri, I know that. There would be reasons to go on living. I would find them. But right now I can't imagine what they might be."

Teresa: "Coming here, to the States to live—for a single year, I thought then—I felt as Columbus must have felt. I was falling off the edge of the world, leaving civilization behind me. Then I discovered malls! fast food! credit cards!"

Me: "Once in the sixties I remember seeing spray-painted on the wall of a K&B: Convenience Kills."

Teresa: " 'For arrogance and hatred are the wares peddled in the thoroughfares.' "

B.A.: "Yeats."

Me: " 'A Poem for My Daughter.' Now *I'm* the fifty-year-old, unsmiling, unpublic man."

"I think we need to give some thought to food," Teresa said. "Food seems essential."

"I think we're all still waiting for that conductor," Beth Ann said.

22

The sun was edging up by the time we climbed into Teresa's car to head for a restaurant out on the loop. I sat between her and Beth Ann in the front seat. Morning light filled our conversation, too; shadows fell away. When they dropped me back at the motel an hour or so later, after two pecan waffles and a gallon of coffee, I'd begun filling slowly with light myself.

I showered, put on real clothes (Verne called them "grown-up clothes," I suddenly remembered) and went to the hospital to see what I needed to do. Day Administrator Katherine Farrell, a woman in her late fifties and more handsome than pretty, striking nonetheless, expressed her condolences and said that Mrs. Adams had already signed the necessary papers.

I found her sitting in the covered bus stop outside the hospital. I sat down beside her. We watched traffic go by.

"Ain't the first or the last time either of us lost something," she said after a while.

"No, m'am."

A workhorse of an old Ford pickup, fenders ripped away, heaved past, wearing the latest of several coats of primer. A beetle-green new Toyota followed close behind. Rap's heavy iambs, its booming bass, washed over us.

"I want you to know I've been talking to those nurses in there. They tell me you loved that little girl, that you're a good man. And judging from what you said on the way here, my daughter turned out a fair good woman."

"Yes, m'am. She did. She always was."

"Been wrong before."

"Yes, m'am." Then, after a moment, nothing more forthcoming: "Thank you."

I stood. "My car's in the lot, Mrs. Adams. I'll drive you back home now, if you're ready."

She put her hand out and I took it. It was like holding on to dry twigs.

"I'd appreciate that, Lewis," she said.

I was back in Clarksville by midafternoon and, after a quick meal at a place called The Drop, stretched out at the motel for a few hours' sleep. I'd got almost half of one of those hours when the phone rang.

I struggled to the surface and said, "Yeah?"

"Sorry about the kid. I know how that feels, and that nothing I can say's going to help. You know who this is, right?"

I nodded, then came a little more awake and said, "Camaro." The world was swimming into focus, albeit soft.

"You okay, man?"

"Fine. Just haven't managed much sleep this last couple of days."

"Know how that is, too. I can call back."

"No reason to. What's up?"

"Well . . ." It rolled on out for half a minute or so. "Probably shouldn't be calling you at all. Last time I did, from what I hear, you went apeshit and ralphed those boys right into the hospital. You ever hear of asking a guy first?"

"I asked."

"Oh yeah? Remember to say please?"

"I'm sure I did. Rarely forget that. I may have left off the thank you, though, now that I think about it."

"Ever had your jaw wired, Griffin?"

"Came close a few times."

"I bet you did. Probably chew the wires up and spit them at people. Well, what the fuck, those boys are pretty much garbage anyway. You don't take them out to the curb, someone else will."

"So: you called up to give me a few hot tips on navigating the complex social waters of postcolonial Mississippi. Or just to chat, for old times' sake? Not that we share any old times."

"We all know you're *bad* by now, Griffin."

"Yeah, well, I need sleep more than I need bullshit right now."

"You also need help finding your girl. Though damn if *I* know why anyone'd want to help you."

"It's my honest face. My purity of heart. My high position in antebellum society. And the twenties I spread around. What do you have?"

"Thought you always remembered to say please."

"Please."

"There's a girl, Louette, that's been kind of living at this dealer's house just over the state line. I mean, they finally took a look around and realized she's been there at least a month. Helping out at first you know, doing the guys when they were able or whatever, but since then just hunkering down there, riding a big free one. Even *they* know that's not good business."

"Thank you."

I wrote down the address he gave me.

"One thing," he said.

"Yeah?"

"Try to keep from going nuclear on this one? You're not in the big city now. We try to keep a lower profile out here, not draw too much attention to ourselves."

I told him I'd do what I could. Neither of us believed it.

The house was up in West Memphis, on the outskirts, in a part of town owing its existence to the spillover from Memphis military bases during World War II, a warren of apartment-size simple wood homes set close in row after row like carrots in a garden. Narrow, bobtail driveways had eroded through the years, cowlicks of grass and hedge pushing through them; many of the carports had become extra rooms, utility sheds, screened-in porches; trailers were grafted onto some. Abandoned refrigerators, motorcycles and decaying cars sat in yards beside swing sets and inflatable pools.

I pulled to the curb at 3216 Zachary Taylor. Out my side window in the distance I could see the winglike curve of the Arkansas-Mississippi Bridge. I'd had to drive on into Memphis, drop onto Riverfront Drive, and loop back across the bridge into Arkansas. I started up the brief walk, hearing what sounded like reggae country music from inside. Marley in Nashville, maybe. Jimmy Cliff and His Country Shitkickers.

Remembering Camaro's admonitions, I knocked politely at the door. No one responded, so I knocked, politely, again. Then, with still no response, as politely as possible I started kicking.

The door opened and a man maybe half my age stood there. Brush-style blond hair, fatigue pants with a white Hanes T, lizard cowboy boots. Pumper muscles and an earring. Tumbler in hand. Tequila, from the smell of it.

"What is your *prob*lem?"

Behind him, from different rooms, both Randy Travis and reggae were playing at high volume, crashing onto one another's beach, from time to time blending in an oddly beautiful way.

"Oh. Sorry. Didn't think you'd heard me."

"We heard you. They heard you over in Little Rock, man."

"Good. It's so hard to be heard in this world. Thank you."

"Mama brought you up right, did she? Manners like that, I'd think you couldn't be anything but one of those biblebeaters that come through here every week or so. They're always wearing a coat and tie, too. Don't nobody *else* 'round here."

He took a sip of his drink.

"But of course you ain't no biblebeater, are you?"

"Nosir, I have to tell you I'm not. But I do wonder if you might do me the favor of answering a question or two. I won't trouble you to take much of your time."

"And why would I answer any questions you'd have? Unless you have a warrant, that is."

"Warrant?"

"Come on, you got cop on you like slime on a snail."

Another, shorter man with a close-cut helmet of hair, vaguely elfish, had joined him at the door. Squinting beneath monumental eyebrows he said, "Yeah, man, this the *new* South. Nigger cops ever'where."

"You go on back inside now, Bobo. We're doing just fine out here."

"So that's the way it is here in America. What made us great," he said to me. "You come back with a warrant, or the next time it's clear trespass. You hear what I'm saying?"

Uh-oh. This guy watched cop shows; I was in trouble.

He shut the door.

When it stopped against my foot, he glanced down.

Then he looked back up at me and, for a split second before he caught himself, over my shoulder.

It was enough.

I went down, rolling, as the guy behind me swung and, meeting no resistance, connected with Mr. Warrant midchest, a glancing blow, then toppled himself.

I pivoted back like a break dancer and slammed my feet into Warrant's kidneys. His glass bounced off the front wall and rebounded, spinning, into the small entryway, came up against vinyl coping and stopped there, rocking back and forth. I hooked fingers into his neck now that he was down. Put a heel hard against the other one's balls and felt him curl in on himself.

"Your call," I told him. "Funny how so much of life comes down to attitude, huh?"

"Hold on, man," he said. "We can talk about this." And the minute I started backing off his windpipe and carotid: *"Bobby Ray!"*

Who trotted in from a room to the right where the face of some talk-show host filled a TV screen like an egg in a bottle, nailing live audience and viewers with sincere clear eyes.

Bobby Ray had a sincere Walther PPK in one hand.

I had a coat rack.

It caught him full across neck and chest. Remember Martin Balsam pedaling backward down the stairs in *Psycho*?

His head came up off the floor like a turtle's, trying for air. Didn't get it. The head went back down. He was still.

I set the coat rack back down in the corner. A few well-anchored coats swung to a stop on its hooks; most were on the floor.

"You have a right not to move," I told Mr. Warrant. "You get up and I use you to clean furniture. You hear what I'm saying?"

He nodded.

I picked up the PPK and walked into the next room. Faces turned toward me. Petals on a wet black bough. A modest buffet of drugs was set out on a card table: joints, bowls of colored pills, a couple of small covered plastic containers, a marble cheese board with razor and some remains of white powder on it.

Feeding time at the zoo.

"Our savior."

"*Ecce homo*. And I do mean mo'."

"Show-and-tell time, obviously."

"Black's definitely beautiful."

"Validate your parking ticket, sir?"

"Pizza dude's here."

"Help."

Alouette said nothing.

I found her in the back bedroom, lying on two stacked mattresses, nude, between a skinny black man and a fat 44-D blonde. They were passing a fifth of Southern Comfort back and forth over her. The *Green Acres* theme erupted from a bedside TV.

I dug into the hollow of her neck. There was a pulse, albeit a weak one.

"Where's the phone?"

He looked at me and, without looking away, handed the bottle across to the blonde. She grappled and found it, hauled it in, breast swinging.

In one continuous move I took it from her and smashed it against the headboard. Held a most satisfying handle and bladelike shard of glass against the man's throat as I watched his hard-on dwindle to nothing, with the impossibly sweet reek of oranges washing over us.

"Now," I said.

His eyes swept toward the floor. Again, again. I reached under the bed and pulled out the phone. Dialed 911.

"Thirty-two sixteen Zachary Taylor," I said. Overdose, I was going to say, but heard instead: "Officer down." There'd be hell to pay. But the ambulance was there in four minutes.

While we were waiting, new muscle came into the room. Three of them.

"That's the guy did Lonnie," one of them said. "Busted his jaw."

"Son of a bitch."

"Oyster time."

I lifted the PPK.

We were still facing one another off when the ambulance and four police cars careened into place.

23

Time to remember lots of prison films. Lisping Tony Curtis chained to a black stud, spoon handles ground down to knives against cement floors, lights dimming all over town as Big Lou got fried moments before the stay of execution came, college students on summer vacation in the South pulled over by big-bellied cops and railroaded onto chain gangs. And the novels: Malcolm Braly's *On the Yard,* Chester Himes's *Cast the First Stone.*

On the way in, in the squad car, one of the cops asked me what the hell I thought I was doing.

A good question.

A *very* good question for this fifty-year-old, unsmiling, resolutely unpublic man.

What *was* I doing?

Besides sitting in a holding cell in West Memphis, Arkansas, that is —home at last, or close enough.

Besides not telling mostly indifferent juniors, seniors and a scatter of grad students about modern French novels—which is what I was *supposed* to be doing.

The thought occurred to me that I'd disappeared from my school as precipitately and incommunicably as, a few years ago, my son David had vanished from his.

I really *was* getting far too old for this.

And besides, basically the whole thing just wasn't any of my business.

And so I sat there, watching dawn lightly brush, then nudge, then fill a single high window, drinking cup after cup of coffee deputies brought me and declining their offer of cigarettes, my mind curving gently inward, backward, toward things long shut away.

David: his final postcard and consummate disappearance, those moments of silence on the phone machine's tape.

Vicky: red hair drifting in a cloud above me, pale white body opening beneath me, trilled *r*'s, unvoiced assents, *I can't do this any longer Lew.* Seeing her off and for the last time at the airport as she emplaned for Paris.

LaVerne.

Till the drifting mind fetched up, finally, on a shore of sorts.

I thought of two photos of my parents, the only things I'd kept when Francy and I went through the house after Mom died. After these, taken the year they were married, they became shy; only a handful of snapshots remain, and in them, in every case, my parents are turned, or turning, away from the camera: looking off, averting faces, moving toward the borders of the frame. But here my mother, then in a kind of mirror image my father, sit on the hood of a Hudson Terraplane, so that, were the photos placed side by side, they would be looking into one another's eyes. And that image—their occupancy of discrete worlds, the connection relying upon careful placement, upon circumstance—seems wholly appropriate in light of their subsequent life together, Chekhov's precisely wrong and telling detail.

All their silent, ceaseless warfare came later, of course. Here in these photos, momentarily, the world has softened. She is full of life, a plainly pretty woman for whom life is just now beginning. His mixed heritage shows in cheekbones and straight, jet-black hair; his skin is light, like Charlie Patton's. They are a handsome, a fine, young couple.

As I myself grew older, into my early teens, I began to notice that my father was slowly going out of focus, blurring at the edges, color washing out to the dun grayish-green of early Polaroids. I can't be sure this is how I saw it at the time; time's whispers are suspect, memory forever as much poet as reporter; and perhaps this is only the way that, retrospectively, imaginatively, I make sense for now (though a limited sense, true) of what then bewildered me.

My mother by then had already begun her own decline, her own transformation, hardening into a bitter rind of a woman who pushed through the stations of her day as though each moment were unpleasant duty; as though the currencies of joy had become so inflated they could no longer purchase anything of worth.

How had those two young people on the Terraplane ever become the sad, embattled, barricaded couple I grew up with? What terrible, quiet things had happened to them?

How do *any* of us become what we are, really: so distant a thing from what we set out to be, and seemed?

How, for instance, does a part-time college instructor, part-time novelist who believed he'd put his past behind him where it rightfully belonged (and what he couldn't put behind him, into his books), come to be sitting in an interrogation room across from a quartet of cops at nine in the morning in West Memphis, Arkansas?

Which is where I was but minutes later.

The guy who seemed to be in charge had oiled-down hair, a bushy mustache and rolled-up sleeves. I felt a moment's terror that a barbershop quartet had been sent in to interrogate me. Any moment they were going to start singing "The Whiffenpoof Song," and I'd tell them everything I knew. Hell, I'd tell them things I *didn't* know. As a writer, I was good at that.

"Can we get you anything, Mr. Griffin, before we start?"

Had to be the baritone. He and a wiry little guy, probably the tenor, sat at the table. The others sat against the wall behind them on folding chairs. The table between us had nothing on it. Table, floor and walls were spotless, scrubbed. The air smelled faintly of disinfectant and lemon.

"No, but thanks."

"Then could you explain to us why on the emergency line you represented yourself as a police officer?"

I tried to think of a snappy response. Marlowe certainly would have had one.

"Strictly speaking, I didn't," was the best I could do.

" 'Officer down,' I believe you said."

That kind of set the pace for the whole thing. They'd ask a question and I'd answer it, they'd ask another and circle back to an earlier one. It was a lot like the chants kids use when they're jumping rope. Or gamelan music.

"I needed help fast. The girl was in bad shape."

We were all very polite, very businesslike. There were things, practical things, to get done, and we were men of the world. Members of the quartet changed from time to time. Toward the end, two hours or more into the morning, Sergeant Travis of Clarksville's finest came in and sat against the back wall.

"You went there for a drug buy and the deal went bad," one of them was saying just then. "We know that, Griffin."

I looked across at Travis. He shook his head sadly, looked at the floor.

This went on a while, as it had been going on, and eventually Travis stood, nodded to me, and left. I had become a tape loop.

Ten minutes later he walked back in behind a guy in a suit and said, "Come on, Griffin, let's go."

I followed him out into a long bare hallway, voices raised and clashing behind us.

"Last I heard, extradition didn't work like this."

"All in who and what you know," Travis said. "Those boys are kind of pissed, right now. They've been planning a raid on that house for three weeks. It was finally set to go down tonight. And here you went and spoiled their party. Luckily, Douglas and I went to high school together. Guy in the suit? He's the chief here. Caught a hundred long passes from that man if I caught one. You play?"

"Hate football." Didn't dance, either.

"Look like you could have, easy."

We were standing outside the station now. I felt strangely weightless. Travis stopped and turned toward me.

"They're not charging you with anything. But godal*mighty* are they pissed."

"Give me a lift?"

"Be glad to, but you don't need one."

He smiled. Handed me an envelope: wallet, pocket contents, keys.

"Your car's in the lot around back. I had a trustee go out there and bring it in."

"I don't suppose you want to tell me how it was that you happened to show up here?"

"Not really. But in my experience, there's very little in life that just happens. Know what I mean?"

"No. And I don't guess I'm going to."

"Doesn't matter. You'll be coming back down to Clarksville?"

"I don't know. Not right away, at any rate. There may be no reason to. First I have to find out about Alouette."

We'd walked around to the back. I opened the car door and reached to shake his hand.

"Thanks. I appreciate what you've done." Whatever the reasons.

"The girl's over at Baptist Hospital, tenth floor. Across the bridge, find Union Avenue and you're almost there. She's going to be okay, Griffin. For now, anyway."

I got in and started the engine.

"Thanks again, Sergeant."

"Nothing to it."

"Tell Camaro thanks for me, too, when you see him?"

"I'll do that. If I see him, you understand."

It's still a hell of a river, even if it did seem bigger when I was a kid: not only endless, but also impossibly wide. It was full of boats then, with sandbars the size of islands; and ferries nosed back and forth across the wake of the big ships, cars crouched on their decks, people peering out from within, waiting for things to change.

24

Hospitals, like bus stations and prisons, are all much the same. Their makers conjure up the soul of the thing, then drape skin around it. This one was like the one where I woke all those years ago, light like fists in my eyes, with Vicky's face hovering over me; like the one unseen in which my father died; like the one that broke Cordelia Davis's long fall; like the one in which Verne had lain dying.

Tenth floor was a limited-admittance wing, and after being turned away at the nurses' station I had to go back down to the administrative offices, where the atmosphere was so different that it was like stepping into another world, to clear permissions. I gave my name and relationship to Alouette to a walleyed young man whose expression suggested that he found what he saw out here perpetually just beyond his understanding, and added that he might call Travis for corroboration.

"Oh that won't be necessary, Mr. Griffin," he said, handing a small paper across to me. "Sergeant Travis has already called. Let me wish you and the girl both the best of luck. It's tough, I know."

I shared the ride back up with a stretcher and two attendants, probably a nurse and respiratory therapist. An old lady with skin like dried mud flats lay on the stretcher surrounded by monitors, oxygen cylinder, IV bags and portable pump, a compact drug box, charts, a box of disposable diapers. Tubes and drains snaked out from under the sheet covering her. She was trached, and the attendant at the head of the stretcher was squeezing an Ambu bag regularly, monotonously, to give her breath. Her eyes locked on to mine and I was surprised at how clear, how filled with intelligence, they were. Those eyes followed me as I got off on the tenth floor.

I handed over my scrip to the nurse at the gateway. She'd summon Charon, who'd ferry me across. But she only looked at it and signaled to another beyond the double doors. That one buzzed the doors to unlock them, holding her finger on the button until I was in.

A young woman sitting behind the desk just inside stood. "Mr. Griffin?" She was in her midtwenties, a blonde with perfect fair skin and a bow in her hair. Typical valley girl sort, but she was wearing jeans, cowboy boots and a denim shirt with snaps for buttons. Barbie at the Bar-B, I thought inanely.

She held out a hand to shake mine. "I'm Mickey Francis, a social worker on the staff here. We don't have very much information about Alouette, I'm afraid. Do you have a few minutes to answer some questions? It would be a great help to us."

"I have the time, Miss Francis. But I don't know if I'll have any answers for you."

"Anything will help."

So we went down the hall to a conference room looking much like the police interrogation room back across the river, poured two cups of coffee and sat down. A calendar on the wall showed a swatch of New England forest in the throes of fall, an impossible array of gold and scarlet and chrome yellow; each leaf on each tree seemed a different color. Starting with Chip Landrieu's arrival at my doorstep, backtracking to Verne's and my lengthy relationship, jump-cutting forward to Baby Girl's death, I told her what I knew.

As I talked, she made brief notes in a pocket memo book. I thought of Eddie Lang, who kept the cues for the entire Whiteman Orchestra repertoire on an index card. And of how he had tried so hard, in those amazing duets with Lonnie Johnson, to transcend his heavy, European style. Lang could hear the difference, that loose urgency, in Johnson's playing—sensed but somehow couldn't seize it.

"Do you mind if I contact Richard Garces?" she asked when I finished. "He might be able to get some of the information we need. Legally I suppose we're going to have to notify the father, but we can probably hold off on that for a while."

"When you do, be prepared for the descent of the Valkyries."

"Oh, we're used to Valkyries around here, Mr. Griffin." She stood and held out her hand. "Thank you for your help. We'll do what we can. But as you know, Alouette will have to do most of it herself. Jane, at the desk, will take you in to see her. The police have cleared her from the jail ward, by the way: she'll be moved to a regular ICU as soon as a bed comes available. Good luck."

She walked away. Because the boots' heels tipped her forward and she leaned back just a little too hard against it, she seemed above the waist to carry herself stiffly and unnaturally straight. But her legs, long and looking still longer in jeans and heels, moved freely.

Jane escorted me into a four-bed room just within the double doors. To the right, propped on his or her side with rolled pillows, lay a hairless individual with intersecting scars like two zippers across the crown of his/her head. He or she was trached, and an aerosol generator in the wall above the bed, hissing, delivered continuous humidity to the airway through a corrugated tube and T-piece, outflow disappearing when the patient breathed in, spuming back into the room on exhalation. In the bed behind this one, a middle-aged woman sat upright, eyes following my progress into the room, face and eyes equally blank.

Alouette was in the rear left corner, past an unoccupied bed. Soft restraints at ankles and wrists were tied to the bed rails, and a half dozen sandbags chucked along her sides helped hold her in place, so that she could move only her eyes. Towels covered breasts and abdomen. She had peripheral IVs in each arm, happy-face patches for the cardiac monitor on her chest, yet another line in her neck. An endotracheal tube was taped in place at her mouth and connected to a ventilator alongside the bed. Its bellows rose, hesitated and fell, accordionlike.

A nurse had just finished bathing her and was gathering up the plastic basin half filled with water, washcloths, talcum, bottle of liquid soap, toothbrush, toothpaste. "Are you the father?"

I shook my head. "A friend."

Alouette's eyes had locked on to me. I imagined that I saw all sorts of things in them. Perhaps I did. She tried to speak, prompting a loud buzz and flashing light from the ventilator.

"You can't talk, sweetheart, remember?"

She put down the basin and reached for a clipboard on the bedside table.

"I'll undo an arm, honey, if you promise me you won't try to pull anything loose. And then I can leave you folks alone a minute."

Alouette looked at her and blinked several times.

"You'll have to help her," the nurse said to me. "Things are still pretty thin for her. Will be, for a while."

She started to untie her right arm, but when I told her that Alouette was left-handed (like her mother), she redid the knot and pulled the other free instead. Handed me the clipboard.

I walked around to the side and held it up for her, gave her the pencil. She made several tries at it—lines huge and shaky and often not meeting, other times overscoring one another, tip of the pencil lead breaking away at one point—before I could make out what it was.

Lew.

I nodded, surprised that she knew who I was.

I—

Hope? hate?

She tried again.
No: hurt.
I HURT.
And what I said then, unintended, unexpectedly, came in a rush.

25

I had been in New Orleans a little more than a year when I met your mother. I was a fatback-and-grits kid from Arkansas who'd read a few books and thought they'd taught him whatever secrets he needed to know. I had this black gabardine suit that I'd wear all the time, press it and one of my three shirts every morning, put on a tie of some kind, buff my shoes with a towel. I wasn't drinking much, then. That came later. But I always tried to look presentable.

I'd been in and out of several jobs by that time. Bellhopped at the Royal Orleans for a little while, worked the ticket counter at the bus station, even did some short-order cooking and janitored at a grade school when times got really hard. I was living with half a dozen or more people, the number kept changing from week to week, or even day to day, in a house on Dryades, an old camelback double. People used to kid me because everywhere I went I wore that suit.

I was sitting at the counter in a diner one morning about four, nursing a cup of coffee, wearing my suit. I'd been fired the day before for "talking back" to my supervisor (actually, I'd told him to go to hell), and I left the store, went out and got drunk by midafternoon, somehow got home and passed out there till thirst and jittery nerves shook me awake a little before midnight.

Someone sat down beside me. When I looked at her, she smiled, sipped her coffee and said "Nice suit."

I thanked her, and after a moment she said, "Things kind of slow for you tonight too, I guess."

And that was your mother, the first time I ever saw her. And that's all we said. But the next night I was there at that same diner from two to six, and the *next* night she came in, around five, and sat down by me again when she saw me, and we talked. So then we started having breakfast together most mornings. And after a couple of weeks I asked her to have dinner with me that night. "You mean, like a date?" she said. And I said, "Yeah, like a date."

By the end of the month I'd had two more jobs, quit one and got fired from the other, and had moved in with her on a more or less permanent basis. She helped me get another job, someone she knew from her work knew someone else, that kind of thing. It was with this furniture and appliance outfit over on Magazine. They'd sell all this stuff on time at inflated prices and have people sign contracts agreeing to forfeit everything if there was ever a missed payment. Mostly poor black people, and most of them not even able to read the contracts. But the company was considerate. They always sent their man around to try to collect before they were forced "to invoke the terms of contract." And I was their man.

So I'd go humping all over town doing what I could to help these people keep their things. I'd explain what the contract said, tell them if they didn't scrape a payment together by Friday, or Monday, or whatever, the truck would back up to their door and haul it all away and they'd *still* owe the company money for whatever payments were outstanding at the time of repossession. A couple of times I even threw in some of my own money.

Then one day the owner wants to see me in his office. "You doin' okay, Lew?" he says. Then he tells me word's got to him how I've been going about my collections, that I know damn well that's not the way it's done and he never wanted to hire me in the first place, and I had better get my black butt in the groove or out of his store, did I understand.

It went on like that a little while, not too much longer. Finally I just reached across the desk, pulled him toward me by his shirtfront and started pounding at his face. Afterwards, I went on home.

The police picked me up within the hour. I was sitting out on the porch, cleaned up and dressed in my black suit and waiting for them. The officers and I were polite. A few days later, the judge was polite. He said, politely, that I had a choice: prison for assault and battery, or the armed services, who might be able to put to some good use my, ah, talent for mayhem. A squad car delivered me directly from courtroom to recruiter who, once I'd signed papers, took over. I never even had a chance to call your mother.

It didn't last long. The army didn't think I was nearly as desirable as that judge had. And when I got out, your mother was there at the bus station in New Orleans waiting for me. Wearing, since she was working that night, a blue satin dress and blood-red heels, and looking unbelievably beautiful.

After that, we were together, even when we were apart, for almost thirty years. She never let me down. She was always there when I needed her, even when I didn't *know* I needed her, even though I was a mess for a long time—more years than you've been alive. All that time, I didn't do much besides hurt myself and other people. Your mother was the one I hurt most.

I'm trying to tell you that I know a little about what you've been through. And that I'd like to help, however I can. If you want that help. If you'll accept it.

And that I loved your mother.

26

Three days later, when she was up and about, we told Alouette that her baby had died and she said, "Yeah, I thought so." She was still on sedation, her eyes dull stones.

I went out that afternoon and bought clothes for her. Jeans and sweatshirts, for the most part, but also a plain cotton dress. That's what she chose to wear when I came by to take her, out on pass, to dinner.

"Well?" she said, standing at half-slouch in the doorway of her room. She had pulled her hair, damaged from months of poor nutrition and utter lack of care, behind her head with a barrette and tried to fluff it out, to give it some body. She wore lipstick that, pale as it was, only emphasized her waxy, sallow complexion. She'd borrowed shoes, navy pumps, from one of the nurses, I guess, along with the lipstick and barrette; I'd bought her a pair of knockoff Nikes.

"Well," I said. "Your mother's daughter. No doubt about it."

"Yeah? Well you can be pretty charming for an old fart, even if you are full of shit."

"I'll take that as a compliment."

"Take it any way you want. Where we going?"

"Up to you. Kids still live off pizza?"

"I don't know. Next time I see one, I'll ask."

"I stand corrected, and apologize. How about burgers?"

"How about steaks?"

"That was going to be my very next suggestion."

"Big ones. What time do the gates slam shut on me here, anyway?"

"Ten. So there's plenty of time for a movie too, if you'd like."

"You're pretty ordinary, aren't you, Lewis?"

"I try."

"Okay," she said. We stepped together out of the hospital into a warm fall evening, day's final light fading in a blush of pink and gray just above the trees. "I'll try too."

The place we decided on, with the improbable name of Fred's Steak-Out, looked as though it had slipped through a crack in time from Dodge City or Abilene circa 1860. You could see space between the bare boards of floor and wall, the tables were slabs of wood nailed to lengths of four-by-four and covered with butcher paper and drinks came in old canning jars. The spitoons must have been out back for cleaning. And of course the food was wonderful.

Alouette had prime rib that looked like about half a small cow, a baked potato the size of a football, and mixed greens, mostly kale and collard greens, from the look of it. I ordered grilled tuna with a Caesar salad. We both had iced tea. Lots of iced tea. She still complained of a sore throat from having had the tube in, and thirst from all the drugs.

That night I talked to her more about her mother and me, about our time together. Specific things, things she asked, like had we ever gone here, or done that, and how had it felt when Verne got married and I didn't see her for so long, did it bother me when she was on the streets, what made her decide to give it up finally, how had she managed to do that. We talked, too, about what was going to happen when she got out of the hospital, where she'd go, what her options were (as everybody says these days), and by the time I delivered her back to the hospital, there were glints of light deep within her eyes, stray emotions tugging at the hard lines of her face. Or at least I imagined there were.

Alouette wasn't the only one who needed to check in with reality.

I went back to my room and dialed Chip Landrieu. He'd obviously been asleep.

"Lew Griffin," I said.

There was a long silence.

"It's usually only bad news comes in the night," he finally said.

"Not this time. Look, I'm sorry I haven't been in touch. I'm calling from Memphis, and I've spent the last few weeks down in Mississippi. But I wanted to tell you I've found Alouette."

Another silence. A breath.

"Is she all right?"

"I think so, basically. She's been on some hard drugs, and it's going to be rocky for a while. But I've talked to her a lot these last few days. I think she has a good chance of making it."

I told him about the baby, about Mississippi and my straggling path toward Alouette.

"She'll be getting out of the hospital soon."

"What then?"

"I'm not sure. We've talked about a treatment center up here, or some kind of halfway house. She may want to come back to New Orleans. Right now, it's still one-day-at-a-time time."

"You *will* let me know if there's anything I can do to help, won't you?"

"Absolutely."

"Thanks, Lew. Keep me posted."

"I will."

"You need anything? Money?"

"I'm fine."

"Let me know if you do. Guess I'll owe you a few dozen lunches when you get back."

"You're on."

I sat looking at the phone for a while, finally dialed again but when Clare's answering machine came on the line, hung up.

A minute or two later I called back and told the machine: "It's Lew, Clare. I'm in Memphis. I found Alouette. Sorry I haven't called, but I have been thinking of you."

After hanging up again, I realized that I should have left my number and thought about calling back, but decided to put it off till morning.

I pulled out my notebook and looked up Richard Garces's home number. His machine came on the line, its recorded message in rapid-fire, oddly staccato Spanish, but then Garces himself broke in with "Rick."

I told him who it was and he said, "Hey," stretching it out like a yawn, "good to hear from you."

He'd spoken with Mickey Francis from the hospital and was up to date on pretty much all of it.

"I need some help, Richard. Advice, really."

"You've got it."

"What's Alouette's legal situation?"

"Shaky—as it always is when contentions of mental health are part of the package. Of course in this case there's really no established history of mental health problems, and the girl *is* in her majority."

"If her father doesn't know by now, he will soon enough. I'm expecting lawyers to swoop down on her like a pack of crows."

"I'll have to check to be sure. Laws could be different there; a lot of them are, since everything here is based on the Napoleonic Code. But there's no formal charge as far as the courts are concerned, right? No talk of sanity hearings, anything like that?"

"None."

"That would probably be the way he'd want to go. Claim that the girl was financially dependent, stress her runaway status, abandonment of the baby and its subsequent death. That's all public record. The lawyers could lean hard on her overdose as a suicide attempt. After that, mostly it would depend on the judge. Down here, I could pretty much call it according to whose court it was set for. There, I just don't know. But they'd probably get *some* kind of exclusionary ruling. Commitment to one of the diagnostic centers for observation, possibly, or mandatory court-monitored therapy."

"Is there anything we could do to counter it?"

"This isn't science we're talking, Lew. Not even law, really—and law itself is unpredictable enough. More like magic where the correspondences are skewed and whatever rules there are, keep changing. Let me do some checking. I'll get on the network and see what I can turn up. I have some contacts scattered around up there. I'll get back to you. May be a while. The girl able to sit up straight and say what *she* wants?"

"Yes. Once she decides."

"She look okay?"

"Yeah. A little shopworn."

"Good. That counts for a lot. Okay, let me fire up the circuits and read some smoke. Where you gonna be?"

I gave him my phone number and said if I missed him, which was likely under the circumstances, I'd check back with him sometime tomorrow.

I hung up and sat remembering light gouging at my eyes.

Once years ago, surfacing briefly in a diner during a week-long drunk, I found Mephistopheles himself sitting across from me in the booth, pouring Tabasco sauce into his coffee. At the time it seemed the most natural thing in the world. We talked a while (I remember the waitress coming by to ask if I needed anything, and a couple of times to ask if I was all right, and some other people staring over at us), I declined his offers, and he left, telling me to keep up the good work.

Naturally, I later used the whole thing in a novel.

Tomorrow morning, too, I would call the university, try to mend *that* tattered sail as best I could, if it were mendable at all. Then Clare. Hoping for wind and calm seas.

27

I found her standing at the side of the two-lane highway near a gas-station-and-foodstore crossroad, wearing the cotton dress and navy pumps.

My phone had chirred that morning at eight. Crickets were devouring the Superdome, then there were incoming missiles. The door to my elevator wouldn't close despite a formless something lurking out there in shadow. When my beeper went off, the thing tracking me turned its head suddenly, tipped by the sound—then the sound was only a phone.

Someone's hand went out and got it.

"Mr. Griffin?"

I admitted it.

"Doris Brown, at the hospital. I'm one of the nurses on Three East. We were wondering if you'd seen Alouette."

I came suddenly awake.

"Not since last night. I brought her back about nine-thirty."

"The nurse on duty remembers her coming back, but somehow

she never logged back in. And when Trudy made a bed check about two A.M., Alouette was gone." She turned her head away, coughed. "I'm sorry we've been so long getting in touch with you, but we had trouble locating a number for you. You have no idea where Alouette is, then?"

"No."

"Will she contact you, do you think? Or is there someone else she might get in touch with? Her hospitalization became voluntary upon release from the jail ward, of course, but we're concerned."

"I understand."

"You'll let us know if you hear from her?"

"I will."

I hung up and stood in the shower a long time, turning the water ever hotter as I adjusted. I'd been awake much of last night, finally falling into agitated sleep just as dawn's fingers tugged at the sill. A sleep in which restless dreams billowed soft and soundless as silk parachutes and dropped away.

I'd spent those hours preceding my shabby, ragged *symphonie fantastique* remembering an incident, itself almost dreamlike, from years ago.

Every teacher has stories of students who suddenly give way under pressure. They start coming in during office hours all the time for no discernible reason, they just one day vanish and are never seen again, they disrupt class with objections and urgent queries or sit in the back and never speak, the essays they turn in have little to do with the subject and everything to do with themselves.

Oddly enough, in all these on-again, off-again years, I'd really had only one instance.

The young man's name was Robert. He dressed neatly, chinos and oxford cloth shirts mostly, and when he spoke, it was with a demure, softly southern accent; he had the deferential look of men raised by women. His French was extraordinarily good. He easily followed everything that was said, evidenced fine vocabulary and grammar on all written work, but had trouble whenever things shifted over to speech, as though words and phrases caught in his throat like some kind of phlegm and only with great effort could he expel them.

During conversation one afternoon—we were discussing Montaigne, as I recall—Robert passed twice, and when it came around to him again, simply sat there watching me blankly until I directed a question elsewhere. When I glanced back at him moments later, he leapt from his desk and stood in a crouch beside it.

"Ça va?" I asked him.

Whereupon he straightened, announcing in a loud voice, and in perfect French: "There is a conspiracy against me, Mr. Griffin. Surely you know that."

"No, I wasn't aware of that, Robert. But can you tell me just who is involved in this conspiracy?"

He looked around him wildly, but said no more. The room was absolutely quiet. No one moved.

I said: "I'd like for everyone who is not directly involved in this conspiracy to leave the room, please."

The others quickly gathered their things and slipped from the room. I walked over to Robert, who remained standing stock still by the desk.

"So it's down to just us now," he said.

And looking into his eyes, I realized that he wasn't talking to me. I don't think he even knew I was there any longer.

Security came, and Robert let them lead him away without protest. A few weeks later, at a department meeting, Dean Vidale told us that Robert had got up one night at the state hospital, gone into the shower stall, and hung himself with a strip of ticking torn from his mattress.

I was thinking about it again that morning as I climbed back into the car with a huge cup of coffee and a bag of doughnuts and pulled out onto Highway 61. I'm not at all sure why this came to mind. I hadn't thought about it in years. But now that I had, I couldn't seem to shake it.

There was only one place for Alouette to go. And only two reasons for going there, the first of these, and far the least likely, her grandmother.

I'd driven less than an hour, coffee long gone, half a doughnut left in the bag, when, ahead, I saw a semi pull onto the opposite shoulder to let someone off, then pull back into traffic without looking, sending a panicked Camry into the oncoming lane. A panel truck in front of me hit its brakes and swerved onto the shoulder. It fishtailed and came to a stop nose-down in a shallow ditch at roadside, one wheel hanging free. I worked my own brakes, slowing by increments, and at the end of the curve, after the Camry had retaken its lane and shot by me, fell into an easy U.

I watched her face change as I approached and pulled off beside her.

"Thought you might need a ride."

"Guess so. Last one's price was one I didn't want to pay. Man, you get straight and people start *smelling* bad, you know what I mean?"

She got in, crossing her legs beneath her on the car seat.

"He wasn't even going the right direction. I hitched him at a truck stop down the highway and he told me he was bound for Vicksburg. But then we get to the highway and he turns north. And when I say something, he just says, 'What difference does it make, little girl? Places is all alike.' "

"So how'd you persuade him to let you out?"

"I told him I just *couldn't* go back toward Memphis, cause my daddy the sheriff had all-point bulletins out on me up there."

I sat with motor idling. The panel truck backed out, wheels spinning, throwing up dust and stray gravel. A piece flew across the road and banged into the Mazda with a strangely nonmetallic *thunk*.

"Anytime now," she said. "I'm in. We can go."

"Okay. Which way?"

"You mean you didn't come out here to haul me back?"

"Why? You don't want to be there, you'd just leave again. Not much I can do about that. Not much anyone can do about it."

"But me, you mean."

I shrugged.

After a moment I said, "Something I used to do a lot was, I'd line everything up against myself so I had to get slapped back down. Work myself half to death sometimes, just getting it set up that way."

"When you were drinking, you mean?"

"I still drink."

"When you were a drunk, then."

I nodded.

"And you're saying that's what I'm doing."

"No. I'm only saying that I try not to do that anymore. If you want to go back to Clarksville and whatever's there, I'm not going to try to stop you."

"But you came after me."

"Only to talk. You don't want that, we'll shut up, both of us. You don't want to come back up to Memphis, you just open the door and get out. Or you can ask me and I'll drive you to Clarksville myself."

"That's it, that's where I want to go," she said.

"Okay." I waited for a couple of cars to pass, pulled the Mazda back onto the highway and started gaining speed.

"Lewis?" she said.

"Yes."

"You don't preach to me, tell me what's right, what I need to do, like all the rest."

"No."

"Why is that?"

"I figure you know what's right, as much as any of us do. You'll either listen to that, or you won't listen to anything—me, least of all. And you're the only one who can say what you need. Whatever it is, you have to go after that. Everybody does. But needs change, and you don't always notice. Besides," I added, "who'd be fool enough to take advice from me?"

"Let he who is without sin . . ."

I smiled, remembering the last time that came up: when I was hospitalized for DT's, back when I first met Vicky.

"Something like that. But look who's preaching now."

We rode on in silence.

After a while she said, "Lewis, I think you took a wrong turn back there."

There weren't any turns, only farm roads stretching out like dry tongues to the horizon.

I looked at her.

"Memphis is back that way." She hooked a thumb over her shoulder.

"You sure?"

"I'm sure."

"Memphis it is, then." I pulled off to the shoulder. "And on the way, maybe some lunch?"

"Why thank you, sir," she said in a broad Hollywood-southern accent, "I'd mightily admire to have lunch with a fine, strong man like yourself. One that's paying." She sighed dramatically. "A lady carries no money, you know."

As we rode back, I told her about Bob, how he'd suddenly caved in during class that day.

She sat quietly for a while when I was finished, then said: "Why'd you tell me that?"

"I don't know."

A tractor pulled over to let us pass, rocked back onto the road behind us.

"I think I do."

"I'm listening."

"Because you feel responsible somehow. You think there's something you could have done, that you should have noticed something was wrong. But none of us can be responsible for other people and their lives, Lewis. At your advanced age, you should know that."

She was right.

I should.

I looked over at her, noticing now that her dress was torn under the arm. Her eyes were amazingly clear, and she was smiling. I tried to remember if I'd ever seen her smile before.

28

The crows swept in that next day, dropping onto us out of a bright, clear sky.

I sat looking out on that day from an alcove tucked away at the end of the hall. Even the clouds shone with what seemed their own internal white light.

Two were older, one of them about my age, another sixtyish with silver hair and eyebrows like frosted hedges. With them was a lank man in his midtwenties whose law degree from Tulane had gained him the enviable position of carrying their briefcase. He was dressed like the others in dark three-piece suit and rep tie, but had a haircut reminiscent of old British films. A forelock kept falling into his face; he kept brushing it away with two fingers.

They came off the elevator in V formation and marched almost in step to the nurses' station, where Eyebrows announced that they were here to see Miss Alouette Guidry, presently going under the name of (he glanced at Haircut, who fed it to him) McTell.

Jane asked if they were relatives.

"We are attorneys retained by the girl's father to represent her." He made a slight hand motion over his shoulder and Haircut dealt her a business card.

"Hmmm," Jane said. She picked up the phone, spoke into it briefly, hung up. "Alouette doesn't wish to see you," she said.

"I'm afraid that is not satisfactory, young lady."

"Probably not, but unless you gentlemen have further business, I'll have to ask you to leave."

"What is your name, young lady?"

She pointed to the nametag prominently displayed on her uniform front.

"Then I suppose we must ask to speak with your superior. A supervisor? The physician legally responsible for this unit, perhaps?"

It played out from there, the ball rolling on to a head nurse, an intern and then his resident, and finally to the walleyed young man I'd seen in the administrative offices, who came off the elevator blinking.

"We're here—" Eyebrows began as he disembarked.

"I know why you're here, Mr. Eason."

He patiently explained to them, as had all the others, that Alouette was in her majority; that she, not her father, was the patient here, and the only one whose medical or other needs concerned them at this time; and that, should they wish to pursue the matter, they might best proceed in appropriate fashion through proper channels, as they undoubtedly knew, and *stop* badgering the hospital's employees, taking them away from what could well be urgent duties elsewhere.

"I don't know about Louisiana, gentlemen, but we take our patients' rights seriously here in Tennessee. And now, you *will* please leave."

As though on cue, the elevator doors opened and two security guards stepped off. They stood at either side of the doors as the lawyer trio climbed aboard, then got in with them. The doors shut.

"Jane, let me know at once if there's any further problem," the administrator said, then, turning, saw me sitting in the alcove and came over.

"Mr. Griffin." He held out his hand. I stood, and we shook. "I know about yesterday, of course. We're all rather glad you are here."

"Right now, we're all rather glad *you're* here."

He looked puzzled a moment, then said, "Oh, that. We're used to it. They're serious, or have half a leg to stand on, they've already been to a judge and have paper. Otherwise, it's just a pissing contest."

"Still, it's appreciated."

"What I do."

"Think they'll be back?"

"Up here? No. But we'll be seeing more of them downstairs, I expect. I wouldn't worry about it. Meanwhile, if there's anything I can do to help Alouette, or you, please let me know."

We shook hands again. He took out a key and pushed it into the control plate beside the elevator doors; within moments, a car was there. He nodded to me as the door closed.

I sat watching pigeons strut along the sill outside, past locked windows. One was an albino, wings and tail so ragged it was hard to believe the bird could still fly.

A moment later Jane answered the phone and said to me, "They're ready, Mr. Griffin." I thanked her and walked down the hall to a conference room. Sitting at the table inside were Alouette and Mickey Francis. The social worker held a styrofoam cup, rim well chewed.

"Thanks for coming, Mr. Griffin. Can I get you a cup of coffee?"

"No thanks."

"I called you to come in because Alouette asked me to. I hope it's not an inconvenience."

"Not at all. Nothing much going on at the motel this time of day."

Uncertain whether or not that was a joke, she settled on a smile. Waited two beats. I thought of other such interviews, in rooms much like this one, when I myself was on the home team.

"She and I have talked a lot about what happened yesterday. And over the past several months. I know the two of you have discussed her plans once she's released. Treatment programs, halfway houses, that sort of thing. We all feel it's imperative that she get follow-up care."

"I think she agrees."

"She does. And the time for us to shape these decisions is fast approaching."

"Not *us,* Miss Francis. It's her decision all the way."

"You're right, of course." She looked down at the stack of folders on the table before her. "Alouette has expressed to me a desire to go back to New Orleans. Not to remain here."

I nodded. It was home, after all, whatever else it was.

"She would like to find a job, to live independently while participating in an outpatient program."

"Sounds good to me."

"She was wondering if you might be willing to give her a place to live while she did this. She would like to come back to New Orleans with *you,* Mr. Griffin."

I looked at Alouette. She nodded. "Yes, Lewis. That's what I want. If it's all right with you. I know it's a lot to ask."

"You can think about it, Mr. Griffin. You don't have to decide right away. This must come as something of a surprise."

"I'm not much of a role model," I said, "but that house has always been too big for me alone. It would be good to have someone else living there again."

Alouette looked down at the floor a moment, then up at me, smiling. With her mother's eyes.

29

Ad hominem time.

The following Thursday at nine in the morning, I arrived at the hospital to take Alouette home, stepped off the elevator and found her in conversation with a stately, lean man in blazer, knit shirt and charcoal slacks who, following her eyes, turned and immediately walked toward me. Italian shoes of soft cordovan.

"You must be Griffin," he said, holding out a hand. His shake was firm, relaxed, momentary.

"Lewis, this is my father."

I nodded.

"When I refused to see his lawyers, he canceled everything and flew up himself. He wants to set me up in my own apartment, even has a job arranged for me—no questions, no obligations."

"A generous offer. Not many free lunches left these days."

"I'm sure you'd do the same in my place, Griffin. Do you have children yourself?"

I suspected he knew the answer to that, along with my financial status, personal history and (not inconceivably) the contents of my trash.

And I supposed the answer to his question must be no, so I said that.

Alouette spoke to me over his shoulder: "I told him thanks, but I was going home with you."

"Which I'm certain you must realize is just not . . . possible," Guidry added, smiling. Between men.

I smiled back.

White teeth gleaming.

Maybe I should break into a chorus of O massuh, how my heart grow weary.

"I see. Then I have to assume you're no more willing to listen to reason than she is."

"It's her decision, Guidry. Not yours, not mine."

"She's a child. A confused child."

"Laws say that she's an adult, and protect her rights the same way they protect yours or mine."

"One has to wonder what *you* expect to get out of this."

"Wonder away."

Instinctively, he had squared off with me. Now he backed away a half step. "I know about you, Griffin. You're a weak man. Always have been. One hard push, your knees'll give."

"Push away. Find out."

"A drinker. And inherently a violent man—a killer, some say. That's no environment for a troubled young woman who needs desperately to work out her own problems."

He turned back to Alouette without moving closer.

"I sincerely hope you'll take time to think this whole thing over, come to your senses. See what needs to be done here. I've always taken care of your needs. I always will."

"Needs change," she said with a glance toward me. "Maybe you can't take care of my needs anymore, Daddy."

"And this man can."

"I don't know. Maybe only I can. Or maybe I can't. That's part of what I have to find out."

"I'm telling you here and now that this will *not* happen. I simply can't allow it."

"I've talked to the social workers and hospital lawyers, Daddy. Short of alleging burglary and having me thrown into jail, there doesn't seem to be much you can do about it."

"We'll see about that."

"Do what you think you have to. That's all I'm doing."

"I'll see you both again then—very soon."

He walked to the elevator and stood with his finger on the down button.

"Daddy."

"Yes?"

"There's something I never asked. You always made me feel I couldn't ask it, but I don't feel that way any longer."

He held out an arm to keep the elevator doors from closing. They bucked convulsively. "What is it?"

"Why did you think you had any right to keep me away from my mother?"

He stood looking at her, a squall of emotions ticking at his face in the moment before calm restored itself, then turned and stepped into the elevator.

We spent the next hour extricating Alouette from the hospital's coils. A formal discharge visit from her attending physician; a trip down to the administrative offices where our walleyed champion had prepared the way and we were in and out in minutes, Alouette signing papers to pay off her bill in low biweekly installments; a ride back up to retrieve the clothes I'd bought her and say good-bye to staff and patients.

Then we were walking out into another bright, clear day. Were in the Mazda curving along Riverside Drive. I asked if she wanted to stop for something to eat since there wouldn't be much chance for a while after this, and she said no. She found music on the radio, cranked both that and the seat down low, leaned back and fell promptly asleep. Tunica, Mound Bayou, Cleveland and Greenville rolled over her closed eyes. Hollandale, Redwood. But mostly the same furrowed fields, the same narrow straight roads and blanketing dust, huge spindly irrigation systems linked together like Tinkertoys, little more than hoop wheels and perforated pipe.

Erratic traffic as we approached Vicksburg brought her awake in late afternoon. She opened one eye to peek out the windshield, turned it on me and said hoarsely: "Food?"

Which we partook at a truck stop just off the highway, in accordance with her express desire (when I asked more specifically what she might want) for "food, just food, in large quantities, with lots of grease."

Neither wish was disappointed.

Nor did we fail to attract looks, just looks, also in large quantities, also (for lack of more appropriate synonym) greasy.

It was a place of basics: stand after stand of fuel pumps out front, Spartan restaurant area, cashier's counter with boxes of cheap cigars, pocket knives and belt buckles under its glass top and a rack of T-shirts with clever slogans alongside, bunkerlike bathrooms with rentable showers for truckers.

Clouds had been gathering for some time, bumping up against one another, and as we sat over burned-smelling coffee with oils afloat on its surface, several of them coalesced into one, like a dark fist closing, and rain began pounding at the windows and blacktop outside.

I'd spent those hours on the road thinking of many things.

That, for instance, I'd never got around to calling the university after all.

Or got back to Chip Landrieu.

Or talked to Clare.

Composing in my mind, between Tunica and Shelby, the second chapter of what was to become *Mole.*

And thinking how, during travel, the mind instinctively shifts mode. Eyes fix on something far off, something unattainable, as you go on about mechanics appearing to have little to do with end or destination: steering, stopping for gas, working pedals; and time itself, unfolding into a plane, a kind of veldt, a portable horizon, all but disappears.

That was also as good a description as any of the life Alouette, and in reflection I myself, would have to live over the coming months.

Perhaps after all, for all our talk of change, redemption or personal growth, for all our dependence on therapists, religious faith or mood-altering drugs both legal and non, we're doomed simply to go on repeating the same patterns over and over in our lives, dressing them up in different clothes like children at play so we can pretend we don't recognize them when we look into mirrors.

After lunch, as we drove on through Vicksburg and veils of rain toward Natchez, Alouette began talking about the hospital. Though barely conscious at the time, she remembered the intubation, fighting against it, to her mind then a worse violation than anything sexual, worse than anything possible.

"But then, suddenly, I broke *free.* Really free. I was floating, drifting, nothing could touch me, nothing could hold me down. I remember thinking: How wonderful this is, I don't even have to breathe now."

Later, pain made its way in, though a pain she could at first easily ignore: therapists drawing blood from her radial artery for ABG's, as she later learned.

"For a long time I was floating just under the surface of things. I could decide whether to come to the top or stay where I was, or at least it *felt* like I had that choice—though I always stayed right there."

But then after a time, half an eternity, the time it took to rebuild the world, light flooded in. "Light everywhere, so much light that it hurt. God, how it hurt!"

She settled back in her seat and closed her eyes, staring, I suppose, into the face of her own pain and the world's, as I drove on.

We reached New Orleans a little before nine that night.

30

Across the street new apartments were going up. *Broussard General Contractors* had torn down the 140-year-old Greek Revival manse with its rotting gingerbread, burst columns and disintegrating friezes, left wing for years drooping at an ever steeper angle. Doorways, newels, mantels and windowwork had been stacked in trucks and carted off for resale. Only a few stanchions still stood totemlike near the lot's borders, exposing a once-enclosed central courtyard, the bare heart around which new luxury apartments would be constructed. On the balconies of these apartments in four months, or six, young men and women would stand squinting into the sun, memories watching silently over their shoulders.

We sat outside at steel tables painted yellow and green, under a sky whose sagging bellies of clouds reminded me of the upholstered walls and draped ceilings of old Russia. Every few moments wind puffed its cheeks and Clare put a hand on her napkin to hold it in place.

"I'm sorry, Lew," she said suddenly.

I'd been telling her about Alouette's baby. "It's for the best."

She shook her head. A gesture I'd seen often before, when the wrong words came, or when words wouldn't come at all. "I don't mean that."

I looked back at the clouds, lower now. Something was blowing in across the lake, groping for new ground here.

"I don't know how to say this. I don't even know what it is I want to say. And I was never good at speeches—even before."

A sketchy wave touched at the length of her body, hinted at the difficult thing her world had become.

"But I won't ever understand it, won't even *begin* to understand it, if I don't."

She moved her fork in a gentle sweep through pasta. There was a *fleur-de-lis* on the plate, and she had pushed sautéed bits of green pepper into one leaflet of the trefoil, red into another.

"I never wanted anything to work out more than I wanted this, Lew. Not that I ever really thought it would."

I reached across the table and put my hand over hers.

"Somehow as women we learn to say that all the time: 'I'm sorry.' As though it's our all-purpose social formula, good for any occasion, one size fits all. And a lot of time we're not sorry at all; we don't mean to apologize, only to say 'I understand' or 'too bad.' But right now, that's exactly what I mean."

She looked at me, smiled.

"Where do messages like that come from? How can we learn to read them so well without even recognizing that they exist?"

I remembered a poem I'd seen recently in a magazine at Beaucoup Books: *We must learn to put our distress signals in code.*

"That's what socialization is, Clare. Most of the messages—maybe all the most important ones—are silent."

"I guess."

She took a mouthful of pasta, chewed slowly, sipped at her wine. Pacing herself, making herself hold back. Like a runner, or like a hard drinker taking the first one slow, half convincing himself for the few minutes it lasts that this is only recreational drinking.

"I think I love him, Lew. I think he loves me. And I have to do everything I can to give this a chance. Maybe later on we'll be able to see one another again, if you want to. But for now . . . It bothers him, Lew. He doesn't say anything about it, but I can tell. It hurts him, in some very quiet way he probably doesn't even know or understand himself. But I see it. And I can't do that any longer."

Clenched about her regret and misgivings, her hand had become a small fist beneath mine.

"It's okay, Clare."

"No, it's not okay, Lew, not at all. But it's how it has to be. Do you think we could go now?"

On the way to her car, wind swirling torn paper wrappers and magnolia leaves around our ankles in tides, I asked how Bat was.

"Gone. I got home last Tuesday and he wasn't there on top of the refrigerator where he always was. Or anywhere else. I still don't know how he got out. Or why, for that matter, since he never seemed to have much interest at all in going out. I waited, thinking he'd show up again. Last night I finally admitted he wasn't coming back and put his things away in the pantry, his bowl and all."

She unlocked the door and I reached around to open it for her. I told her I was sorry about Bat.

"Life goes on," she said. We kissed and said good-bye. "I'll call, Lew. When I can."

I watched her drive away, holding my hand up in a wave as she took the corner onto Joseph. I walked back, crossed the street and stood for a while in the empty courtyard, looking across at the restaurant with its yellow and green tables and chairs, its laughing, chattering people. I imagined the new apartments going up around me in stop-time, slowly shutting out that world, marooning me here in this ancient, sequestered place.

31

When I got back to the house Alouette was on the phone, as she'd been on the phone pretty much nonstop since the morning before. Thus far she had set up two job interviews, attended another, arranged for information to be mailed concerning GED testing and night classes at Delgado, Xavier and UNO, and spoken with an MHMR counselor about vocational programs. Now she was talking to Richard Garces about outpatient therapy and local support groups.

Not long after I came in, she hung up, scribbled one final note and shut the notebook.

"How'd it go?"

I shrugged.

"That bad, huh?"

"Maybe a little worse."

"I'm sorry."

So of course I had to laugh, then explain why.

"Did you know Richard was a hippie? And a junkie? A long time ago, of course."

"It doesn't surprise me."

"Were you a hippie, Lewis? You know, wearing vests without shirts and bell-bottoms and flowers in your hair? Back in the sixties, I mean."

"What I was in the sixties, mostly, was drunk—at least from about '68 on. I didn't pay a lot of attention to social movements. Or to other people, for that matter."

"You were a bodyguard then, right?"

I looked up, surprised. Not many people knew about that. Verne had, naturally. And Walsh, because that was how we'd first met.

"I haven't said anything before, but I know quite a bit about you, Lewis. More than you think."

I poured tea into my cup, added milk.

"When I was in grade school I had this friend, your classic nerd type, glasses and ugly print shirts, the whole thing, but he was a computer whiz. What everybody calls a hacker now. He was really weird. Look, this is kind of a long story."

"I'll drink slowly."

"And probably a dull one."

"About me? Impossible."

"Yeah, right. Well anyway, Cornell's dad was an engineer with IBM or Apple or someone, and he always had these new computers around the house, products they were developing, or marketing. Cornell told me he grew up with these things as playmates instead of other kids. He thought everybody did. And he could do anything he wanted with them.

"I was twelve or thirteen. And I just decided one day that my father couldn't really be my father. Mother was gone, I was hopelessly miserable. I couldn't talk to him, or to anyone else in the house, and I knew there was just no way I belonged there."

"Most children go through that at some point."

"I know that, now. I think I kind of knew it even then. I was never lucky enough to be stupid."

"But you had to set yourself apart."

She nodded. "And I knew a little about you, just from things I'd heard. So I decided *you* had to be my father. It made a lot of sense at the time; it was the only thing that did. This was about when Cornell and I started being friends. Neither of us had ever had friends before, and I can't remember now how it happened, but somehow he started coming over after school, spending recess and lunch hour with me. One afternoon we sneaked into this office my father had at home, though I wasn't ever supposed to be in there, and Cornell showed me how to use the computer. If you knew how, you could dial into all kinds of information banks, he told me; you could find out almost anything you wanted to know.

"I thought about that for days. Then the next Saturday when Cornell came over—my father was at work, as usual—I told him about you. What little I knew, and a lot more I made up. And Monday he brought me this folder full of stuff. Copies of official forms, printouts of what I guess had been newspaper articles, parts of some kind of dossier the FBI had on you. That one said you killed a man."

I nodded.

"A sniper, according to the dossier. It said he'd killed at least eight people."

"At least."

"You stopped working as a bodyguard after that."

"I stopped doing much of anything. Just kind of drifted into it. Drank a lot. It was a bad time."

"Every night I'd get out that folder and read it. It was like making constellations out of stars: just raw information, that you could fill out any way you wanted. So every night I'd look at some facts, facts I knew by heart by then, and use them to make up stories about you. Those stories became more real to me than the world around me, more real than anything else, and for a time, far more important. Though all along I knew it wasn't true. I knew you weren't my father."

"And that I wasn't a hero."

She nodded. "And that life is just doing the things you have to do: staying alive, getting through the day, turning into your parents.

Maybe I was wrong about that part, huh? Maybe there's something more to it?"

"Maybe."

"Can I make you another pot of tea? That has to be cold by now."

"Only if you'll have some too. I'm already sloshing when I walk."

"Deal."

We went out to the kitchen. I leaned against the sink thinking of meals I'd prepared long ago for Verne, for Vicky and Cherie, remembering their laughter, seeing their faces, as Alouette emptied the kettle, drew fresh water and put it on to boil, filled the pot with hot water from the tap.

"Transportation's going to be the biggest problem," she said. "I figure between work, group meetings and whatever classes I settle on, I'm going to be piling up a lot of miles. I'll centralize what I can, find locations closer in to home. But some of it, like work and school, won't be so easy."

"Give it time. We'll see. Things start working out so that you decide you need a car, I'll match whatever money you can save up for one. And I'll take you to a friend who has a used-car lot and owes me a few favors."

"All *right.*"

She emptied the pot, measured in Earl Grey, poured water, stirred once and set it to steep under a brocade cozy Vicky had sent me from Scotland years back.

When the tea was ready, we went back into the living room. Alouette settled on the couch with her notebook, feet tucked under her. I sat in my chair with a copy of Queneau's *Zazie dans le métro.* I looked up at her after a while and thought how strange this tableau, this quiet domestic scene, was for both of us. Then how very alone I had been all these years, and how good it was to have someone here again.

32

Queneau once remarked that just about anyone could learn to move characters around, getting them from place to place and scene to situation, pushing them through pages like sheep until finally one arrived at something people would read as a novel. But Queneau himself wanted the characters and their relationships—to one another, to the sprawl of human history and thought, to the book itself—to be structured, wanted those relationships to be in the word's purest sense *constructed:* in short, he wanted something more.

There are those who would argue—*engagés* like Sartre, or perhaps in our own country the late John Gardner—that, in eschewing the tenets of "realistic" or mimetic fiction, he wanted less.

This strain of what we might call irrealism, this motive of artifice, in French fiction reaches back at least to Roussel, whose *Locus Solus* some of you may have encountered in Jack Palangian's magic-realism seminar, and persists today in the work of Georges Perec, the group

OuLiPo—cofounded by Queneau, incidentally—and American expatriate Harry Mathews.

Le Chiendent, Queneau's first published novel, in fact consciously, deliberately parodies most all the conventions of realistic fiction.

It is a rigorously structured novel. Ninety-one parts: seven chapters each containing thirteen sections, each of them with its three unities of time, place and action, each confined to a specific mode of representation, or narrative: narration only, narration with dialogue, dialogue alone, interior monologue, letters, newspaper articles, dreams.

The novel, a meditation on the Cartesian *cogito,* in fact had its beginning in Queneau's attempt to translate Descartes into demotic French. It opens with a bank clerk, Étienne Marcel, coming to consciousness, surfacing out of the slough of his unexamined life, while looking into a shop window. Taking substance from this sudden self-consciousness, *and* from the objective existence accrued from Pierre le Grand, who has happened to see him there at the window and become curious about him, Étienne is plunged headlong into a series of adventures—into the thick of life itself.

At one point le Grand, through whose eyes we witness much of the book's early action, says: "I am observing a man." And his confidante replies: "You don't say! Are you a novelist?" To which he replies: "No. A character."

As things go on, and as still more characters and situations are introduced, many of them truly bizarre—it's rather like those jugglers who begin with a small cane or club and end up piling chair atop chair, all of it tottering there far above them—the novel turns ever more fantastic, drifting further and further from the moorings of realistic fiction, until at last the reader is forced to abandon any pretense that he's reading a story about "real" people or events and to admit that he is only participating in the arbitrary constructions—reflective, complex, but always arbitrary—of a writer. A sophisticated game-playing.

From one of the novel's many discursive passages:

"People think they are doing one thing, and then they do another. They think they are making a pair of scissors, but they have made something quite different. Of course, it is a pair of scissors, it is made to cut and it cuts, but it is also something quite different."

A character muses: Wouldn't it be wonderful to be able to say what that "something else" is? And that is exactly what Queneau attempts, here and in all his work: to touch on that "something else" we sense, yet never locate, in our lives.

Yet because he has a kind of horror of seriousness, it's often at their most profound moments that his books and poems turn outrageously comic, dissolving into puns, bits of allusive and other business, vaudeville jokes, slapstick. One often thinks they are books that might have been written by an extraordinarily brilliant child.

Which brings us, quite naturally, to *Zazie,* a best-seller for Queneau and perhaps his most easily accessible novel.

As the book opens, murderous dwarf Bébé Overall has abducted little Zazie from the department store where her young mother was choosing fine Irish linen and has taken her into his underground lair far beneath the Paris *métro* lines, a place frequented by old circus performers, arthritic guitar players and legless Apache dancers, ancient socialists with Marx-like beards and tiny Trotsky spectacles. There Bébé—

Yes, Miss Mara?

I see. You may be right; perhaps in my enthusiasm I am not describing Queneau's novel at all, but rather some alternate version, some *possibility,* of my own; have begun, as some colleagues might say, deconstructing it. Why don't *you* tell us what *actually* happens in *Zazie dans le métro?*

33

I was, in a sense, singing for my supper. A latter-day minstrel show for ol' massuh, ol' massuh in this case being Dean Treadwell, who had chosen today—my first day back, after yesterday sheepishly calling my department chairman, apologizing for my absence so profusely that I began to stammer, and finally pleading a family emergency—to audit, as was his custom once each term with every course offered under his aegis, my class.

Miss Mara acquitted herself well, the students had actually read *Zazie,* and discussion was lively. One of the young men took a particular, keen delight in Zazie's Uncle Gabriel, pitching his voice throughout the discussion in a high, thin flutter he obviously imagined similar to the uncle's own during his performances as a female impersonator.

As the students filed out, Dean Treadwell came up to me and held out his hand.

"Fine class. Somehow you have a way of making it all real to them, making them care. I wish half my other teachers could do that."

"You caught me on a good day. Most others, the snoring would have distracted you."

"Fascinating. And I never even *heard* of Queneau before this."

"Three weeks ago, none of the students had either. A semester from now, most of them will have forgotten him."

"You have a minute, Lew?"

"Actually, I have about four hours—till my seminar after lunch."

"Walk with me, then. I'll buy you a coffee."

"Sure. But if the coffee's from one of the faculty lounges, I'll pay *you* not to have to drink it."

We ambled out into the hallway and along it, heads together like two monks strolling the cloisters as they kicked Boethius back and forth.

"I don't know how you'll feel about this . . ."

I let it hang there.

"I understand from some of the faculty members, and from my wife as well, that you worked for many years as a detective."

"Worked *at* it, anyway."

Two of my students from Advanced Conversational passed us. One of them said *Bonjour,* the other Hey, how's it going?

We wound up off-campus, at one of the coffeehouses that suddenly seem to be springing up everywhere in New Orleans. This one was a Tennessee Williams set: a hodgepodge of rickety ancient tables and chairs, crumbling plaster walls, windows so hazed you could safely watch eclipses through them, door open onto a dank inner patio where a three-legged cat furiously eyed all trespassers. A massive mahogany counter built directly into the tiled floor and topped with a slab of green marble dominated the room. A cork bulletin board took up most of the back wall, scaled in layers of handbills for alternative music, scribbled ads offering musical equipment for sale, notices of tutors and roommates wanted.

Like many such places in the city, it was a museum exhibit in other ways as well: here, an unregenerate hippie in jeans, work shirt and vest, scraggly hair stuffed into a bandanna; a fifties young professional in polyester "smart" frock and bouffant hair, or facsimile beatnik with goatee, shades and beret; over there, a black man natted out in suit and impossibly wide tie dating from the forties, slicked hair close to his scalp under a wool slouch hat. People have a way of getting stuck in time here in New Orleans. Once a student fresh from New Hampshire asked "Are all these strange-looking people here for Mardi Gras?" and another student told her, "Those are the ones who live here."

"Why did you give it up?" Treadwell asked me when we were seated over tall, untouchably hot glasses of *café latte*. "Detective work, I mean."

"I'd tell you I found honest work instead, but you know better."

He laughed silently, a single brief paroxysm, and looked off toward the patio. Sitting in the doorway with its stump raised for cleaning, the cat glared back at him.

"You've been married, haven't you, Lewis?"

"Once, a long time ago."

"And you had children?"

"I did. A son. He's gone now."

Treadwell's eyes came back to me.

"Gone?"

I shrugged. "It doesn't matter. But all this has to be leading up to something."

"I was married once, when I was younger than seems possible now. It didn't last long, and afterward, I was by myself for a long time, one of those academic bachelors who comes out of the house on his way to classes slapping dust and crumbs off his coat. I never imagined I'd live any other way. But— What's the old saying? life's all conjunctions, just one thing after another?"

"More like punctuation, I think. Colons and exclamations for some, dashes for the rest."

"One day in Victorian Life I looked up from my notes and, I still don't know why, noticed a young woman sitting there in the front row. Older than the other students, but still young to me. And while I was looking, while the fact of her existence was slowly sinking in as I prattled on about the monarchy or somesuch, she winked at me. Not coquettishly at all, you understand, but with this amazing sense of maturity somehow, of being very much her own person . . . solid.

"I dismissed class shortly thereafter. That was on a Thursday. And by Monday we were married. Twelve years ago. Twelve years. From the first I felt as though I'd packed up everything and moved to a new country. A different language, different customs, different weather—who knows, maybe even different physical laws. *Everything* changed."

I waited. Good interviewers never have to say much; they turn themselves into voids, into receptacles.

"Laura *is* my life now, everything else revolves around her, her and the university. But I have a son by that first, youthful marriage. He's an adult himself now, of course. We never had much to do with one another, never communicated much; he grew up on the West Coast, mostly. But a couple of months ago he moved back here, to New Orleans, and we began seeing one another. He'd call every week or so. We'd meet for lunch, a glass of wine. It's an ambiguous relationship, at best. Would you like more coffee?"

I declined, and after a moment he said, "I'm afraid he's in trouble. I wondered if you might be able to help him." Then he added: "Laura's dead against my getting involved."

This is none of your business, Griffin echoed far back in my head. I said: "I'd have to know two things. What kind of trouble—"

"Drugs. I don't know how deeply."

"Then your wife may be right. The other thing I'd have to know is what you'd expect me to do. There's probably not much you, or I, or anyone else *can* do. You have to know that."

He nodded, head remaining momentarily bowed. "I suppose in a sense I've dedicated my life to the belief that knowledge, that learning, intellect, reason, *matter.*" He looked back up. "Yes, I know. I've dealt with this in my usual manner: I settled into the library and read everything available. But now I seem to be flying in the face of all that, don't I?"

"If not flying, at least taking one hell of a leap of faith."

"Too close to the son," he said. I wouldn't have thought he had it in him.

And because of that, as much as anything else, I told him I would do it.

I got the son's address, a snapshot (his only one, he told me as he pulled it from his wallet) and as many details of his son's life as he knew. There weren't many: a workplace that might or might not be current, a bar he'd mentioned a couple of times, a few friends' first names. His son drove an old mustard-color Volvo, loved spicy food and war movies, was not a reader and had no particular taste for music.

"I want to know how bad it is," Dean Treadwell said, "how deeply he's into this. That's all I expect of you. Maybe then I can find a way to help him."

"I'll do what I can. I still have a few contacts out there. I'll ask around, turn over some stones."

Treadwell had pulled a checkbook out of his coat pocket and was uncapping a pen.

I shook my head. "This is a favor. Besides, it may well come to nothing."

"I insist."

"So do I."

"Very well, then." He clipped pen to checkbook and slipped them back into his pocket. "At least promise that you'll come over for a meal with Laura and me, soon."

"I'll be in touch."

Outside, he turned back.

"Lew. I almost forgot: my wife made me promise to ask when there's going to be a new book. She's read them all, and said to tell you she loves them, especially the ones set in New Orleans."

"Tell her thanks, but I'm not sure. Lately I seem to be getting distracted by life a lot."

Neither of us knew, of course, that the next book when it came, written in a two-week binge of twenty-hour days and published just before *Mole,* would be the story of his own son's last days.

34

It was much worse than he said, of course. Probably even worse than he thought.

The first thing I did that afternoon, from my airless, shared office in the basement of Monroe Hall, was call Walsh. They couldn't find him for a while, and I sat listening to a rumble of shouts and clatter, indecipherable conversations, other phones buzzing. Finally he came on with "Yeah?"

"Lew."

"Listen, I don't care how much you beg, I'm not buying you any more dinners."

"Two desirable bachelors like us, both our calendars are probably filled anyway, bubba."

"Well, I might just be able to squeeze you in—but you'd have to buy."

"I'm not that desperate yet."

"You will be."

"So I'll call you back when I am."

"Sure you will." Someone spoke to him, and he turned away briefly, came back. "How's the girl?"

"Doing okay, this far."

"Good sign. Any word from Clare?" When I said nothing, he went on. "Yeah, well, I'm sorry about that, Lew, I really am."

"Life goes on."

"Yeah. Such as it is. So what kind of favor you need this time? Not a big one, I hope. The city just dumped a new load of shit on us and now the mayor and his boys are down here smearing it all around."

I told him.

"You at home?"

"School." I gave him the number.

Twenty minutes later, he called back.

"What about the mayor and his boys?" I asked.

"Hey, urgent police business came up. It happens like that. They're cooling their buns on the bench out in the squad room, staring at me in here. Told them I'd be right out, soon as I took care of this emergency. First time I've sat down today."

"Maybe I should thank them."

"Maybe you should shoot the whole lot of them."

"So what's the story?"

"Well, it looks like your boy's cut himself a little swath down the coast from Seattle to Portland."

"Drugs?"

"Initially. Possession, PI, sales. Then your man went to school somewhere: suddenly B&E, suspicion of auto theft and attempted fraud start rolling up. No convictions on any of it, so a lot of this isn't on the record, but he became a familiar face. A couple of short falls, one for assault and battery, the other for, get this, unpaid traffic tickets. He's been lucky. But the captain I talked to up there said he's a body ready to drop. That help?"

"You bet. Thanks, Don."

"You want me to keep the net open on this?"

"No. Good enough."

"This guy's in town, I take it."

"Yeah."

"Yet another fine example of scuz rising to the bottom. I'm sure he'll be in to say hello sooner or later."

"Good chance of it."

"So I have to go feed the lions now, right?"

"Guess so. Pull a tail for me."

"You got it."

I could have just called Dean Treadwell then, of course. It was what he wanted to know—more than he wanted to know. My favor was done. But I didn't want to break the old man's heart, I told myself, not in such an impersonal fashion.

If you're in New Orleans with time to kill and a taste for alcohol, sooner or later you run into Doo-Wop. And sooner or later you'll probably buy him a drink and get into a conversation with him.

Every day Doo-Wop makes his steady round of bars from the Quarter up through the Irish Channel and along Oak Street. That's what he *does,* that's his job, and he pursues it with single-minded devotion. And because after all this time he's as much part of the city landscape as palm trees or the buildings along St. Charles, he gets free drinks, a lot of them from the bartenders themselves, a lot from bar regulars, some from drop-in drinkers. Anybody who buys Doo-Wop a drink buys a conversation too.

And if you ever had one of those conversations, Doo-Wop remembers it. He can't remember if he ever had another name or where he's from, he doesn't know the year or who the president is and probably can't tell you where he stayed last night, but if you talked to him, last week, last month, or back in the summer of '68, Doo-Wop's still got it all.

I found him after a couple of hours, in the twelfth or fourteenth place I tried. He was seated on a stool at the bar, drinking tequila since that's what the guy buying was drinking, and talking about his days as a Navy SEAL. I doubt he was ever a SEAL, but he'd probably spent a few hours with one sometime in a bar much like this one. That's what he did with all that conversation, why he collected all those stories. They were his stock in trade, the product he traded for drinks and companionship of a sort.

"Big guy," he said as I came in, looking into a mirror so silvered that it turned the whole world into an antique photograph. "Long time." He was wearing high-top black tennis shoes laced halfway up, a purplish gabardine suit, plaid sport shirt with thin black tie.

"Too long." I signaled the barkeep, who shuffled over and simply stared at me till I said, "Two more tequilas for these gentlemen and whatever's on draft for me."

"No draft."

"An Abita, then."

"No Abita."

"Dixie?"

He nodded and shuffled toward the bend in the bar, sliding his feet along stiffly as though on skis.

"Big guy, this's . . ."

We both waited a moment.

"Newman," his companion said.

"From Missoula, Montana." Doo-Wop hurriedly threw back what remained of his old drink before the new one got there. He didn't like things in life getting ahead of him. "Has him a little ranch up there, breeds horses." He nodded toward Newman in the mirror. "Next time we run into each other, remind me to tell you about that Arabian stable I worked at down in Waco."

Since he'd finished the drink Newman bought him, the subtle morality of Doo-Wop's enterprise allowed him now to cut Newman loose in my favor, and he motioned toward a booth in one corner. We waited at the bar for our drinks, then settled in there.

"So what's up, big guy? Who you looking for?"

"How do you know I'm looking for someone?"

"Big guy. You ever come see me just to have a quiet drink? You got your business, I got mine, right? And sometimes they kind of fetch up against one another. Way the world works. Damn glass empty again."

I motioned for the barkeep to refill it and showed Doo-Wop the snapshot Dean Treadwell had given me.

"Twice. Once at the Cajun Bar on Tulane, the other time over on Magazine, the Greek's place."

It wouldn't do any good to ask when; time didn't exist for Doo-Wop.

"From Washington. Near Seattle, he said. Did a stretch or two up there. Not very interesting. Didn't have any stories that amounted to anything, didn't pay much attention to mine."

"I don't suppose he wrote his address on a matchbook and gave it to you?"

"Not as I recall."

"That was a joke, Doo-Wop."

He thought about it a minute. "Never did quite get the hang of that joke thing."

"What I meant was, did he happen to say anything about where he was staying."

"Not a word. Said he had a couple of things going. Usually means a man's right next to eating rats off the street."

"Okay. Thanks, guy. You see him again, and remember to, you call me?" I laid a ten-dollar bill and a business card on the table.

He picked up the bill, leaving the card. "I already got one of those from last time."

I stood to leave, Doo-Wop to move back to the bar.

"Ask the Greek," he said. "Guy did some work for him. Heard that, anyway."

I got a twenty out of my wallet and handed it to him. He stuck it down in his shoe with the other bill.

"You come have a drink with me sometime when it ain't business. I'll buy," he said. "You know where to find me."

35

The Greek wasn't Greek, but Puerto Rican. He *was* from a foreign country—New York—and wore the sort of bushy, untrimmed mustache often seen on Mediterranean males. His name was Salas, which upon his arrival in New Orleans had sounded to someone enough like the Greek surname Salus to earn the sobriquet he'd had ever since. He'd worked as *maître d'* for years at restaurants from Kolb's to Upperline before a heart attack dropped him flat into a client's swordfish steak with béarnaise at age twenty-nine. Coming out of the hospital, he'd simplified his life: got rid of most of what he owned, bought this place, a decaying, abandoned corner grocery store on Magazine with Spartan apartment above, and turned it into a neighborhood bar, a remarkably laid-back, low-key one, even for New Orleans. He served some of the best gumbo and sandwiches in town, if you didn't mind waiting a while.

The weekend after papers were signed, an army of uncles, brothers and cousins had appeared from nowhere and set about shoring the place up. It was as though they converged on a derelict grocery store, swarmed briefly and stepped back from a bar; and not much had changed since. The beams and supports they'd fashioned from two-by-twos, still bare wood but now gone green with mildew and mold, still propped up corners and ceiling. Cracks in the plaster troweled over with little or no effort to match the color of new plaster to old now looked like skin grafts long since rejected.

Living in a third-floor apartment across the street at the time, with nothing much to do on weekends till seven o'clock rolled over and I allowed myself to begin the night's drinking, I'd watched the whole thing. The Greek's was on my parade route, the place I started and more often than not ended my nights. It was also one of the few bars in the city I'd never been thrown out of. There had been a name on the window at one point, but no one ever paid any attention to it, and when the name faded away, it was never replaced.

Carlos was sitting on a footstool behind the bar, one hand gently swirling ice around the bottom of what remained of a glass of lemonade, the other holding open a paperback book. I might have been gone twenty minutes, instead of twenty years.

Carlos wanted to know about me, so I gave him a two-minute version. I asked the same in return, and he shrugged and moved his head to indicate the bar.

"Get you a drink?"

"Not today, Carlos, I'm in a hurry. Let me come back when I have more time."

He smiled and nodded, waiting for me to say what I'd come for.

I showed him the snapshot of Treadwell's son. "He been around?"

"Last I heard, you'd quit doing detective work."

"I have. This is more like a favor. You know him?"

"Teaching, I heard. Always thought that was something I'd be good at, if things had turned out a lot different."

"The picture, Carlos."

"He in trouble?"

"Not yet."

"But he's planning something."

"I don't know if he's planning it or not, but he's about to break an old man's heart."

"Old man?"

"His father."

Carlos shook his head. "That's bad. What can I tell you?"

"Where he's staying would be a good start."

"Couple weeks ago, he was staying with a guy named Tito, over on Baronne a block off Louisiana. I don't know if he's still there. Or the address, but it's this huge blue monster, textured plaster, at the edge of an open lot. Tito's place is upstairs on the left. There's a separate staircase up to it."

"This Tito a salesman?"

"So they say."

"And a relative of yours, by any chance?"

"A cousin, as it happens. Tito's never there in the afternoon. That would be a good time for you to drop by."

"Then that's what I'll do."

I thanked him and said I'd see him soon, looking at the clock over the bar as I left. Almost five. My seminar students had walked long since. But it was still afternoon, at least.

I caught a cab at Jackson Avenue, had the driver take me up St. Charles to Louisiana and got out there. Walked two blocks to Baronne. I saw the building as soon as I turned.

It was a shade of blue not found in the natural world. The texturing on its plaster sides reminded me of Maori masks. Two cars and a pickup truck were stacked up in the driveway alongside like planes waiting for takeoff clearance, but they'd been waiting a long time.

The railing at the top of the stairs was hung with towels and a washcloth, an orange cotton rug, a shirt on a hanger. I knocked at the screen door, waited a moment, then opened it and knocked on the glass of the door inside. When there was still no response, either from within or from curious neighbors, I pulled out an old plastic ID card I keep for this very purpose and slipped the lock.

The door opened directly into the kitchen. A quarter inch of leftover coffee baked to black tar on the bottom of its carafe. Grease half filled the gutters around the stove's burners. The whole apartment smelled of cat, equal parts musk and pee, with the heady, sweet reek of marijuana beneath. Furnishings were minimal, cast-off clothes in abundance.

I found some Baggies of grass and crack stashed among provisions—mostly unopened jars of spices, sacks of flour, sugar and baking soda, and canned goods like corned-beef hash and stew—and put them back. I found a .38 under the cushion of one of the chairs in the living room and put that back too.

Off to one side was a windowless, odd-shaped little room of the sort often seen in these huge old places that have been chopped into apartments again and again. A mattress had been crammed into it. One corner was bent back like a dog-eared page where the room took a sudden turn; an edge lapped over the baseboard. A nylon athletic bag lying on the mattress had been used as a pillow. I opened it and found in a manila envelope stuffed with scraps and folds of paper an expired Washington driver's license issued to Marcus Treadwell. Most of the rest was people's names and addresses, with notations in a tiny, precise script, in what I presumed to be a code.

I stepped back into the living room and discovered that the .38 was no longer under the cushion. It was now in someone's hand, and pointed at me.

"You must be Tito."

He nodded.

"I'm a friend of Carlos."

"Carlos don't live here, man."

"I know. I was just down at the bar talking to him. He thought you might be able to help me."

"What you need help with?"

"I'm looking for something."

"Just something for yourself? You don't look like a user, man. And I don't do wholesale, know what I mean?"

I shook my head. "Not drugs."

"I'm willing to believe that."

"The guy who's been sleeping here."

"What you want with that pile of shit?"

"Just to talk."

"Yeah? Well, you find him, I want to talk to him too, but I won't be talking long."

"Guess you guys didn't hit it off."

"Hey, I thought he was okay, you know? Till I come home yesterday morning and find him with the back of the crapper off, going after my stash. I'd already moved it, but that don't matter. But I guess he heard me coming, 'cause he was out the window and gone in about half a second. Wouldn't have thought the boy could move that fast."

"You saw him?"

He shrugged. "Who else would it be?"

"Listen, are you going to shoot me or not? Cause if you're not, I'm going to reach into my pocket for a picture."

"Nah, man, I ain't gonna shoot no one." He stuck the gun in a back pocket.

"This the guy?"

"Yeah."

"And you haven't seen him since yesterday morning?"

"No."

"What time?"

"Nine, ten, something like that. He try to rip you off too?"

I shook my head.

"You got a message for him, that right?" Tito said.

"More or less." I handed him a card. "If you do see him again, think about giving me a call."

"There money in it?"

"You never know. For now, let's just say it will be much appreciated."

He looked at the card, then up at me. "Lew Griffin. I heard of you. People say you used to be bad."

"I used to be a lot of things."

"Yeah. Know what you mean."

"I might drop by again tomorrow or the next day, just to check, if that's okay."

"Sure. You do that, Lew Griffin. Just don't forget to lock up again when you leave."

He grinned, gold bicuspid flashing. I suddenly remembered that my father had one just like it.

36

Walsh and Richard Garces were coming for dinner that night. I'd done most of it ahead, a cassoulet and flan, and Alouette was in charge of the rest. When I stepped through the door at seven-twenty I found them all sitting together in the living room. Richard had a glass of wine, Walsh a tumbler of bourbon, Alouette one of those prepackaged wine cooler things. No one got up, but three faces swiveled toward me.

"There goes the party," Garces said.

"And the neighborhood." Alouette.

"Buck seems to be stopping here." Walsh.

"What would you like, Lewis?" Alouette again. I followed her out to the kitchen, pulled an Abita out of the fridge. The kitchen was warm and full of wonderful smells.

"Everything set?"

"Cassoulet's heating, bread's in the oven with it, salad's made except for the dressing."

"You've been watching reruns of Donna Reed."

"Who?"

"Never mind. Anything I can do?"

"Go sit down, drink your beer and talk to the guys. I'll throw this stuff together."

"You sure?"

"Shoo."

It had felt good being in the kitchen again last night, preparing for this, and it felt good now sitting with friends, talking about nothing in particular, anticipating more of the same. I laid my head back, felt tensions go out of my body. My mind rippled with stray thoughts, then became still water.

"Had a call from a friend of yours today," Walsh said. "Sergeant Travis up in Mississippi. Asked how things were going down here. And wanted me to tell you things are a lot duller there now that you're gone."

"I hope you don't mind," Garces said, "but I've asked Alouette to see *Torch Song Trilogy* with me this weekend; they're doing it at the Marigny. It's sold out—which means about twenty tickets—but I have friends in unimportant places. It's Saturday night. That's all right?"

"Sure. Do her good to get out. She's become kind of monomaniacal about this whole thing."

"She has to, for a while."

"I know."

"She seems to be doing well. I have a good feeling about it."

Moments later, Alouette called us to table. We all went out to the kitchen to help her bring things in, forming a culinary chorus line on our way back through the open double door, me with cassoulet, Richard with salad and a huge basket of bread, Don with a tray of condiments and a pitcher of iced tea, Alouette with serving spoons, trivet and a pot of coffee.

The usual dinnertime conversation—politics, jokes, anecdotes, compliments—mixed with grunts of satisfaction and the clatter of silverware. The coffee disappeared fast, and before long I went out to the kitchen to make another pot. When I came back, Alouette was saying: "I can't plan too much ahead. I mean, I want to, but I know I just can't do that, that it doesn't make sense."

"You're right," Richard said. "That's part of what addiction's all about. The personality type, anyway. You start setting up a scene in your head for how things *should be,* and before long you'll look at what's there and how far it is from what you envisioned, from your expectations—and fall into the gap."

" 'I fear those big words that make us so unhappy,' " I said.

Everyone looked at me.

"James Joyce."

"We . . . *fear* . . . change," Alouette said.

"Wayne's World." Garces. We were an allusive, cultured bunch.

Walsh asked about Treadwell then, and I filled him in.

"Your dean's going to have his face rubbed in shit, any way you look at it, Lew. He ready for that?"

"Hard to say. At some level or another, he probably already knows. I think he wants me to be able to tell him everything's all right. But I also think he knows that's not going to happen."

We sat around the table long after dinner and the second pot of coffee were finished. I'd put music on low, a Yazoo anthology of early jazz guitar including the Eddie Lang-Lonnie Johnson duets (for which Lang had used an assumed name, since black and white musicians didn't record together in those days), and a recent CD by New Orleans banjoist Danny Barker.

Walsh bailed out, bleary-eyed, about eleven, Garces within the hour. In each case I threw my arms across the door and explained that they had to take cassoulet with them or would not be allowed to leave. As usual, the cassoulet had gone upscale from a small skillet to the kitchen's largest ovenworthy vessel.

Alouette and I for a while made motions toward cleaning up, mostly just picking things up in one place and putting them down somewhere else. Finally we abandoned pretense and sat at the kitchen table to finish off the iced tea. Out in the front room Danny Barker was making his third or fourth trip of the night down to St. James Infirmary.

I started telling her about David, how I hadn't been around when he was growing up, how we'd at last got to know one another a little, not really as father and son (though I guessed those feelings were there) but more as two adults living in very different worlds.

"He'd gone to Europe for the summer, and sent a postcard or two. Bored gargoyles on one of them, I remember. But we had this pattern—nothing at all for months, then one of us would write a ten-page letter—so I didn't think anything of it. But then his mother called to say she hadn't heard from him either and couldn't seem to get in touch with him."

Alouette listened silently.

"I started trying to find him, figuring there'd be nothing to it. He was in Paris. Apparently he boarded a flight to return to the States, and a cabdriver thought he remembered picking him up at Kennedy and letting him off near Port Authority. But then it was as if he'd dropped off the edge of the earth. There was no trace of him, whatever I did.

"Once about this time, someone called me and said nothing but stayed on the line until the answering machine automatically broke the connection. And somehow, for no good reason, with no idea why he might call like that, or why he wouldn't speak, I knew it was David."

I didn't tell her that, like one of Beckett's mad fabulists, I still had the tape with that silence on it.

Alouette waited, and when she was certain I was through, said: "You never found him, or found out what happened?"

"Nothing."

She reached across the table and laid her hand loosely on mine. "I'm sorry, Lewis. It must hurt terribly."

"It should. But what it really feels like, is that the hole in me, the one that's always been there, just got bigger. And now I know it won't ever be filled."

I removed my hand to pat hers briefly and retrieve my tea. "Well. That last beer seems to have carried me right past philosophical and poetic drunk straight to maudlin."

"In vino veritas."

"I never found any. And God knows I spent enough years looking. Right now—I've been giving this some thought—I've decided that I may have just enough energy left to crawl up the stairs to my room."

We walked up together, and at the head Alouette turned back. "Why did you tell me about David, Lewis?"

Because it's the deepest, most guarded thing in me that I have to give you, I thought.

"I don't know," I said.

37

I spent most of the next day chasing snipe. No one in any bar in New Orleans had ever seen anyone remotely resembling Treadwell's son. Most of them couldn't even be bothered to look at the snapshot. He had not registered at any of the employment services, applied for a driver's license or library card (how's that for desperation?), rented storage space or a postal box from one of the private facilities. No parking tickets had been issued to any vehicle registered in his name. Local credit and collection agencies had received no inquiries.

At four that afternoon I was sitting in a coffeehouse on Magazine, Rue de la Course, gulping my second large *café au lait* from a glass and watching downtown workers bolt for an early start out of the CBD. Nineteenth-century testimonials to the social position and restorative powers of coffeehouses, hand-lettered, hung on the wall at eye level, at least a dozen of them, most with cheap frames askew. It had been some time since anyone took note of them.

Because I could think of nothing else to do, yet remained more or less in function mode, I called Tito, and was surprised when he picked up.

"Hey," he said. "I was gonna call you and couldn't find that card you gave me. It's here somewhere. Cause I heard from the guy you were asking about. Told me he got picked up in the Quarter a few nights ago and he's been in jail all this time, so I guess it wasn't him that tried to rip me off after all. You still got a message for him, I wanted you to know he says he's getting out in the morning."

"You be there a while?"

"What for?"

"Thought I might bring by some solid appreciation."

"Hey. It's a favor, man. Like I say, I heard about you. And besides, it's the second week of the month. Got to go see my parole officer. Cute little thing. Always got a bow in her hair, different one each time. Great ass, for a white girl."

"Has a lot of good advice for you, I bet."

"*Deep* conversations. *She* know what it like here, no doubt about it."

"Tito: thanks, man."

"Just don't forget, Lew Griffin. Next time, maybe *I*'m the one needs a favor, who knows. Happens."

"It does indeed."

I walked to Prytania, got a cab and gave the driver my home address. Halfway there, I told him to swing over to St. Charles and drop me at Louisiana instead.

I was working on pure intuition—maybe the closest thing to principle I had. Connections were being made, switches getting thrown, at some level not accessible to me. I only had to go with it, ride it.

I went up those stairs and into the kitchen as though it were my own. Heard the rasp and scuttle of someone else in the next room.

I stepped in and saw Treadwell's kid bent over the mattress in the niche. Late sunlight threw a perfect print of miniblinds against one wall.

"Find what you're looking for?"

How often does it happen, after all?

He straightened. "Who the fuck are *you?*" He came up and

around and had a gun in hand. The .38 from under the chair cushion. I saw his eyes and knew what was going to happen.

The choice was clear: stand still and get shot straight on, or move and possibly, just possibly, minimize damage.

So instinctively I dove to the left. It felt as though someone had slammed the heel of his hand, hard, against my right shoulder. I was watching his face, then suddenly the back wall. Couldn't feel my right side at all. Then I was out for a while.

I came to on the stretcher. Saw my father's face upside down as they hoisted me into an ambulance. Lots of other faces watching.

"I've been wanting to talk to you," I told him.

"You're gonna be okay," he said. "It's not bad. Take some deep breaths."

"I miss you, Dad."

"We've stopped the bleeding. Try to be still. There's a needle in your hand, for fluids, just a precaution."

"You both were sitting on the car. You looked so young, so happy. What happened?"

"You've been shot, Mr. Griffin. You're going to be okay."

I caromed down a hall and into a room with bright lights overhead. An authoritative voice: the resident. Deferential ones: staff nurses. And one other.

"Mr. Griffin. Lewis. I know you can hear me. You're going to be all right. Listen to me."

A British accent. Wouldn't you know.

38

It was good theater, as they say, meaning that the playwright's contrived a way to get all his themes and characters and the underwear of his plot with its bad elastic crowded onstage at play's end for the big finale.

The old man lies on his sickbed and people file in and out, dragging behind them like bags of wool the very stuff of his life: his forfeitures and silences, his assumptions, his regrets.

So, propped up on pillows in my float of a bed with arm and shoulder taped firmly in place, for several days I held court, an improbable Rex, as faces streamed by: Walsh, Chip Landrieu, Richard Garces, Tito, Alouette.

Once, early on, I dreamed that Treadwell's son was there. Standing against a blue plaster wall, otherwise surrounded by sky, he held a gun loosely in hand. A flag had come out of the gun's barrel and unfurled; it read *Bang*. He said: You will not find me, get this sad certainty firmly in your head. Quoting Cocteau.

Another time LaVerne was there, eyes brimming with the world's pain and all the things left unsaid between us as she silently approached and leaned down to kiss me. Take care of my girl, she said. I awoke with a jolt of disorientation and loss.

Sometime on the third or fourth day, Walsh brought Treadwell by, as I'd asked, and I told him what I knew, sensing the spill of despair into his life. He kept his head down, thanked me and left. Walsh and I sat looking at one another a moment, then he shook his own head and followed.

Alouette was there when I first awoke, and came by the next two afternoons, after work. Things were fine at home, she told me, and she'd be starting school in January. Her father had called once or twice, but just to talk. And oh, yeah, before she forgot, a couple of things had come up at the house that she needed money for. I gave her most of what I had on me and said if she needed more, let me know.

But I *did* know, of course. Knew as surely as I think Dean Treadwell must have known. Even if, at the time, I declined putting it into words.

Alouette didn't show up the next day, and when I called the house, I got myself on the answering machine. I tried again two or three times that night, then again in the morning.

I was standing in front of a mirror, trying to figure out what to do with the other half of the shirt I'd managed to get my left arm into, when the doctor who operated on me came by on rounds. His name was Kowalski, he was chief resident on the surgical service, came from Chicago and was a rock climber. Most of our conversation had been about the last. Three years ago in Arizona a friend climbing beside him, another resident, had fallen and broken his back. Kowalski had immobilized him with climbing rope and sections he hollowed from saguaro cactus, lashed together a rough travois and carried him out. The friend had made a full recovery. Somehow you got the idea that nothing in the surgeon's formal practice was ever going to live up to that one bright segment of improvisation.

"Good. You're up," he said.

"Up. Yes, and going home."

"I'd have to recommend most urgently against that, Mr. Griffin."

"Recommend away." I turned to face him. "Look, I appreciate what you've done. And I'm more than willing to accede to whatever continuing treatment you prescribe. But the truth is, I don't have insurance, I can lie around at home every bit as well as I can here, and meanwhile there are things to be taken care of."

I suppose I should have said *truths are*.

"You'll promise to come in first thing in the morning?"

I nodded.

"Through ER. Just tell them I'm expecting you for a follow-up, and to beep me. It's against hospital policy, but they're used to it. I'll be here—somewhere. That way I can officially discharge you now and you won't have to go AMA, which can always lead to problems farther down the road."

"American Medical Association?"

"Against medical advice."

He helped drape the shirt and button it, then went out to the desk to do the paperwork. I joined him there eventually, shook hands and thanked him again.

"They're going to ask for a deposit downstairs at the business office. I'm sure they'll even insist that it's mandatory, but it isn't. The hospital's supported by public funds and legally they can't demand payment. Just tell them you don't have any money with you."

I didn't have. And as it turned out, they didn't ask, probably because I didn't go by the office.

I got a cab outside the hospital, had the driver take me home and wait while I went in to get money. Like most people who've been poor and on the streets, I had cash squirreled away in various spots around the house. Alouette had found some of the stashes, but others were intact. I took the driver a ten, doubling his fare, and came back in for the damage report.

Everything was still in her room except for clothes, personal items and a small suitcase. It seemed to me there were a few vacancies on the shelves, with books canting into them where others had been removed, but I couldn't be sure. Maybe I only wanted it to be so.

I found her note in the kitchen, on the table around which, in the best southern tradition, we'd sat night after night talking.

Lewis,

I think you're okay, your arm I mean, and I think by now you have to know something's wrong. You probably have a good idea what it is.

I tried so hard, I really did. I hope you can give me credit for that. But everything's so *ordinary* now, so *plain.*

I can't do this any longer. I don't want to hurt you, and I know that I will unless I go now. Of course, I'll hurt you either way, won't I? There's just not any way to win.

It would be nice if I could believe I'm doing something good by leaving, but I guess that would only be fooling myself. And I don't need any more practice at that.

Thank you for everything you did and tried to do for me, Lew. And thank you most of all for loving my mother. Yes, I remember that.

Alouette

39

Years were to pass before I saw Alouette again.

I rented a car that very afternoon, of course, and drove back up to Mississippi, scouting roadsides the whole way. I had midnight dinner with Sergeant Travis, left my suitcase for a few days at Dee's-Lux Inn but was mostly away from the room, spent two nights at a Quality Inn in Memphis. Then drove one-armed and empty-handed back to New Orleans. No sign of Alouette anywhere.

Mardi Gras is just over as I sit on a bright Ash Wednesday by the window in the upstairs front room writing this. All week I've looked down to watch crowds swarm toward St. Charles for parades, people stroll past at all hours in mask and costume, young women in pairs with backpacks and cotton sweaters, men with the plastic webbing of six-packs looped into their belts. Now the street is awash in trash: beer and soft-drink cans, waxed paper cups, containers from Popeye's and Taco Bell, discarded strings of beads, broken doubloons. The old house creaks around me. A tree limb screeches at the pane, and from somewhere behind, deep within the house, a dull moan starts up each time the wind peaks.

Some inchoate equation between the masking and forced revelry of Mardi Gras, the expert self-deception Alouette recognized in herself, and my own in this account, suggests itself. Finally there's little enough difference between them.

I remember that Robbe-Grillet, at work on *Le Voyeur,* traveled briefly to the Brittany coast to refresh his memory of its setting and found that he had no interest in actual gulls, that he cared now only for the gulls of his fiction.

This much is true: Alouette was gone. And I was left thinking, in that self-engaged manner we all have when suddenly alone, that it all had been for nothing.

But maybe (I thought then) something would come of it after all. Maybe we do good things, things that matter, without ever realizing it. Maybe those are the best things we do.

Or maybe, just as Alouette tried so hard to believe her departure might be virtuous, that is just something I want to believe. We betray ourselves into going on; but it's also given us to choose the form of that betrayal.

Alouette was gone. Gone into the darkness that took my son, the darkness that took her mother, the darkness that is so much in us all.

I sat looking for a long time out into that darkness. It was almost midnight, with a chance of rain. The phone's ringing brought me around. I answered.

"Lew," and when she took time getting the next word out, I knew it was Clare. "How are you? I just heard, a few minutes ago. About Alouette."

"It's not like it's wholly unexpected."

"That does nothing to diminish the pain."

"No," I said. "It doesn't. Except maybe in movies about boys learning to be men."

"Pain can be good, Lew. The same as other strong feelings. Love, fear, devotion. It can give us reasons to go on when there aren't any others. It can become a new center for a new self."

Or an excuse for all sorts of evasions.

But I said: "You're proof of that, Clare."

"Of course, it can also give us a reason to make a perfect fool of ourself at eleven o'clock at night."

"Is that what you're doing?"

"God. I hope not." She was silent for a few moments. "I guess what I'm doing, really, is using the situation as an excuse to call and say how much I miss you. Yeah. I'm pretty sure that's it."

"I miss you too. More than you can know."

"You could have called."

"No, Clare. I couldn't."

"Okay. So I never was much good at these coy, girlish ploys. Give me credit for trying. I was supposed to call *you*. And now I'm doing that."

"It's good to hear your voice," I said after a moment.

"I'd like to see you, Lew."

A moth fluttered into my window's light again and again.

"Okay."

"If that's all right with you."

"It is."

"You understand . . ."

"I think so. I'd like to see you, whatever I do or don't understand."

"Maybe we could have a drink."

"That would be great. Where?"

"I don't know. Tip's, maybe?"

"Ça va."

"Want me to pick you up?"

"I've had enough car for a while. I'll walk. See you there. Give me fifteen, twenty minutes."

"Oh, Lew, I almost forgot: Bat came home. I went out Tuesday morning and there he was, sitting on the car, like nothing ever happened."

"Nearest thing he could find to his fridge, I guess."

"I guess. God, I'm looking forward to seeing you."

"Then go saddle up your car, scrape off any stray nesting cats and drive if you'll excuse the expression like a—"

"Don't say it!"

"—good friend."

"I hope so, Lew. I do so want to be."

"See you soon. Calm seas, Clare."

And I walked out into the darkness toward her.

Four streets up, hearing voices close by as I came to a corner, I turned my head. Further down the block, a mugging was taking place. It had begun that way, at least; now it seemed to be progressing. One of the men had the woman's purse over his own shoulder. He knelt at her head, holding her down with hands flat against her shoulders and licking upside down at her face while the other one's hands burrowed roughly under her skirt. As I watched, that one reached up and slapped her hard on the cheek, then took her neck in his hand.

I shouted and started toward them, instinctively turning to keep the injured arm out of sight. Both jumped to their feet. The one who had been at her head ran. The other stood his ground till I came closer and slipped my hand into my coat pocket. Then he also bolted.

"Are you all right?" I asked. A plain woman in her early thirties, inexpensively dressed.

"I think so."

"Don't be afraid," I told her.

Then I, too, was running.

THE PROM

a novel

Based on the hit Broadway musical

by **Saunda Mitchell**

with **Bob Martin, Chad Beguelin, and Matthew Sklar**

VIKING
An imprint of Penguin Random House LLC, New York

First published in the United States of America by Viking,
an imprint of Penguin Random House LLC, 2019

Visit us online at penguinrandomhouse.com

Based on the Broadway musical *The Prom*.
For more information, visit theprommusical.com.

LIBRARY OF CONGRESS CATALOGING-IN-PUBLICATION DATA IS AVAILABLE

ISBN 9781984837523

Book manufactured in Canada

Set in Jenson Pro   Book design by Mariam Quraishi

1 3 5 7 9 10 8 6 4 2

I love you, Mommy.

Thank you for giving me the world.

— SM

THE PROM

Broadway Score! scores a chat with Dee Dee Allen and Barry Glickman on the set of their new show, *ELEANOR*!

(cont. from page 2)

Glickman and Allen invite me into the inner sanctum, backstage at the Alliance Theatre. There are signs of the show in production everywhere. A row of foam heads sports the steel gray wigs and dental prosthetics Allen wears to transform herself into Mrs. Roosevelt, and of course, FDR's wheelchair sits in a corner, its seat taken by a cigar (real) and a pair of glasses (prop). Despite the serious subject matter of the show, Drama Desk winner Glickman and Tony winner Allen are all laughs with each other—and us.

BS!: What does it mean for one of Broadway's grand dames—

BG: I guess this question is for me, Dee Dee!

DA: Just try to cut me out of the spotlight, honey!

[We laugh and rephrase.]

BS!: What does it mean for *two* of Broadway's greats to come together on a show like *ELEANOR*?

DA: I truly feel like I'm changing lives. Don't you, Barry?

BG: Indeed. I've come to realize that there's no difference between a celebrity and the president of the United States.

DA: By the time I get tuberculosis in act 2, even the people who are dead inside will be on their feet.

BG: And knee-deep in tissues! If the audience doesn't leave depressed, we haven't done our jobs.

DA: It's power. Literal power.

BG: Not to quote a certain show that destroyed a producer, a pop star, and a comic book hero—but with great power comes great responsibility.

DA: And I think we're great enough to handle it.

Excerpt from a *New York Times* theater review

If FDR Could Stand for This, He Wouldn't

. . . Dee Dee Allen inhabits Eleanor Roosevelt in the same way a demon inhabits the monstrous Annabelle doll from the self-titled horror film series, but with less grace and charm. Allen doesn't so much present the first lady's activism to the audience as she shoves it down their throat: a Molotov cocktail of American flag soaked in syrup and set on fire.

One would think next to Allen's shrill, scene-chomping antics that Glickman would offer a respite. One would be wrong. Glickman's FDR just might be the most insultingly misguided and offensive performance this reviewer has had the squirming misfortune to endure. The aging Glickman has none of the former president's fire or finesse, and the actor's attempt at a mid-Atlantic accent is so laughably lost, it lands somewhere west of New Jersey.

If you were considering buying a ticket, do yourself a favor. Find a way to contract tuberculosis instead. It's a terrible way to go, but worlds better than watching this Eleanor hack herself to death in slow motion.

1. Edgewater, Indiana

EMMA

Note to self: don't be gay in Indiana.

Actually, that's a note for everybody else. I'm already gay in Indiana, and, spoiler alert, it sucks.

I told the internet before I told my parents—on my YouTube channel, Emma Sings. It's me, my guitar, and mostly cover tunes of whatever's popular at the moment. People leave more comments if you sing songs they know, and I like that. I don't have a lot of friends, so those little digital hellos make me feel less alone in the world.

I'm not trying to get discovered or anything like that. First, that literally never works, and second, the idea of fame terrifies me. I already feel like everybody knows my business. Of course, that's because they actually *do* know my business. One slip, and it was everywhere.

So, this is what happened.

Picture it: the summer before freshman year. Picture me: mousy and shy, with thick-rimmed glasses that give me owl eyes. I'm at a youth group picnic hosted by the Vineyard, which is a church. You know, one of those new churches with branding and youth pastors with drum kits.

They really tick off churches like First Lutheran and Missionary Free Baptist and all the other traditional places of worship packed into Edgewater, Indiana. The cheesy signs in front of them that used to say stuff like WHAT'S MISSING FROM CH CH? U R! started to get very snarky when the Vineyard opened.

Naturally, this means all the teenagers want to go there. High-level rebellion, right? *No, Mom, I'm going to the cool church, where I can wear jeans during the service!* And naturally, this means that all the youth group invites that used to lead to punch and cake parties in dingy fellowship halls suddenly lead to big outdoor picnics that still feature pretty unfortunate food, because it's still a church pitch-in.

That's how I end up with a plate of mini meatballs in barbecue sauce. I've heard too many horror stories about potato salad and egg salad and macaroni salad and basically any salad that uses mayo as glue, and I've also read that baby carrots are rejected regular carrots that are bleached and shaved down, so those are also a big no.

A Crock-Pot full of steaming hot meatballs doesn't exactly say summer fun (maybe in Sweden?). But the contents seem safe. I loaded up on them, but now I'm trying to figure out how to eat them without making a mess. These things are impervious to plastic forks and knives, which is what I have on hand.

There's a line at the food tables, and I don't really care to stand in it long enough to get a spoon. Also, I kind of don't feel like drawing attention to myself by cutting in line with an excuse, *Oh, I just need a spoon!* Even extremely adorable people get side-eye for jumping ahead in the food line at a church potluck-slash-picnic, and I'm awkwardly cute at best.

Additionally, who eats meatballs with a spoon? Meatball Spooner wouldn't be the first name people ever called me, but in this moment, it feels like it would be the worst.

Spoiler alert: it's not the worst. But I'll get to that.

So, I'm standing there, trying to ninja food into my face, and *she* walks up. Wavy auburn hair, bronze skin, dark eyes, and she stops. I stop. The world stops. Probably the universe stops; I can't explain the physics of it.

I can only explain the magic, because in that moment, Alyssa Greene looks at me and turns into a goddess. A brilliant, kind, smart, funny goddess in shimmery lip gloss that I suddenly want to taste.

You guys, I'm not surprised to find myself hard crushing on Alyssa Green. I've always liked girls. I was once a teeny, baby lesbian. In sixth grade, I was crazy into Madison from *Talk to the Hand,* and *not* because I wanted to be her friend. And now, I'm a regular, teen-sized lesbian. I have thoughts about Ariana Grande (impure thoughts), and I feel like if I could meet Lara Jean of *To All the Boys I've Loved Before,* I could help her start the sequel, *To All the Girls Who Eclipsed Them.*

But I *am* surprised when Alyssa reaches past everybody at the dessert table and presents me with a giant skewer. With a blinding smile, she says, "This is the only thing that works."

I'm not surprised that she's nice, but that she noticed me. That I'm somehow actually visible to the most beautiful girl ever to breathe air. The surprises keep coming, because she touches my hand. And stands with me while I impale meatball after meatball. She even lets me share one with her. RIGHT THERE. AT THE CHURCH PICNIC.

On the lawn, people play cornhole—which is legitimately the name of a bag-tossing, target-hitting game—and Christian rock blares from a speaker, courtesy of Pastor Zak's iPhone playlist. The sky is endlessly, perfectly blue, and Alyssa Greene puts her phone number into my phone. Then she makes me text her, so she has my number, too.

That night, I recorded a TSwift cover for Emma Sings. Everything inside me was so fantasy and cotton candy that I told the world I was in love with a beautiful girl without a thought. Without the slightest hesitation. I uploaded, I picked a cover thumb that looked semi-decent, and I went to bed.

My mother woke me up.

I'm sure one day this will be a hilarious story, but she shook me awake and shoved a printout of my YouTube page into my face. And when she demanded, "What is this?" all I could say was, "I don't know!" because I didn't!

"We didn't raise you like this!" she yelled.

"Like *what*?!" I asked, because again, literally woken out of a dead sleep with a piece of paper crammed halfway up my nostrils.

My mother rose up to her full, not all that impressive height of five foot four. "You know exactly what I'm talking about, Emma."

But I didn't! They didn't raise me to . . . sing on the internet? Post videos in the deeply awesome salmon jammies my nan got me for Christmas?

I mean, to be fair, after a couple of seconds, the old brain kicked in. Last night, I posted a video full of shameless, unfiltered heart-eyes for a girl who'd given me a marshmallow skewer. (And an extremely passable rendition of "Our Song," if I do say so myself.)

And after I'd posted, someone in town must have watched it and—their delicate sensibilities inflamed—immediately informed my mother. (Mom printed out my profile page like it was a recipe for Crunchy Ramen Noodle Salad; there's no way she found it on her own.)

And in that moment, I guess I was too stunned to be scared of my parents, whom I knew, for a fact, to be lifelong members of a church that officially hated gay people but in practice was "too nice" to say anything about it in public. I must have taken silence for approval, which historically has been an extremely bad policy position. So I told the truth.

"I just like her," I said.

"Well, you can just stop," she snapped, as if I could cancel the gay like Netflix. "Not in this house! Not under my roof!"

If this were a heartwarming, *Chicken Soup*-y kind of story, this is the part where I'd say, yeah, it was hard for a while. But eventually my parents remembered that I was their precious only child, and they loved me unconditionally. They joined PFLAG and started wearing really embarrassing T-shirts at pride parades that said FREE MOM HUGS and FREE DAD HUGS. I brought my girlfriend home, and by graduation, they'd stopped calling her my "friend."

Sorry. Your soul is going to go unsouped this time.

They argued about it for weeks: conversion camp or eviction. And ultimately, they let me take my guitar and my school stuff, reclaimed my key to the house, and kicked me out. All my clothes, my laptop, the box of birthday cards I'd saved since I was six—well, I heard they burned what they couldn't donate. What a couple of drama queens, right?

So now I live with my grandma, Nan, two blocks from my parents' house, in Edgewater, Indiana. I'm the only out queer kid at school, and it's a good thing I still have my YouTube channel.

It's aggressively ordinary, and I know I'll never go viral. But I do have subscribers, and their responses feel like friends. Like-minded, queer friends. I need them. I need them so desperately, I treat it like QUILTBAG Pokémon: I gotta catch them all.

There are places where it's in to be out. New York, San Francisco . . . imaginary places, in imaginary lands, far, far away from here. But Indiana is not one of those places. So yeah, that's my advice to you: don't be gay in Indiana, if you can absolutely help it.

There's nothing here for you but heartbreak.

2. Edgewater, Indiana

ALYSSA

You've probably never been here, so let me tell you, Indiana is a beautiful place.

Sometimes at night, the moon is so bright behind the clouds that the sky is pearl silk. I get up at five A.M. to go to school, and the roads are lined with silvery fog. Just before the sun starts to rise, as my bus makes a left onto State Road 550, everything turns purple, then lavender, then pink.

In the summer, we have acres of fireflies. There's a pond in the woods that's clean enough to swim in. Raspberries and mulberries and blackberries grow along fences, free for the taking. Come fall, we have a riot of autumn color and apple orchards where you pick your own. Have you ever had a piping-hot fried biscuit with apple butter? Deadly good.

We have the kind of winter you see on Christmas cards. Rolling fields, blankets of white, the whisper of snow falling, and nights so dark, you can see the Milky Way. On the clearest days, the fields drift on toward forever. It's a silvered, glittering expanse, stretched until it surrenders to an icy blue horizon.

Indiana is small towns, and Fourth of July parades, and basketball. A lot of basketball. Way too much basketball, actually. It's the state sport-slash-religion. If you make it to high school without swearing allegiance to the IU Hoosiers or Purdue Boilermakers, they throw you in a pit of voles for all eternity.

(Special dispensation given for the Fighting Irish; you're allowed to love Notre Dame, but you're also a little suspect.)

Supporting our school team, the James Madison Golden Weevils, is key in Edgewater. When we have homecoming, it's not for the football team. Nope. *They're* ranked third to last in the state; they're dead to us.

Homecoming is for the basketball team. The prom court is for the basketball team. The pep rallies, the bake sales, the wrapping paper sales, the industrial-sized-cans-of-flavored-popcorn sales, all dedicated to b-ball. Go Golden Weevils!

Consequently, the basketball team is the reason that prom tickets are strictly rationed. Between varsity (first through third strings), and junior varsity (two strings), and freshman prep (*four* strings!), we have a guaranteed hundred and fifty athletes, with a probable hundred and fifty athlete dates, and the fire marshal says we can't have more than four hundred people in our school gym.

Thus, when the Future Corn Keepers of America set up their table to sell prom tickets in the Hall of Champions (aka the front hallway with all the trophy cases), they have three essential items:

1. A cash box. This is a cash-only dance, and don't even try to bring a check from your parents. The

FCK spit on your mom's Precious Moments checks.

2. A stack of tickets designed by the one kid in school who knows how to use Photoshop well. (*Well* being the operative word; everybody around here knows how to filter for Insta, but when it comes to text, it's like a subreddit got font poisoning and started puking Papyrus and Comic Sans.)
3. The list. The list has two columns: Your Name. Date's Name. They are inextricably entwined; there are no stag tickets to our prom. The list is the reason why I've been having a serious discussion about prom with my girlfriend.

It's our senior year; this is our last chance. And I do, I really do want to go and dance under a cardboard moon and aluminum foil stars. I want to look into her funny hazel eyes that sometimes turn blue and sometimes green, depending on what she's wearing. I want to wrap my arms around her and let the whole world slip away.

But it won't slip away.

Not here. Not with my mom watching.

I want to make it clear: I'm not ashamed to be a lesbian. I love love, and I love my girlfriend. I love quiet murmurs and secret kisses. I love snuggling next to her on her grandmother's strangely velveteen couch, watching movies when the rain presses in from the west. I love that our hands are exactly the same size, but she has tiny feet with super long toes. When she sings, I love her even more. So much that it actually hurts, like there's a hand reaching in to squeeze my heart until it's a diamond.

She flickers like a firefly, because her hair is gold but almost brown; her eyes are blue but almost green. When she takes off her glasses, I like to press my nose to hers and just gaze in. It makes her laugh and blush, her cheeks suddenly pink as her lips. It's hard to whisper our love instead of shouting it to the skies.

But the thing is, my mother, she's not ready for it. She's fragile right now. She's *been* fragile since my father left. It was so easy for him. He just packed a gym bag and waltzed out into the night. Started a new family—well, based on when my half sibling was born, he started the new family *before* he walked out.

And since then, Mom has lived in this delicate crystal bubble. She thinks if she goes to church more, if she prays harder, if she cleans the house better, if she loses twenty pounds, if she raises me right, if she finally nails that pot roast recipe her mother-in-law gave her, Dad will come home. You can see the belief sparking in her eyes; she's a transformer hit by lightning. Everything pours out, hot and fast and endlessly.

That fire means I have to be the best daughter. My grades have to be all As, with weighted classes so my GPA breaks that 4.0 ceiling. My safety schools have to be other people's first picks. I have to teach Sunday school, and my kids have to have the best crafts, the ones that make their parents tear up at the preciousness.

But I'm president of the student council because *I* wanted that. Because I thought I could change things that needed to be changed and strengthen things that needed to be stronger. Still, I have to go to the prom in a lilac, spaghetti-strapped, knee-length dress that Mom worked sixty-hour weeks for a month to afford. It has Swarovski crystals on the bodice. Swarovski. Crystals.

And why? Well, she's the president of the PTA (remember: perfect in all things), and they're the chaperone hosts of the prom. This year *will* be perfect, and it will be perfect with me in *that* dress, on the arm of a boy in a tux.

Some boy. Any boy. Mom doesn't know who—but she sure has suggestions. Like Paolo, for instance, the exchange student who goes to our church. He's a real-life college sophomore and looks like TV sophomores look: cut and sculpted, walking with knowing hips. Don't get me wrong: he's hot. But he's also secretly sleeping with our choir director, so shhh, that's between us.

The point is, my mom's bubble is going to burst. She thinks she's working domestic magic, but she's really just lying to herself. Lying to the world. Any minute, everything is going to come crashing down on her. The spell will end, and I need to be able to put her back together again.

That's why I don't want to be the clock that strikes her midnight. And that's why I'm not-arguing-but-discussing-seriously the prom with my girlfriend. She wants one magical night, and I want that, too. But we live in Edgewater, Indiana, and signing that list with our names—Emma Nolan, Alyssa Greene—side by side, that's more than buying two tickets to the school gym.

Emma knows, better than anybody, how this story goes.

Her mom and dad still go to my church. Every week. Same pew. Same stony faces gazing up at the stained-glass Lord behind the pulpit. He gathers lambs at his feet; his hair is almost golden when the light streams through.

My dad's already gone. My mom's in la-la land, probably complete with magical dancing and show tunes. For me, saying yes to the prom is more than putting on a dress and buying a corsage. It's choosing to be the flawless, ideal daughter or to pick up a bat and shatter my mother into a million pieces.

And still, I want to fly free and say yes and kiss Emma under the glimmering light of a borrowed disco ball. So, we're discussing. Not arguing. I don't want to fight. It's spring and Indiana is beautiful again. Between us, and the blue skies, and the budding pear trees, and the tulips sending up little green tendrils toward the sun, I'm leaning toward yes. I want to say yes.

We'll see.

3. Subterfuge

EMMA

I have one hundred dollars in my pocket, but I'm not approaching the ticket table just yet.

I can't; Nick Leavel is putting on a production of *PROMPOSAL!* right here in the Hall of Champions. Standing room only, but mostly because it's the front hallway of a high school and nobody who values their life is going to sit on (a) the stairs or (b) the FCK prom-ticket table.

Excitement runs through the unwitting crowd. Nick has a brigade of junior varsity guys behind him. Carrying poster boards close to their chests, they have (what I'm guessing are) gas station carnations clutched in their teeth. Strobed out in sunglasses, his letter jacket, and *the* shiniest shoes I've ever laid eyes on, Nick puts two fingers in his mouth and whistles sharply.

Everyone in the Hall of Champions stops and turns. I kid you not, Nick pauses to take a quick gander at the gaggles who came to witness his wonder and glory. It's not enough for him to prompose to Kaylee Brooks, he has to make sure he's going all out. When you're the star center of the Golden Weevils, you have to shine.

"Kaylee," Nick says, taking her hands. He spins her around, and hilariously, he has to untangle their arms a little—he pretends it was all smooth. His slick dress shoes scrape against the floor as he turns to kneel in front of her. He looks up, but he doesn't say anything.

Instead, he nods and the junior varsity swoop in. Like, you can tell they've practiced this. Standing in a semicircle behind Nick, they drop the carnations at Kaylee's feet. And then, one by one, they flip the poster boards.

On the one hand, this is practiced and thoughtful and the tiny sliver of sentimentality lodged deep in my heart makes me smile. But let's be real, it's a bunch of tenth-graders fumbling with poster boards like it's a third-grade play about making flowers grow. Plus, it's happening in a high school hallway. In front of the yellowed JUST SAY NO posters. It's legitimately hilarious, but I keep my laughter to myself.

"Kaylee," the first JVer says, holding up his sign. It has a *lot* of writing on it, but helpfully for the audience, Nick reads it aloud. He literally glances over his shoulder to make sure he's in the right place.

Clutching Kaylee's hands, he says, "Girl," like he's a late-night DJ, "ever since freshman first string, everybody has been all up on this. You know I'm the OG around here, but it's lonely at the top."

My eyes roll so hard, I feel a little twinge before they roll back. Because, let me clarify for you: this OG is the whitest kid in our mostly white school. Light brown hair, pale blue eyes, he's the tallest, foamiest glass of milk in southern Indiana. Kaylee's lapping it up like a rescue kitten, too.

The next poster board falls, and I hover near the stairs because yes, I'm watching this, but no, I don't want to be caught watching this. As I cling to the straps of my backpack, I shiver suddenly. Not from cold, or excess cynicism—it's her.

When Alyssa gets close, I tingle everywhere. Everywhere. She doesn't stand *too* close, because nobody knows. But she's near enough that I catch a hint of the coconut oil she uses in her hair, the rich vanilla from her hand lotion, and if I'm making her sound delicious, well, obviously.

When Nick gets to the third poster board in his set (*Then something happened, girl, you turned my life around*), Alyssa murmurs to me, "Are you sorry we're not doing this?"

I muster a smile. "What, sonnets in the key of duh? Not sorry at all."

Her fingers brush the back of my arm, and she says, "You know what I mean."

Her skin is like silk on mine. I want to wrap myself in her, bury my face in the warm curve of her neck. I'd love to get on one knee for her, or write her a song and sing it from the balcony here at school. I really would. But it's easier to be sarcastic about something I'm never going to get than to admit that I want it. I'd go beyond big if Alyssa would let me. But she won't, so why think about it?

With a quick look back, I say, "I just want to go to prom with you."

"About that," she replies, and she already sounds like she's negotiating with Principal Hawkins for off-campus lunch for seniors. Not a promising start to a conversation I thought we were almost done having. She says, "I had a thought."

Welp. Time to pull down the metal shutters and chain off the old heart. Deliberately, I stare at Nick and his All-Star Carnation Revue, my brain full of Wonder Bread romance that they don't even appreciate.

Sure, yeah, Kaylee jumps up and down and makes Wookiee sounds before she says yes, and maybe Nick is into that. Behind her, her best friend Shelby pretends to be happy, but it's obvious by the way she stares longingly at her boyfriend, she's peeved this moment isn't hers.

But this is a show we've all seen before on YouTube, except with way worse production values. It's so *easy* for them that they don't even try. They don't *have* to try; people will remember this like a classic movie scene because it happens all the time in movies . . . for them.

I don't want my disappointment to come out when I answer Alyssa, but it might. My throat's so tight, I can't tell. "Let's hear this thought."

"We'll go together," Alyssa says diplomatically, "but let's sign up separately today. I need to be able to ease my mom into this. I think she's starting to come around."

I almost make a Wookiee sound of my own, and not a cute one. Baffled, I turn to look at her. "What's the difference between telling her today and telling her three weeks from today?"

"She's not ready yet, and you know she has this place on lockdown," Alyssa says. "If we buy tickets together, she'll know before I get home. I want to tell her. Present it exactly the right way, and that takes time."

The argument is there, and fair. The longer we wait to buy tickets, the less likely there will be tickets to buy. Since neither of us will be arriving on the underwhelming arm of a James Madison Golden Weevil, time is of the essence.

But, I point out, "I'm going to have to put down somebody's name. And you realize this means we're paying for two extra tickets we're not going to use. That's basically a gay tax."

"I'll pay you back," Alyssa says. She touches the back of my arm again, a secret touch no one should see because we're lingering under the stairs like bridge trolls. She swears, "I'll make this up to you."

Cash money is *not* on offer. Instead, it's everything. It's one night that's just ours, without hiding and sneaking and pretending we're something we're not. And I know it's hard—only out gay kid in my entire school, remember? And also the gay kid who didn't get to tell her parents on her own terms. And, *finalement,* the gay kid who lives with Grandma now. Truly, honestly, really, I get it. Lying about who you're with isn't quite as hard as lying about who you are, and yet . . .

"I just want to dance with you," I tell her, as I reach back and catch her hand, our fingers touching. For just a moment, she holds my hand, and we're together in the bright light of day. I see no one but her; I swear, I feel her heartbeat instead of mine. My lips sting for a kiss, but I let go before she can. Not here. Not now.

"Is that a yes?" she asks.

"Watch this," I say, some weird strain of bravado flowing

through me. I walk straight for the FCK table, because my thought is, I'm going to buy those tickets right now and show my girlfriend I'll do whatever it takes to have the most romantic night of our lives together.

Buuuut, I fail at the down low, because our star center just promposed, so of *course* all eyes are on the sign-up table as he pays for tickets while his girl watches, clutching a bouquet of sophomore-slobbered flowers. Now everybody's huddled around the table, buzzing about the spectacle, and *now* THE ONLY (OUT) GAY GIRL IN EDGEWATER just hopped in line.

The FCK doesn't care who buys prom tickets. They want their money (25 percent of ticket sales goes to their club to—I don't know—buy luxury pesticides or something), and my fee disappears into the lockbox before I can say hello. Breanna Lo slaps down two tickets, ready to inscribe my name and my date's name on them, while Milo Potts shoves the clipboard under my nose.

"Your name here," he says, tapping the first column. "Date's name here."

I say something really intelligent, like "Uh," then sign my name very slowly. I even say it out loud, as if Breanna might not know who I am. Emma Nolan, that's me, that's for sure, definitely write down *Emma Nolan* on that first ticket!

"Who are you going with?" Kaylee asks facetiously. This is quite possibly the first time Kaylee has spoken to me since ninth-grade English, when she asked me to trade seats because the fluorescent lights were, and I quote, making her eyelashes twitch.

Shelby perches at her elbow, Kaylee's perpetual garbage minion. "Yeah, who are you going with, Emma? I didn't know we had more than one lesbo in town."

This is when I want to look back. When I want to turn and see Alyssa standing there. The strength of her dark eyes would hold me up. We'd be connected; I wouldn't be alone. But that would be endlessly obvious. I can't do that to her. So I stiffen my neck like it's a vampire convention and stare at the blank line. Date's name. Date's name.

"You have to have a date," Breanna says curtly. The daggers in her eyes imply that I'd better not have just made her ruin a ticket for nothing.

"Your left hand doesn't count," Kaylee says. Nick snorts a laugh that makes me take back any benefit of the doubt I might have given him for his cheese-factory promposal. I'm also a big enough person that I don't stab him with the pen when he says, "Righty doesn't either."

Oh, the devastating wit.

Clenching my teeth, I scribble the first name I can think of, and it's not my fault I thought of it, it just happened. Here's hoping that the gathered brain trust isn't bright enough to make the connection. The only thing I can say in my defense is that she's a cute brunette and I have a type.

Kaylee reads over the top of the clipboard. "Anna Kendrick . . . son?"

"You don't know her," I mutter.

"Is she an exchange student or something?" Shelby asks.

"Sure."

Nick detaches his lips from Kaylee's ear long enough to

ask, "Then why don't you exchange her for a guy?"

With every bit of patience I have, I ignore them. I thrust my hand under Breanna's nose and say, "Tickets, please."

Kaylee all but falls back against Nick. "I can't wait to meet your really real gay prom date, Emma! Anna Kendrick . . . son sounds so *cute*. Doesn't she sound cute, Nick?"

He twines his arms around her, like she's bricks and he's ivy. The combined IQ is about right, anyway. With his chin resting on her shoulder, Nick nuzzles Kaylee's ear in a way that I find genuinely cannibalistic, then he spills a tanker's worth of smarm when he replies, "Not as cute as you, babe."

Without another word, I tuck the tickets into my backpack and turn. The smile I was about to shoot Alyssa dies. She's not even turned this way.

Her mother has appeared from nowhere, as she is wont to do. There are days when I see Mrs. Greene around here more than I see Principal Hawkins, which is saying something. She might be the slightest bit overinvested in all things Alyssa.

Mrs. Greene holds both of Alyssa's hands. I can tell they're talking about the prom, because Mrs. Greene keeps gesturing toward the table. The look on Alyssa's face is somewhere south of nauseated, but she nods. She nods and smiles and then takes one mechanical step in my direction.

There's a whole dance to being in and being out, and I know the steps. I'm supposed to disappear now. So I do, ducking my head and drifting past Nick's JV chorus line. They cough, "Gay, gay, gay," as I pass, and as Alyssa passes me, she says nothing.

Escaping, I chant back to myself, *She's worth it, she's worth it, she's worth it.*

4. Strategic

ALYSSA

I think—no, I know—I am the worst person in the world.

Mom shows up at school far too often these days, and this was the positively worst time. I didn't hear what Kaylee and her crew said to Emma, but I saw the look on her face. Her heart-shaped, freckled face, her face that I love more than any other face in the world.

When I have to pretend we're not together, it's like giant hands reaching down to break me in two. I feel the break, right in the middle of my chest. It exposes my marrow and my nerves, and I'm nothing but a walking wound.

"What's all that about?" my mother asks sharply. As we walk around Emma, we both hear the JVers barking, "Gay, gay, gay."

They do it to Emma sometimes, like it's supposed to be an insult. I guess they think it *is* an insult, instead of a statement of fact. Most of the time, I say something. But most of the time, I don't have my mother frog-marching me up to the prom-ticket table.

I swallow my anger, my frustration, my embarrassment. I

push down the hurt I feel because I can't say anything, and the shame that I don't. I put on my perfect-daughter smile and shake my head like it's light and worry-free. "No idea. Wow, a hundred dollars. I don't know if I have—"

Five twenties fan out in my mother's hand. She's so proud; she hands it to Milo. "I've got that covered. And now, little missy, you have to give up this big secret you've been keeping."

Pinned to the floor in a panic, I say, "I'm not keeping any secrets!"

With a practiced, carefree laugh, my mother plucks the clipboard off the table and a pen right out of Milo's hand. With a flourish, she fills in my name, then fixes me in her gaze. "Your date, sweetheart? You've been talking him up, and now it's time to reveal all."

My hummingbird heart beats so fast, it feels like it's stopped. I *have* been talking up my date. Very carefully, without pronouns. *I think you'll like my date, Mom. My date's so brave, so talented, so cute. You're definitely going to meet my date soon.* But I am not prepared to come out in the middle of the Hall of Champions, in front of Kaylee and Shelby. They have the biggest mouths in James Madison. They do *not* get to see my mother break. This will *not* be the next group-text intrigue.

"John," I say finally. What a nice, generic name. What a nice, nobody-you-know kind of name. Except my mother's brows are arched; they're question marks. That presses some primal button in me, the big red one that says, *Answer her right now or ELSE!* Stunned, I hear myself say, "Cho."

Oh no. I just told my mother I'm going to the prom with hot Sulu. My face stings; I wait for her to bust me. Instead, she simply lights up and scrawls his name beside mine. She doesn't suspect a thing, because she asks with quiet delight, "How do we know John Cho?"

My blush deepens, but I keep it together. "Model UN. I met him at Model UN. He was Australia."

"Oooh," Mom says, pretending to fan herself. "He comes from a land down undah, does he?"

From the weird accent to the expectant way Mom looks at me, it's like I'm supposed to get something out of it. Well, what I get out of it is that I just set my plan to ease Emma into my mother's sights back by three weeks, easily.

Why did Mom have to be here at this exact moment? Why couldn't she just stay at work and phone in her school interest like everybody else's mom?

I take the tickets from Breanna and force my smile wider. "Yeah, I guess so."

"Well, I can't wait to meet him."

Is everyone in the Hall of Champions staring at me? It feels like it. It's like someone turned a blinding spotlight on me and I forgot my lines. I shove the tickets in my purse and nod. "It's going to be exciting."

"I bet," Mom says. She starts to hand the clipboard back to Milo, but her expression changes. There's a darkness in the furrow of her brows. She clutches the sign-up sheet a little harder and reads aloud the line just before mine. "Emma Nolan and Anna Kendrickson?"

Please, please, floor, just open up and swallow me right now.

I pluck the clipboard from her hands and try to return it. "Sounds about right!"

"Two girls?" Mom lifts her chin. "The rules are very clear: no stag dates. There are too many people who want to come to prom and not enough tickets to go around. Couples only!"

"Oh, that *is* a couple, Mrs. Greene," Breanna helpfully supplies. She doesn't sound the slightest bit mean as she informs Mom, "Emma Nolan's gay."

Ice crackles around my mother. "Excuse me?"

Milo has perhaps spent a little too much time breathing the fumes in the cattle barn. He can't tell that my mother is about to get full dragon queen up in here; he thinks he's just clearing up some lingering confusion. "Yeah, she came out freshman year."

My mother lands just shy of mocking Milo's tone. "How lovely for her." She starts flipping through each page, her eyes sharp and scouring. When she gets back to the front, she informs Milo and Breanna, "You're done selling tickets for the day. Move along."

They look baffled, but this isn't their first rodeo with my mom. They zip their lips, lock the cashbox, and disappear.

An abyss swirls around me. It gets wider and deeper. The dark presses in from every side. I try to smile and lighten the moment and make this right. I'm desperate to make this right. "There's still another half an hour left of lunch, Mom. You can't close up shop early."

"Oh, I can, and I am," she says adamantly. She stares at the list again, disgust curling the arch of her lips. "I don't know who this Emma thinks she is, but we have standards here. We have morals."

"It's just a dance, Mom. It's fine."

Summoning up her full height, my mother glares at me. "It is *not* fine, Alyssa. Nothing about this is fine! I don't think so, and neither will the rest of the PTA, I guarantee you that."

"Why are you making a big deal out of this?" I ask. I already know what she's going to say. I already know because I've imagined variations on this conversation for three whole years. No matter how I approach it, I could never make this, make *queer*, okay for my mental mother. And god, now that it's happening for real, it's like I'm being torn in pieces. "It's one couple!"

"It's the principle of the matter!" Nostrils flaring, she looks away, some switch going off in her head. She points toward the office, thinking out loud. "I need to go have a word with Principal Hawkins."

Catching her by the hand, I say, "Mom, please!"

A thread of suspicion wraps around her. "You seem awfully invested in this, Alyssa."

Here, I could confess: *Because she's my girlfriend!* I could say, *Because she's my date. Because she loves me and I love her. Because there's nothing wrong with that. In fact, there's everything right with it!* But I can see my mother's fury and her fear. She grows with it, until she looks ten feet tall. She towers and glowers, all that stone wrapped around a heart of vulnerable flesh.

I guess I'm a coward. Instead of making any of the arguments I could make, I say, "I'm not."

For a moment, I think Mom sees through me. It's in the

way she tilts her head to the side, in the angle of her gaze as it sweeps across my face. It's like a strobe light goes off, and everything's illuminated for her. Then the dark comes again, and she pats me on the cheek. "Good girl. Let me worry about this."

I really am the worst person in the world, because I say nothing as she walks away.

5. Pitchforks Strongly Encouraged

EMMA

Thanks to Mrs. Greene, it's Emma season at school.

Of course she talked to Principal Hawkins. I don't know what he told her, but Mrs. Greene then called an *emergency* meeting of the PTA.

Never in the history of education has there been a PTA emergency. Like, omg, we don't have enough crepe paper for Spirit Week, we have to hit the Walmart like the fist of an angry god and correct that *immediately*!

Apparently, they also have to correct my existence.

The day after I volunteered as tribute—I mean, the day after I bought prom tickets for me and a celebrity that I'm definitely not asking to prom on the internet in the vain hope she'll actually show—the PTA sent an email to all the parents and students. It read:

> Dear James Madison Family,
>
> As you know, the PTA and the Future Corn Keepers of America host the annual prom

for our school. Excitement builds all year long for this event, and it's a highlight for our graduating seniors. We feel the need to remind everyone that attendance at prom is a privilege, not a right. As there have been questions, we want to clarify the requirements students must meet to attend:

GPA of 2.5 or above.[1]

Gentlemen are expected to wear a suit and tie.

Ladies are expected to wear modest evening attire, with dresses no shorter than knee length, no strapless gowns, no gowns that show belly or feature slits in the skirts to reveal skin above the knee, no material that is see-through or transparent, no material that is designed to appear see-through or transparent, no unusual materials (i.e., no duct tape dresses), and nothing that is designed to be sexually provocative, which will be determined at the discretion of the chaperones.[2]

Tickets will only be sold to boy/girl couples.[3] Due to space constraints, there will be no individual tickets sold, and no tickets sold to friends of the same sex. We want to make sure that everyone who has earned the right to attend this event with their date has the chance to.

Because prom tickets are limited, and because prom is meant to be a reward for our students at James Madison, only enrolled, eligible James Madison students[4] will be permitted to attend. No outside dates.

Thanks for your time, and we look forward to having a great prom this year!

Sincerely,
Your PTA
Go Golden Weevils!

So, uh, that letter, wow. Let me tell you, I tore it apart on YouTube, point by point, starting at [1], that GPA requirement.

You know why it's that low? Because otherwise, half the basketball team would be barred from the prom. And that, of course, can never happen, because it would literally signal the Hoosier apocalypse. I've heard teachers aren't allowed to let the players' grades dip below that average, period. How lucky for them.

Moving on to [2], way to enshrine the patriarchy and gender binary. Only guys can show up in any old jacket and tie, but woOooOoo, beware the specter of a girl (and only a girl!) in a dress that shows her knees. Can you believe this one? You should, because that's the "classy, formal" version of the school's regular dress code. Guys who were assigned male at birth? Show up in some clothes, thanks. AFAB ladies, let me unfurl the scroll of respectability and modesty. Other genders? You don't exist.

Don't you love [3] and [4]? Those rules are brand-new. And they are stunning in their elegance. I'm almost proud of the bigots in our PTA, who CYAed twice without even once saying no gays allowed! It's almost like they know what they're doing is wrong! I mean, built-in plausible deniability, Golden Weevils PTA, well done! I would applaud them, but I can't. I'm too busy protecting myself from their demon seeds at school.

See, their kids tortured me all through freshman year and most of sophomore year but kind of got over the everyday offensive until just recently.

Recently, as in the minute this PTA letter was sent out and I got a bunch of online comments on my takedown. It's my channel, so most of the comments were on my side, you know? Can't have that!

Also, since Nan informed the school that I would be attending prom with anyone I wanted to, and if somebody had a problem with that, she had the ACLU on speed dial (whatever that is).

To be fair, she did ask me first. She only fights the fights I want her to—after I begged her not to go to the principal about the everyday awful stuff that happens because I knew it would make it ten times worse. But she gave my parents an epic talking-to, and when it made no difference, she cut them off like skin tags. While I cried in her arms, she promised to always be there if I needed her.

So after the email from the PTA, she held my chin in my hands and looked into my eyes. She asked, "Is this something you want, baby girl? You know it's going to be hard."

Maybe I hesitated, but not for long. My YouTube peeps are on my side, and that helps. And you know what? What I want doesn't hurt anybody. I've put up with their abuse since ninth grade, and I'm tired of it. I want to say goodbye to senior year with my date, at prom, like everybody else.

With tears in my eyes, and some caught in my throat, I told her, "I just want to dance with her, Nan."

She bobbed her head sharply. "Then we're doing this."

And she marched into school with me this past Monday morning. Swept me into the front office and demanded to speak to the principal. Said she'd sit on the counter until he was available, because, well, Nan has a way of making a point when she wants to.

Principal Hawkins, I need to tell you, is really nice. First, he listened. He covered Nan's white hands with his brown ones and listened to every single word she said without interrupting.

Then, when she was finished, he turned to me and said, "Prom isn't sponsored by the school. It doesn't come out of our budget, we don't plan it. We allow the committee to throw it here for free."

"But the money goes to a school club," I said. "It's run by the PTA."

"And I'll point that out in the meeting, Emma. You just have to understand that I only have so much power over this. If it escalates, I'll go as far as I can. You just have to know that I can't stop this all by myself."

It didn't seem right or fair that the principal couldn't make the rules about our school prom. But there it was. To be honest, I thought I should cry, but all I felt was numb. Nan reached over and stroked my back; it was like a ghost of a touch.

Principal Hawkins waited a moment, then said, "I can warn them that their prom includes you, or they need to find another site. Hopefully, that will turn things around. Money's pretty tight all over since the plant closed down."

"Okay."

"There's still a chance it could make things worse. This is a big deal, Emma. Are you sure you want me to go forward?"

Was I? I was. And yet, even though I got a rush of adrenaline, somehow, I couldn't get enough breath to say yes. So I nodded instead. The deal was sealed. He promised to talk to the PTA, and I know he kept his word.

How? Well, the PTA did *not* send out a new email. Instead, they whispered a rumor and made sure it spread like sparks in the night: if Emma Nolan insists on queering up this year's prom, then prom is gonna be canceled. They can't afford to host it anywhere else; this is all my fault.

And you know, we don't have a lot going on in Edgewater. I think you can probably tell. Sometimes a tent revival will come to town, and that's exciting because people fall down and speak in tongues.

There's fair season, when everybody's competing with prize calves and wedding ring quilts.

And let's not forget the wonder and glory of cruising the Walmart parking lot on Saturday night. (Yes, we have a movie theater, but it shows one movie at a time, and usually something super old.)

Friends, Golden Weevils basketball games, and prom? Those are *the* social highlights of our limited calendar. And now everybody thinks one of them's about to get canceled because of *me*.

And that means all the abuse from freshman year is happening again, only this time, with purpose. The chanting is back—annoying but ignorable. There are worse things people could whisper at me, but I have to say, "Gay, gay, gay" offends on an artistic level.

It lacks creativity. There's a whole internet out there for people who can't think for themselves; it's literally a gateway to thousands of slurs with bite, with real shape to them. Instead, these doofuses pick the dictionary definition of me and croak it like a choir of narrow-minded frogs.

Oh, and bow down, because I'm now the Moses of southern Indiana. Wherever I go, seas part for me to pass. Hall of Champions, English class, cafeteria, doesn't matter: students who had forgotten they cared I was gay suddenly recoil again. I am my own personal cootie factory, open for business for the first time since *kindergarten*.

Oh, and this morning, I had to relearn the importance of keeping *nothing* important in my locker. See, during freshman year, people squeezed packets of Zesty French dressing from the cafeteria through the vents and ruined my favorite jacket.

To this day, I tense up when I smell sweetness and vinegar.

I started using the locker again when things tapered in junior year. I didn't store anything super important in it, but guess what?

Today, the very clever students of James Madison High found a way to squirt lotion through the vents. When I opened it after lunch, I found everything coated in a thick, pearly layer of Jergens. Including a history textbook that leaves out the reason for the Civil War.

I took it to the office to get a new one, and the secretary (whose desk Nan threatened to sit on) told me *I* have to pay to replace it. She didn't care why it was ruined or who had a hand in it. My book, my responsibility. That'll be eighty dollars, please.

My nan doesn't have that kind of money just lying around, so I'll have to cash out my Patreon savings. So much for a new guitar this year.

Through all of this, normally, I'd lean on my girlfriend for support. But outside of school, I haven't seen Alyssa in almost two weeks.

Once her mother started leading this particular mob of angry townsfolk, she ended up on lockdown. We text at night, stolen moments during econ homework, quick Snaps so there's no evidence left behind. And, you know, I know why she's hiding. Most of me is glad she's safe in her invisibility.

I just wish I didn't have to be visible all alone.

Principal Hawkins says he's doing everything he can behind the scenes, Alyssa is heartbroken behind our screens, but that leaves me by myself, in front of *them*.

I make myself go to school. I make myself show up for each class. Every day, each step is heavier as the clock ticks toward three, then I burst out of my seat the second the last bell rings.

Seniors get to leave their classes first. We have a whole twenty-minute passing period—mostly so people who drive can get out of the parking lot before the buses leave. Car riders wait at the front doors, and this week, Nan's been picking me up because . . . well, her *forty*-year-old car seems safer than a fairly new bus full of enemies and no way out.

Today's only different because it's raining, and I have to wait inside. Arms wrapped around myself, I stare out the front doors while I watch for Nan's blue VW Beetle. I have my Moses circle around me, isolating but safe, right? Then I hear something behind me. A weird shuffling, a concentrated rustle.

Pushing up my glasses, I look back.

Everyone's eyes are turned away from me. I know all of these faces; they're not even the most popular kids at school. They're medium-ordinary. They just think they're better than me because they're straight.

They talk at each other so hard, it looks like their jaws might fly off. It's not natural, but they're not *doing* anything. I try to warn with a dark expression, but I'm afraid it comes out plaintive instead.

I turn back to the doors. My breath steams the glass as I lean on the metal frame. There's no point in texting. Nan always puts her phone in the glove box. Therefore, I try telepathy. *Nan, come on, please hurry.*

Then it happens.

Something hard bounces off the back of my head and falls

to the floor. Instinctively, I throw a hand up, but there's no cut. No blood. Probably not even a bruise. It takes me a second, but I find the projectile wobbling to a stop on the floor.

A quarter.

Like, somebody has enough pocket change that they skipped the pennies and nickels and dimes and went straight for a quarter. Once again, I cast a look at the people around me. Once again, they're coincidentally all craning in other directions. It doesn't keep them from laughing, though. Little, trapped snickers escape them.

Even as my insides turn to sick, green goo, I lean over and snatch up the coin. With a wave, I make a show of shoving it into my pocket. "Thanks. Now I have enough money to take your mom on a date."

Then I punch through the doors and into the rain.

6. Camouflage

ALYSSA

Shelby Kinnunen opens the door for me, and I back into the gym with a giant box of cardboard.

It's reclaimed, from the recycling program the student council started this year in the cafeteria. Even though it smells like corn dog nuggets, it's free, and it's plentiful. Hefting the box a little higher, I say, "We're going to make so many stars with this."

"Don't know why we're bothering," Shelby says, twirling off the door and following me inside. There are people at work as far as the eye can see. The president and vice president of every single club at school have shown up to work on prom decorations. It's tradition; it really makes the dance our own.

"We're making it nice," I reply. "It's more special this way, isn't it?"

Shelby rolls her shoulders lazily. She's here as the cheer captain, but I feel like we're friends. I mean, I feel like everyone here is at least friend*ly*. It's not a big school, or a big town, so we all have a lot in common.

When I move to put my box of boxes down, Shelby leans in to help and whispers to me, "I heard it's getting canceled."

An icy drop of panic falls on my heart. I've heard that, too—from my mother. Not directly, but she's not exactly quiet on the phone these days. Her voice falls to a murmur, but I hear her campaigning with the other parents. They workshopped the new PTA prom rules together and celebrated when they sent them out.

Somehow, they didn't see it coming, that Emma's grandmother would fire back. I could have told Mom. I've been secretly having dinner with Emma and Nan Nolan for three years now. When Nan decides to do something, she goes all in. She painted her house purple, I'm not even kidding. Actual, grapey, Jolly Rancher purple—with lime green trim.

So if my mother had thought about it for even a second, she would have realized that bringing in the ACLU wasn't just a threat—even though that's exactly what it felt like. Oh yes. And then it made her even madder when Principal Hawkins said he *agreed* with Nan. Oh my gosh, Mom went from annoyed to red-flag-in-a-bullfighting-ring mad, baseball-bat-against-a-hornet's-nest kind of mad.

Since then, she's been gauging support for a cancellation, and I think that's my fault.

I pointed out to her that if we can't take outside dates, that means I can't go with John Cho. (Let's set aside the fact that he's famous, grown up, and has no idea I exist.) Theoretically, Mom's rule meant no perfect, perfect prom for me either.

With a wave of her hand, she said, "Oh, Alyssa, you know that doesn't apply to you."

"Uh no," I told her. I actually stamped my foot, and felt ridiculous when I did it. "The rules are the rules. They apply to me or they don't apply to anyone."

Mom walked away from me. And then the whispering started. The phone calls and frantic messages. Her fingers flew so fast, the chime of incoming texts sounded like an arcade. She talked to the PTA and everybody's parents at our church, who, of course, told their kids, and that's how rumors get started.

The one thing that keeps me from completely losing it is that everybody's feelings are mixed when it comes to calling off the prom. It's the usual *seniors won't get their senior year back; not fair to punish everybody because one person wants to break the rules* kind of stuff. For once, entropy is on the side of good.

So I feel comfortable telling Shelby, "That's not going to happen. Prom is for everybody, and everybody looks forward to it."

Twisting the dark coils of her hair into a loose braid, Shelby shrugs again. "I get that. You get that. Why doesn't she? Is it really going to kill her to stay home and *not* shave her legs that night?"

Fire blazes in my stomach. She knows *nothing* about Emma. She doesn't have the first inkling. There are so many beautiful things in Emma Nolan that we're lucky to have her in Edgewater at all. Her heart is so big when she doesn't have to protect it.

I mean, she feeds the squirrels on purpose—she feels bad for them, because everybody else tries to keep them out of their yards. When Emma turns her attention on you, it will break your heart because you've never been so *seen* in your life.

All these little people, with all their little minds, constantly spitting on her—for no reason. Because their pastors say so, because their parents say so. Not because they care, or think, or decide for themselves. And I want to say all of that, but instead, I sit on the polished wood floor and reach for the scissors. "That's really mean."

"I'm joking," Shelby says, not joking at all. "But I'm super sad, Alyssa! Kevin was *supposed* to prompose to me, like, the day after Nick did Kaylee. But they quit selling the tickets, and now he, like . . . wants to wait and see what happens. It's like I'm personally being punished."

My whole life, I've been lucky that when I get mad, I don't get hot in the face. The tips of my ears, yes. And across my chest, definitely. But I don't *look* angry. The sound of it doesn't come out in my voice. That makes it easier to try to talk sense to people who have completely lost the plot. "Well, she's being punished, too."

Shelby stops, the glue she's pouring into her paper plate still dripping. "How?"

Calmly, I repeat, "Prom is for everybody. Emma included."

With disgust, Shelby puts the glue down and starts stirring it around with a broken piece of leftover cardboard. We're going to slop that onto the stars I'm getting ready to cut out of nugget boxes and then dip them in the glitter tray. At least, we are if we can get through this conversation and back to work. "There are rules."

"Rules the PTA *just* invented."

"No, they were just unspoken rules before."

I sigh and catch Shelby's gaze. "Did you care if Emma went to the prom *before* she signed up?"

Oh. Oh, there it is. A tiny flicker of self-awareness; of course she didn't. Before Emma signed up, all Shelby, and Kaylee, and everybody else cared about was getting *their* promposal and getting *their* special night. But instead of admitting that, Shelby stares me down. "I'm kind of wondering why you care so much *after*."

Danger! Warning! The heat spreads across my chest and down into my belly. Is she clocking me? Shelby's never struck me as all that observant, but maybe it was an act. Can she look into me and see that I'm not *just* arguing for Emma? That I want this night for me, too?

I cannot let that rumor start. Not now. My mother has to find out from me, at the right time, in the right way. Hands shaking, I put down the scissors. "I'm the president of student council. I work for every student, not just the popular ones."

Out of nowhere, Shelby's boyfriend, Kevin McCalla, slides on his knees and right into our pile of cardboard. At the last second, he ditches onto his back, like he's crashing into a pile of autumn leaves.

He thinks this is charming; you can tell by the way he cheese-grins at Shelby when he comes to a stop. He's practically in her lap. That's probably against some unspoken rules, too, and yet, there he is. "Why so serious, babes?"

"Just talking about Emma," Shelby replies.

"You mean Ho-meo and Juliet?"

My temper slips; I slap a hand down on the cardboard by

Kevin's head. Stray flecks of glitter leap up like fleas. "We have a no-tolerance bullying policy in this school!"

He laughs, baffled. "I didn't say it to *her*."

"That's not the point."

Shelby looks me over again. "Again, you're getting very LGBTOMG over this, Alyssa. Something you want to share?"

"You know what I want to share?" I ask, pulling it all back in. Swallowing it all down. It's ridiculous, but I literally feel like Elsa in *Frozen*, and how sad is it that a cartoon is the only thing I can think of to calm myself down? I can't *feel* this right now. I can't let it show. Kevin and Shelby aren't exactly bloodhounds, but if I lose my temper . . .

Talking with my hands, I say, "I want to share my prom night with anybody who wants to be there. Because I don't want anybody to stand in the way of me and the dance that I have been thinking about since I was twelve. I already have my dress. I already have my tickets. I want to have this. And I want you to have it, too. I want us *all* to have it. Is that so wrong?"

I don't think Shelby or Kevin feels bad at all, but they both shrug. She says, "Whatever."

He says, "Whatever, who cares?"

Twin whatevers in the face of something so monumental, and they can't even see it. I'm glad they don't see it.

Yes, I hate myself for hiding it. But I'm doing what I can—as much as I can—to help this blow over. With all of the push-back Mom's getting over canceling, I really feel like the PTA is close to deciding it's not worth the fight. If the Shelbys and Kaylees and Kevins and Nicks of James Madison High decide they want their prom more than they want to keep Emma away, that *helps*.

They'll put pressure on their parents; Principal Hawkins will push back from the school. If we can just ride this out, just a couple days more, I really believe my mother and the rest of the PTA will give up on this. They just need to be able to step back quietly, without losing face.

And the sooner that happens, the sooner I can sit my mother down and talk some sense into her. Or at least talk some understanding into her. I promised Emma that we'd go to prom together, and I meant it.

I can't be—I *won't* be—one more person in her life who loves her then lets her down.

7. Enter Stage Left

EMMA

One more day out on my own, ducking my head and making myself as small as possible as I move between classes at school.

Alyssa thinks the rumors are dying down. I think she's wearing the thickest, rosiest glasses in history. It's easy for her to think it's getting better. She's basically in the next county, watching the tornado snake along in the distance. I'm the spinning cow, whirling around inside it.

My back aches under the weight of my bag. Now that I can't use my locker at all, I'm carrying around fifteen thousand pounds of textbooks, a conservative estimate. The diesel-sniffing mob around me doesn't know that, though.

So as I turn down the hall toward my locker, I feel eyes on me. It must be a Spidey sense at this point. I know when they're lurking, watching, waiting.

If they want to keep throwing quarters, I'm good with that. But no, apparently somebody taught them the value of money because that's not what awaits me this time. People edge back from me; I take each step warily.

"Gaybo," someone mutters.

Another whispers, "Lezzie."

The insults sink into my skin, tangling into a black knot that permanently lives in the pit of my stomach. I thought I was over caring what people say about me, but I guess not. The sad thing is, I don't even want people to like me anymore. I just wish they'd leave me alone. I have a feeling that I would be very forgettable if I lived anywhere else.

When I steal a look up, I see two red balloons bobbing above our heads. I don't have to get closer to know they're the *X* that marks the spot. But oh, what treasures await me?

During Spirit Week, the cheerleaders decorate all the jocks' lockers. It's not unusual to see signs, balloons, ribbons, tiny awnings and faux gems, silk curtains and streamers. They've got this down to a science, with their perfect stick-and-bead hand-lettering and their eye for accessories. I'm sure all of these skills will come in useful later in life.

But let's be real, y'all. There's just one locker decorated right now, and this may come as a surprise to you, but I'm not athletic at all.

Voices drop; the hallway goes eerily quiet. Is this an improvement over the constant chatter of people three centuries shy of whispering *burn the witch* at me? I don't know. What I do know is that whatever's on my locker, I'm going to ignore it. They don't get the satisfaction of a reaction.

I lift my chin but look down and forward. I'm probably all Hunchback of Notre Dame right now, but so? Just breathe, Emma. Just walk, one foot in front of the other.

I try to summon the picture of golden, sandy beaches, or even just the grayish-beige shores of Indiana Beach.

Think about holding Alyssa's hand at Holiday World. It's small and soft; she feels delicate next to me. She'd want me to smile and nod; I don't think I can. Namaste and pray to get the hell away from here, that's the best I can do. There's a Greyhound ticket in my future. I don't even care where it goes. Focus on that. On freedom and escape and—

Yes. Good. Breathe. I'm breathing, and I'm not listening, and I'm not looking—not, not looking except I just caught a glimpse. Now I can't tear my eyes away.

This time, it's not lotion or dressing. It's not even graffiti for the custodians to scrub clean. No, it's two red balloons to mark the hanging of a rainbow teddy bear. Somebody took the time to make a *noose*. They took the time to string it through the locker vents, so a pride-flavored Beanie Boo could bite the dust.

I can't breathe through this. I reach out and yank the noose free. I feel small and sharp and brittle, cutting looks at the people around me. They hold back like a wave. They want to crash over me, but they don't dare. They're cowards, every single one of them.

"Nice," I say, waving the Beanie Boo at them. "Real nice."

Breaking free from the crowd, Kaylee washes up against me. With a sickly sweet smile, she asks, "Do you like it? We got it just for you."

"Yeah, you know what? I'm pretty sure this is one step past breaking school rules, Kaylee. This is a death threat."

Kaylee's eyes widen with disingenuous sincerity. "It's our way of saying thank you, Emma!"

Now that Kaylee broke the seal and spoke to me, her centurion Shelby steps up and adds, "Yeah! Thanks for canceling prom!"

When I wave my shaking hands, I feel myself lose balance. My backpack is too heavy, my heart is too broken, my brain is too fried. My voice cracks when I say, "Prom isn't canceled!"

Just then, Alyssa appears. At once, it's like the sun rises, and hope fills my heart. She's trying to save me, even though she has a secret. Even though she risks exposure when she takes my side. Her gaze slides past mine, but she steps between me and Kaylee. "That's enough. Leave her alone."

"We're just talking," Kaylee says. She looks around Alyssa, threatening me with a smile. "Right, Emma?"

I don't say anything. I refuse to degrade myself. I refuse to be complicit. But it's like my presence answers for me. Just by standing there, I'm making them angry. Just by breathing, I make it worse. I want to grab Alyssa and run away with her, far away from here, somewhere we can just be. Instead, I stand stock-still and try not to cry.

"Walk away," Alyssa says, gathering the full mantle of the student council presidency around her.

"Oh, is that how it is?" Cocking her head to one side, Kaylee sounds the slightest bit hurt. That dissipates instantly, converted into pure primary school bile. "So you're on her side."

"No," Alyssa says, a shot right through my heart. "I'm just not in third grade."

A muffled roar laps the hallway. Someone is two seconds from yelling, "Fight, fight!" Then Nick and Kevin melt out of the mob like twin grease stains. They back up their girlfriends in a way that I, if I were their girlfriends, would dump them for on the spot.

Nick says, "Kaylee. Babe. It's okay. She can bring her queer-bait girlfriend to the prom if she lets us watch."

With a leer, Kevin nods. "Add some memories to the spank bank."

Suddenly, a voice booms out. My knees go out from under me in relief. Principal Hawkins stalks down the hallway. Students peel away and disappear as fast as they can. Recreational felonies are only fun if you don't get caught.

"Gentlemen," Principal Hawkins says, then, "Ladies. I don't know what's going on here, but it's over."

Kaylee shrugs and goes to walk away. She makes a wide circle around Alyssa, just so she can "accidentally" bump my shoulder. With a purposeful whisper at my side, she says, "Oh, Emma. Unlike your social life, this is *not* over."

Whither goest Kaylee, so goes her ragtag nation of troglodytes who are going to peak in high school. Shelby vines herself around Kevin, and Nick throws an arm over Kaylee's shoulder. When they finally drift around the corner, I exhale and collapse. Though I know they're on my side, it's hard to face Alyssa and Principal Hawkins.

"I'm sorry," I say, even though it's not my fault. I hold up the bear helplessly.

Principal Hawkins eyes it in my hand. His kind face hardens, and he straightens his back. "This is unacceptable, Emma. We'll find out who did it, and they'll be handled appropriately."

"Please don't," I say. "Things are bad enough as it is."

Alyssa puts a hand on my arm. Her dark eyes are liquid,

too. I feel the pull between us; it's hard not to give in. If I could collapse in her arms, everything—well, it wouldn't be all right. But it would be better, at least for a moment. Softly, she says, "If you let them get away with it . . ."

"No, it's not worth it." Folding into myself again, I can barely say it above a whisper, but I do say it: "Maybe none of this is worth it."

Principal Hawkins shakes his head. "No, uh-uh. You have rights, Emma. I have an email from the ACLU liaison. They're prepared to step in if they have to. In fact, they said your case has already attracted some attention online."

"Besides on my channel?" I say, stunned.

"Oh yes. This is a big deal," Principal Hawkins says. "For you, absolutely. But for all the kids just like you, too."

I blink in disbelief. "What are you saying? I'm like a gay, white Rosa Parks?"

Principal Hawkins gives me *a look*. "Uh, no. I'm absolutely not saying that."

"You're the gay, white Emma Nolan," Alyssa says. "You're leading *this* charge."

"Exactly. And I'm proud to be a part of that," Principal Hawkins says. "This is so much better than dealing with students on meth."

At that, Alyssa and I both rear our heads back and say, "Wut?"

Principal Hawkins waves it off. "I've got a principal friend in Terre Haute. All he deals with are bad smells and meth, all day long."

For some reason, that breaks the heaviness of the moment.

I laugh in spite of myself. No, not myself. In spite of everyone else. I laugh because I'm not on drugs. I laugh because the legal cavalry is coming. I laugh because . . . because I need it. I even slump against Alyssa. Just a little bit, just for a moment.

"Well, I'm not on meth yet. We'll see how the next couple of days go."

"We'll get you through this," Principal Hawkins promises.

And then Milo Potts, the FCK treasurer, comes screaming around the corner. Both figuratively—he's running at top speed—and literally, his voice cracking. "Principal Hawkins! Principal Hawkins! Come quick!"

Calmly, Principal Hawkins approaches him. "Everything's going to be all right, Milo. What's going on?"

"There are people outside," Milo shouts. "They have picket signs about prom!"

Oh. Crap.

8. The Invasion

ALYSSA

There is trouble right here in Edgewater, Indiana. Crammed behind three sets of double doors that lead into the parking lot, I stand with Emma as we stare at the picketers outside.

We're not the only ones. It feels like most of the high school is pressed in here with us. The small space buzzes like a beehive, and it's unbearably hot with so many bodies and so little room. Also, it smells like at least half the people in here just finished gym class without hitting the showers. But we have to be pressed to the glass, because we can't miss the biggest show ever to hit James Madison High.

Outside, Principal Hawkins stands on the curb, his back to us. He's got one hand on his hip, and the other—I'm guessing—clapped to his brow. Though we're all dying to hear what's going on out there, Principal Hawkins told us to stay inside, and he said it in a Stern Dad voice that would make most of us feel legitimately guilty for letting him down. It feels like there are hundreds of cell phones flashing, all turned toward the parking lot . . . and the strangers with protest signs that fill it.

"Who are these people?" I ask under my breath.

Emma subtly loops her pinkie with mine and squeezes. "I don't know."

Nearby, somebody reads one of the signs as it turns toward us. "Classically trained singer dancer activist?"

"What the hell?" somebody else says.

I'm speechless. Literally. A dark-haired woman carries a sign that reads ANNIE GET YOUR GIRL, and the sign is the least striking thing about her. Her hair is short and tight, and her lipstick is one shade darker than blood-red. She's wearing this jumpsuit-pantsuit thing in the same scarlet, and her heels are sharp enough to serve steak-on-a-stick at the county fair. When she stops to talk to Principal Hawkins, she talks with her whole body: shoulders thrown back, hand gesturing at the sky.

Whatever she's saying, Principal Hawkins hangs on every word. He's a moth caught in her light, nodding and nodding and nodding.

From behind us, Nick and Kevin boom out, "Go! Go! GoooooolDEN?!"

Everyone else calls back, "WEEEEvils, go, go!"

With that display of athletic privilege, Nick and Kevin cut through the crowd. Arms held out straight, they shove open the front doors. And since they're the most popular guys in school, everybody else pours out behind them.

In the rush, I lose hold of Emma's pinkie and we're swept out of different doors. I can't even hope to get back to her until everybody stops pushing.

"Hey," a guy yells, "it's Mr. Pecker!"

And . . . he's right! My mouth drops open, and I stare at the heavyset man with the NO MORE MR. NICE GAY sign.

He's probably Principal Hawkins's age, but he has a perfectly smooth face that's instantly recognizable. He used to play the weird neighbor on *Talk to the Hand,* which we all watched in middle school.

He was so popular, they even aired extra webisodes with him. They're probably still online, in fact. Whenever the kids on the show got into some kind of trouble, he'd randomly burst in and try to solve everything. Usually in ways that blew up in his face and threatened to destroy property.

And now he's at James Madison High, in a silver-gray suit, carrying a blatantly pro-LGBTQ sign. When people recognize him—and you can tell they do, because suddenly there's an echo of "Pecker, Pecker, Pecker!" in the air—he throws his head back ever so slightly. Like he's soaking their attention up, like it has a reverse-aging effect. His skin *is* really smooth—maybe it does.

"All students," Principal Hawkins booms, his voice rising over the crowd, "need to return to their homeroom classes immediately!"

"Why?" booms the brunette woman. Impressively, her voice carries better than our principal's does. She's shorter than he is but somehow takes up all of the space in their tight little circle. "Are you afraid of a little truth? Are you afraid these young Indianans will be exposed to . . . the truth?!"

Principal Hawkins raises his hands. "No, this is a matter of safet—"

The woman cuts him off. "Sir, I am *the* Dee Dee Allen, and

the spotlight only dims when I will it! I read three-quarters of a news story about dear little Emma Nolan, and I knew I had to come!"

I turn my head so fast, I think I pop something in my spine. Across the way, Emma freezes. I recognize that look on her face, the flight-because-she's-not-going-to-fight face. Suddenly, everyone's looking at her. It couldn't have been scripted more perfectly. Emma's face is bright red, and she clutches the strangled teddy bear in her hands.

"This," Dee Dee Allen, mysterious picketer, continues, "is an OUTRAGE! You act like a mob of angry villagers while poor Emma's heart breaks! And let me tell you, I've played Mrs. Potts in *Beauty and the Beast*; I know all about angry mobs!"

"Ms. Allen," Principal Hawkins says, but she interrupts him.

"The prom should be for everyone! Straight and gay and LGBTQIA! Plus all the other letters I don't know, but are all equally worthy of love!"

Now the kids around me start to roil and boil, a kettle full of indignation. People shout back, but it's a mush of sound. The kind of mush that signals the beginning of a riot, actually.

Little spikes of panic race through me. I don't think anything really bad will happen, but this . . . this feels like something really bad might happen. I look to Emma again. Her face is strained and anxious. I know she feels the turn in the crowd, too. And she knows—*we* know—that if they turn, it'll be on her.

I am the student council president. I have a responsibility.

The last thing I want is for everyone to stare at me and speculate about me. But actually, the last thing I want is for everybody here to hurt Emma. They already threatened her today; this could be the spark before the bang.

Without another thought, I act. Jumping up on the concrete benches, I throw my hands out. As loud as I can, I call out, "Go! Go! GoooooolDEN?!"

And like it's built into their DNA, my fellow students all turn toward me and bellow back, "WEEEEvils, go, go!"

Now that I have all the attention, Ms. Allen and—I hate to call him Mr. Pecker, but I don't know what else to say—Mr. Pecker look incredibly annoyed. I don't care. They're not my concern. My classmates are.

With everyone looking to me expectantly, I try not to let the woozy feeling in my chest spread too far. Fainting would probably put an end to this dangerous situation, but taking a header into cement seems like it would be counterintuitive.

Rubbing my hands on my jeans, I say, "These fine people, whoever they are, have a right to their opinion. And . . . and so do you. Everybody should be heard. People have been whispering about prom for too long now. As your student council president, I am saying here and now, let's have that talk. I'm officially inviting everyone to a public meeting in the gym tonight at six thirty to hash this out, once and for all."

I'm absolutely sure I hear Ms. Allen mutter, "Who is this broad?" but I don't care. Emma catches my eye, then jerks a thumb over her shoulder. She's not dumb—she's getting out of here before she gets hurt. Since all eyes are on the parking lot,

Emma slips back into the school and disappears from sight. I don't know if she's going to bail on the rest of the day or what, and I don't need to. Wherever she's going, she's safe, and that's what matters.

My mouth is instantly dry, but I wave a hand at our picketers. "Ms. Allen, Mr. . . ." I don't want to say *Pecker*.

Graciously, the man waves a hand in a flourish and projects, "Glickman. Barry Glickman, star of stage and screen!"

"Thank you, Mr. Glickman. You and Ms. Allen are welcome to come tonight." I turn to the students, who stare at me, and I can't even make out their expressions. Their faces are rapt but unfocused. I hold out my arms to them. "And you're all invited. So are your parents. Everybody gets a say. This is our school. We *will* protect it. But this is also our community, and we *will* respect it. All of it."

Now that the spell is broken, Principal Hawkins puts a hand on Ms. Allen's arm—a really kind of familiar hand, if you ask me. But he regains his authority, and the sharp look that makes even the most beef-hearted senior quail.

"Thank you, Miss Greene! Now that we've set a time to discuss the issue, this gathering is over. Everyone, and I mean everyone, needs to return to their classes immediately."

"But, Tom," Ms. Allen says, intoning his first name like they're long-lost friends, distress written across her face in broad strokes. "We haven't even met the girl!"

"Later," Principal Hawkins tells her.

My classmates break and trickle back inside. Slowly, because you never know when something else might happen, but they keep moving. They straggle until there's no one left outside but me, Principal Hawkins, and a handful of strangers with picket signs.

Emma's gone. Long gone. And even though I put a stop to the human tsunami that threatened to drown her, guilt gnaws in my stomach. I could have done more. Or better. Or something. Because now that the blur of adrenaline is fading, suddenly the realization of what I've actually done settles in.

I just asked everybody in Edgewater to come testify at Emma's witch trial.

Oh no.

A little dizzy, I sink down to sit on the bench, rather than stepping down and staying on my feet. Principal Hawkins exchanges a few more quiet words with Ms. Allen and Mr. Glickman, then strides over to me.

Even though I've never been in trouble at any point during my four-year high school career, I crumple a little as he approaches. To my surprise, he sits down beside me and puts a hand on my shoulder. "You showed an incredible amount of leadership just now, Alyssa."

Weakly, I say, "Didn't I make it worse?"

"No," he says. His voice is warm and low and comforting. "I think you did what we should have done weeks ago. You've dragged this out of the shadows. You're insisting we handle this civilly and discuss the issue like human beings."

Glancing past him, I see Ms. Allen and Mr. Glickman in their own discussion huddle. To Principal Hawkins, and only to him, I admit, "*They* forced the issue. I was just trying to calm everyone down."

"And you don't think that was worthwhile?"

For a moment, I'm quiet. Finally, I shake my head, "No, I do."

"Don't let perfect be the enemy of good, Alyssa. Every step we make toward better is a step in the right direction."

At this moment, I can hear Emma cracking a joke about how Hallmark card that sounds. But also laughing at his sincerity—not in a cruel way, just in disbelief. In surprise that anyone can be that optimistic, that full of hope.

I don't think it's funny, though. Those words lodge into me, right between my ribs, the tip of their arrow just nicking my heart.

Don't let perfect be the enemy of good.

Not perfect. Just good.

Wow.

9. John Proctor Problems

EMMA

In general, going back to school after the school day is over is not high on my list of good times to be had.

And it still isn't. Nan and I pull up to the school at a quarter till six in the hope that I can find Alyssa and talk to her first. But there's no way that's happening, because a veritable river of people pour off a bus that says BROADWAY ACROSS THE STATES on the side of it. They have signs, they wear bright colors, they have hair lengths that are inappropriate for both the guys *and* the girls around these parts.

Streaming across the parking lot, they march toward the single illuminated door in the dark school: the one that leads to the gym. Their voices ring up to the night sky, singing snatches of show tunes I don't recognize and barking out cadences I do. They're here, they're queer, and they cordially invite the people of my high school to get over it.

They crash into the Extremely Angry Parents of James Madison High on the sidewalk, mingling like a violent smoothie that no one in their right mind would want to taste. They force a bottleneck at the doors, with people shot through them seemingly at random. The parents yell at the Broadway people to go home and, even *better*, to go back where they belong. Right in front of all the reporters, who round out the melee.

Parked along the curb, there are two news vans: one from Evansville, which isn't far from us, and one from Indianapolis, which is both far *and* our state capital. They have lights and video cameras, complementing the reporters with just camera-cameras who keep trying to fish people out of the stream to give statements.

Mr. Thu and Mr. Gonsalves, our school security guards, are doing what they can to keep everyone calm. The way they gently urge the horde inside results in a process about as graceful as stuffing a cattle chute. Which is to say: people move, but it ain't pretty.

Nan and I straggle back a little. She clutches my hand, sure and strong. "Bet they wish they'd just let you go to prom in peace, huh?"

"I'm starting to wish we'd just gone with boys and ditched them after we got there," I reply. That's only 15 percent true. Maybe 25. The number falls and rises with each step I take. Angry voices spill from the gym already. The meeting's not supposed to start for another half hour, but it's already bedlam when we get inside.

The bleachers on either side of the gym are pulled out, but hardly anyone is using them. The Broadway people wave their picket signs on one side, and the only local over there with them is our resident anarchist-slash-goth, who is basically on whatever side causes the most trouble. She ran a student council campaign on the slogan *End the Tyranny of Tater Tots at Lunch.* (She lost.)

The locals shake their spirit cowbells (ten dollars each, available at the bookstore or the box office at any Golden Weevils home game) angrily on the other side. They don't chant. They don't sing. But they do yell at the Broadway people, so loudly that the veins on their collective foreheads jut out in syncopated time.

I've never spent a lot of time picturing what sound looks like. Buuuut, I've just walked into Hieronymus Bosch's *Cacophony,* gouache on board, 2019.

My fingertips tingle. So do my toes. Something heavy keeps thumping into my ribs from the inside, then crashing against the inside of my skull. I could be having a heart attack. Or a stroke. Or both! That would probably make me a modern medical miracle, way more newsworthy than falling in love with a girl and wanting to go to prom.

Alyssa, my Alyssa, stands next to Principal Hawkins. Her dark hair falls in perfect cascades over her shoulders. She's wearing the same outfit she wore to Model UN, a gray jacket and pencil skirt, black patent heels. She looks so professional up there, so accomplished.

And yet, she holds a megaphone and stares at the mess her meeting has already become. There's despair in her eyes and discontent on her coral lips. When she texted me about it, she made it sound like a tea party. Everyone gathered to respectfully discuss whether or not I deserve civil rights. I mean, she didn't put it *that* way, but the emphasis was on how orderly it would be.

Well. This is super orderly, if you're into turf wars. On the left side, the Sharks with their picket signs. On the right, the Jets with their cowbells. No guns, no knives, but make no mistake, there will be absolutely no survivors.

Finally, Alyssa realizes one very important thing. She has the megaphone. She fiddles with the buttons, and suddenly, a loud siren fills the gym. The sound bounces off the concrete block walls and hardwood floor, and people will probably still hear it echoing in two hundred years.

But it does the job; people hush.

Alyssa raises the megaphone and speaks into it. "Thank you all for coming to this town hall meeting. My name is Alyssa Greene; I'm the student council president."

Mrs. Greene snatches the megaphone and squawks into it. "And I am Elena Greene, the president of the PTA! I'm here to represent the parents of this community. I have listened to their concerns and have taken them as my very own. Together, we established rules for this year's prom! Rules that affect everyone, not just Emma Nolan!"

Now, I've met Mrs. Greene. She's used to getting the very last word on everything. I cover my mouth to keep from laughing out loud when Dee Dee Allen reaches across the aisle and snatches the megaphone from her. "Oh, you established some *rules*, did you? I know what's going on here, and frankly, I'm appalled!"

It's horrifying in a very real and concrete way that everybody is in this gym because I want a date night with my girl. But it's also really gratifying to see somebody stand up to Mrs. Greene on my behalf.

Gently, Principal Hawkins takes the megaphone for himself. He waves calming hands, encouraging everybody to sit down. Nan and I sit near the very people protesting my entire existence, just because it seems like it would be weird to sit with strangers. But it's weird over here, too. Moses circle, still in effect. People slide away from me on the bleachers, creating a little island, population: Nan and me.

"Thank you all for coming," Principal Hawkins says. "Thank you all for your concern. And thank you to Alyssa Greene for stepping up and taking control of this situation. She's a remarkable young woman and the kind of leader that makes James Madison stronger. Everyone, Alyssa Greene."

Politely, people applaud. And you can tell it's just polite, because voices rumble and shrill in the stands. Each side is talking to itself. Everyone's just waiting for their turn to talk. My best guess is there will be no listening here tonight. But hey, my tiny Hoosier town that greeted daylight saving time like it was the work of the Devil is absolutely welcome to prove me wrong.

Alyssa thanks Principal Hawkins. Her hands shake—I see them from here. I wish I could catch them between mine and calm them. I wish I could whisper into her ear how great she's about to be. This moment is huge, not because she's out—but because she's *not.*

She's risking everything with her mother to speak up for me; she's risking exposing herself to everyone at school. Yes, I want people to know that we're in love, but right now, I just want them to appreciate how brave she is.

"Students, parents, guests," she says. At first, she stands stiffly, staring vaguely into the distance. But as she goes on, she warms and softens. She looks from one side to the other, even moves between them as she speaks. "Prom is a celebration for every student at James Madison High. It's a celebration of our achievements and of our potential as we move toward our futures. It's a celebration for all of us. *All.*"

Mrs. Greene jumps up. She doesn't need a megaphone to be heard now that the crowd has quieted. "I want to remind everyone that prom is not a school-sponsored event! Principal Hawkins refuses to fund the prom—"

"It's not in the budget," Principal Hawkins interjects. "Our textbooks are ten years old, and our technology is even older!"

As if he said nothing, Mrs. Greene goes on, "This is a social event that *we*, the *parents*, host, and as such, we're entitled to decide who may and may not attend! We are not going to let the government or the ACLU tell us what to do!"

"We're not the ACLU," Dee Dee cries. She waves at the rabble behind her. "This is the touring cast of *Godspell*, and—"

"My son will not be forced to go to a homosexual prom!" some mom shouts, cutting Dee Dee right off.

"It's not a homosexual prom," Alyssa says. "It's an inclusive prom!"

"Will there be homosexuals there or not?"

"Yes," Alyssa concedes.

Barry "Mr. Pecker" Glickman jumps up, tossing his sign. "And so what if there are? There's nothing wrong with being gay. Look at me! I'm an internationally known thespian, a Drama Desk winner, and gay as a bucket of wigs!"

A gasp fills the room. Like, a literal, coordinated gasp of horror. Edgewater is in the middle of nowhere, but it's not like it's the fourteenth century or anything. We get *Drag Race* here.

And there are quietly gay people in town. Gay people who have "roommates" or "friends," who don't hold hands in public and definitely didn't go out and get married once Indiana joined the rest of the country (dead last) and legalized marriage equality.

But nowhere in Edgewater—like, ever—has anybody jumped up in the middle of a school assembly and yelled that they were gay.

Ever.

Actually, I don't think I've ever said it like that myself. On my channel, I said I was in love with a girl. To my parents, I didn't have to say anything, or to my nan. Or . . . wow, I came out freshman year, but I've literally never told anyone I'm gay. And now that I've heard that collective gasp, I may never.

Barry steps into the center ring and looks around. "Emma! Where are you?"

The bench does not, conveniently, fall into a sinkhole and take me with it. Everyone's looking, and it's not like I can pretend to be somebody besides the lesbian in question. After all, I'm the only girl here in plaid flannel and sensible shoes. Slowly, I raise my hand.

Flinging himself toward me, Barry throws out his arms. "Look at this poor creature! Wasting away under your judgment! Your criticism! Your off-the-rack offerings!"

Emboldened, Dee Dee jumps forward. In fact, she jumps in a way that I'm not entirely sure she hasn't practiced. "We didn't come here to make a scene!" Her head pivots, and she addresses Shelby, who has her phone raised to take in all the action. "Darling, if you're going to take pictures, make sure you hashtag 'broadway crashes the prom,' hashtag 'dee dee allen,' hashtag 'no filter'—"

"This! Is not about us," Barry says, flinging an arm around me. He is solid and he is *strong*. He also smells like really expensive soap. He turns toward most of the senior class, their parents, and two reporters to declare, "This is about you and prying open your tiny little minds!"

Nick's dad—recognizable as such because he wears his son's jersey, for real—stands and bellows, "Just who the hell do you think you are?"

"We," Barry says and—hand to god—places a palm on his chest like this is the Pledge of Allegiance, "are liberal actors from New York!"

Tilting toward Nan, I murmur, "Why didn't he just say Satan and his minions?"

"And we represent liberty and justice for all," Dee Dee adds. "We're here for America!"

"This is not America," Mrs. Greene says. "This is Edgewater, Indiana! We have morals here. We have a way of life that we're proud of! We believe in God and country, and we believe there's a right way and a wrong way!"

Before this turns into an all-out brawl between Mrs. Greene and Dee Dee, and honestly, it's looking like that might still happen, Principal Hawkins steps between them. "Ladies, ladies, can we please, just for a moment, hear from the person this affects most?"

What the what?! I didn't come here to talk! I came because Alyssa asked me to and because I was curious about the protestors. Because it was kind of nice to see that there were more people on my side than my nan, my girl, and the principal. It's one thing to talk to my YouTube channel. Those comments are nice, and focused on my guitar work, and safe on the other side of my laptop screen! I don't want to stand up and talk to people who look like they'd bite me if they weren't afraid of catching the gay!

Principal Hawkins reclaims the megaphone and approaches me with it. "This is Emma Nolan. An honor roll student since freshman year. She's a very talented musician, and she's been a model student here for four years. Emma *is* James Madison, and now she'd like to go to the prom. Emma, can you tell us what this means to you?"

I feel the fire of a thousand stares on me. I feel the weight of a thousand churches on me. I feel the crushing grip of an actor around my shoulders.

My parents aren't here; they threw me away. But everybody else's parents are here in their place. They stare at me, stony. Their eyes are gray and angry. Their hands are folded tight, so tight, their knuckles are white. Can't Principal Hawkins see how much they hate me? Doesn't he realize that it doesn't matter what I say?

Apparently not. He stands beside me and looks at me expectantly. Barry gives me an encouraging shake. I steal a look at Alyssa, but I can't linger. Her mother is here. The town is here. I'm not alone right now, but right this second, I feel it.

My voice warbles when I speak into the megaphone. And

hang on to your butts, you're never going to believe the stirring and inspirational thing I say. Are you ready? Here we go:

"I just want to go to prom like everybody else."

It's the least profound thing I could have possibly said. And at the same time, I may as well have thrown a beehive into a hair salon. The screaming. Oh my god, the *screaming*.

"You can't make us have a homosexual prom!"

"She's here! She's queer! Get used to it!"

"This school cannot condone discrimination!"

And once again, it's everybody howling, nobody listening. As I watch them tear into each other—and some of the Broadway people start to sing selections from *Hamilton*—I just stare. All of this because of me. I am a seed of Chaos. Heck, maybe I'm the Red Rider of the Apocalypse.

Hilariously, if I am, that means that literally nobody in my hometown got called home to Jesus. They all got left behind.

A hysterical laugh escapes me, projected by the megaphone. Pushing it away, I shake my head. I think I say *thanks* to Barry, and *I'm sorry* to Principal Hawkins, but I slip out the side door and into the cool night air. As nice as it is to finally have people on my side, I've got to get out of here. Pulling my phone from my pocket, I text Alyssa, `So that was fun!`

She pings me back instantly. `I'm so sorry.`

So am I. But that, I keep to myself.

10. Mama Who Raised Me

ALYSSA

The ride home from the meeting isn't quiet. I almost wish it were. It would be so much easier to sit next to a mother who stews in silence. It would be so much easier to believe I haven't disappointed her in every single way.

"And what was that, with *The prom is a celebration for us all?* Honestly, Alyssa, I raised you better than that."

"Actually," I say, "you raised me to be a strong woman. To stand up for what I believe in."

"I raised you to be a good Christian!"

My stomach hurts, and it's telling my brain to shut up. *Shutting up doesn't mean agreement,* it wheedles. Thomas More died to prove that. Then again, Thomas More *died* to prove that. I mumble, "And I think that's what I'm being. Love thy neighbor as you love thyself?"

Mom turns to look at me so sharply, her neck pops. There's fury in her eyes; it sizzles all the way to the tips of her blowout and threatens to jump off and start a wildfire. Every word that leaps from her lips is an ember ready to catch. "I'm not telling you to hate that girl. Hate the sin, love the sinner. It would be loving the sin to encourage her to swan around our prom with some out-of-town girl. Especially after she dragged those crazies from New York here to embarrass us—"

"She didn't invite them, Mom!"

Shaking with anger, Mom clutches the steering wheel and buries the needle on the speedometer. Our car shakes, too, when we hit seventy-five. It's twelve years old and on its third set of tires. Somehow, my mother manages to explode with rage but also drive in a perfectly straight line. "Oh, don't give me that, Alyssa. She all but begged outsiders to get involved in this when she mocked our rules on the internet!"

"Because you guys made them just to keep her from going to the prom! She's one person, Mom. What does it hurt?"

"What does it hurt? Everything. You can't compromise your values or you compromise who you are! If we let that girl come to the prom, then what's next? Boys dressing up like girls to get into the locker room? One sin leads to another, and that leads to damnation!"

I flinch when she says these things, because . . . look, I always knew that my mother would have a hard time with me being queer. But I didn't realize how deep that . . . I don't want to call it *hatred*. I don't want to call my mother a homophobe and a transphobe, but, god, it's all right there on the surface.

"None of those things are going to happen! Leaving gay people alone hurts *nothing*."

"Oh no?" Mom counters furiously. "Gay marriage is suddenly legal and your father leaves?"

"He left for a weather girl in Kansas!"

"After the Supreme Court told him that the bonds of marriage didn't matter! They made us compromise our values, and one compromise leads to— Alyssa, one day, you will understand. You're in a broken home right now. You're confused."

"Mom, I'm not confused."

She waves that off, the rationalization and denial working overtime. "It's all right. When your father gets back, we'll go to counseling at the church. Pastor Jimenez is a wonderful man, it will be good for all of us. You'll see."

I scrub my face with both hands. I'm trying, so hard, to keep my mother together. But it's starting to feel like keeping her together is tearing me apart. My dad isn't coming back, and I'm not even allowed to be angry about that. She doesn't give me any room or any breath to feel my *own* feelings about the fact that he started a whole new family. He replaced me with a brand-new baby, and I only know that because his cousin messaged me on Facebook!

Instead, I have to spend all my time making *her* feel better, keeping *her* from any more upset or heartbreak. I'm three months away from eighteen, four months away from college. If she hasn't gotten over this by then, this *obsession* with perfection, this certainty that she can make everything right and my father will come running back, am I going to keep propping her up?

Or am I going to be like nice Ms. Reynolds, who sells tomatoes on a table in her front yard and pretends like Ms. Gloria's not her partner? Am I going to ask Emma to lie for the rest of her life, just to be with me?

Emma's ready to stop lying *now*. How long until she decides I'm not worth the fight?

How long does my mother's happiness have to come first?

Swallowing hard, I look out at the fields I love, newly furrowed for the year. The rows are so neat, so orderly. They're nothing but lines drawn in the earth, but in a few weeks, they'll announce spring with brand-new shoots.

New life, new greenness, stretching out in every direction. I want to be part of that orderly pattern. I want to fit in, in my own town, in my own house. And I want it as I *am*. Not the way Mom wishes me to be.

"We can go to counseling all day long, Mom, but I'm not going to change my mind about this. Prom should be for everybody."

My mother pushes her jaw forward; she always does this when she's beating on a problem and trying to solve it. "I don't know where you got this wild hair, Alyssa."

"I took an oath," I say firmly. "I'm the president of student council. Not president of the students I pick and choose. I didn't think the basketball players deserved new jerseys this year, but I voted to get them anyway. It's important to them! And this is important to Emma."

"Emma, Emma, Emma," my mother mocks, waving a hand. "She must be loving all of this attention. Those people do. I mean, look at that disgraceful display tonight!"

"But that was them, not her."

"It was *for* her, so what's the difference? You'll never convince me she didn't orchestrate that!"

I can't remember ever raising my voice to my mother, so it startles us both when I rail at her. "It never would have happened if there wasn't something to protest! And I bet you a million dollars they're going to *keep* protesting until *we* change!"

"Alyssa, enough!"

My mother's voice is a blade. It slices between us, severing our conversation. Her perfect veneer falters, revealing all the cracks underneath. She's so close to breaking. We pass beneath a traffic light. Her face glows green for a moment, then goes dark. And when the dark comes again, everything's smoothed back into place.

"So, tell me about this John Cho," she says, as if we weren't just arguing. As if she can hit reset on our lives and move forward in a more pleasant direction. "If you met him at Model UN, then he must be smart. Not as smart as my baby girl, but smart."

"Mom," I say, warning.

"You have to be careful," she goes on. "Boys don't like it when you're *too* smart. But look at that face. That beautiful face. That will distract him every time."

"Mom, I canceled, okay? You changed the rules about outside dates, so I called it off."

With an expression of pure dismay, Mom cries out, "Alyssa, honey! Why would you do that? I told you that didn't apply to you."

"It should have," I say flatly.

It's all written on her face: this ruins everything. There's a perfect night to be had, and it has to be had with me on my date's arm. For a moment, it looks like she might cry. But then she finds some well of strength and waves off this obstacle like an errant fly.

"There's still time. Call him back! Hey, do you know what? I'm so glad we went to Edinburgh to get your dress. You're going to outshine everyone there. It's just a shame you refused to run for the court. Kaylee will probably win now, and she's not half as pretty as you are."

Carefully, I ask, "Does this means prom's not canceled? For sure?"

My mother's laughter, light and airy, fills the car. She glances over at me, her smile perfectly fixed, her teeth perfectly white. She's so perfect, she sounds like the fairy godmother from a Disney movie when she says, "As if I would ever keep my own daughter from her senior prom."

Wary, I look at her. Did I change her mind? I don't know why, but I'm afraid to ask. It would be such good news if she just decided to give in. But I honestly can't tell if this is surrender or if her break with reality just became permanent. I say nothing.

Mom reaches over to take my hand and squeeze it. "I'd love to take pictures in front of the fireplace and under the swinging oak. Is he taller than you? If he's not, it's fine. You can wait to put on your heels. Do you know when he's going to pick you up?"

"Mom, I told you I canceled," I say, schooling my voice to sound normal, as if any of this is normal. "He's not coming."

"And I told you to call him," Mom says, wriggling happily in her seat.

I start to argue. Then I realize that it's foolish to argue about my imaginary date's imaginary social calendar. It's easier to be quiet, and unsettled, and just feed my mother the nodding agreement she wants. It changes nothing, but it brings a bit of peace to the ride home.

For now, peace is good enough.

11. Wouldn't It Be Loverly?

EMMA

For some reason, Nan wants to talk to the Broadway people.

So we follow their tour bus to the Comfort Inn by the highway. I'm relieved that they didn't end up at the Knights Inn on the other side of the highway. That one rents by the hour; truckers love it.

The tour bus is parked at the back of the lot, and half the *Godspell* people are gathered in knots just outside. Two of the guys tangle in each other's arms—I don't think they're trying to keep warm, either.

Moving through them, I watch in amazement as one of the girls grabs the curve of one foot and raises it above her head. She just perches there on the other foot, arching her back and carrying on a conversation at the same time.

"Put your eyes back in your head," Nan says, amused, and ushers me inside. The foyer is more of the same, only this time with a guy sitting in a girl's lap on the couch by the front door, and excited conversations exploding next to the luggage racks.

But we're here for two specific Broadway people; they're

standing at the front desk. Nan waves a hand, calling out, "Mr. Glickman! Ms. Allen!"

Barry stops mid-monologue at the hotel clerk—surprise, surprise, there's no sauna and no room service at the Edgewater, Indiana, Comfort Inn. Also, no suites. I mean, it's only three stories high—what did they expect? He smooths the front of his jacket and walks toward us.

"Emma, honey," he says, and instead of shaking my hand, he captures it between his and squeezes. There might even be a little bow involved; I'm not quite sure. "What are you doing here?"

"We wanted to thank all of you," Nan says. She steps ever so slightly in front of me, a tiny, bingo-playing wall of protection. "*I* want to thank you, for coming all this way for my Emma. She's had a rough row to hoe the past couple years."

"Farm metaphors," Dee Dee says, turning her roller bag and snapping the handle closed with precision. "How charming!"

Barry lets go of my hand and nods. "I never got to go to prom. Okay, correction, I went to fourteen proms—just not my own. And I—"

"We," Dee Dee interjects.

Barry gives her a look. "*We* couldn't let that happen to you. Not in this day and age."

"It's tough out here for this little girl," Nan says, ruffling my hair like I'm a toddler. Slightly embarrassed, I lean away. If she moves on to squeezing cheeks next, she's going to have to grab Barry. Who knows? He might even be into that.

I say, "I just don't understand why this is such a big deal."

"It's ignorance," Dee Dee announces with certainty. "It's backwater ignorance! These hayseeds don't learn because they don't *want* to learn."

Even though I live here, even though I mostly hate living here, my hackles rise. Dee Dee's from New York, a magical fairyland where apparently you can make a living pretending to be other people onstage, and also, public transportation actually exists.

She's standing here talking about ignorance when she doesn't even know that we have no hayseeds in Indiana.

We don't grow much wheat here. No wheat, no hayseeds, hello. We grow corn and soybeans; we're dairy farmers and hog farmers. (Also, we export limestone and natural gas. You're welcome.) It's one thing if she calls us rednecks. People around here do get the backs of their necks sunburned working in the fields. But hayseeds? Not so much.

And I can't even believe I'm mentally defending this place, but I am. I live here. I know all our faults. If I want to talk Hoosier trash, well, bring the chicken and noodles on mashed potatoes, because I will. *My* trash is *accurate*. Dee Dee, however, is about to get an attitude adjustment, courtesy of this baby gayseed.

"Can I steal this delightful little sugarplum for just a minute?" Barry asks.

Nan looks him over, then glances at me. Touching her nose, she points. "I better be able to see you at all times."

So much for schooling Dee Dee. I'm still itching to mouth off to her, but my temper fades the farther we get from her. Barry and I end up in matching green chairs by the cookie table—after he shoos a couple of chorus kids out of his way. They look at him like he's a god. I'm guessing a Roman one, who likes his feasts and libations.

A tray of chocolate chip and snickerdoodle cookies sits beneath a sign that welcomes anyone to have a bite. No tongs, though. If you want one, you're gonna have to grab it with your grubby hand like everybody else.

Despite this, Barry takes a cookie and breaks it. He offers me half and fixes me with a sympathetic smile.

"I've been exactly where you are," he says, and his eyes are so kind as he glances toward Nan. "I mean, at least you've got your mother?"

"Actually," I tell him, "that's my grandmother. She took me in when Mom and Dad kicked me out."

"How did *that* happen?"

"Nan says she must have dropped Dad on his head too many times when he was a baby." I shrug and offer a game smile.

But instead of laughing along, Barry murmurs the most sympathetic sound. The regret on his face is so real and so present that I tear up. He's still Mr. Pecker in my head, but he's a better version of him. Sweet, sincere.

Abandoning his half of the cookie, he rests his chin on his hand just so, then says, "That's rough, kiddo. And . . . I've been there, too."

"I'm sorry."

"Me too." He looks to the distance, but then snaps back to the present. "But I'm here to tell you, people like us? We get to choose our family. And when we see each other, across the room or across the country, we care. Instead of your uncle who tells racist jokes at Thanksgiving, you get me now."

"The uncle who pickets my school?"

"Honey, the auntie who's going to change your life." With a flourish, he smiles; he snaps.

He is seriously the gayest person I've ever met, and I've been to third base with my girlfriend. I guess I should say, he's the most stereotypically gay person I've ever met? He's the queeniest person I've ever met? I don't even know!

I might be showing my own internalized homophobia right now. Because Barry looks perfectly comfortable in his skin, and I'm perched on a hotel chair with a cold cookie in my claws, a gargoyle too basic to make the grade for the church bell tower.

"And do you know what?" Barry says, leaning toward me and lowering his voice. "There's a way out of here. I watched the rest of the videos on your channel. You're talented, Emma. There's always room for talented people—session singing, background singing, overdubbing tuneless blondes in yet another *Mamma Mia* sequel? I'm such a petty bitch, pretend I didn't say that last one."

I'm surprised by my own smile, my own sudden laughter. He's saying all the things I want to hear. Here's somebody who's completely, totally on my side. Who's been through what I'm going through now. Who made it to the other side. When they say *it gets better*, this is what they mean.

"Barry . . . can I call you Barry?" I say, testing the weight of his name on my tongue when he nods. "I really appreciate you coming all this way. But after tonight . . . I'm not sure it's a good idea to keep pushing. You saw how mad all the parents are. And when you showed up at school today, you literally interrupted a death threat in progress."

"But, Emma! That's *exactly* why we're here!"

"You don't think this is going to make it worse?"

Picking up his chair by the arms, Barry turns it toward me and drops it with a heavy thump. He catches my hands again. "Absotively not. We won't let that happen. Between me and Dee Dee, this is going to be the most watched prom in the country. They wouldn't dare."

"That's really nice of you, but we still don't know if there's going to be a prom. And also?" I roll my shoulders ruefully. "Even if there is, I don't think my girlfriend's going to come."

Barry looks like he's about to say something sassy and possibly inappropriate. He thinks better of it and rubs his hands together. His voice lilts, almost like he's singing, when he asks, "Who's your girlfriend?"

Boy, do I appreciate the gobsmacked look on his face when I say, "Alyssa Greene, the student council president. Her mom's the head of the PTA; she's the one who hates my guts."

Scandalized, Barry asks, "Does she know?"

"Nooooo," I say. "Not about me and not about her daughter, and she's not going to find out until Alyssa's ready, got it?"

"I'm here as an agent of Cupid, not a sower of discord, darling." Barry nods firmly at that, then says, "You know what? You work on your date, and I'll work on everything else. Leave it to me, Emma. There *will* be a prom, and it will be perfect. I'll take care of your flowers, your hair, your shoes—you have a dress?"

I stammer, "Uh, no," but fail to say I had no intention of wearing a dress.

"Oh, sweetheart, I've got so much work to do. Where's the nearest Saks?"

"We don't have one."

He shudders but amends, "Macy's?"

I shake my head. "Sorry. We have a Walmart?"

"Oh good god, you're going to prom, not a hoedown. All right. Breathe. Center. Exhale. Good." He claps his hands and ends his impromptu meditation session. "No Saks, no problem. Tony Award–winning costume designer Gregg Barnes owes me a favor or two. I'll have him FedEx a selection and bring them by."

"To school?"

"Your humble abode, Emma." Barry considers, then asks, "If your grandmother won't have a problem with a middle-aged man prancing around your bedroom."

We both glance at her at the same time. She's petting one of the young picketers; his long, golden hair does look irresistible. I say, "She's gonna make us leave the door open and keep both feet on the floor."

"I'll do my best," Barry jokes.

My cell phone gurgles with a school alert. I pull it from my pocket, but I don't look at it. My throat is dry and my heart is still. I tell Barry, "That's something from the school."

"Read it," he says. "If it's a battle, we must prepare. Wouldn't want to show up to a slap fight barehanded."

Unlocking the screen, I touch the notification. It takes a minute for my mail to load. Signal reception is hit or miss around here because of all the limestone, and also because we live in the middle of nowhere. The screen finally flashes white, and there it is. A letter from the PTA.

"Regarding this year's prom," I say shakily, then read on. "After much consideration and consultation with friends, family, and the community, the James Madison PTA has decided to move forward with plans to host the prom at its original date and time. We will be in touch with more information as necessary. Thank you for your passionate advocacy. We are proud of our students and our class of 2019 Golden Weevils. Sincerely, Elena Greene, PTA president."

"We did it," Barry says, so quiet it's almost a whisper. Then he leaps up and shouts into the other room. "Dee Dee! Non-equity cast of *Godspell*! We did it! Emma's going to the prom!"

A roar fills the hotel foyer. Jazz hands and kicks-ball-change (kick-ball-changes?) break out everywhere. The news travels fast, shouted out the sliding front doors with ecstatic glee. There are so many bright, delighted faces around me that I can't help but laugh. This is a mob scene I can appreciate.

"Yay *us*!" Dee Dee shouts, throwing her arms over her head.

Nan raises an eyebrow. "More like yay Emma."

"It can be them," I concede. "Everything changed when they got here."

With that, Barry sweeps Dee Dee up in a very choreographed waltz (I'm guessing—how should I know? This is Indiana 2019, not Versailles 1719—although there is a Versailles, Indiana, and guess how many of those *S*s and *L*s we pronounce. Spoiler: all of them).

As people cheer around me and burst into song—they've been here a minute, and I've already noticed that happens a lot—I bask in stunned silence. My phone weighs a million pounds, but I'm as light as air. I'm going to prom.

I'm going to prom!

12. Something Begun

ALYSSA

I push open my car door, and Emma jumps in.

Throwing my arms around her, I kiss her. I kiss her hard and fast; I kiss her softly. I kiss her until our lips are sticky and my windows are fogged. She tastes like bubble gum and electricity, a sweet summer storm that rolls through me and rumbles on and on.

Even though we're still parked in her grandmother's driveway, I kiss her again and again, apologies and promises, greetings, but no goodbyes for once. Not yet. Not tonight.

When Emma pulls back for a breath, she presses her brow to mine. Her fingers slip through my hair; I shiver. She's familiar and constant and untouchable all at the same time, and I feed her my relief on soft caresses that fall on her skin. We've been so far away lately—I was afraid we might not snap back together, but we do.

We fit, my hands in hers, my lips on hers, my heart against hers. A little trill runs through my chest, and I'm dizzy for a moment. She makes me dizzy.

"How'd you manage a prison break?" Emma asks, her lips teasing in a smile.

"Tunneled out behind a picture of Ruby Rose on my wall."

Laughter fills my car, and she hugs me fiercely. When she pulls back, she leans her head against the headrest. She plays with my fingers between hers. Her fingertips are rough from playing the guitar; they create their own kisses on the palm of my hand. "Seriously, though?" she asks.

"Seriously? Her manager at the Red Stripe threatened to write her up if she missed any more shifts."

"Yikes," Emma says, furrowing her brow. "I guess when you get into the grocery deli game, it's hard to get out."

My laugh is soft; my eye-rolling amused instead of annoyed. Even though my mother has made Emma's life exponentially harder, she doesn't hold it against me. She's not cruel about her, and sometimes—especially lately—I really feel like she kind of has the right to be.

My mother is a complicated disaster, but she's my complicated disaster. And she's really all I have. My grandparents retired to New Mexico; my only aunt lives in Des Moines. They exist solely in Christmas and birthday cards, on Facebook and text message. My dad . . . well, you know all about my dad.

"I've been thinking," I say, and my skin goes hot as soon as I say it. "The prom is back on, and obviously, that wouldn't be the case if Mom hadn't softened a little—"

"What, you don't think it was the Broadway invasion that changed her mind?"

"Emma."

"They're doing a number at the truck rally this weekend, just to make a point. Can you *imagine* the looks in that crowd? *Sunday, Sunday, Sunday! We'll sell you the seat, but you'll only need the edge, edge, edge—and a taste for show tunes.* I tried to warn them."

Covering my face with my hand, I shake my head, "Why, even? They got what they came for."

"The show must go on?" Emma says, more like a question. She shrugs, and then her face changes—her tone, too. To something soft, almost wondrous. "Barry's calling in a favor from a costume designer. For my outfit."

"You're on a first-name basis now?"

Emma nods, her dark hair bobbing, her glasses slipping down her nose. "Apparently I am. And I think his idea of formal wear for me doesn't match *my* idea, but . . . we talked for a long time last night. It was really nice."

Guilt coils inside me. She's doing this all alone. Worse, this is all my mother's fault *and* she's doing this alone. Mr. Glickman and Ms. Allen seem a little . . . intense, but I guess I can't blame Emma for embracing them. I make myself smile and ask, "Was it?"

With her gaze out the window, something plays out on Emma's features. It's like she catches herself up in a memory. She sounds wistful when she says, "Yeah, it was. It's like he's the very first person who really *gets* me."

My smile falters. "Ouch."

"You know what I mean," Emma says. All of a sudden, she's moving, filling my car with flying hands and animation. I haven't seen her this excited since she found out the new *Sabrina* was going to be freaky-scary instead of goofy-silly.

"He's just *out* there," she goes on. "His mom pushed him out, too. And he said that people like us, we get to choose our families. We get to choose the people around us, and I never thought about that before. If family is love, then the people we love are family."

I'm not sure why, but unease snakes through me, low through my belly. I feel like I'm holding on to a balloon too tight, afraid that it'll slip from my grasp. I interrupt this train of thought and say, "I don't want to change the subject or anything, but I do . . . I mean, so you know, I do still want us to do it—go to prom together."

She stops short. "I thought that was already settled."

"It is, it was!" I say. "I just didn't know, with everything that's happened . . . if, I don't know, maybe you'd changed your mind."

With that, Emma leans back and looks at me. Really looks at me. "You realize I'm the only thing that *hasn't* changed in all of this, right? I didn't ask for your mother to turn this into a referendum on my personhood. And I didn't ask for Broadway to picket the school. I didn't ask for any of this."

"No, of course you didn't!" I hold up my hands. "Please, I don't want to fight."

"I don't either." Emma looks so disappointed, but then she catches my hands. "And you know what? I don't want to start a riot. I don't want to blaze a trail or be a symbol—and I don't care what other people think. I just want to dance with you."

When the tears spring up, they catch me by surprise. *That's all I want, too,* I want to say. To dance together, and let the world melt away, and to just feel right about it. To feel no fear. I love Emma so much it hurts, and I hate that the way I've been loving her hurts her, too. Finally, I say, "I just want to hold you."

"And I don't want to let you go," she says. Tears glimmer in her eyes, too. "Two people swaying, that's it. Nobody knows how to dance anymore anyway. So it'll be you and me, shuffling awkwardly to music nobody was ever supposed to dance to. I don't know why that scares them so much, but I don't care, Alyssa. All I care about is you."

I turn away to sniff. I'm a gross crier, and when I kiss her after this, I don't want to slime her. "I promise you. When we get there, it's going to be just you and me and a song."

Emma falls into my arms again, and I hold her so tight. I rub my cheek against her hair and squeeze until I feel her exhale a breath. It's not right that something this good, this *perfect*, can cause so much trouble. No—that other people let something this good, this perfect, bother *them*.

A soft rain opens up, and the hush of drops spilling over the roof of my car does that thing that Emma wants—it makes the world melt away. Right now, here in the dark, in the mist, beneath the fall of rain, there is no world, just this. Just now.

Just us.

13. Razzle, Also Some Dazzle, Plus, Pound Cake

EMMA

I hear Barry and Dee Dee on the porch before they knock on the door.

More specifically, I hear Dee Dee doing something that sounds suspiciously like a few steps of tap dancing. Then, when she knocks on the door, it's bright and strident. I leap up from the bright yellow lounger in the living room to answer.

"I was expecting them to be fashionably late," Nan says, pulling out a bread knife to slice the cake she made. The whole house smells like sugar and vanilla, and even though I'm nervous, I open the door with a smile.

"Nous sommes arrivés," Dee Dee announces, stepping through the door like a showgirl. She catches me up in her manicured hands, pressing her cheek to mine and mwahing right next to my ear. When she lets go, I practically spin across the floor. She's been in my house for less than ten seconds and I'm already out of breath.

A clothing rack comes through the door next, Barry pushing it from behind. His perfect skin is slightly pink, and when he gets in, he pulls a handkerchief from his pocket and daubs it across his face. When he finishes, he literally closes his eyes, takes a breath, and then comes back to the present.

"Emma!" he says, lighting up. He doesn't spin me across the room, thankfully. He just grabs my hands and squeezes them. "How are you, darling?"

Overwhelmed. Excited. Slightly nauseated? I say none of those things, because none of them answer the question. I'm all of them, and more. I feel like a weathervane, spinning toward ecstasy, then back toward despair. So I offer a smile instead and lead him inside. "I'm good, thank you, how are you?"

"Recuperating," Dee Dee answers for him. She turns, as if looking for somewhere to perch. We have a couch, a love seat, a rocking chair, and the yellow lounger, but Dee Dee seems out of sorts. Finally, she manages to arrange herself against the fireplace. Placing a hand dramatically over her heart she says, "No one appreciated our performance at the rally. They threw things!"

"Did they really?" Nan asks, hiding a smile.

"They did! Do you know how many people would pay good money to see us in New York?"

"It was probably the up-and-down weather," Nan says. "People get a little loopy when spring is almost here. Would you like some refreshments?" She ferries thick yellow slices of pound cake onto paper plates. I can't wait to see what Dee Dee does with disposable dishes.

Dee Dee peeks at the cake and quickly shifts her attention away. "I couldn't possibly," she says. Then, just as quickly, she reverses herself. "But it would be so terribly rude to decline. Just a tiny slice for me?"

"I want to get these out of the garment bags for Emma," Barry says. "Which way to the boudoir?"

"Uh, if you mean my bedroom, it's this way," I say, gesturing toward the hallway.

Barry puts my hand on the rack and walks off toward my room. I guess he's about done driving this thing around. Amused, I pull it along behind me. It's incredibly heavy, and I can hear things scratching and shaking behind the thick vinyl bags. My guess is rhinestones. At least, I hope that's all it is.

"Oh, I recognize this," Barry says as he sashays into my room. "This is where you record your videos!"

I still can't believe he bothered to watch them. With a shy smile, I sit down on my bed and say dryly, "Yep, this is where the magic happens."

"Well, believe you me," he says, turning to the rack, "it's about to get one thousand percent more magical in here, starting now!"

"You know," I say quickly, "maybe we could mix it up a little. I was thinking a vintage tux, some high-tops . . ."

Appalled, Barry turns to me. "Could we? Yes. Should we? Dear god, no. Sweetheart, I'm begging here. Let me dress you for the prom."

"Okay," I say. I mean, he's from New York. He definitely knows more about fashion than I do. Folding my hands, pressing my knees together, I nod at him encouragingly and wait.

Barry unzips the first garment bag, then throws it back like he's revealing a new piece of art. I recoil, because for a second, it looks like whatever's in there is going to shoot out and stab me with a million little icicles.

When *fight or flight* fades to *slightly anxious in my own skin,* I see that it's a red spangly dress covered with rows upon rows of dangling crystals. The dress shimmies when he pulls it free; it sounds like a hundred whispers all at once when it moves.

"Wow," I say, stunned.

Barry leans in. "Good wow or bad wow?"

"Just wow."

I hate to say no, because it's obviously gorgeous. And I don't want him to think I'm not trying here, but there's no way I'm going to prom in a red hot jazz baby dress like that. It's forty-two inches of va-voom violation of the dress code, and the only accessory I can think to wear with it would be a machine gun. All things considered, that might come off as a tiny bit aggro.

Finally, I come up with something I can say that isn't wildly ungrateful. "It's a little flashy for me."

"Fair enough," he says, and *whoosh!* He flings off another garment bag to reveal a white gown with black ribbon at the ankles, and the waist, and the neck. And ruffles, whoa, so many ruffles at the neck.

It definitely covers all of the body parts I'm required to cover—and then some. The sleeves puff out at the shoulders and taper to tight wristlets. Barry waggles his brows at me. "There's a matching hat, three feet wide, white ostrich plumes for days."

I laugh. "That's just daring all the roosters around here to attack."

At that, Barry chuckles. In the other room, I hear Dee Dee

belting a few lines and Nan singing something back in her crow-like rattle. She's the worst singer I know, but she loves doing it more than anyone I know, too. My grandmother is out there bonding with this Broadway invasionette over pound cake and . . . what sounds like "Swing Low, Sweet Chariot"??

All the tension that's in me, that surrounds me, melts away. It's okay if I don't love this dress; there's another one right behind it. It's okay if I'm an ordinary girl from an ordinary place. Barry makes me feel like there's more to me than this bedroom, this town, this moment. It's easy to get caught up in his enthusiasm, and you know what? I'm gonna let myself.

It's the first time in weeks that I've genuinely laughed. And breathed. And worried about nothing except what frilly Lovecraftian confection might be in the next bag. My house is so much bigger now. Fuller and brighter, somehow. It's just . . . alive. I can't remember the last time my life felt . . . full.

Barry reveals the next dress with a slow flourish. It's pink and fitted, not really me at all. But this one, at least, looks like a dress I could wear to a high school prom. Or to a midday business meeting with a select group of venture capitalists and tech gurus. Easing the hanger free, Barry says, "This one, you have to try on. It's something special."

"Okay," I say. Why not?

"I'll wait for you in the living room. But don't make me wait too long or you'll meet my drag alter ego, Carol Channing Tatum."

"Is that supposed to make me *not* want that?" I ask with a laugh.

He points imperiously. "Go. Now."

With that, I duck down the hall to our bathroom. Stripping out of my flannels and tee, I pull the dress over my head. It's strangely heavy, and I feel packed into it. I never wear clothes this tight.

Looking into the mirror, I try to smooth and flatten . . . and then I try to scoop up my boobs so they sit front and center in this thing. The wide straps cover a lot of my shoulders, but not everything. It's so much skin. It's so revealing.

I have never wanted to be a lacy girl. There's nothing wrong with it—Alyssa is all soft frills and fitted everything, everyday heels and skirts that range from ankle to knee. Her makeup is always soft, mascara framing her big brown eyes, lipstick teasing out the perfect bow of her lips. I love a lacy girl.

But I'm not one. I feel like my joints are ten times too big to walk around in a dress like this. As I slip out of the bathroom and down the hallway, I'm Godzilla in Gucci, tromping through Tokyo Fashion Week.

In the living room, Barry laughs with Nan and Dee Dee. They're waiting to see the dress on me. To be part of my big makeover scene. That's how this works, right? I get a fairy godfather, a glittering gown, glass slippers, a ticket to the ball . . .

I tentatively make my way into the room, and all eyes turn to me. Nervously, I ask, "What do you think?"

"We're getting there," Dee Dee says, unhooking herself from the hearth and handing off her cake to Barry. "Good shoulders, terrible posture. Posture is half the battle, Emma. It rights so many wrongs, makes C cups of so many barely Bs . . ." Clasping my shoulders, Dee Dee looks me in the face and says, "Zazz."

Uh . . . what?

"That's what's missing," she says, whirling around me. She pulls my shoulders back and presses a hand in the middle of my spine. "Breathe in, from the diaphragm."

I take a breath, and I don't say anything. Dee Dee moves in a flash, adjusting my posture, even tipping my chin up with a quick flash of fingers. When she stops in front of me, she stares into my eyes for a long moment and says, "We need to see it in your eyes."

"You want me to smize?"

Crisply, Dee Dee steps into a pose. She's Wonder Woman without the bracelets, suddenly taller, her shoulders appear broader, taking up angular space in a way that simultaneously reminds me of Picasso and praying mantises. "Zazz is style plus confidence. Now let's see it."

"It's just so . . . pink," I say finally.

That's when Barry leaps to his feet. "Sweetheart, I told you this was special." He tugs a ribbon on the side of the dress. "Spin!"

And like a crazy, out-of-control top, I do. I feel the ribbon unfurl; I spin and spin and suddenly, the pink dress turns blue. I don't even know how it happens. The skirt turns fuller and longer, kissing my knees. The top is softer, the shoulder straps turned to cap sleeves. I'm Katniss freaking Everdeen, and I'm gonna be the last girl standing at prom!

"Look at you," Nan says, admiring.

I am never going to be a lacy girl, and I'm never going to love wearing a dress. But this one? This one I can handle. This one is special. It's magic, and these people are, too.

They're magic in Indiana, and maybe—just maybe—a little bit of me is magic, too.

14. It's Raining on Prom Night

ALYSSA

I am in so much trouble. The countdown to prom is in minutes, and I haven't told my mother yet.

The back of my head still burns from way too long under the space bubble hair dryer at Joan's Curl Up 'n' Dye. I've never had this much Aqua Net or glitter in my hair before. When I reach up to touch it, two things happen: first, it crunches a little beneath my fingers, and second, my mother smacks my hand away.

"I've been peeping at those makeup gals online. They all do this," Joan tells her as she paints my face with another round of foundation. "It's called *wake and baking*."

Choking on my gum, I say nothing. There's not enough money in the world to get me to explain to my mother what that really means. If she doesn't know, she'd demand to know how I do. Existing in 2019 would be the answer, but not one she would appreciate hearing.

What *I* don't appreciate is how I haven't had a moment alone with Mom all day. It's like every single time there's been a breath in her nonstop pre-prom prep list, she's flung herself as far from me as possible. I open my mouth to say one serious thing, and her phone blows up on cue.

Oh, there's a balloon emergency. No, the DJ absolutely cannot deviate from the playlist. What do you mean we don't have a punch monitor?

I glance at my phone, so far away from me on Joan's station. Less than an hour until prom starts and I've said word zero to my mother about my date. My very real date who was, last time she managed to text, being semi-felt-up by Dee Dee Allen after the introduction of something Emma would only call "Nightmare Panties by Feather Boa Constrictor."

Meanwhile, my mother hovers over my shoulder, alternately watching her hairdresser pageantify me and barking voice-to-text orders at Shelby's mother through the phone. She stares into the mirror with fiery intensity. It's like she's measuring my face, over and over. Calculating the angle of my updo and quantifying the looseness of the tendrils that fall against my shoulders.

"Mom," I say, "I was hoping we'd get to talk a little before things got crazy."

Joan lunges in with immaculately spray-tanned hands and orders, "Look up!" before attacking me with more mascara.

"Honey, you don't have to say anything," Mom says, catching my hand before it strays toward my hair again. "Just enjoy this. You won't get another special day like this until your wedding day."

"Amen," Joan says, switching to the other eye.

Mom lowers her voice, like she's being naughty. "And

you'll have to share *that* with your mother-in-law."

From the way Joan laughs, my mother is the funniest woman she's ever met. Maybe she used to be, but I'm pretty sure Joan's laughter is a nod. A tribute to the woman most likely to tip well when all of this is through. "Lord, you're not lying. By the time I got to the altar, I was just about ready to tell Nathan it's me or her!"

"Looks like he chose the right one."

"Well, I still have to put up with her and her god-awful ambrosia salad at Christmas, Thanksgiving, Easter, and Race Day . . ."

Just like that, they're chatting about appropriate food for your Indy 500 party and how men's mothers ruin everything. I'm not even here. I'm just the disembodied doll head being decorated within an inch of its life.

A knot tightens in my stomach. I hold very, very still as Joan coaxes a smoky eye out of a mostly pastel palette, and I try not to frown when my mother chooses the shade of my lipstick.

"It's important," I tell my mother, when Joan turns away to open a tackle box full of cosmetics. That's not a joke. She has the same bright yellow plastic organizer that half the guys in town have rattling around in the beds of their pickup trucks.

Mom holds up a finger. "Hold on; Shelby's mother doesn't know if anybody bought the sherbert."

Because nothing says *classy evening of elegance* like a massive punch bowl full of ginger ale with melted rainbow foam in it. But to be fair, it *is* served at wedding receptions, baby showers, and anniversary parties all over town. The way people fuss over the punch, you'd think it was a recipe handed down across the generations and not copied off a Schweppes label sometime in the last century.

And if I didn't know better, I'd think my mother is deliberately avoiding me. Every time I gather the words in my mind and the courage in my heart, she darts away again. *Stop being paranoid,* I tell myself. *She's like this with every event she plans for school.*

Forty minutes before homecoming last fall, she was hanging—lit-er-ally hanging—from the top of a ladder, trimming the crepe paper streamers in the gym to exactly the same length. She's not going to relax until the last balloon drops and the final fleck of confetti settles on the dance floor. It just feels like she's avoiding me because I've been putting this off for so long.

"Here we are!"

Joan surfaces from the tackle box and puts a plastic dish in my hand. Carefully, she selects a glimmering crystal from the container and dots the back of it with eyelash glue. One after the other, Joan affixes three little gleaming gems at the corner of my eye, then steps back.

Admiring her own handiwork in the mirror, she waves my mother over. Joan mouths, "She's beautiful," and my mother mouths back, "Thank you."

Their pride lasts half a second. Then Mom, with the phone to her ear, pushes the hanger with my dress on it into my hands. Half whispering, she says, "Go on, get changed. We're running out of time, and I want to get some pictures of you."

"Mom, I—"

"Vamoose, Alyssa," she says. And then she gives me a swat

on the butt, like I'm six years old and we're running late for church. Into the phone, she says, "Yes, I'm still here. Did you look in the freezer? Not the cooler, the freezer?"

The salon's bathroom smells like perm solution and vanilla candles. The scent is thick, and it makes me queasy, but I manage to get out of my street clothes and into the overtime gown without incident.

I'm careful not to yank the straps on my dress too hard. For some reason, I remember them being a lot more substantial in the store. Now, they're just thin, jeweled threads that definitely do not meet dress code.

A wash of lavender satin and tulle surrounds me. The full skirt murmurs when I move. A perfect fit. Exactly right. My makeup matches perfectly, even if it is a little thick for my taste. Trying to turn in the tight space, I wobble, and wonder if my hair will shatter if it hits the wall. I'd better not find out.

I wonder what Emma's doing right now. When I Marcoed her last night, she sat her phone on her dresser to stay in frame. All nerves and excitement, Emma's anticipation shone in her bright pink cheeks, and eyes that glittered like Christmas lights. She kept rolling onto her back, then onto her stomach, unable to lie still.

My guess is, she's surrounded by Nan and Mr. Glickman and Ms. Allen, enduring hair and makeup just like me. She told me Mr. Glickman conned her into a dress, but she refused to show it to me. She wanted it to be a surprise. So right now, she's probably counting down the minutes until all the waiting is over. Until it's finally the two of us.

And most of our high school.

And my mother.

Who still doesn't know.

The thing is, I'm trying. I'm really trying! Mom hasn't stopped long enough to breathe, let alone have a heart-to-heart. Everything happened so fast after prom was officially back on that time just slipped from my grasp.

But it's fine. As soon as I'm dressed and the pictures are over, all that's left is the drive to the school. Mom won't be able to get away from me then. I have a semi-thought-out plan. First, I'll turn down the radio. Not all the way, just low enough that she can hear me over it. But not so low that I have to fill the silence all by myself.

Then I'll hold her hand; she loves it when I do that. I think it reminds her that I'm still her baby, even if I'm not a little girl anymore. So yes, I'll hold her hand and I'll start by thanking her. For being my mom. For being funny—she used to be funny, before Dad left, and I know she could be again. For being a part of every big moment in my life, for celebrating them with me.

For loving me.

For loving me unconditionally.

And then I'll just say it. I'll open my mouth, and I will—

"Alyssa!" my mother calls through the door, rapping on it sharply. "What's taking so long? Do you need help with the zipper?"

I want to laugh, but I'm wound too tight. No matter how much I want to convince myself that this will all be okay, I know it won't. Darkness creeps up inside me, and I want to tear off the dress, scrub the makeup off my face. I want to run. But that's not going to happen, so I have to admit this, to myself, so I can move forward:

My mom's not going to pleasantly surprise me with her reaction. I know her. I know how this goes.

At night, when I put my hands together and try to think of something to pray for that isn't selfish, I ask for peace of mind for my mom. For acceptance. Or even tolerance. I sit with this huge secret, praying for divine intervention, because I know I haven't misjudged her.

She's on a razor-thin edge with Dad leaving, yes, that's going to blow up on her, sooner rather than later, yes, but I think—no, I know.

Even if everything were perfect—if my dad had stayed, if Mom were still a housewife and stay-at-home mother instead of a junior deli clerk at the age of forty-eight, my being a lesbian *still wouldn't be okay with her*. She doesn't even have the vocabulary to understand who I am. In her world, in her mind, there's gay and there's *normal*.

And that means, if I'm not straight, I'm not normal.

I wasn't there, exactly, when Emma's parents kicked her out. Slightly before my time. But I've heard the story. She's lain in her bed at Nan's house, with her head in my lap, trying to find some meaning to it. Trying to figure out if her mom and dad actually loved her before, and somehow, she destroyed that by existing . . . or if they never loved her at all. Not really. Not unconditionally.

My mother's love has conditions. I already know the price of admission in the Greene house is perfection. *Normal* perfection.

If mom kicks me out, I have nowhere to go. My grandparents are just as religious as Mom is, maybe even more so. They're yard-sign people, handwritten harangues about whatever moral ills are in the news on any given day. Last June, they had one that said *The rainbow is God's promise, not Satan's flag.* They could have forty-seven extra rooms; there wouldn't be one for me in their house. Not once they knew.

That leaves my dad. My dad, who threw away the life that included me, and got as far from Edgewater as possible. The dad who doesn't call, doesn't write, doesn't pay for my textbook rental or new sneakers. He has a new wife. He has a new baby. If I knocked on his door, what would he say? I bet it would be something like, "I'm so sorry, I thought I canceled my subscription to you."

Things are tight for Emma and Nan, so even if I thought they would take me in, I could never ask. It's too much. Too big.

Call me selfish; maybe I am selfish. But I'm selfish *and* afraid. I've done the research. Forty percent of homeless teens are queer. A quarter of queer kids get kicked out when they come out. It's a long, long summer before college starts in the fall. I mean, at least I have a car. The title's in my name. She can't take that from me.

Wow. That's my silver lining. I have a car I can live in when my mother inevitably kicks me out.

Because I know, in my heart, that Mom didn't soften up about *the gay issue* and prom. She changed her mind because she didn't want *me* to miss *my* prom. And, based on the increasingly desperate hammering on the bathroom door, I'm about to miss it anyway.

My heart pounding, I step into the shoes Mom dyed to match my dress. I catch my breath, then sweep open the door. Somehow, I end up in a cloud of my mother's hugs. I hold on for so long; I don't want to let go. I know what happens next, and I want this moment—when she still loves me—to linger just a little longer.

These are the arms that taught me to ride a bike, and comforted me when I had nightmares. These are the arms that lifted me up when I fell, and pushed me toward things I wanted but wasn't quite brave enough to grasp on my own. One last time, I gather my strength in her embrace.

Mom pulls away, swiping at her eyes. "You're the most beautiful girl in the world."

"Thank you, Mommy," I say, barely keeping it together myself.

"What a shame John Cho can't see you like this. You deserve to have a date tonight."

Now. I have to do this now before I lose my courage again. I don't want to . . . I can't . . . God, prom is almost here, and I have to do this. The words taste like ash, and I force them out. "Mom, about that. I have to tell you something."

"Not now," she says as she takes my wrist, sweeping me toward the front door. She grabs my clutch and forces it into my hand. There's the slightest hint of annoyance in her voice, but it's fond. "The first part of your surprise showed up early."

For a millisecond, my heart convinces me that she's going to open the salon door and Emma will be standing there. But the thought flits away almost as quickly as it arrived. The cool evening air hits me, and I swear it hisses on my skin.

The girl of my dreams isn't standing there with flowers in her hands.

Instead, waiting at the curb is a limo. A stretch SUV, as a matter of fact. Shelby and Kaylee pop out of the moon roof. Music pours out, and they throw up their arms and squeal when they see me. They're already corsaged, and from the sounds of it, pre-gaming with a hit of secret schnapps.

"Get in, loser, we're going to prom!"

"Mom," I shout, "something's going to happen tonight. You need to know—"

"Don't spoil this," she says, catching my face in her hands. "I've worked very hard on this night, and I want to enjoy it, too. You're going to have a wonderful prom, like a normal girl. I've made sure of that."

"What does that mean?" I ask, but it's too late. She pushes me into the limo's open door. I'm engulfed by a wave of heat and the funk of too much cologne on brand-new leather. It's like being kidnapped by Abercrombie & Fitch.

The door slams closed behind me, and the SUV takes off at top speed. What is happening? *Why* is this happening? I can't even get settled as I strain to look out the back window. The last coherent thought I have as I watch my mother grow smaller and smaller in the distance is:

I didn't even get to tell her I loved her, one last time.

15. On the Steps of the Palace

EMMA

As promised on prom night, there are flowers. And limos. And pictures.

Oh my god, so many pictures that I'm seeing nothing but flashbulb leopard spots. Oh, and the occasional glimpse of the bouquet of tastefully selected orchids, lilies, and roses I clutch in my hands. Their rich perfume goes straight to my head, but that's okay. Everything's been happening so fast today that it's good to have a chance to stop and literally smell the flowers.

Barry sits next to me in the limo, handsome in his tux—it doesn't change colors, I already asked. Next to Dee Dee, he'll be the best-dressed chaperone in the whole county. She's positioned herself closest to the window that separates us from the chauffeur. She talks so fast, he doesn't manage to reply, but that's okay. I think this is how Dee Dee flirts?

Barry, on the other hand, has a quiet serenity to him tonight, which is a whole new side. Clutching the bouquet tighter in my sweaty hands, I ask him, "Nervous?"

"Contemplative," he says. "How are you feeling?"

"Like I swallowed an angry bag of snakes. But I'm going to make you proud."

"Sweetie." Barry turns toward me. "This isn't about me. This is about you, and I promise, you're going to have the time of your life."

I can't even say, *I hope you're right.* Like, it catches in my throat. The bag of snakes gives a good, solid twist, and the only thing that comes out of me is a weird little squeak.

Warmth pours from Barry when he asks, "What's your date wearing?" He's trying to distract me, and I'm going to let him.

"I don't know. Her mother bought it for her, but I haven't seen it."

"What, no fashion show?"

Poor, sweet Barry. He's been out so long, he has no idea what it's like to be in. I can't even imagine that—going a whole day without checking myself. Without looking too long in the wrong direction, without cautiously measuring the things I say. I'm glad it's far behind him, but it makes him seem just a little more out of reach. "I've never been to her house. Her mom doesn't know about us, remember?"

He shakes his head. "How long have you been together?"

"A year and a half," I say. "And before that, it was a year and a half of really clumsy, careful flirting. I knew I was crazy for her the day I met her. But I couldn't just, you know, make a move."

"My heart!"

"She's coming out tonight," I say, and I can't believe I let the words out. I've been holding them so close to my heart, close enough to feel the shimmer of hope but too tightly to really let it grow.

Alyssa's been talking about coming out for a long time now, and there's always a reason why it can't happen. She says tonight, and I believe her. But I didn't want to jinx it by saying it out loud. It feels like tempting fate, but it's too late to worry about that, I guess.

"That's a big deal," Barry says. "If I'd known, I would have baked a cake!"

Instead of laughing, I choke on a sob. All the feelings I've been pushing down come up at once. Everything that's happened in the last couple of weeks, it's like getting hit by different trains, over and over. Joy and fear and hatred and hope and . . . I confess to Barry, "I'm so scared."

"Oh no, honey, we don't cry on prom night. Hey. Come here."

He slides toward me and raises an arm. I slip beneath it and remember all the times I sat like this with my dad—before. When I was little, and still perfect in his eyes. We'd sneak and watch scary movies. When it got to be too much, I'd hide my face against his shoulder and he'd tell me when it was safe to look again. God, I miss my dad, and how can I miss him when he threw me away?

"Talk to your auntie," he says. "What are you scared of? An unfortunate selection of evolutionary dead ends?"

That's good. If I can remember it, I'm going to steal it. I glance up at him and say, "They all hate me. They don't want me to be here tonight."

"Hey, look." And he waits for me to look. I feel like there

should be an orchestra warming up nearby, but he doesn't burst into song. Instead, he chucks my chin and says, "You know what? I didn't go to my own prom, because just like your mystery girlfriend, I was scared out of my Buster Browns."

I have no idea what those are, but I nod.

"But you? You're a queen. When you walk into that gym tonight, you know what your haters are going to see? The bravest person on the planet, and she's going to look fabulous in blue."

"Or pink," I say, trying to joke. "Or green. It *is* a Gregg Barnes original."

"You bet your bottom dollar it is. Emma, honey. You're scared. Fine. Be scared. On the inside. On the outside, be the soft butch you were always meant to be. Life is not a dress rehearsal. You're afraid they're going to look at you? I say, *Good! Look! Take it all in!*"

"I'm not sure—"

Barry presses a finger to my lips. "Shhh. You wanted this. You fought for this. And you're going to walk in there and make it clear that tonight belongs to *you*. This *school* belongs to you."

I start to shake my head, but then I realize: he's right. I fought this fight. I won this battle. I could have walked away—I wanted to so many times. It would have been easier. Looking away is painful, but it's easy. Absorbing hurt instead of pushing back against it—painful, but easy.

Right now, everybody at James Madison High knows my name. They know my power. Broadway literally came to Indiana to stand at my side. I'm not alone. And I'm about to have the night of my life.

"You're right," I finally say.

Barry fans himself with one hand. "My favorite words."

I barely have time to laugh before the limo stops. My snakes turn into butterflies—big, beautiful butterflies soaring and flying and defying gravity. Barry holds me back when I go to open the door. "Oh, girl, you have so much to learn."

Then, when the chauffeur opens the door for us, Dee Dee takes his hand and glides to her feet. She's decked out in gold leopard print, from head to toe, and I think I just heard her purr.

The chauffeur releases her and reaches back for my hand. I take it and haul myself onto the sidewalk as gracefully as I can manage. A breeze whips up my skirt, and I clutch it in a panic.

Behind me, Barry . . . well, he slinks out of the limo. There's no other word for it. He's instant diva, and it's a little disconcerting. He's been so godmothery that it never occurred to me that he might flirt with someone. For real. After an over-appreciative look at the chauffeur, Barry says in a brand-new baritone, "Thank you, darling."

"You're welcome, sir," the chauffeur says, and he looks back! He glances at Barry's face, and then . . . Barry's cummerbund. That was not a hallucination; he totally checked Barry out! The gaybies are blooming in Indiana!

I'm pretty sure I hear Dee Dee mutter, "Bitch," at Barry.

In return, Barry cheerfully murmurs, "Harridan."

Maybe tomorrow, after the ball, I'll ask Barry and Dee Dee if they're actually friends. But that's tomorrow, and I'm gazing in wonder at tonight. Balloons bob from the lampposts, and the lights flooding from the school seem enchanted. There's a glow in the air; the clouds are low, and they reflect the golden brightness beneath them. The sky is like silk, washing in elegant swirls overhead. The air is cold and crisp. It's like a sudden kiss in the dark, and boy howdy, in this dress, I feel it everywhere.

A heavy bassline thumps through the concrete block walls, reverberating all the way out here. I can't make out the song, but I don't care. It's prom night. It's finally here.

"May I?" Barry asks, offering his elbow.

"I'd be delighted," I say, taking it.

We walk up to the school together, Dee Dee outpacing us easily. The front doors are pushed open. I go here every day, but it's different tonight. Bright and buzzy and . . . really weirdly empty. Everyone's probably already in the gym. We're supposed to stay in the gym during dances—no wandering the halls.

Allegedly, some guy named Winston McCarthy discovered the access tunnels under the school and ran an extremely (from what I hear) profitable casino down there. It lasted three whole semesters before he got caught. What a legend. It's a shame he doesn't have a trophy of his own in the Hall of Champions. Instead, he lives on in oral tradition, like all good folk heroes should.

"Where are we meeting your inamorata?" Barry asks.

"Inside," I say. I'm strangling her bouquet. I'm afraid if I loosen my grip I might drop them. I'm about to see her face; we're about to show the world we're in love. Tonight, everything changes. Every step toward the gym feels like a step toward destiny.

We're about to open the doors of the gym when I hear

Principal Hawkins shouting from behind. "Emma! Wait!" He's jogging down the hall toward us.

We turn, and to my horror (and delight, lbr), Barry whistles under his breath at him. I mean, Principal Hawkins looks really distinguished in a tux, so if I were into super old humans and also guys, I might whistle, too. Instead, I smile and call back, "Principal Hawkins!"

Except . . . he's not smiling.

And he's not alone. Nan is doing the scary speed walk she usually reserves for Black Friday sales. Her grim expression sends a wave of fear through me. I clutch Barry's arm a little tighter. "What's going on?"

"I tried to catch you before you left home," Principal Hawkins says when he catches up. He's not breathless; he just sounds broken. "Emma, I'm so sorry."

Alyssa's not coming. Of course she'd be responsible enough to leave a message with a trusted figure of authority. Of course she'd be too afraid to tell me herself. All the snaky butterflies inside me turn to ash. I have a prom, but I don't have a date.

Dee Dee's voice explodes behind us, filling the air. "What have they done?!"

Barry and I turn at the same time. Dee Dee throws herself in front of Nan so she can get to me first. She grabs my shoulders and drags me to her chest. Her comforting pats are like ninja death slices, all up and down my back. She keens, her voice echoing down the hall. "How could they? How *dare* they?"

Pulling myself free, I look at all of them. "How could they what?"

Dee Dee's hesitation is the flicker of an eyelash.

Previously, I've mentioned that I'm not particularly athletic, but when the world grinds to a halt, it turns out I move pretty fast.

I burst past Dee Dee and run into the gym. It's decorated with glittery moons and tinfoil stars overhead, with indigo streamers and flickering white lights. There's a table with punch and cookies, and a photo booth with a box full of props like top hats and boas.

The stage is hung with silver streamers, but the DJ isn't a DJ. It's an iPod in a Bluetooth dock, blasting out somebody's personal prom playlist. The floor is empty. The seats are empty. The gym is empty.

I've never wanted more to faint in my life than I do right now. But I'm not that girl, apparently. I'm the girl who keeps on standing, no matter how hard you hit her. I absorb those blows. I take those hits. The flowers slip from my hand, dropping to the glossy hardwood with a plaintive sigh.

The adults press in behind me. I hear their voices; I feel their presence. But it doesn't matter what they're saying. I thought I had imagined the worst possible scenario: that Alyssa wouldn't show. I'd even prepared for it, a tiny little bit.

But this.

Who could have imagined anything like this?

"Pictures started showing up on social media about a half an hour ago," Principal Hawkins says, from far, far away. "And I have a text from the PTA. They say they did their due diligence. They threw an inclusive prom for Emma. It's not their fault if their children chose to attend a private dance at the Elks Club instead."

He said the message came from the PTA. But the PTA can't text; it's an organization, like the Klan or the Kardashians. No. That text came from Mrs. Greene, and that means she plotted this. Planned it. Executed it like a crime boss.

But I don't understand, because I have texts from Alyssa. She's been texting me, like, all day. Talking about her crazy mom, and last-minute crazy, and crazycrazycrazy. Texts that stopped . . . about an hour ago.

They planned this. Mrs. Greene planned this. Shelby and Kaylee and Nick and Kevin and everybody else in school *planned* this!

Flattened, Barry says, "I think I'm going to cry. They went behind her back? The whole *town* kept this from her?"

"How could they do this to us?" Dee Dee wails. "This was supposed to be an easy win! God, somebody wake me from this PR nightmare!"

Nan rounds on Dee Dee. "Excuse me, easy win?"

Principal Hawkins turns on her, too. "Wait. Is that why you came here? For the publicity?"

I look to Barry. Barry in his tux. Barry who brought me dresses I didn't even want. Auntie Barry, Barry who swears he knows just what this is like. Sympathetic, sweet-talking Barry.

Numb, I say, "I'm just a publicity stunt for you?"

"This is what we're going to do," Barry says, ignoring my question. His face is pink, and his brow is starting to shine. "We're getting right back in that limo, and we're going to that other prom, and we are going to—"

"Stop it! Just stop!"

I shout it above the noise of the iPod DJ, above the sound

of Barry's and Dee Dee's egos. This was never about me. Not for them. Principal Hawkins was just thrilled I wasn't on meth. Nan fought the fight because I asked her to; I guess I never asked if she thought I *should*. And Alyssa . . . no. I can't even think her name right now.

Barry reaches out. "Emma . . ."

I shove his hand away. "I don't want any more help, okay? Go ahead and go to the other prom, Mr. Pecker. I'm sure you'll have no trouble getting in!"

And then I walk away. I don't even try to run. I walk, with my big dinosaur bones, and my big monster feet, in this stupid monster dress I never wanted to wear, right out of James Madison High.

Maybe for good.

16. The Nicest Kids in Town

ALYSSA

"Where are we?" I ask when the limo stops.

I have to ask that, because this isn't James Madison, therefore, this can't be prom. My thoughts spin like mad, trying to make sense of this.

Mom said something about *one* of my surprises. I assumed that a ride with people who haven't really been my friends since third grade was enough surprise to last a lifetime. But no, now we're at an undisclosed location.

Nobody answers me. Instead, Kaylee holds out her phone and goes cheek to cheek with Shelby. They hold up peace signs, trying to look as cute as possible before the flash goes off, and then Kaylee instantly pulls up the snap. Present-moment Kaylee smiles at digital, two-seconds-ago Kaylee.

"I hate to sound conceited," Kaylee says disingenuously, "but even I would do me."

"I'd do you, too," Shelby chimes in. Then she instantly amends, "No homo."

It will come as no surprise if I tell you that Nick and Kevin agree with all levels of hotness proposed by the girls who were very recently semi-permanent residents of their laps.

The guys spill out of the limo, leaving the three of us to see ourselves out. Once we do, it's pretty clear we're all glowing under the light of the Elks Club sign.

All around us, people stream toward the doors. Each time they open, a blast of music escapes. Laughter drifts around us, excited squeals punctuated by the bright pop of phones on selfie sticks.

I put a hand out, holding Kaylee back on the sidewalk. "I'm not kidding, what's going on?"

"Look," Kaylee says, her voice a cauldron of pure, unadulterated nasty-nice, "realize that we're doing you a favor and say thank you, Alyssa."

"It's okay that you don't care about being popular, but we're saving you from yourself." Shelby nods, and her dangling earrings swing like pendulums. They catch the light: bright, then dark, almost hypnotic.

Leaning in, Kaylee whispers, "We know about you and Emma."

Her words punch through me, knocking the breath from my lungs.

"You don't want to be a messiah," Shelby adds.

Jaw dropped, I hear myself correcting Shelby instead of processing what they've just said. "You mean *pariah*."

Cheerfully, Shelby links arms with Kaylee and shrugs. "Whatever. It's prom. It's our night. Let's go and have fun!"

"No, wait," I say sharply, staying them with a hand. "What do you mean you know?"

Kaylee rolls her eyes. Her thick, spider-leg lashes flutter as she shakes her head. "Anna Kendrick and John Cho? Two mysterious dates from other schools, one for the town lesbo and one for the student council president who thinks she's subtle when she holds her hand in public? I mean, come on."

"Plus, you're always standing up for her," Shelby notes casually. "And you let those weirdos from New York come to our meeting. It's kind of obvious."

"Why didn't you say anything?" I ask, feeling faint and slightly sick.

Annoyed, Kaylee chooses her words carefully and speaks them very slowly. "Because we didn't want your mom to cancel prom, dummy."

"Yay prom!" Shelby says, throwing a victory hand to the sky. "Come on, it's starting, let's go!"

Cocooned in a numb haze, I go along as Kaylee and Shelby manage to hustle me inside. All this time with Emma, I've been careful; we've been *so* careful. Kaylee and Shelby aren't idiots, but they're the most self-absorbed people I know—and *they* caught on? My heart slips between beats and my ears ring as we walk inside.

Red and gold cover everything. Cardboard genie lamps hang from the ceiling. Big loops of red gauze ring the tables. Little paper camels scatter across the refreshment table. They graze among gold plastic cups and red paper plates, next to a massive plastic bowl full of jewel-red punch. Even the picture station is a vaguely Middle Eastern tent with a banner over it that says: 1,001 NIGHTS.

I'm mortified, especially when I see some of the basketball

team wearing turbans. This is not the prom we've been planning since Christmas. This is some racist monstrosity, pulled from an alternate universe.

And Emma is nowhere to be found. I reach for my phone and realize that I don't have it. It's still on Joan's station at the salon. Kaylee and Shelby peeled away as soon as we hit the door, which leaves me alone to search for Emma.

It feels like a funhouse in here, red lights pulsing across familiar faces, the shadows distorting them. The laughter is too loud, and it vibrates on a frequency that goes straight down my spine. No one's touching me, but I feel pushed and pulled and shoved, fighting through the haze of a smoke machine and the sharp daggers of lights that flash on the floor.

I search everywhere: the dance floor, the bathrooms, even the kitchenette, where PTA moms are shoveling sherbert into a backup punch bowl at breakneck speed.

Breathless and panicked, I duck back into the main room. Leaning against the wall for support, I squint and stare, scanning the crowd over and over, hoping to see one face, *that* face.

None of this makes sense. This time yesterday, I was still helping set up the gym for A Night to Remember. My mother mentioned nothing about a change of venue; she was way more interested in waterproof tablecloths and signing off on the DJ's playlist. I don't understand when all of this could have happened.

Somehow, over the roar of the crowd, I hear my mother's voice behind me. She must have gone in the side door and straight to the kitchen. When I turn to walk back inside, she fills the door. The worst, most devastating thing is, she looks *happy*. Like, genuinely happy, in a way I haven't seen since before Dad left.

"What do you think?" she asks, waving a hand at the Arabian Nights around us.

"I think I'm confused, Mother," I say. "Why did you move prom? *When* did you move it?"

"At the last minute. There was a problem that had to be dealt with."

Well, no wonder she's been on her phone all day. I'm afraid to ask when she started planning this move and how apparently everybody knew but me. Was it this morning? Last night? Suddenly, heavy lead melts into my feet, pulling me down. I feel so weighted that I could drop right through the floor. Did she decide to do this the night of the public meeting? When I pushed? *Because* I pushed?

Wait.

I look around again, and a needle of ice threads through my heart. New place, secret location, a problem to be dealt with. It's agonizing to take a breath, but I have to. I have to open my mouth, and I have to ask.

"Mom, where's Emma Nolan?"

My mother laughs lightly, without a hint of steel beneath it. "I'm quite sure she's at her inclusive prom, Alyssa."

"Mom, you didn't . . ."

"I don't like it when strangers presume to come to our community and tell us how to live. Our rules were a problem? Fine, fixing little problems is what I do. And now everyone is happy. She has a prom, and we have our prom."

Stunned, I don't know what to say. I had no idea my mother

could be this cruel. Smoothing her hands down my arms, Mom looks me over again, her smile widening until it's almost maniacal. "I wasn't going to let you miss a night like this, Alyssa. This is for you. I did this all for you."

"This is not—"

She interrupts me. "Now, you go have fun. I'll be here to make sure everything is perfect."

I back away from her, because I don't know this woman. This calculating, manipulative person masquerading as my mother is terrifying. She stepped right out of *Game of Thrones* and into *Game of Proms*. And she won.

I have to get away from Elena Lannister Greene. If I look at her for one more second, I'm honestly afraid I might throw up.

When I whip around, I stumble onto the dance floor, into the throng. Since I can't turn back, I have to wade through a sea of people having the times of their lives. Bodies crash all around me. The music, the voices, they fill my head until they beat against my eardrums to get out. Everything swirls and melts together like a nightmare; I wish I could wake up. I'm not even sure where I'm going—all I know is *away, away*.

Kaylee grabs my arm and jolts me back to the present. "We need to get our picture taken together."

"No. I can't. I have to go—"

"You're part of the prom court, Alyssa. Don't make me get ugly."

My mother really has arranged everything. I can't get away. I can't call for help. I can't even warn Emma. The urge to vomit lurches back up. I clap a hand over my mouth, just in case, and that's all Kaylee needs to drag me off balance and over to the photo booth. The photographer crams me in the middle, with the couples on either side.

She tells them to smile, they say cheese, and a single tear streaks down my cheek.

17. Step Out of the Sun

EMMA

The good thing about your entire life imploding is that people stop questioning your poor choices. I've worn the same pair of pajamas for two days now, and I'm on a strict diet of melted ice cream and chocolate Teddy Grahams.

Today was supposed to be my first day back at school since . . . well, you know. When Nan looked in on me this morning, I didn't even move from my perfect, lumpen position in bed.

"I'm not going," I said.

She closed the door quietly and said nothing.

I know that Barry and Dee Dee have been at the house. It's impossible to miss the reaching-for-the-back-row quality of their voices. Thankfully, Nan keeps sending them away. It saves me the trouble of getting out of bed to find heavy objects to chuck at them.

When I got home from prom, I posted a one-minute video on Emma Sings because I knew people would ask how it went. Then I called Alyssa four thousand times and left four thousand voice mails, in between googling Dee Dee Allen and Barry Glickman. Guess what I found out!

No, don't guess. I'll tell you.

Right before they showed up in Indiana, their new musical bombed. It bombed hard. It bombed so hard, even people in New Jersey hated it. I don't know how long a play is supposed to be on Broadway, but I'm guessing that closing after one night is *bad*.

So, their careers took a header and they picked me as the poster child for their image-rehabilitation tour. Like, they did *interviews* about it—they did a photo shoot with the picket signs before they even left for Indiana.

In a way, I'm not surprised that Dee Dee wanted to use me. Honestly, I wouldn't be surprised if she ate little baby harp seals for breakfast and washed them down with melted polar-ice-cap water—zazz!—but Barry's betrayal exposed a nerve.

I can't believe how stupidly, how easily I trusted him. I can't believe I didn't realize that none of that was for me. Or even *about* me. How could I have been so naive?

Oh, did Alyssa ever call back? Glad you asked, friend. She did not. But there *are* pictures of her reigning in the shadow prom court with Kaylee and Shelby. They all have tiaras, isn't that cute?

Because I'm all about the pain, I scrolled through the #jmprom19 tag for a while. Real prom looked like it was banging, one of those clubs with the velvet rope and very selective guest list. Picture after picture, I studied the details. Memorized the faces. Made a mental inventory with a neat little tab at the top: enemies.

And picture after picture, I searched for signs of Alyssa in them. I only found a couple, mostly with the gruesome twosome. But! There was one super adorable mommy-daughter picture from the photo booth.

Mrs. Greene was auditioning to play the Joker in hers, her lips a slash of scarlet lipstick and her mouth full of hundreds of big white teeth. Alyssa's smile was more pained, but it was there.

Yep. She still had a smile left in her. At the absolute worst moment of my high school career, my girlfriend smiled for the official photographer of James Madison High's actual real prom for actually real people.

I tortured myself with that for a while, screenshotting the pictures and arranging them in their own album. Back and forth, just looking at Alyssa. Analyzing her face. I mean, I've been studying it for years, and I can tell she's not having the time of her life. But I can also tell that she's at the *secret prom she didn't tell me about*.

After a while, I turned off my phone and threw it at the pile of laundry in the corner of my room. And there it remains. Hence the Nan alarm clock and the engulfing silence in my room. It's good. It gives me a chance to sleep. Sleep and I go way back; a growing girl totally needs eighteen or more hours a day of unconsciousness, right? Bring on the dreamless dark; I'll just Rip Van Winkle my way through graduation and summer break.

Except, I've slept so much the past couple of days that my back kind of aches, and I'm not tired at all. Instead, all the squirrels in my brain got into some caffeine, and my mind lurches from dead stop to top speed.

It kicks in with all the things I've been trying not to consider, like what the hell is wrong with me that this stuff keeps happening? Was I a serial killer in my past life and that's why this one sucks? Am I atoning for metaphysical mistakes? Or am I just cursed in this one? Maybe I ate some witch's radishes and cabbages when I was a toddler.

This is stupid.

I roll out of bed and onto my feet. If I'm going to hate myself, my life, and everyone in it, I'm gonna need more ice cream. Pulling a robe over my pajamas, I studiously ignore the mirror. Y'all, I'm experiencing the sensation of my hair sticking up in a giant wing on one side and being matted flat on the other. I don't need visual confirmation.

My palms itch as I pass the pile of clothes where I threw my phone. My brain tells me to keep walking, there's Rocky Road waiting in the kitchen. But my stupid, stupid heart wants to see if Alyssa ever replied. I stare at the pile for a second, debating what to do, but I already know what I'm going to do.

I plunge my hand into a tangle of inside-out jeans and snatch my phone; I'm a bear in a salmon stream. First try, and I got it. A wide streak of nausea breaks through the numbness as I wait for my phone to turn back on.

When it finally boots, it makes one chirpy text sound, and then it blows up. Text notifications scroll like it's the latest Star Wars movie. YouTube sent me a ton of notifications, too. Oh, and voice mails—eight of those.

Before I can start my deep dive, the phone rings. I yelp in surprise and almost throw it across the room. The ID flashes on the screen. Alyssa. Just seeing her name is a punch in the gut, and I consider rejecting the call. But my stupid, stupid thumb touches the green icon and I say, "Hello?"

"Emma," Alyssa says. Her voice is hoarse; it sounds like she might have been crying. "Are you there?"

Sinking into my laundry pile, I struggle to speak. Finally, I manage, "Yeah, it's me."

"Oh my god, are you all right??"

I laugh. Seriously, I laugh. Is that a real question? "No, I'm great. I'm fantastic. I mean, sure, my girlfriend went to a secret prom with people she swears she can't stand and left me hanging at A Ghost Town to Remember by myself, but it's fine. It's all fine. I'm *so* fine."

"I'm so sorry, Emma," Alyssa warbles. "I swear, I had no idea."

Oh good. Anger just showed up to the party. I like anger. It's nice and clean and specific. "How could you not know? Your mother was the host; you were on prom committee!"

With a sniffle, Alyssa says, "They hid it from me. And then Kaylee and Shelby dropped a bomb on me. They figured out that we're together, and they wanted to make sure prom happened. The whole PTA was planning behind my back."

"I don't believe you."

Shock crackles on the line. "Do you really think I would do something like this to you?"

"I don't think," I shout. "It happened. I saw the pictures. Nice tiara, by the way."

Alyssa pleads, but it's laced with irritation. "What is it going to take to prove it to you? Because I didn't know. My mother stalked me the whole night. I didn't have my phone, and I couldn't sneak out, and I'm so, so sorry, Emma, but I didn't know they were going to do this to you. I've been shaking and crying for two days."

"Well, that makes two of us."

"Please, Emma. Please."

"Fine," I say, because this hurts. It feels like an axe to the chest, splitting me right down the middle. Hearing Alyssa cry makes me want to comfort her. But knowing why she's crying makes me want to scream. "Come see me. Tell me face-to-face, so I can look in your eyes."

"I can't."

Ha. I ask for one thing, and it's already a no. Thumping my head back against the wall, I ask, "You can't, or you won't?"

Lowering her voice, Alyssa says, "My mom is here. I think she knows, and she's doing everything she can to *not* know. She's watching me every second."

Everything she just said is a slap in the face. All of this fighting, all of this negotiating for months about prom, and whether we'd go together, whether we'd tell people, and . . . she thinks her mom already knows? I can't hide my frustration. If my hair weren't so greasy, I'd pull it.

"Oh my god, Alyssa, if you think she knows, just tell her! Tell her we're in love! That was the plan, right?"

"I can't," she says, plaintive and small. "It's bad enough that Kaylee and Shelby know."

Oh. Oh wow. My anger keys up to white hot, so hot I barely feel it anymore. I have so much heat, I could punch through the atmosphere. I could boil oceans and scorch the earth.

She's been using her mom as the reason she can't come out

for months, and suddenly I realize, it's not a reason. It's an *excuse*. Yeah, her mom is obviously a bigot and a homophobe, but it looks like Alyssa's carrying some of that on her own.

Slowly, I repeat, "*Bad* enough?"

"That's not what I mean."

"And yet, that's exactly what you said," I snap.

"Emma, I'm sorry."

What is she apologizing for, exactly? The wrong words? Or for the way she really feels about us? It doesn't matter. I'm out of bandwidth. I can't fake cheerful, but bitter works. "Okay, great. That fixes everything. Thanks for calling!"

Then I hang up. I hang up on Alyssa Greene, the girl at the church picnic, my first love, my first kiss, my first everything. So true, on so many levels, because she was my first real secret, too. She was the longest lie I ever told. I wanted her to be happy; I didn't want her to lose everything like I did.

We're so freaking close to college. She's so close to being free from her mom and her mom's neuroses, and I thought, I really thought that this time, she'd come out and we'd be together, for real, no more hiding.

But all this time, I thought her mom was the only thing holding her back. Her family. Truly, I believed that until fifteen seconds ago when she said it was *bad enough* that Kaylee and Shelby knew.

Now Alyssa Greene's my first heartbreak, and I think I'm going to die of it.

18. Five Hundred Twenty-Five Thousand Six Hundred Minutes

ALYSSA

I have watched the video Emma put up on prom night a thousand times.

"This is how it went," Emma tells the camera, combing her fingers through her hair. There are still hints of makeup on her face, but she's already changed into a T-shirt. Specifically, a T-shirt that reads: BEHOLD THE FIELD IN WHICH I GROW MY F*CKS, LAY THINE EYES UPON IT AND SEE THAT IT IS BARREN.

Adjusting the laptop screen, she gazes down into its glow. "Well, it didn't. I mean, yeah, the gym was decorated and there was music playing, but I was the only one there. It turns out, I was the only one who wanted to go to the inclusive prom. Everybody else, including—no, let's just say everybody else—went to the secret, *not*-inclusive prom. But hey, at least I got to take all these cool pictures for my Insta story!"

And then there's this brief, awful slideshow that she set to the sad angel song from the dog commercial—pictures of the gym, empty. Of the chairs and tables, empty. Of the stage, empty. Of party favors and punch bowls untouched. The screen goes black, and this glittery font swirls across the screen: *Happy Prom Night!*

It's short, and Emma's wrecked. I keep watching it because I'm hoping that . . . I don't know. That the past will change? That the hurt will fade? That somehow it might end differently? I don't know what I hope, but I hate that I see her heart break in real time.

But I'm glad she didn't come to school today. Everybody's talking about her video, and it's really weird. Some people are mad she won't drop the issue; others have started to feel guilty. But all of them are obsessed with the number of views she's getting and the semi-famous people who've shared the link—I'm pretty sure anyone who's written a young adult novel in the last three years has tweeted about it, as have tons of Broadway people . . . and plenty of journalists.

Which is why Principal Hawkins completely changed our end-of-day routine. We're not allowed to go out the front doors like usual. We're exiting directly into the student parking lot through the gym doors and going straight to our cars or buses.

A fleet of reporters showed up just after lunch and set up in the front lot. They have cameras and glossy-haired reporters with microphones, and we've been told explicitly that we're not allowed to talk to any of them without a parent present.

Breanna Lo touches me on the shoulder. When I turn around, she's holding up her iPhone. "I'm doing an episode of my podcast about the promtroversy, can I get a quote?"

"It was unkind and unfair, and it never should have been an issue to begin with."

"Love it," Breanna says. She scrolls on her screen, then asks,

"And just for the record, we're speaking to Alyssa Greene, our student council president. Alyssa, can you tell us which prom you attended?"

My tongue fills my mouth, and I shake my head. I should have listened to Principal Hawkins—no talking to reporters of any kind.

With as much grace as I can manage, I bail on Breanna and duck outside to get to my car. Even though we're not supposed to be filmed, plenty of people are dragging themselves past the cameras, just casually making sure they'll be seen.

Mr. Thu comes out and starts to hurry people along, but there's only so much narcissism he can tamp down on his own. I try to keep my head lowered as I pull out of the school lot. But as I turn toward home, I catch a glimpse of a car that looks just like—no, it *is* my mother's.

Craning around, I'm shattered with cold when I see her standing in the field across from the school, holding her coat closed and talking to a news crew from Indianapolis. Oh god, what is she saying now? Why can't she just leave this alone?

I look back at the road just in time to slam on my brakes. My whole body stiffens, and the shock pushes the breath out of my lugs. I almost hit the car in front of me. An accident, right in front of James Madison, is the last thing I need right now.

Traffic crawls into town. This is ridiculous; I'm going four miles an hour. At this rate, I'll get home next Thursday. I throw on my turn signal and pull into the Walmart parking lot. I don't need anything, but it's a good place to hang out. There are tables out front, and the Coke machines are cheap.

When I pull in, it's obvious I'm not the only person who had this idea. A bunch of the guys from the basketball team are slow-rolling their pickups past the entrance, leaning out of windows to holler at the girls at the table. It's what this place looks like on a Friday night, except it's full daylight and we're all in our school clothes.

"Heyyy, Alyssa," Shelby calls as I walk up.

Kaylee gives me a little finger wave. "Come sit, queen."

Inside, I feel hesitation, but my legs carry me right over. I don't want to sit with them. I don't even want to look at them, and yet somehow, my mother has reengineered my life. I'm back in elementary school, when she picked my clothes and my friends and dictated everything about my day. I'm a leaf in the wind, helpless to choose my direction, at the mercy of outside forces.

"Did you know our school is on CNN?" Kaylee says, turning to let one of her sub-minions braid her hair.

"What?" I say flatly.

"Yeah, the home page." She makes a sour face, then quotes the headline. "'Edgewater, Indiana, overflows with bigotry.' Like, seriously? They're acting like we're monsters."

Shelby bobs her head like a good hench-cheerleader. "Seriously. We gave her a prom, god."

I start to say something—I'm not even sure what—but there's a quiet roar that runs through the people collected on the tables. Suddenly, someone shouts, "It's Mr. Pecker!"

We all crane our necks, and then more people call out. It's a hailstorm of *Pecker!*s, and I can't believe that Mr. Glickman is walking out of the Walmart with a little bag clutched in his hands. I didn't realize he was still in town; I assumed he and Ms. Allen packed up after prom night and headed back to New York City.

"Say it!" Shelby yells, cupping her hands around her mouth to amplify it.

Nick and Kevin bound out of the bed of a pickup to join us, and they chant it, too. "Say it! Say it!"

Mr. Glickman takes a deep breath and rolls his eyes. Without much enthusiasm, he spits out Mr. Pecker's signature phrase from *Talk to the Hand*. "It's Pecker time."

Everybody roars and cheers. Kaylee nudges Shelby, pressing quarters into her hand. "Can we get you something to drink, Mr. Pecker?"

He wraps a hand around his throat. "This . . . is a finely tuned instrument. I will not insult it with"—he takes a look at the cans on the table—"Diet Mountain Lightning."

Nostrils curling, Kaylee rolls a shoulder. "Fine, then."

Mr. Glickman takes a few steps like he's leaving. Then he spins on his toe, coming back around to face us. It looks kind of practiced, but to be fair, everything Ms. Allen and Mr. Glickman do looks rehearsed. "You know, I think I've been unfair. Coming to your charming little hamlet, making demands."

"You made my mom cry rage tears," Shelby volunteers.

Mr. Glickman puts a hand to his chest. "Oh no, did I? How?"

Shelby waves a hand around, "You know. Trying to make our prom all gay."

"I see, I see, I see," Mr. Glickman says. He doesn't catch my eye—he probably doesn't even remember who I am. But his gaze seems to slide past me. Which is good, because I was right—this isn't entirely spontaneous.

I have a feeling he's about to make an argument he's made before—a performance pretending to be a conversation. This is exactly the way I talk to people who want the student council to make 4/20 a school holiday, or Domino's the official sponsor of our cafeteria.

Kaylee leans back on the table and eyes him. "So, are you sorry?"

"Exquisitely apologetic," Mr. Glickman says. "Do you object to me?"

"Nah," Nick says with a laugh. "You're Mr. Pecker!"

"Then could one of you darling little urchins explain to me why you didn't want Emma at your prom?"

"Because, you know, it's wrong." Kevin says this like it's the most obvious answer in the world. Then, to bolster his case, he says, "It's in the Bible."

"And we believe in the Bible." Shelby nods and nestles down beneath Kevin's arm. Kevin stretches out his arm around Shelby's back and subtly tugs on the cup of her bra. She giggles but doesn't shoo him away. Charming.

Mr. Glickman surveys them slowly. "I see. It's in the Bible, and you're true believers. If that's the case, aren't you afraid?"

"Of what?" Nick asks.

Ohhhh yeah. Here we go. I see where this is going now, and it surprises me that they don't. Well, no, I guess it doesn't surprise me.

We all have Bibles with white leather covers, presents for graduating from Sunday school to Youth Celebration! But we're not exactly encouraged to read from beginning to end.

We have discussion guides that focus on certain stories, that tell us how we should feel and think about said certain stories. Usually, they're parables and miracles, occasionally inspirational women or acts of faith. It's not a deep dive by any stretch of the imagination.

Gracefully, Mr. Glickman slides to sit on the bench. With a wave of his hand, he gestures at Kaylee's foot. "Well, I see that this lovely young woman has a charming dolphin tattoo on her ankle."

Kaylee warms back up, now that the topic of conversation has turned back to her favorite subject. "Spring break, last year. The guy said I had the best ankles he'd ever inked."

"I bet he did," Mr. Glickman says agreeably. "Too bad you're going to Hell for it."

"Excuse me?" Kaylee yelps.

"Well, it's in the Bible."

Setting her face in a scowl, Kaylee says, "No it's not."

"'Ye shall not print any marks upon you,'" Mr. Glickman says. "Look it up, it's in Leviticus."

Kaylee whips out her phone. She doesn't even have to google it; she has a Bible app right there on the home screen. It's visible the very second she finds the passage in question. Some of the fire goes out of her—more because she's wrong than because she's really worried about going to Hell, would be my guess. She slaps her phone facedown and says, "That doesn't count."

"So, you can pick and choose?" Mr. Glickman asks. He doesn't let her answer, though. He rolls his head to look at

Kevin. "Because let me guess, sir. You see plenty of action."

"I get mine," Kevin says, pulling on his varsity jacket, and Shelby giggles against him again.

"Well, then that means everyone at your church gets to throw rocks at your precious, precious head until you *die*."

Shelby looks distressed. "Nooooooo. Not my Kevin's head!"

"There's no way that's in the Bible," Kevin says, because he obviously didn't learn his lesson from Kaylee looking up a verse not two seconds ago. And, since she's not about to be the only one who gets shamed this day, she helpfully does just that.

Flashing her phone at Kevin and Shelby, Kaylee says, "Ope, sorry, guys. You're getting stoned, and not the fun way."

With a snort, Nick points at Shelby and Kevin. And then, out loud, he literally says, "Ha ha!"

"Don't think you're out of the woods, young man," Mr. Glickman tells Nick. "If I'm not mistaken, that's a polyester jacket and those are denim blue jeans. To Hell with you for wearing two kinds of cloth!"

I press my lips together and watch as they look it up, as everyone else around us starts to murmur.

"Who loves beefy nachos supreme?" Mr. Glickman asks, and then announces gleefully at the hands that go up, "Hell for you, and you, and you! Don't you know the Bible says you can't mix meat and milk in the same meal?"

The murmurs grow a little louder. Other people have pulled out their phones to fact-check this. They skim through, and I hear pop-up whispers around me. Milo from the FCK curses under his breath because he found a rule about planting two kinds of crops in one field; someone else is baffled by *tearing your clothes*. This is probably the closest any of us have read the Bible in our lives . . . and I think it might be working?

"This is a lot of rules," Shelby says quietly.

Kevin adds, "I didn't know any of this was in here."

While I marvel at the sudden change at the table, Mr. Glickman stands up, smoothing hands down the front of his suit. "There's one more thing in there you should look at. You should know that I have played Jesus Christ on three separate occasions, in *Superstar*, in *Godspell*, and in my shiksa aunt Dorothy's living nativity. And do you know what I've taken away from it?"

Since no one else says it, I volunteer. "What, Mr. Glickman?"

"First, it takes a Jew to play the messiah with authority," he says, gesturing at himself extravagantly. "And second, when asked which law was the most important, the man himself said that *love thy neighbor* was the only rule he cared about."

Fingers fly across screens, now searching for that phrase. Heads bob all around, and eyes raise to Mr. Glickman. Fighting back a smile, I watch as he plays my classmates like fiddles.

He says, gently, "And if you ask me, I don't think anybody showed Miss Emma much love on prom night."

Kaylee frowns. "Stop trying to get into our heads."

"I mean," Shelby says, "he's not wrong. We used to hang out with her."

"Before she turned gay!"

"If she turned, that implies she had no choice." Mr. Glickman shrugs expansively, as if to say, *I don't make the rules.*

"And if she had no choice, doesn't that mean God made her that way?"

"That's not how it works."

Mr. Glickman turns his gaze to Shelby. "Oh no? When did you choose to be straight?"

"Never," Shelby says. "I just am."

Mr. Glickman is silent for a minute, watching Shelby's face until understanding finally dawns on her. With a little bow of his head, Mr. Glickman spreads his hands. His point is made. Then he stands up and gathers his purchases. The thin plastic of the bag reveals a box of Throat Coat tea and a *People* magazine.

"I must be off," Mr. Glickman says warmly. "But say it with me, once more?"

And then the Walmart parking lot fills with dozens of voices, all crying out at once:

"It's Pecker time!"

19. Their Voices Soft as Thunder

EMMA

When I emerge from my misery cocoon with my laptop, Nan scrambles to turn off the television.

"Subtle," I say as I sit beside her on the couch. Pushing the screen back so she can see, I tell her, "I know it's on the news."

In fact, that's why I came out at all. I finally decided to look at the comments on my prom night video and found that my story went viral. Or at least, the version of the story people can piece together from my video and all the interviews outside the school went viral. Shockingly, except for angry tweets that night, Barry and Dee Dee have been silent.

Nan puts an arm around me and rests her chin on my shoulder. "I'm sorry you have to bear all this, Emma."

Leaning into her, I say, "Yeah, me too. It sucks. And it's not just me, you know? Listen to some of these comments."

I load my channel again, hitting pause on the video. It's not like I need to hear myself explain what happened on prom night again. Instead, I scroll to the comments—and yeah, there are some jerkwads and douche canoes dropping their turds of wisdom. But most of the responses are from kids like me. All over Indiana and the Midwest. Hell, all over the country.

Safe beneath the curve of my grandmother's arm, I start to read. "This girl's from Muncie. She says she was allowed to take her girlfriend to the prom, but they kicked her out because she wore a tux. And this transboy from Seymour actually got the most votes for prom king, but the school wouldn't give it to him. There are, like, six comments from people who said their teachers refuse to use their proper pronouns. Here's a bisexual girl in South Bend who got suspended for wearing a rainbow-flag pin. Nan, it's everywhere. They hate us everywhere."

With a soft sigh, Nan hugs me to her side. "Some of them are scared. And some are ignorant. And yes, some of them are full of hate. We can do something about the first two-thirds, and the ones left over, we leave to God to sort out."

An overwhelming wave of despair crashes over me. Is this going to be my whole life? Constantly explaining myself to the ignorant, always trying to convince people that I'm about as scary as rice pudding, and learning to run and hide from the ones with teeth and claws? This is my forever? I'm suddenly exhausted again.

We're told to hide this beautiful part of ourselves, the falling-in-love part, the dizzy infatuation part. Don't hold hands in your Uber; don't kiss at the movies. Think hard about whether you want to correct a stranger when they ask about your significant other and get the gender wrong. Carefully consider everything you say so these strangers don't spit on you—or worse.

Nan is the one person in my life who can almost read my mind. She shakes me and leans around to make me look in her eyes. "I won't tell you this isn't a trial. But I will tell you this is not the end."

I start to cry. Nan sets my laptop aside so she can wrap both her arms around me. And I just bawl, because the numbness has faded and everything that's left is agony. I don't want to be a news story; I don't want to be a cause. All I wanted was a dance. One night. Barely anything, and I couldn't even have that.

Somewhere, in this same town, my parents are probably watching the news. And they're probably *happy*. Oh, they might pretend to feel bad for me, but it would be in their twisted way. *What a terrible way for Emma to learn the wages of her sin. Maybe this will make her change her mind and her behavior. Maybe she'll repent and we can welcome her home.*

I swear, I didn't come out of my room to cry. I wanted to share the comments on my video. If Nan hadn't seen it, I wanted to show her the terrible things Mrs. Greene told Channel 13 in Indianapolis. Awful, just like the new rules were awful, because people like her have learned to use our words against us. They don't come right out and call us *fag*. Instead, they say things like:

"What happened here was not the result of an elaborate plan to humiliate this girl, as has been reported in the press. The James Madison High PTA felt that Emma would not be safe unless we offered the option of a separate prom for students and parents who objected. Unfortunately, there are people in our community who are offended by her lifestyle, and we felt this arrangement, while not ideal, was the only course of action available to us."

Leaving out the part that she's one of the people in the community, and that she couldn't care less if I'm safe or not. Totally ignoring the part where she's the one who stirred everyone up to begin with.

But it sounds good, doesn't it? It sounds *reasonable*. It sounds so much better than the truth. And it looks like, as long as people learn to lie the right way, they can get away with murder.

My sobs fade after a while, but my chest still hurts. With every single breath, I ache.

Nan proves her love for me once more by mopping up my slick, snotty face with a handful of napkins. Her touch is gentle, her palms warm. She takes my face in her hands and strokes my now-dry cheeks with her thumbs.

She had no idea this is where she would be in her old age, I'm sure. Raising me instead of tearing it up on the riverboat casinos in Rising Sun. Or, I don't know, spending winter in Florida, teaching snowbirds to play euchre so she could whip them at it. Instead, she's stuck here with me. Looking at her, I feel the urge to cry come back up again. I've made everything so hard on her.

"I'm sorry I dragged you into this," I tell her.

Nan takes a deep breath and strokes her fingers through my hair. "Emma, do you remember your great-uncle Donnie?"

The name is vaguely familiar, but I shake my head.

"Well, double great to you. He was my uncle," she says. "He served in the Pacific during World War Two, met his lifelong beau there. Of course, that's not how he introduced him. Frank was his *friend*.

"They went off to live in California, far away from us, to hide their lives. And even though they came to every Thanksgiving and Christmas, even though we ended up calling him Uncle Frank, everybody pretended they were just war buddies. They were together forty-seven years when Uncle Frank passed, and even then, Uncle Donnie never said it out loud.

"They'd been together a quarter of a century before the first pride parade ever happened. They both passed before marriage equality. And I'm telling you this because what you're going through now is terrible. Inexcusable. There are people around here I'd set on fire if I had the chance, and people I wouldn't walk across the street to spit on if they *were* on fire.

"So. If you want to go when you graduate, to New York or San Francisco, I'll do what I can to get you there. I know you planned to go to IU in the fall, but if you want to take a year and settle yourself somewhere more accepting, I won't blame you one bit. I've got some money saved up, even.

"I just want you to know that you are the dream that Uncle Donnie never dared to dream.

"You're seventeen years old; you know who you are. The world knows who you are. It might not mean much to you now. But believe your nan when she tells you that your fight, right here, right now, matters."

My breath shudders as I lean back against her. I had no idea I had a gay uncle and . . . well, that's a problem right there, isn't it? Wrapping Nan's arms around me more tightly, I say, "I'd like to think it does, but I just don't know anymore."

"That's all right, baby," she says. "You don't have to be sure right now. And we can always come back to this later."

"That would be nice, actually." I really mean that, too. There's been way too much talking lately, and too many people talking *for* me, too. Some quiet, inside my head and outside of it, would be a good thing. And I feel safe here, tucked away behind the lime green door in my nan's quirky purple house, two strange ladies who belong under the same roof.

Nan hugs me, but she also peeks over my shoulder at me. "Changing the subject, we should probably discuss my alibi."

My brow furrows. "For what?"

"Well, I'm not saying that I plan to run Elena Greene over in the Red Stripe parking lot next time I see her. But I'm not *not* saying that, either."

For the first time in days, I smile.

20. Small Town in Slow Motion

ALYSSA

Here I am, sitting on the hood of my car, underneath the water tower, all alone.

A couple of hours ago, I texted Emma and begged her to meet me. She didn't reply, but I came out here anyway. The sun is trying to shine, but hazy gray clouds blot the sky. Sometimes, spring in Indiana is daffodils and tulips, but it's also sheets of rain and impotent thunder.

I look at my phone again. No texts from Emma, and I've already waited fifteen minutes longer than the time I proposed. She doesn't owe me anything; I know that. I just—she asked me to look her in the eyes and tell her that I knew nothing about the prom switch. There's the thinnest gap of time between getting out of school and Mom getting home from work, and it's getting thinner by the minute.

A cold wind blows across the fields, and I pull my hands into my coat sleeves. In my bones, I know she's not coming, but I wait just a little longer. Just in case. The gaping hole in my heart won't close until I have a chance to see her. Talk to her. Explain. I've practiced this talk more than I practiced coming out to my mom—which is a huge part of the problem, I admit.

The wind whips my hair around my face, and strands of it stick in the tracks of my tears. She's not coming, and that's fair, I tell myself. Because it's true. That doesn't mean there's no hurt involved. I fought for her as hard as I could, and yes, I screwed up . . . but the fact that she believes I knew about the prom switch feels like a hot poker in my belly. I would never, and I thought she knew me better than that.

Just then, an engine's buzz catches my attention. I turn, looking in both directions. About a mile off, I see a little dark spot that could be a car heading this way. My throat tightens as it comes closer, closer, and I jump to my feet when I recognize the familiar shape of Nan's Beetle. They only have the one car, so Emma doesn't usually drive—but it's Emma behind the wheel now.

She pulls in next to me and slowly steps out. Bundled in a blue hoodie and a pair of blue sweats, she looks like she's surfacing for the first time in days. She even squints at the sun a little as she approaches me. Dark circles ring her eyes, and I'm guessing that beanie she's wearing is hiding bedhead. Stuffing the keys into her hoodie pocket, Emma keeps her hands in there as well.

Uneasily, I shift. Her whole body is closed off, and her face is stony. She stops more than a foot away from me. Even though I didn't expect her to throw herself into my arms, I guess I didn't think she would be so walled off. It's fair, I tell myself. No matter how much it hurts, it's fair.

"Thank you for meeting me," I say, fighting the urge to touch her. "I didn't know if you would."

Sharply, Emma shrugs. "I didn't either. What do you want?"

Wow, okay. My brain whispers, *This is fair*, but my heart protests. She's treating me like a stranger, and whether I deserve it or not, it's painful. I'm so used to her warmth that this iciness makes her into a stranger. Drawing myself up, I say, "Okay, well, first, I guess I want to say I'm sorry."

"You *guess?*"

I can't help it. I step closer. "I mean I *am*. I'm so, so sorry."

Emma bites her lip, then narrows her eyes. "What are you sorry for, exactly? Actually, just tell me: Were you in on it?"

I throw myself closer still and see the agony in her eyes. The video she made on prom night plays on an endless loop in my head. It's just hard to make it better when I can't hold her. When I can't squeeze her hands and kiss her tears away. "I swear to you, I wasn't. I didn't know about it until I got there. My mother rented a limo and threw me in it. I had no idea."

With a tip of her head, Emma considers me. There's bitterness in the curve of her lips. "Nobody told you. Not even your new BFFs?"

"What?"

"Shelby and Kaylee? You guys looked like you were having a pretty good time to me. They didn't mention anything about the big plan?"

"They are *not* my friends," I say furiously. "My mother *thinks* they are. She set everything up."

Emma looks away, weak sunlight glinting off her glasses. Her skin is so gray, except where the wind rasps pink into her cheeks. She looks like a porcelain doll, fragile and painted in stark colors. "And somehow, your mom planned a whole second prom and you had no idea."

"Emma," I say, spreading my hands. Pleading. "You know me."

When she turns back to me, I see her swallow hard. She's trying not to cry. No, she looks like she's trying not to blow away in the wind. "Do I?"

Catching her shoulders, I step close. Close enough that I smell her skin and feel her warmth. My body burns up with the sudden contact. It's been so long; it's been too long. "You do. I'm a coward, I know, I put things off too long, but you know what you mean to me!"

For the first time ever, Emma doesn't catch me up in her hands. They stay in her hoodie pocket, hidden and protected.

"No, I don't." Her voice has no edge to it; it's defeated. "I've had a lot of time to think, and I'm like . . . maybe I'm just an experiment to you. Or maybe you're trying to piss off your mom, I don't know."

Stung, I step back. "An experiment? What else, Emma? Are you wondering if this is just a *phase*?"

Emma's eyes flash. "That's not what I meant and you know it."

"It's what you said." I let go of her.

The stones fall, and suddenly Emma's expression collapses. She moves, in mourning, running her hands through the grief tangled in her hair. "Do you know what it was like standing there in that *stupid* dress alone in the gym? Knowing that people got together and planned the best way to hurt me? To humiliate me? I mean, the only thing you guys left out was a bucket of pig's blood!"

"It had to be awful," I sob, tears shaking through me.

"It was. But the worst part was that you didn't come. Even though you knew what happened, you didn't come. You didn't hold my hand, or take me out of there, you just let it happen."

It takes two tries to find my voice. "I couldn't come."

"You *should* have."

"I should have, but I couldn't. You know what my mother's like," I say, and I reach for her again.

This time, Emma flinches away from me. The wall comes back up, and she nods. "Yep. I do. I saw her on the news. She's trying to make it sound like I'm the bad guy. Like I called 1-800-Broadway and asked Barry and Dee Dee to come out here to destroy prom for everybody."

"I saw Mr. Glickman at Walmart," I say stupidly. "He was trying to change people's minds about you."

Emma seems rattled by this. But then she shakes her head and shrugs. "Whatever. Good luck with that. Look, I'm going to make another video. I'm going to tell the whole story. Will you do it with me?"

The question catches me off guard. I have a feeling the whole story is going to paint a huge target on my mother's back. And I know she's been a monster.

But I also know I listened to her this morning, leaving a message for my father again. Telling him how much she misses him and how much I need him. Admitting that things here aren't perfect and haven't been perfect since he left.

I don't know how to explain to Emma that I agree with her and I'm on her side, but I also still, despite everything, love my mother. So what I say, instead, is a weak and anemic "I want to, but . . ."

Emma smiles ruefully. "You know what, Alyssa? I believe you have feelings for me, but I can't do this anymore. It hurts too much."

Even though it doesn't come as a shock, it still hits like one. It feels like a sonic boom, shattering the sky. "Is this . . . Are you breaking up with me?"

Neither of us says anything. Emma looks into the wind, baring her face. I wrap my arms around myself tightly and wait. I will her to say no, I pray she says no.

"Yes," Emma says, punctuating it with a nod. "We're done. This is done."

And even though I want to throw myself at her and step in front of her car and beg her to stay, instead, I watch her walk away. She backs out, and as her car moves farther and farther away from me, all I want to do is scream and scream, until my voice shears into ribbons and disappears completely.

I have done nothing but achieve, jump through hoops, and put on smiles. And it's not enough. The blue ribbons and first-place trophies, my extracurriculars and my Sunday school class—I have done every single thing my mother wanted . . . for nothing. Because she's never going to stop wanting me to be perfect Alyssa Greene, and I'm never going to actually be her. Never.

Slumping against the hood of my car, I cover my face with my hands and start to cry. The one thing that was mine, the one beautiful thing that I chose, that made me feel whole and human and alive, just drove away.

And I let her.

21. Look to the Western Sky

EMMA

By the time I get home, I have no more tears left to cry. And this time, I really mean it.

This past month has been the hardest of my life, and that includes being kicked out of the house by my parents when I was fourteen, and my really unfortunate mullet phase. I'm not happy and I'm not over it, but boy, have I learned a lot.

For one, I learned that it's possible to sideline myself from my own life.

And I also learned that it's possible to convince yourself you're happy with a scrap when everybody else has the whole meal. I finally understand what they mean when people ask if the ends justify the means. Barry and Dee Dee were on my side for all the wrong reasons. Maybe Principal Hawkins was, too.

My heart is broken, but it's still beating. My town turned on me, but I survived it. I'm done waiting for my life to start. I'm over being a pawn in other people's games.

So when I pull in and see Barry and Dee Dee's rental car in front of the house, I say *bring it*. If Alyssa's to be believed, Barry thinks he's still fighting the good fight on my behalf. And you know what? Maybe he is, but I'm going to fight my own battles from here on out.

Inside, Nan sits with Barry and Dee Dee—and she jumps right up when I come in. "Emma, they have something they'd like to talk to you about. But if you're not interested in hearing it . . ."

I look from Nan to Barry, and his expression is so tentative. So hopeful. Now I remember why I trusted him so easily. I've seen that look on my own face in the mirror; I don't think he was lying when he said he knew what it was like for me and Alyssa. He probably told me a lot of truths when he swept into my life. He just didn't bother to mention that his motives weren't pure.

But Barry doesn't speak first. Dee Dee does. Of course she does. Sweeping out of the chair, she gathers the spotlight around her, even if it's just in her own mind. Pressing a hand to her chest, she says, "If I may. We have to admit that we have made matters worse. And I think the best thing we can do for Emma is to go home and put it all behind us."

Barry cuts a look in her direction. It's pretty clear there's been some discussion, and it's also pretty clear that leaving right now is not what they discussed. Imperiously, Barry tells her, "We're not leaving."

"We are *always* not leaving!" Dee Dee moans.

"We are staying until we fix this," Barry says with authority. "We're going to turn this around, Emma."

I wonder what they think there is left to turn around at this point. The prom is over. My senior year is almost done.

Most frustratingly, they've shown up and written yet another script without sharing it with me. This isn't going to happen again—I don't care about their plans. I think I know what I'm going to do next, and if they're going to be a part of it, they're going to follow. Not lead. And they're *not* going to follow until they cough up some remorse. "Okay, first of all. You two? You owe me an apology."

Dee Dee looks like I just started speaking Martian. "I did apologize."

"No," Nan says, faintly amused. "You said you made things worse."

"Which is an acknowledgment of wrongdoing," Dee Dee insists. She looks to me. "We failed to get you to prom."

"Still not an apology," Nan singsongs.

I step in, because Nan's enjoying this way too much. "And it's not what you should be sorry for anyway. You didn't come to help me. You came to help yourselves."

"Help me, help you," Dee Dee says airily. "What's wrong with that? People who need people are the luckiest people in the world, don't you know?"

Barry raises his voice, swiping his hands through the air. "Emma, I'm sorry. I'm sorry that we took your story and wrapped ourselves in it like a pashmina on an autumn day. It was wrong, we know that, and now . . . we'd like to help you. Just for you. I want to invite you and your nan to come back to New York with me. Now, or when you graduate. I have a darling little walk-up, Manhattan-adjacent—"

Dee Dee snorts. "Oh please, you live in Queens!"

Barry sends a poisonous glare at Dee Dee, then rolls his

head to look back at me, picking up where he left off. "With plenty of room. Come to stay. Come to NYU. Emma, you'll love the city. And New York City will love you back."

There are so many times I would have jumped at that offer in the past—some of them not even that long ago. It's tempting—more than tempting. It sounds like a miracle, a transformation better than a Gregg Barnes color-changing dress. It would be a whole new world, and a whole new me, and a whole new life.

But I want mine.

"That's . . . I mean, that's huge, Barry, but you know what? If every gay kid in Indiana leaves, then that means every gay kid in Indiana has to do this alone."

Nan murmurs something, I don't catch what. But her face is bright and warm, full of pride. She winks at me and gives me a little approving nod. All along, I've had her. I've never been entirely alone. And as far as I'm concerned, the next kid gets me on their side—if they want it.

"Then a press offensive," Barry says. "We'll get you on Fallon."

"How the hell are you going to get her on Fallon?" Dee Dee asks.

"I'll figure it out," Barry says through gritted teeth. He turns back to me. "You'll be the face of this story, not that PTA witch sucking up all the airtime right now. We'll get you on TV so you can show the world who this story is really about."

They're doing it again. It's almost funny; like, they can't stop taking up all the air in the room. They're literally trying right now, and failing so hard. And you know what? It makes me smile. These absolute teaspoons have been floating around being famous for so long, they don't know how to adult like normal people anymore.

"Okay, guys," I say, trying to back them down like two oversized Siberian tigers in a Las Vegas show ring. "I wouldn't do Fallon if my life depended on it. I'm still mad that he played pet the Nazi. I'd consider Kimmel—"

"My ex-husband knows Kimmel," Dee Dee says quietly, like she just volunteered for dental surgery. "He's been dying to get the house in the Hamptons from me for years."

"Mmm, he has," Barry says agreeably.

Dee Dee's jaw is so tight, a muscle in her neck pops out when she says, "Do you know how many Broadway cruises I had to book to pay for that house? I'd rather suck my own eyes out with a vacuum cleaner than call that leech . . ."

We all watch her; this seems like a monologue, but who knows if it's the end? I think there must be something that comes next, and I'm right.

"But I will. If I have to." Dee Dee swallows the knot in her throat and reaches for my hand. "If you want me to."

Shaking my head, I squeeze her hand. "I don't want you to give up your house, Dee Dee."

She collapses with a faint *Thank god* and peeks at me through the dramatic hand across her brow. "Go on, then."

"I'm going to take a stand. And you know what? I owe you guys a thank-you for coming out here. My life was blowing up with or without you, and at least you gave it some zazz."

"That's not what that means," Dee Dee whispers, then puts on an attentive face. "I'm listening!"

My hands start to shake, and my heart feels like a Jell-O mold in the trunk of a car. It wiggles like crazy; it might even come apart. But even though it's hard to get a whole breath, I'm not going to change my mind. I won't back down.

I look at my nan, who has always had my back, and Barry, who really does know what all of this is like, and even Dee Dee, who can be forcibly nudged in the right direction. I really look at them, and everything instantly clears.

"I'm doing this my way. I'm going to record a video, and I'm putting it on my channel. I have a *lot* more subscribers now. And thanks to Mrs. Greene, people keep hitting it, looking for more of the story."

"That's true," Dee Dee says.

"And considering how much we screwed this up, you probably know better than we do," Barry agrees.

I sit on the coffee table in front of them, an offense that would normally get me told off, but *good*, by my nan. But this time, I get a raised eyebrow and curiosity about what comes next. Clasping my hands together, I nod as the plan forms in my mind.

"I'm going to do my thing. And some people in town are going to listen, and they may even cry because they'll realize what they did was wrong. And there will be shouting and meetings, and there will be a reckoning.

"It'll spread to other towns and other cities and other states. Shouting and meetings and reckonings, and maybe next year, there will be a kickass prom in Edgewater, Indiana, for everybody, no matter who they are, no matter who they love."

So far, the making-people-cry part of this plan is working. Nan is dewy, and Barry is outright sobbing. Even Dee Dee does one razor-sharp swipe beneath one eye before her mascara streaks her cheek. Normally, I'd feel bad about leaving people in tears, but I'm proud of these. I earned them. I worked for them.

Barry reaches for my hands, and I let him take them. "Emma, that would be wonderful."

"And you know what? When that happens, Barry? I want you to be my date."

"What about—"

"We broke up," I say, and a sudden well of hurt rises up through the optimism.

"Oh, honey," he says.

I nod. This time next year, we'll both be at college and I'll be a memory. Maybe one she'll keep in a shoebox and pull out from time to time—or maybe one that she'll bury deep and pretend she never had.

I don't know. And I hate that. But I can't make her do something she doesn't want to do. I can't make her be who I want her to be. Alyssa is Alyssa, and she has to find her own way.

So I shrug that aside and tell Barry, "Anyway, this will be a prom for every kid who never got theirs, and that includes you."

"Can I wear the silver tux I never wore? I still have it." Barry looks into the distance. "It needs renovations, but I happen to know—"

Nan, Dee Dee, and I all say, "Tony Award–winning costume designer Gregg Barnes!" at the same time.

"You all think you're sooo funny," Barry says, but he laughs softly. Squeezing my hands, he asks, "So when are we—when are *you* making this video? You're going to do all the work, but the least we can do is make sure you get all the attention you deserve."

Standing up, I say, "I'm going to go do it now. I've been working on a lot of music lately, and I know what I'm going to lead with."

"Godspeed," Dee Dee cries.

Barry salutes me. "And good luck."

22. For Good

ALYSSA

It's a little terrifying when I get to school and everyone is on their phone.

Technically, there are rules against having our phones out in the hallways, even though we all sneak from time to time. But this is a full-out insurrection.

As I move through the hall, people are clumped in groups, watching something together. I hear tinny sounds that might be music, but it's hard to tell with so many of them playing at once.

Turning slowly, I spin the combination to get into my locker when Shelby appears out of nowhere to glom onto me. Her face is pink and shiny with tears, but her makeup is perfect. When she throws her arms around me, she does it precisely, part drama and part genuine emotion. I think. It's hard to tell with Shelby sometimes.

"Oh. My. God," Shelby says, sniffling on my shoulder. "Did you see Emma's video?"

I feel every pore in my body close up. It would be so nice to sink into my sweater and turn into a small gray stone, but unfortunately, I'm the student council president, not the student council magician. Emma's prom video is burned into my mind. Over and over, it plays in my head, stuck there like a song. "I watched it on prom night, Shelby. Why?"

"Nooooo," she keens into my ear, squeezing me tighter. "The new one. Oh my god, I can't believe you haven't seen it. Here. Watch it. Watch!"

Shelby shoves her phone in front of me. I have to lean my head back so I can focus on the screen as she keeps pushing it closer. Finally, I take the thing from her. If I'm going to be forced to watch my ex-girlfriend's latest vlog on heartbreak, I'd prefer to do it from a reasonable distance.

Like an octopus, Shelby snakes an arm around me and pushes play. "Watch!"

"I am," I tell her, annoyed. I mean, I'd rather not, but apparently, I have no choice. And what the heck, I probably deserve it. I mentioned a while back that I am the worst person in the world, and the last two days have done nothing to change my opinion on that.

After a little ad plays, Emma's face fills the screen. The ache in my chest grows, because she looks better than the last time I saw her. Under the water tower, her skin was gray and her lips slate and her eyes bloodshot from crying. She wore every inch of her agony on her face, but she looks fine in this video. She looks *good*. And all I can think is *Oh god, she's already over me.*

The screen blurs, but I stand there anyway. Shelby breathes hotly on my neck as she re-watches, too. Her fingers dig into my shoulders, and her weight threatens to pull me off balance. Or maybe *I'm* just off balance, because Emma sits there in her lavender bed, beneath her green walls, and explains everything from the beginning.

As she speaks, her fingers touch the guitar strings without playing. They move by some memory, as she explains how the PTA threatened to cancel prom if she brought her girlfriend. How Mr. Glickman and Ms. Allen showed up to protest. How the PTA decided to hold a fake prom just for her. Her fingers strum silent chords; her shoulders move with music that's just in her head. And I realize for the first time:

She never once outed me. She never told anyone that her girlfriend went to the other prom. That her girlfriend's mother is the reason this all got started and ended up so out of hand. She never blamed me; she never named me. She never even mentioned that we agreed to go together and I backed out on her.

All this time, she's been protecting me, and I didn't even see it until now.

And then, she plays. The silent chords suddenly have voice, and she sings words that she *said* to me what seems like a million years ago.

I don't want to start a riot
I don't want to blaze a trail
I don't want to be a symbol
Or cautionary tale
I don't want to be a scapegoat
For people to oppose

What I want is simple
As far as wanting goes

To my shock, Shelby starts to sing along quietly, sniffling between lines.

I just want to dance with you
Let the whole world melt away
And dance with you
Who cares what other people say?
And when we're through
No one can convince us we were wrong
All it takes is you and me
And a song.

When Emma stops singing, I can't see her face anymore. Tears cloud my vision, and I can barely hear her voice over my own sobs. I wanted so badly to give her all of that, and I couldn't. I failed.

I'm not the perfect student, I'm not the perfect daughter, and I'm definitely not the perfect girlfriend. I'm the worst person in the world, and—

"Do you hear that, Alyssa?" Shelby asks, squeezing me tighter. "She just wanted to dance with you."

I try to say yes, but the only sound that comes out of my throat is a broken sob.

Shelby shakes me, then starts stroking my hair. "I'm really sorry we ruined that. We suck so hard."

If Emma were here, she'd say something like *That's why*

Kevin likes you, but something like that would never leave my lips. If Emma were here, I would hold her and dance with her, right here in this hallway. If Emma were here, I'd . . . I don't know. I'd make it up to her. I'd give anything to make it up to her somehow.

Still swaying with me, Shelby says, "I think it's really nice that she wants to try to have an everybody prom next year. I'd totally help with decorations for that. I could sew banners and make a big rainbow arch for pictures and maybe little baby cupids with rainbow diapers . . . I love rainbows!"

"Rainbows are great," I say numbly. Then Shelby fades to me; she's there, but separated by a strange, internal distance.

In my thoughts, I'm alone. And there's a ticking in my brain that feels like an idea. No, like a memory. Maybe both. Suddenly, so clearly, I hear Principal Hawkins reminding me, *Don't let perfect be the enemy of good.*

"I have to go to the principal's office," I say.

"You're not going to get in trouble," Shelby swears, dragging me into the present. "Everybody's on their phone; they can't put the whole school in detention."

"No," I say, laughing incredulously. "I need to talk to him. I need to . . . You said you'd help set up and decorate, right?"

Confused, Shelby nods. "Um, yeah?"

"Can you get the rest of the squad on board?" I ask her. "And the basketball teams, too?"

Shelby blinks at me. "Probably . . . ?"

"All right, do that." I peel out of her grip but grab her arms. "I have to go."

And then I plant a kiss on her cheek and run. The halls are

full of Emma's song, echoing everywhere. Probably, certainly, there are people mocking it. But I see more people crying because of it. Touching their hearts and watching again.

Butcher paper posters on the wall flap as I run by, and when I burst into the front office, the secretary yelps and jumps a little. Her face is tear-streaked, too. I can't see what's on her monitor, but I can guess.

"I need to see Principal Hawkins," I say.

"I can check and see if he's busy—" she starts, but I ignore her and head straight there. Through the window, I see he's on the phone, so I *do* knock first. But I also let myself in without waiting for an answer. Then, I lean back against the door to shut it *and* hold it closed. I'm not going to be dragged away by security or the school secretary.

Calmly, Principal Hawkins tells the person on the other line that he'll call back, and he resets the receiver. With raised brows, he leans back in his chair and steeples his hands. "Miss Greene."

"Principal Hawkins," I say breathlessly. "Have you seen Emma's new video?"

He nods once, slowly. "I have."

"You let the PTA use the gym for free, right?"

"I do."

Throwing my arms wide, I burst out, "I want to use it to throw another prom. Not just for Edgewater. For anybody who wants to come, for free."

Surprise barely registers on Principal Hawkins's face; instead, it rises, then falls to a more general kind of concern. "I think it's a lovely idea, Miss Greene, but you know we don't have the funds for something like that. The DJ, the food, the decorations . . ."

"The cheerleaders are already on board. They're going to help put everything together," I say, and I'm going to believe in my heart that it's not a lie. "The guys on the team, too. And I think I have a pretty good idea where we might be able to get some funding. I just need you to say yes."

Principal Hawkins rubs his palms together. "The PTA may still protest."

"Fine," I say. "Let them."

"Your mother's likely to take serious issue with this."

Ugh, that hits me right in the chest. It's a solid blow, but I'm not perfect. I'm going to stop trying for perfect. And that means standing up to my mother and making her understand that nothing we do is going to change Dad. He's gone; he's not coming back. It's time Mom faced that. I steel myself and say, "Almost definitely she will, sir."

Principal Hawkins considers me for a long moment. He seems a little older than he did at the start of the year. More gray in his hair, a few more lines in his face. It's possible that his older and wiser self will say no. That he's not going to continue to feed the promtroversy fire. The reporters have started to go home.

But he doesn't say that. Instead, he rolls his chair under his desk. He pats a few piles of paper, then opens a drawer. His silence is torture as he fingers through file folders one by one. Finally, he produces one and smooths it open on his desk. Taking a single sheet from it, he picks up a pen and starts to write.

"Principal Hawkins?" I say softly.

"Alyssa Greene, student council," he murmurs to himself, writing. Then he looks up at me. "And you're reserving the gym for which date?"

Clapping a hand over my mouth, I barely contain my shriek.

We. Are. Doing. This!

23. Pride in the Name of Love

EMMA

I'm going back to school today, and I'm going to be seen.

First, I'm definitely seen by the news cameras camped in the cornfield across the road. There are orange cones and striped barriers holding them back, but they surge when I get out of Nan's car. Kissing Nan on the cheek, I back out of the car and then turn as quickly as I can. I don't want to stare into all those glass eyes and lose my nerve.

Hefting my backpack onto my shoulders, I stare at the front doors for a long moment. Deciding to give up fear is one thing. Actually doing it is . . . daunting. My throat's all dry, and my chest is tight. I clutch the strap of my backpack and stiffen up my spine.

This place is just a pile of bricks—sure, full of people who thought it was clever to strangle a teddy bear in my honor, but it's just a place. A place in my hometown, where I was born, where I've grown up. I belong here.

I pull out my phone and check Emma Sings one last time before heading unto the breach. The woozy, swirling sensation in my head reaches its peak when I see the stats. More than six million views. Six. Million. Views. I'm pretty sure that's more people listening to my song than bought Kanye's last album.

More important than the numbers are the people in the comments. So many strangers with stories like mine. They reach out across the distance, saying sorry, saying me too, saying I love you. Barry was right, we do get to make our own families, and mine is growing exponentially.

My family's full of people from near and far, whose faces I've never seen but whose hearts I share. Who want to come to a prom that welcomes everybody. Who just want to dance with somebody, romantically and aromantically, and just *be*.

The biggest shock is that my new family has people from my school in it. From good old James Madison High in Edgewater, Indiana, cheering me on.

Shelby and Kevin both posted, weirdly enough (and the timestamps show them commenting within a minute of each other, so apparently this was a group activity), and so did some of the teachers. Even Principal Hawkins braved the electronic wilds to write, "I'm proud of you."

I'm walking through these doors on my own, but I'm not alone.

I stuff my phone back into my pocket, take a deep breath, and jump. Well, push. Push the doors open into the Hall of Champions.

The trophy cases gleam, and the yearbook committee has a table set up in the middle. That weird industrial-slash-teenage-hormone smell washes over me. My body wants to turn and run. It's got a little panic party going on in the limbs, urging me to *go, go, go* and never come back.

Instead, I walk forward. And as I melt into the morning crowds, the weirdest thing happens. People look at me and . . . say hi.

"Hi, Emma," Breanna says, giving me a little wave. "I love your video!"

"Thanks," I say, smiling in confusion.

Then confusion turns to wonder, because people keep on being nice. Like, guys from the basketball team say hi without snickering. Two cheerleaders wave poms at me when I pass, singing *hiIIiiIiii* like it's a ritual greeting.

Out of nowhere, the president of Key Club falls into step with me. Key Club kids are the busy little volunteers who hold pancake breakfasts to raise money for needy families and volunteer to weed medians in town, that kind of thing. Last year, they repainted old people's houses for free. I think, but I'm not sure, that they grow up to be Kiwanis Club members. Or they become Khaleesi, mothers of dragons. I'm not clear on that.

Anyway, I've seen this chick around, obviously, and I'm pretty sure her name is Dana Sklar. But we've literally never said two words to each other. Ever.

"Okay, you have to know," Dana tells me, clutching her books to her chest, "that you are amazing. The kind of outreach you're doing for LGBTQ teens online just melts my heart."

For a second or maybe two, I wait for her to turn this into a punking. Surely that was the windup, and the punch line should be along any second. Annny time now. Slowly, I realize she's not kidding. She really means it.

Incredulity turns to a little spark of happiness, and I say, "Thanks, that means a lot."

"And if you want," she goes on, pulling out her phone, "I have a bunch of stuff on fundraising and how to put together an event and stuff like that. I can email it to you, if you want?"

"That would be great," I say, my face growing hot. Somehow, this conversation is a really real thing that I'm not hallucinating. It's hard to get my head around it, but I have to admit that my video did this. *I* did this. "Thank you, really. Just, you can send it to enolan dot sings at gmail dot com."

With quite possibly the swiftest thumb in the county, Dana puts my address into her phone and then nods at me. "Okay, great! I'll get that to you. And if you ever want to come to a meeting or anything . . ."

Probably, I do not, but who knows? Maybe I do? After a few more pleasantries, Dana melts back into the general haze of people hanging out in the halls before classes start. I look down and realize my hands are shaking. I don't know what that is—maybe adrenaline? Maybe terror? Maybe . . . excitement? All I know is that my stomach is full of weasels, and they're chasing their tails at top speed.

When I turn down the hall where my locker is, I see something stuck to it. The weasels get drunk and start trashing the place as I approach.

Look, it can't possibly be any worse than the bear, and the lotion, and the salad dressing. This is my school, too; I belong. I'm not going to use my locker, because I'm not *stupid*—but I'm going to walk past it. I'm going to look.

And when I do, I stop short and almost cry. Right there, in

the hall, surrounded by people who slow down to look my way.

Someone has pasted a glittery rainbow, complete with clouds and a sun peeking out, at the top of my locker. And underneath it, there's a long piece of butcher paper cut to look like a scroll. They even drew in the loops at the top and bottom.

On it, in calligraphy, someone wrote out the words to my song. Someone in this school sat and listened to my video long enough to get all the lyrics down. And then they scripted them in beautiful swirls on this faux parchment. Then they drew musical notes around them and dusted the whole thing with more glitter.

I cover my mouth with my hand, because I feel tears threatening. People are looking at me, so I manage to hold it in. But when I glance at them, they're *smiling*. They're here, in this moment, sharing it with me.

Subtly, I bite the tip of my thumb. Really hard. So hard that I'm like, *What the hell, Emma?* But I'm rewarded with a jolt of pain which means *Yup, I'm awake*. This is actually happening. Because I have no idea who did this, I mumble thanks at the people around me. Just anybody in thanking distance, you know?

Deep inside, I almost wish that somebody would walk by and call me a name. Because that? That would be normal. I expect that, not kindness. Not acceptance. It's genuinely frightening to stand here and accept that maybe my song (and, okay, a tiny bit of Barry and Dee Dee's shenanigans) might have really changed them. There's no way it reached everybody; realistically, I know that. But, oh my god, it changed *some*.

This moment feels so fragile, and I feel so clumsy. But I

hold it close to my heart. Carefully and gently. Opening up is the hardest thing I've ever done, but slowly, I lift my head and stand there, feeling more myself than I ever have. When I look around, I meet everyone's eyes. I am Emma Nolan, Hoosier, lesbian, and human being.

And I am proud.

24. Begin Again

ALYSSA

I hear their voices before I see them. I think people probably say that a lot about Mr. Glickman and Ms. Allen. Loud or not, I'm glad they accepted my invitation.

"I can't believe we're back in this place," Ms. Allen says. "In my memoirs, I'm calling this chapter 'Groundhog Day.'"

Mr. Glickman replies immediately. "I thought that was the title of the chapter about your husbands?"

Between their sniping, I hear a low voice of reason. That has to be Principal Hawkins, and I'm glad that he's here. Not that he wouldn't be, but Mr. Glickman and Ms. Allen make me nervous, and I'm kind of glad I've never been alone with them. Their hearts are in the right place; it's all the flying jazz hands that scare me.

When they come into the gym, I wave from my carefully arranged table. There's a laptop, a projector, a stack of handouts, and a diorama. The diorama was probably unnecessary, but I haven't made one since seventh grade (*Scene at Gallows Hill in Salem, 1692*), and I'm kind of good at them.

"Hi, thank you for coming, hi!"

Next to me, the school's ancient laptop starts humming. It had better not blow up before I finish my presentation; quickly, I say a silent prayer for technology. Then I smile as brightly as I can as the adults approach. Ms. Allen's heels click on the hardwood floor in a way that I'm sure would send Coach Strickland into fits.

She's wearing what seems to be one of a thousand pantsuits she owns, and I'm starting to really respect her dedication to a look. This one has no sequins, but the red fabric is shot through with silver thread. The bottoms of her shoes are blood-red, too, and I marvel. Those are probably the only pair of Louboutins ever to grace Edgewater, Indiana.

Mr. Glickman is casual in a jacket and tie, and when he gets closer, I squint at the pattern on the tie. Little white outlines of hair—no, I get it. Wigs. Wigs of all shapes and sizes, arrayed in a graceful grid pattern.

They're so out of place, it's funny, and yet . . . it almost seems like this won't be home anymore if they leave. I offer my hand when they approach. "Hi, I'm Alyssa Greene, the student council president. Thank you for coming. Thank you, thank you for coming, thank you, Principal Hawkins."

As soon as I say my name, Mr. Glickman goes frosty. He looks at me down his nose and crosses his arms over his chest. Well, I guess somebody in the room knows that I'm the ex-girlfriend. That's okay, pretty sure everyone is going to know in a couple of minutes.

I pass out copies of the agenda, and their eyes skim the page. Lots of white space, for easy skimming. Ms. Allen squawks about halfway down, but Principal Hawkins puts a (very familiar!) hand on her shoulder and says, "Please, hear her out."

Picking up the clicker, I advance my PowerPoint to the first slide. It's a still from Emma's video, where she sings and shares her vision for a prom for everyone one day. "As of this morning, more than six million people have viewed Emma's video about an inclusive, open prom."

Mr. Glickman sniffs. "That video just kills me. It's better than the one about the guy being reunited with the lion he raised from a cub."

"Don't bring that up," Ms. Allen says, also sniffling. "I can't even think about it."

Exploding with emotion, Mr. Glickman waves at the screen with Emma's face on it. His eyes glimmer with tears, and he fans his face. "She said she had a plan, and look at her. She's so smart, that kid."

I know if I don't cut him off, it'll be ages before I can finish my pitch. And I don't have ages. Shelby and Kevin just showed up at the gym doors, and they're slinking in to sit on the bleachers. Some of the Golden Weevils basketball team slide in, along with their cheerleader cohort, more of them than I expected, actually. (Notably absent? Kaylee and Nick.) Everyone else settles in, whispering.

I can't make out what they're saying, but it's not important. I raise my voice, and fortunately, it carries in a mostly empty gym. "She asked for one thing, and I think we can make it happen. Not next year, this year."

Power-clicking through my presentation, I go on, trying

not to focus on Mr. Glickman's and Ms. Allen's faces. If I pay too much attention to their reactions, I won't be able to get this all out.

"As you know, the school has no budget for dances, and traditionally, funding has come from outside sources. Now, I have secured the school gym as the event site for free. I've even created a diorama to show the potential design of the dance. And I have a team of students prepared to help decorate. Shelby? Kevin?"

They stand up and cheer and hoot from the bleachers.

"What we're missing, Ms. Allen, Mr. Glickman, is money. Now, I could host a GoFundMe and, with as many views as Emma's getting on her video, probably get that money in time for a prom next fall. I'm not interested in next fall. I'm interested in this year, this place, two weeks from now."

Mr. Glickman shifts from ice to fire. He all but vibrates with excitement. "It's Mickey and Judy time. We'll build this prom with blood and hair if we have to."

"Wait," Ms. Allen says. "According to this cute little line item, you're looking for *fifteen thousand dollars?*"

Even though I feel weak hearing the number aloud, I nod my head. "I've priced everything out. That's a good DJ from Evansville, catering instead of homemade treats, decorations, a photographer, and souvenirs."

Mr. Glickman holds up a hand. "How much are we talking if we really do this up? No hay bales and a cutout cow. A real A-level, Tony Award–worthy prom?"

This time, when I break into a smile, it's genuine. I was hoping someone would ask. I hand them the second printout.

"For everything I already mentioned, plus lighting, special effects, flowers, and professional decorations, thirty thousand dollars."

Ms. Allen swoons. "Jesus."

Without hesitating, Barry reaches into his front pocket and produces a wallet. He hands me a credit card, black, with obvious signs of wear around the edges.

"There's fifteen thousand dollars on there," he says. "That's my limit. It's a long story, but I had to declare bankruptcy after my self-produced gritty reboot of *Peter Pan*."

Principal Hawkins blinks. "That's a lot of money. You're sure?"

"Listen," Barry says, raising his voice so the kids in the bleachers can hear as well. Not that they're paying attention, but if they were, they'd be able to hear him. "We failed at the abstract singing and speechifying. This is concrete. This is buying. This is the American way."

Nodding slowly, Principal Hawkins produces his wallet. "It's not much, but I can put down two thousand."

"Thank you," I say, starting to get misty. This is going to happen. We already have enough for the hometown version of the prom, so it's on, regardless. At that moment, all three of us—Mr. Glickman, Principal Hawkins, and I—look to Ms. Allen expectantly.

Stiffening, Ms. Allen returns the looks. "What?" she says finally.

"Dee Dee, come on." Barry cozies up to her. "I know you have an AmEx with no limit."

Principal Hawkins gazes into Dee Dee's eyes. "I know you

have it in you. All our talks at Applebee's? I know you want to do the right thing."

There have been talks at Applebee's? Talks, plural? Apparently so, and when I look to Ms. Allen, I'm amazed.

Her face, always so studied and perfect, suddenly softens. I'd never, ever tell her this, because I think it might break her heart, but for just a second, I get a glimpse of Ms. Allen the human being instead of Ms. Allen the star. Not that they're not the same person—it's just that one aspect gets all the spotlight, and the other? Not so much.

The star reappears, and she reaches into her purse. She snaps a credit card out of the clutch like it was in a holster and hands it over. "God, why does being good cost *so much money*? Go on. Take it."

Right now, I feel like I could fly through the roof. It's like fireworks and champagne bubbles. I feel like a comet streaking across the sky. There's applause and cheering, but I am so effervescent, I barely hear it. What I *do* hear is my mother's voice cutting through it all.

"Alyssa Greene, what is the meaning of this?"

Quickly, I advance the slide on my presentation. I padded the slideshow with some extra facts on the off chance they were reluctant to donate (cough—Ms. Allen—cough). At first, my voice catches in my throat. It's terrifying, the look on my mother's face. She sees the projection screen, the slide with a big pink PROM FOR EVERYONE on it. She sees the date, the time, and all the different pride flags underneath. And she sees me, standing beneath it, just like I planned. My mother can't resist a PTA obligation, and I told her that's exactly what this was to get her here.

"Mrs. Greene," Principal Hawkins says, but I cut him off.

"I've got this," I say, with more confidence than I feel. Taking a few steps toward her, I let go of my guilt—because I'm not a perfect daughter. I let go of my fear—because I can't change who I am, and she's going to find out sooner or later. And I let go of my responsibility—I'm the *kid* here. She's the parent. It's not my job to take care of her; she's supposed to take care of me.

"I certainly hope there's an explanation," Mom says, waving a hand furiously at the screen.

Just past my mother, there's a shadow in the doorway. I know that shape. I'd know it anywhere, and I'm so glad the note pulled her out of class at just the right time, because she deserves to see this. Standing up straight, I approach my mother and offer her my hand. She doesn't take it, and it hurts, but I don't let that stop me.

"Mom, I love you. And I'm so grateful to you, for all you do for me. For all you've done for me since Dad left."

"Alyssa!" she whispers, scandalized.

I've spoken it aloud, the truth we don't discuss. But I go on. "And I know this is going to be another thing that's hard on you. But, Mom, I'm gay. I've always been gay. And to answer the questions I know you want to ask, nobody did this to me. Nobody hurt me. You didn't do anything wrong. This is who I am; I'm proud of who I am. You know everything about me, and it's been so hard keeping this from you. Too hard. I can't do it anymore. Mom, I'm gay."

Mom laughs, a sound that's wound tight with anxiety. Her eyes dart around, taking in how many people are seeing this, how many are witnessing her humiliation. I see her fighting to keep it together. To look perfect, be perfect. She fights for a smile and whispers at me again. "Alyssa, that's quite enough."

Shaking my head, I say, "No. I've put this off for way too long. And I've hurt someone so precious to me, in a way I can't ever expect her to forgive. I was Emma Nolan's date to the prom, Mom. We were supposed to go together, and I let her down."

Now my mother starts to cry. "Stop it. Just stop it. Alyssa, I'm sorry, but this is not who you really are. Whatever you're feeling, it's not real. You're young and you're confused."

"I'm not confused. I'm in love."

Mom stamps at the ground, jabbing an accusing finger at Mr. Glickman and Ms. Allen. "This is *their* fault. They're putting ideas into your head, and they're forcing me to be someone I don't want to be. You are young, you are impressionable, and I'm sick of this. This ends now."

For the first time since my mother appeared, Mr. Glickman speaks. "If you don't let her be who she is, you're going to lose her."

"Excuse me?" my mother says, all acid.

He steps closer and speaks, low and heartbroken. "I mean, she'll go away to college, and she'll forget to write. She'll move to another state and send you cards on Mother's Day. She'll come home for Christmas for a while, until she has to choose between the family she makes for herself and the family who won't accept that. And soon, you'll count the months between phone calls. The years between visits. Until one day, you'll wonder how it is that your baby left and never came home."

"I don't think—" my mother says tartly, but Mr. Glickman takes her hand.

"Trust me, Mrs. Greene. I *know*."

The gym falls silent, except for some sniffling from the bleachers. I glance over, and Shelby has buried her face against Kevin's chest. The cheerleaders clutch each other, and—well, the basketball players shuffle uncomfortably. There can only be so many miracles in one day.

My mother looks at Mr. Glickman, then she turns to me. And there it is: the face I feared, the one where I can see every hurt and every wound she's suffered in the last few years. The silver in her hair that tragedy put there, the lines on her face that I've caused. But instead of raising her voice, my mother pulls herself together and swipes her face dry.

"This is not what I hoped for you," she says. "This is going to make your life so much harder, in so many ways. And that's the last thing I ever wanted. The reason I've been trying so hard to get your father to come back is so you can have the life you *deserve*. The world isn't a forgiving place, Alyssa."

I tremble. "I know. But it doesn't change who I am."

My mother clasps my face in her hands. They're cool against my skin, but her eyes are warm. She searches my face, and she sighs.

Every muscle in my body is stretched tight, ready to snap. Is this when she gives me up? Is this when I lose my mother for good? I stand so still, it hurts, trying desperately to read the thoughts behind her eyes.

It takes her a moment to find her voice. And even then, she

stares at the floor—trying, I think, to find the words. Finally, she slowly pronounces, "Alyssa, you're my baby girl. My own gift from God. My most precious treasure."

I try to hold still, but inside, I'm squirming. I still can't tell if this is a goodbye or a hello. "Mom . . ."

She raises my face to hers. Her perfectly manicured nails brush against my temples, and she traces her thumbs against my cheeks. Then, finally, she leans in and she kisses my forehead.

Her perfume washes over me, and a million memories flood through me: making cookies with her at Christmas; snuggling beneath a blanket and watching the first snowfall of the year; waking her up in the middle of the night because I had a nightmare and being wrapped so tight, so safely in her arms that all the fear just burned away.

Right now, this moment, my fear burns away when she says, "I love you."

Clinging to her, I whisper, "I love you, too."

She hugs me, an impossibly short hug, and she steps away. Holding my gaze, she slips back and says sincerely, "We'll talk tonight."

Then she turns and walks away. She holds her head high, and her heels click efficiently across the gym floor. Her posture is impeccable, and she sweeps one stray hair back into place with a graceful hand. There's no wavering; she doesn't look back. She knows she doesn't have to. She said what she said. She loves me, and we'll talk tonight.

It hits me in a sudden wave. In a crashing of thunder. I wobble on unsteady legs, gathering my senses and my balance at the same time.

My mom knows.

The secret is out. No more lying, no more pretending. From here on out, when she looks at me, she'll see who I really am. She doesn't have the words yet, but she *knows*.

And—somehow, improbably—she still loves me.

25. Juliet in Converse

EMMA

Mrs. Greene walks past me in a cloud of brimstone and designer imposter Chanel N°5.

The last time I saw a back that straight, I was sitting in the doctor's office, staring at the tiny anatomical model she keeps on the shelf. Mrs. Greene is really rocking the vertical thoracic spine right now. Suffice it to say, I don't think I'm invited to the Greene family Thanksgiving.

And all of that joking is a strong, heavy shield for the soft, vulnerable feelings I contain. The note from the office to send me to the gym was weird, but I got here in time to hear Alyssa come out to her mother in front of a screen glowing with the words PROM FOR EVERYONE.

Barry and Dee Dee stand there with Principal Hawkins, and for some reason, most of the Golden Weevils are hanging out on the bleachers. This feels like a dream I once had, except I'm not naked, and the gym isn't also the China Garden right off I-69.

Wary, I walk inside. My boots sound so heavy, echoing low thunder as I approach Alyssa. Any minute, I expect laughter or jeers from the stands, but it doesn't come. Instead, Alyssa walks toward me, her hands clasped together almost in prayer.

I know we broke up, but that doesn't mean my unruly heart stopped loving her. How could it?

This is the girl who flirted with me at a church picnic. The girl who texted me pictures of otters in the middle of the night and whispered love in my ear. This is the girl who was brave enough to kiss me first, when I was still desperately trying to figure out if she liked me or if she *liked* me.

There's so much history written on our skin, so many firsts that will always belong to us alone. They were secret, and they were ours, and that doesn't melt away in an instant. How could it? Something so real and monumental can only be abandoned. It doesn't cease to exist.

And that's why my heart leaps up, full of strange optimism and hope, but I keep my shield close. Loving her so completely means that she can wound me with a single word. I have to protect myself, because her delicate hands still hold so much power.

As proof, Alyssa stops a few feet in front of me, and her expression steals past my shield with ease. As soon as she's close, I want to surrender. I want to throw myself into her arms and hold her again. The urge is so strong, I swear I feel her already—the warmth of her body and the silk of her skin.

You can't, I tell myself. *Just don't.*

Her dark eyes shine in the low light, and her tentative smile glows. I see her swallow nervously, her fingers squeezing together even tighter.

"What is all of this?" I ask. According to Nan, she who talks first loses, but it doesn't feel like anyone's losing today. I know Alyssa knows what I mean, but I nod toward the screen, and the team, and the . . . diorama? Anyway.

Stroking a long swirl of her dark hair behind her ear, Alyssa says, "It's for you."

"I don't get it," I say, even though I kind of do. I want to hear her say it.

"You asked for a prom where everyone was welcome, and it's going to happen. We have funding, thanks to Principal Hawkins, Ms. Allen, and Mr. Glickman; and we have a committee ready to build it, thanks to Shelby and Kevin. There's a date, and a time, and I hope you'll help us get the word out."

It's too much. Like, my brain is so full right now, it pounds against my skull. My closeted ex-girlfriend and a couple of misguided Broadway stars are bringing this to life? It was a small idea, one that I hoped would develop over time. Something that might eventually come together, something to look forward to.

I didn't think it would happen this quickly or that it would happen this way. And honestly, that's all a way of saying that I didn't think this would happen for *me*.

My lips, the lips that have kissed Alyssa's a thousand times, are numb. They barely move when I speak. "And your mother?"

Alyssa nods. "It was time. I did it for me, but I wanted you to see. I thought you deserved that much."

It's getting harder to stand so far from her. My feet take a step closer without my permission. "Are you okay?"

Alyssa hesitates, like she's taking some mental inventory

before she answers. But then she smiles softly and nods. "Yeah, I am. I have a feeling I'm going to be explaining all the other letters in the rainbow a few thousand times over the next couple of weeks, but yeah. I'm . . . I'm really okay."

I feel like I'm whispering when I say, "I'm happy for you."

Suddenly, Alyssa sweeps forward and catches my hands. She curls her arms around mine and pulls me in close. Pressed against her, I swear I feel her heartbeat on my skin again, and it makes me sweat. She's just a little bit shorter than I am, so when she leans in, her nose rests against mine, and her eyes look up into me. All the way through me.

"I love you," she says, her voice rough with emotion. "And I'm so sorry about before. None of this would have happened if I had just spoken up sooner."

Her apology makes something bloom inside me. Heat washes from my heart to all my ends and beginnings. I've wanted to hear and believe an apology since prom night, but she's taking responsibility for too much. It's just like her. Full of forgiveness, I'm also full of reason. Squeezing her hands, I shake my head. "I won't let you take the blame for things you didn't do, Alyssa. Just say, *I'm sorry I stood you up.*"

"I'm sorry I stood you up," she whispers, her breath warm on my lips.

I take that and tuck it away, deep in my heart. And then it's easy to say the words she deserves to hear, too. "I'm sorry I didn't believe you—and I'm sorry I pushed so hard. Everybody should get to come out in their own time and their own way."

Across the gym, Barry cries out, "And we're sorry, too!"

Alyssa and I laugh, turning to look at him. "For what?"

"For using you," Barry says, and Dee Dee nods. "We got blasted in the *New York Times*. They said we were narcissists, in big, bold font. And it hurt, I guess, because they were right."

This is so bizarre. Seriously, I'm back to wondering if I'm dreaming. But if I am, it's a hell of a dream. "Aren't all actors narcissists?"

Throwing her head back, Dee Dee pronounces, "Yes, but we're *really* good at it."

"We decided to look for a cause, to give us credibility. Get a little good press. We thought about building houses with Habitat for Humanity—"

Dee Dee interrupts, "But we don't actually know how to build anything."

"So maybe we're not the best human beings in the world. But we got here and got to know you and your town . . . and suddenly, that bad review didn't matter so much anymore. The truth is, yes, we came because of a bad review."

Then warmly, more warmly than I've heard Dee Dee say anything, while (alert! alert! alert!) slipping her hand into Principal Hawkins's (!!!!!!), she says, "But we stayed because of you."

From the bleachers, Shelby jumps up. "And we're sorry, too. Aren't we, Kevin?" Despite her tiny frame, Shelby hauls him up like a naughty puppy. He nods emphatically, and he gets rewarded with a very booby hug. Twined on him like ivy, Shelby says, "You deserve to go to prom, just like everybody else!"

"I thought you hated me," I say, somehow slowly tangling

around Alyssa as well. "I thought you all hated me."

"Oh, we did; Kaylee still does," Shelby says agreeably. Then she looks to Barry. "But Mr. Pecker crashed our hang at Walmart and said some stuff that made us think. He's a really good teacher."

Barry takes a tiny bow but also waves Shelby off, as if to say, *No, no, please, that's too much, you're too kind.* It cracks me up that he can take the credit and also pretend to be humble at the same time. It's like his superpower or something.

I don't know what to do with this moment. Historically, my life hasn't worked out this neatly before. It's hard to believe so many people have turned around because of a song and, apparently, a star turn in the Walmart parking lot—I'm going to have to ask about that later for sure.

Instead of blustering, or joking, or any of that, I'm just honest. Turning in Alyssa's arms, I tell her, "I don't know what to say."

"Well," she says, shyly, a little coyly, "there's this prom coming up . . ."

Fireflies light up inside me. "Uh-huh."

A question doesn't come; she doesn't even finish that sentence. Instead, Alyssa, with her reedy voice and uncertain smile, sings to me, *"I just want to dance with you, let the whole world melt away and dance with you . . ."*

And then, all around me, suddenly there are voices singing my song. Shelby sways with Kevin, and literally no one from the bleachers is in tune, but they know the words. I hear Barry and Dee Dee lift their voices, trying to out-emote each other.

Probably, Principal Hawkins sings, too, but once Dee Dee and Barry get going, it's impossible to tell.

They sing my song. They sing my words and my heart. With every note, it feels like I'm being taken apart and scrubbed new and put back together again. There's pride in there, yes, that I created something that suddenly has life outside of me.

But mostly, it's a becoming. I feel new, for the first time in years. I feel special—I feel seen and loved. Being out in Edgewater, Indiana, is something it never was before: beautiful.

My head spins, and all I can do is stare incredulously at everyone else, and melt away in Alyssa's eyes when I look to her. Here I am, back in her arms. Back where I belong, because we fit together without a single space between. My hurt and resentment and frustration burn away like phoenixes. Now they're joy and excitement and anticipation.

Alyssa frees her hands so she can lay them against my face. Her thumbs skim the curve of my lower lip; her nails rasp delicately against my cheeks. Her heat sinks into me, and I am hopelessly trapped in her gaze. Her body lifts and tightens against mine with each breath. My melody vibrates through her, and I feel the crest to each note in her arms. This is the most epic promposal in the world. Bar none, no arguing, the record is set forever.

When their voices trail off, I exhale Alyssa's name in wonder. I never wanted to let her go; I just felt like I had to. Now it feels like I should never set her free again. My cheeks flush hot, and I'm afraid my palms are sweaty, but I cling to her all the same.

Abruptly, Shelby and the cheerleaders chant, like this is

some fan fiction come to life, "Kiss, kiss, kiss, kiss!"

"A kiss is yes," Alyssa warns me.

Warning taken. That's why I engulf her in my arms and lift her off the ground, just an inch, and kiss her until we see nothing but the two of us, the edge of forever, and the end of the world.

26. Let's Put on a Show

ALYSSA

We're really lucky Mr. Glickman and Ms. Allen donated so much to the cause.

As soon as Emma posted about the new prom on her channel, we were flooded with requests for tickets. There are kids coming from all over Indiana for this dance, and a bunch who are coming from out of state. Illinois, Ohio, Kentucky—they're all coming here, so we had to get creative.

Prom won't just be in the gym; it will also extend out into the school parking lot. We cordoned off the entire thing and rented huge white marquee tents with plastic windows in them. Standing at one end of the tent, I wave both hands slowly as the basketball team unrolls four of the biggest carpets I've ever seen. They grunt and huff as they shove the rolls toward me.

"Okay," I say when they finish stomping down the curled ends to flatten them. "Next thing we need are cocktail tables. If you look at the chart I made, just follow that, and they'll be exactly where they're supposed to be. Thank you!"

I take a quick jog up to the open gym doors to peek inside.

Somehow, Shelby got all of the cheerleaders to help, including the junior team from the middle school. The Key Club is here, and National Honor Society. Most of the choir showed up, and I'm pleased that the rest of the student council turned out as well.

We need the extra hands, especially because Mr. Glickman quote, unquote called in some favors, and two days later, several huge crates arrived at the school. Better than crepe paper and plastic bunting, the crates spilled forth with huge, beautiful sheets of blue, glimmering cloth that we draped around the gym and the stage. There were two cardboard boxes in there full of foiled butterflies that flap their wings when you hang them from their invisible nylon cords.

To go along with those, there are burnished gilt lanterns for the tables and thick ropes of flickering fairy lights to string between standup lampposts that really light up.

Finally, there are massive frames with picturesque cityscapes painted on them. They're erected on casters, so they roll with ease, and on the backs are frames for lights, so the little windows will actually glow on prom night.

"*How to Succeed* hasn't run on Broadway for years," Mr. Glickman explained broadly. "They won't miss them!"

And speaking of Mr. Glickman, he's holding court at one end of the gym. Perched in a folding chair, he talks about his many, many successes on Broadway as he inflates a balloon with helium. Once it's full, he hands it off to a handful of FCK kids to tie off.

Then they go into a massive box where they shimmer in pearly, pastel rainbows. We're going to dump them into a net and hang them from the ceiling, so when we play the last song of the night, we'll pull the rope and they'll come floating down onto the dance floor. As far as finales go, it's a little bit tame, but Principal Hawkins nixed the confetti cannons.

Ms. Allen has an eye for arrangement and flow. Every so often, she claps sharply or taps one of her heels against the floor to get someone's attention. Then she walks them through the spaces between the tables. With assertive hands, she points out what needs to happen. Her assistants, mostly guys from the basketball team, follow her and shift tables and chairs until there's a perfect balance. There's no way she was ever going to pick up a table herself.

Posted at the door, Principal Hawkins supervises and signs off on deliveries. So far, he's accepted two cases of souvenir dance cards, a pallet full of pride-flag key chains in multiple orientations, several thousand pronoun pins, and now he's running down the catering receipt.

Kids are coming from so far away, we wanted to make sure they got a meal. The people from the caterers are setting up huge trays that will hold all the stuff for our taco-bowl bar. We have three huge sheet cakes, iced tea, ice water, and, yes, sherbert punch and cookies. I can't abandon tradition.

As everything comes together, I stand in the middle of the gym with my clipboard and slowly take it in. Everything looks so perfect; it's like a dream made real. One of the women from the party-lights place sets up a ladder near me. I watch as she climbs up and hefts a massive gold disco ball above her head.

Once it's secure, her assistant turns on the lights. Fractures of gold dance across the floor and along the walls. With the flickering, shifting brightness, the butterflies seem to come alive. From the far end of the gym, the DJ sends a mechanical hum through the place, then blasts us with some Ariana Grande.

The explosion of music didn't startle me, but hands suddenly around my waist from behind do. Relieved, I sink back against Emma to anchor myself and look over my shoulder. "You're not supposed to be here," I tease. "It's bad luck to see the prom before prom night."

She presses a kiss to my neck and hugs me close. "I promise, I'm not looking. But I don't need to see it to know that everything looks fantastic."

I laugh. "It's really coming together. How are the electronic tickets going?"

Emma set up an evite for up to eight hundred people, and the last I'd heard, tickets were about 60 percent claimed. It was the fairest way we could think of to invite everybody but also be realistic about the fact that we don't have unlimited space.

"All gone," she says. "And I checked with the Comfort Inn; they're pretty much booked up, too. People are actually coming, Alyssa. This is actually happening."

Before I can reply, my mother walks in. She's the last person I expected to see. Just like she promised, we talked the night I came out. It wasn't all good; she still doesn't understand why I can't just date boys. Why I can't just shove it down and be normal. She hasn't been to church in weeks because she doesn't know what to say about me.

But she also told me that she was proud of me, no matter

what. Proud of the woman I was becoming. Proud that I stand up for my principles. (Not thrilled that I stood up for them against *her*, mind you, but baby steps.)

We also talked a lot about Dad. She finally admitted he wasn't coming home. She cried, and I cried, and then I told her about Tinder. She was horrified; I probably should have started with Christian Mingle.

Emma lets her arms slip away; I appreciate that she's going easy on my mom. For all her sarcasm and sharpness, Emma's one of the most generous people I know. And one of the most forgiving, too. I doubt Mom and Emma will ever be friends, but I'm so glad she'll never make me choose between them.

Mom offers a stiff hello to Emma (which is more than I expected, actually), then looks around. Golden flecks of light dance across her face. "You're putting on quite a production here."

"We've had a *ton* of help," I say. "What's up with you? I didn't expect to see you here."

She shrugs slightly and raises the box. "I always lend the prom my grandmother's punch bowls."

Oh wow. I know how difficult this is for her, but I can see how hard she's trying. Emma steps in and offers to take the box from her. Then she slips quietly away to leave me with my mother.

This is still new, and still hard, so I make it as simple for Mom as I can. I throw my arms around her in a hug and squeeze her tight. "Thank you, Mommy."

"It's the least I could do," she says, and hugs me back.

27. Prom Night Again

EMMA

"No, sweetheart, it's walk, walk, pivot, turn!"

Once again, my house is full of Nan and Broadway. Dee Dee sits on the arm of the couch, "sampling" Nan's pound cake again, and Barry waves his hands, trying to direct me as I show off my suit.

They're already dressed in full regalia. In gold, to match the theme of the night, Dee Dee's decked out in a lamé pantsuit cut down to whoa. And Barry? He's totally wearing the silver tux he bought for the first prom he never got to attend. With teal bow tie and cummerbund, he's resisting the pound cake by ordering me around.

I duck back down the hallway to attempt this perfect runway walk he seems to think I can accomplish. And actually, I probably can. Most days, I don't think about my clothes much. They're just there to cover my body and keep me from public indecency charges.

But this outfit is different. Tonight, I feel *good*.

No gowns. Not this time. Instead, I have a black velvet

jacket that makes me feel so boss, I want to go out and sing karaoke in front of strangers. I mean, it's that epic of a jacket. I keep running my hands over my own arms, luxuriating in the warm, soft kiss of the fabric. If Alyssa and I break up again, I might date this thing. I mean, for real.

My shirt is white and fitted, with dark blue edging on the collar and sleeves. My tie is silk, patterned in dark blues and purples, a little galaxy swirling along its length. The pants are lighter blue, cut above my ankles, and made of some kind of slick material that whispers when I walk.

Barry insisted on getting everything fitted, and I have to say, he was right. Darts and tucks do make everything 150 percent more fabulous.

"Let's go," barks Barry, clapping his hands impatiently. "Let's see that walk!"

With a laugh, I throw my shoulders back for some zazz, and then I march the length of the hallway and into the living room. I walk, walk, walk, pivot, and then start laughing before I can manage the turn. It's just too much for this girl to manage.

Tumbling into the couch between Dee Dee and Barry, I look up at them both. These two. They have been the worst, best thing that ever happened to me. I still can't believe they rolled into town with picket signs and crashed a school meeting with the entire touring cast of *Godspell*.

They made things so much harder, but I can't help but look at where I am right now: dressed to the nines and waiting for my girlfriend to show up so we can go to prom together, a dance that's so much bigger than just one graduating class. None of this would have happened without them either.

I have my nan, who loves me more than anything in this world, and now I have two (occasionally misguided, definitely narcissistic) fairy godparents, and that's so much more than so many other kids get. Gratitude fills me with this sweet, golden wave, and I look to Barry, and then Dee Dee, and say, "Thank you."

"For what?" Barry says, playing it off. I know he wants to hear it.

With an arched brow, Dee Dee says, "Buying an entire prom, for one."

He gives her a look, and I laugh between them. Laying my head against Barry's shoulder, I say, "For coming to Edgewater and wrecking my life. I really needed it."

"Well," Barry says, patting my arm, "I like to think of it as renovating."

"Whatever it is, I'm glad it happened. Because I'm here, and you're here, and, oh my god, hundreds of queer kids from all over the Midwest are here . . ."

Barry smiles, but he nudges me. "Hey. Take some credit."

"Yes, take it. Most people aren't going to give it to you, so you'll have to snatch it for yourself, like nature, red in tooth and claw—" Dee Dee interrupts herself with a significant look and then credits herself, "*Tennyson: The Musical,* original Broadway cast, 19—Never mind."

Nan leans forward, her round face comforting and familiar. She's got a lavender streak in her hair for tonight, and a rainbow manicure. The whole look is pulled together with a black T-shirt that says PROM FOR EVERYONE on the front and CHAPERONE on the back. They really did think of everything.

"Dee Dee's right. You helped grow something beautiful out of something terrible, and I couldn't be prouder of you."

Rolling out of the couch to hug Nan, I hear Dee Dee tell Barry, "Did you hear that? *Dee Dee's right.*"

With a good, solid hug, Nan kisses both of my cheeks. Then she straightens my jacket, tugging the lapels and smoothing my tie. There are tears in her eyes, and I wonder if she's thinking about my dad right now. When she kept me, she lost him. I used to feel guilty about that, like I'd wrecked our family. But I don't anymore.

We all make choices, and all those choices matter. I've always been exactly who I am; he's the one who failed as a father. But that's another terrible thing that led to beautiful things for me, because I wouldn't give up my nan for anyone.

She was my champion long before Barry and Dee Dee showed up, and she's my favorite person in the world (even if she does cheat at *Super Smash Bros. Brawl*). I hope she feels the same way—I'm pretty sure she does.

My phone chirps, and it's like a siren. Everyone in the room sits up and looks toward the sound. I don't dive for it, because come on, but I do move expeditiously across the room to pluck it up. Swiping the lockscreen away, I smile at Alyssa's name, all lit up. `Turning down your street right now. Can't wait to see you!`

"Is she coming?" Dee Dee asks.

"Of course she's coming," Barry says, then looks to me nervously. "But she is coming, isn't she?"

I hold out the phone so they can see it with their own eyes. I don't blame them for asking. I barely slept last night myself.

Part of it was knowing that this huge thing is happening and all eyes are on Edgewater again (still?).

In the last two days, a squadron of news vans have shown up, and this time, it's not just Hoosier stations. I saw CNN parked in front of Beguelin's Pancake House in town and NBC, like *the* NBC, not just the local station, circling the school with their camera hanging out of the window.

There were new protestors yesterday, too, but they were banished to the cornfield across the street. They're not even *from* here. They're from that publicity-sucking church out west that does this for a living. In a way, it's almost an honor. Hey, we made the big time: national bands of bigots have arrived!

The best thing about that protest is that the *Godspell* kids came back in costume after their matinee in Terre Haute. The whole front page of our town newspaper had a picture of biblical figures clowning on the out-of-towners. Video of it ran on all the news stations last night, too, and it's still trending on Twitter.

But I admit that some of my sleeplessness was because I was . . . I'm not even sure what the right word is. *Afraid* is too big. *Anxious* is close. It's just that my bones and my body ached, hoping that this time, Alyssa would show up. That everything really would be different.

Most of my brain was fully engaged: Of course she's going to show. Everything has changed! It was just this small, silver worm of worry wriggling through me, squeaking, *But what if?! But what if?!*

As of this text, in this moment, that worm is dead. Now

I'm nervous for a whole new reason, and that's because it's prom night. My legendary suit fills me with power, and I leap at the door to throw it open when I hear an engine out front.

Oops, it's our neighbor, Mr. Martin, pulling in after his shift at the transmission factory. I wave at him, then hang from the door frame to look down the street.

I feel Barry and Dee Dee crowd in behind me, and we all watch in breathless anticipation. After approximately five million years, a dark car appears and glides toward us. It's black and sleek and looks completely out of place in our little neighborhood. It's perfect!

"Get back inside," Dee Dee says. "Act aloof. A little mysterious. Don't make her think you're desperate."

Of course, the second the limo stops, I bound out of the house. I feel like I could jump over roofs, but guess what? Gravity is still a thing! I can barely jump off the porch, and I bobble when I land. It's okay, though, because Alyssa throws herself out of the limo and we all but crash into each other in the middle of the yard.

"You look so good," she says at the same time I say, "Oh my god, you're gorgeous." We babble at each other, and honestly, I have no idea what we're saying. It's all just joyful, positive-sounding yammer, punctuated by kisses. In public! In my front yard!

I don't think cis, straight people realize how many of our kisses happen out of sight. As magical as it is to hold hands at the movies, it's incredible to hold hands on the street. A hug in a park, a nuzzle at a concert—even when you're out in Indiana, those things don't seem possible.

They are; they can be—but they're scary and dangerous, too, because you just never know what the people around you might do when they see it.

So this? This moment? I can barely breathe. I'm so drunk on sunlight and kisses bathed in them that I actually lose my balance. Alyssa catches me, and then I catch her, because we're this tangled-up, gloriously clumsy ball of pure emotion right now. There's glitter in her eye shadow and the taste of strawberry in her lipstick, and I could honestly explode from the feels right now.

"I have flowers for you," she says, gesturing at the limo. "I left them in the car."

Nobody's ever bought me flowers before. I swoon and squeeze her hands. "Wait here, I have your corsage."

Turning, I bound back into my house (nearly missing the second porch step) and almost careen into Barry. I'm so full of love right now, I could explode, and I throw my arms around him. Hugging him tight, I tell him, "You'd better save me a dance."

"As if you even have to ask," he tells me. He takes my hands and steps back, inspecting me one last time before I leave. His face is flushed, and his smile is so warm. If I didn't know better, I'd say he's on the verge of crying. He suddenly waves a hand to fan his face. "Get out of here, kid. Go get your girl."

I rise up on my toes to kiss his cheek, then turn to take the boxed corsage from Nan. She strokes my cheek, and then, like the secret monster she is, pinches it teasingly. "Your curfew is?"

"Whenever," I say, giggling.

"Very good," Nan says, and sets me free.

I look to Dee Dee for any last-minute advice, but she's face-down in pound cake and a box of tissues. I take that as a no, pack myself with zazz, and get the hell out of there. I wave and Dee Dee waves, and then I'm back out the door and down the steps to Alyssa.

The wrist corsage matches Alyssa's dress, lavender ribbon with white and lavender carnations. When I put it on her, she looks at it like I pulled out a bracelet from Tiffany or something. There are too many people tearing up right now, and it's going to make me cry, too.

"It's perfect," Alyssa says.

"I'm glad you like it," I say.

And then, because we can, because we're in the middle of my lawn, because we fought our way up a mountain to get here, because she's beautiful, because I *can,* I kiss her again and linger so long on the petal softness of her lips. I'm alive with spark and fire, and I tighten my hands on her waist.

"You ready to do this?"

"So ready," she says, her dark eyes gleaming.

And just like that, we jump in the limo and drive off into our own personal sunset—which in this case just happens to be our prom.

I never wanted much. Just to hold Alyssa's hand and walk through those gym doors and wrap my arms around her waist while she wraps hers around my neck. To dance slow to fast songs and take pictures under a hand-painted photo booth banner.

All I ever wanted was to watch the lights sparkle across her skin and share a cup of truly regrettable punch in an overheated gym.

And tonight, it happens. This is more than I dared wish for; it's epic, and there's room for everyone. Room for kids from my school. For kids from far away. For gay kids and lesbian kids, pan kids and bi kids. Ace kids are here, and trans kids, too. Nonbinary kids and cis kids. Straight kids and questioning kids and queer kids. It's a whole new family, and we're all coming out for our own big night.

We built a prom for everyone. And with those cameras watching across the street, we're showing the world that it can be done. *Godspell* escorts meet kids in the parking lot: nobody walks in alone. We stream into the gym and the marquee tents; we take selfies and fill plates and cringe as we sip the inescapable nuclear punch.

The beat of the drum urges us to take to the floor, and we do, and we move like nobody's watching. When the music blares, nobody cares who you're with. And all those miserable people across the street, still protesting? I'm sure they can feel the bass; they *have* to feel the joy.

And me? I just wanted to dance with Alyssa. Alyssa Greene, church picnic flirt and student council president. We made it here, and here we are. Under the lights, under the stars, under the disco ball, under the tents, out in the parking lot, up and down the street, everywhere in Edgewater, Indiana, and wherever you're from, too—let's go.

It's time to dance.

Broadway Score! scores a chat with Dee Dee Allen and Barry Glickman at the office of their newest endeavor, PROM FOR EVERYONE!

(cont. from page 1)

. . . a handsomely appointed office in the Flatiron, though not one that affords a view. The space is interior but bright, with photos on the wall from the prom they held last year in Edgewater, Indiana, after a gay teen there went viral with her story of discrimination. Glickman, with his trademark bombast, can hardly sit still in his Aeron chair. Allen sits on the edge of the desk, arranged and ready for a photo at any moment. Their mood can best be described as ebullient.

BS!: So you were booed at the school and the monster truck rally. What happened next?

BG: A tragedy. An absolute travesty. An abomination!

DA: They threw a fake prom for our girl and shattered her delicate little heart. We were gutted. I barely slept for days.

BS!: I can imagine. But then Emma posted that incredible video, and support came pouring in from all over the world. I know I watched it at least a hundred times.

BG: I still get verklempt thinking about it.

DA: I mean, what a star turn! She racked up millions of views practically overnight. We were going to get her booked on Kimmel, but with numbers like that . . .

BG: She did end up doing Kimmel, with Alyssa.

DA: She did. She did. [She looks away for a moment.] I can't remember the last time I did Kimmel.

BG: Fourth of never, darling.

[They laugh.]

BS!: After the video went massively viral, you put together a prom for everyone. You made Emma's wish come true.

DA: We spared no expense.

BG: Alyssa Greene, Emma's sweetheart, was the architect. Definitely the brains of the operation.

DA: But money makes the world go round, as they say! And boy, did we make it go around!

BS!: Which leads us to today. You've opened the PROM FOR EVERYONE organization. That's a nonprofit group you created to host more inclusive dances nationwide. Where will you be opening the doors next?

DA: Iowa.

BG: Idaho.

DA: Another corn-fed backwater hamlet. It's charming; they have one stoplight!

BS!: And after that?

BG: Proms across America. Everywhere Broadway goes in a bus, we'll be there right behind. And we're also working on a little something . . .

DA: We're writing our own show!

[They speak over each other, but after a moment, Glickman speaks for both of them.]

BG: We are, in fact, writing our own show. We've got most of the book done; we have feelers out for just the right composer. In our wildest dreams, Casey Nicholaw comes in for choreography and direction.

BS!: That sounds incredible. What's the show about?

DA: Our journey to Indiana and back again, the agonies, the ecstasies—we'll play ourselves, of course.

BG: We're thinking about calling it *THE PROM*!

ACKNOWLEDGMENTS

This is the happiest project I've worked on, and I'm honored that I got to be the one to bring Emma and Alyssa's side of the story to the page. That never would have happened without the amazing show that Bob Martin, Chad Beguelin, and Matthew Sklar brought to Broadway, and then trusted me with in prose; thank you.

I owe many thanks to Caitlin Kinnunen and Isabelle McCalla, Brooks Ashmanskas, and Beth Leavel, whose chemistry and performances informed every word I wrote; thank you. Heartfelt thanks to the entire team at Viking and at *The Prom* for coming together to make this book happen. It's been a privilege and an honor!

All my love and thanks to my brilliant editor Dana Leydig, who thought of me for this project, and ran through the gauntlet with me. You once said Ravenclaw and Slytherin are a very dangerous mix; we're also a mix that gets stuff done!

Finally, thank you, thank you, thank you to my agent, Jim McCarthy, who has been regularly making my dreams come true since 2012. Thank you for this, thank you for everything we've already done together, and thank you for the future I see more clearly because of you.

—Saundra Mitchell

We would like to thank Casey Nicholaw for his leadership, Dori Berinstein and Bill Damaschke for their intestinal fortitude, Jack Viertel for his cleverness, Izzy McCalla for her humanity, Brooks Ashmanskas for his audacity, Beth Leavel for her belt, Angie Schworer for her legs, Chris Sieber for his hair, Caitlin Kinnunen for her overall, unwavering Caitlin-ness, and Saundra Mitchell for connecting with our show so deeply, and filling in the blanks so brilliantly. Additionally, we would like to thank Cait Hoyt and Erin Malone for making the deal and Dana Leydig and Eileen Kreit from Penguin Random House for making it real.

—Bob Martin, Chad Beguelin, & Matthew Sklar

The producers of *The Prom* musical, Dori Berinstein, Bill Damaschke, and Jack Lane, would like to acknowledge Broadway show conceiver Jack Viertel; director/choreographer Casey Nicholaw; show creators Bob Martin, Chad Beguelin, and Matthew Sklar; the spectacular cast of *The Prom*; and our entire *Prom* family behind the curtain. We'd also like to thank general managers Aaron Lustbader, Lane Marsh, and Nick Ginsberg, and our *Prom* co-producers and investors. A million thanks also to our house and company management team, including Marc Borsak and Alex Wolfe as well as Kenny Nunez and the crew at the Longacre Theater. Thank you to Clint Bond, Meghan Dixon, and the team at On the Rialto; Polk & Co., including Matt Polk, Colgan McNeil, and Kelly Stotmeister; the Situation team, led by Damian Bazadona, Pippa Bexon, and Rian Durham; and our AKA family, including Scott Moore and Jacob Matsumiya. And a special thanks to the wonderful Rose Polidoro.

Turn the page for more about the musical, the show creators, and the cast of *The Prom*!

Notes from Co-Writer Bob Martin on *The Prom*: the musical

May 2010. Chad, Matt, Casey Nicholaw, and I meet with Jack Viertel, venerable producer/writer/artistic director and all around musical theatre guru. Casey has brought us here to the Jujamcyn offices on West 44th street because Jack has an idea he wants to pitch. "A small town girl tries to take her same sex partner to the prom, but the school won't let her. A bunch of Broadway performers come down to fix things. They make it much worse." I'm paraphrasing, but that's how I remember it. Jack pitched us, in a few words, the premise for a rollicking musical comedy with heart; a show rooted in a harsh sociopolitical reality, but littered with ridiculous characters doing stupid things. We said yes.

November 2018. We open on Broadway. Quite a bit happened in those eight years. Yes, a musical was written and rewritten, workshopped, choreographed, staged, and re-staged. But more significantly, the sociopolitical context in which the show was conceived changed dramatically. There was actually a point early on in development when we thought that the show might no longer be relevant. Lots of progress was being made, particularity in the area of LGBTQIA+ rights, and there was a general sense of optimism in the air. Well, incidents of the kind described in the libretto continued to happen, and then a contentious, bitter election split the country in half. Suddenly people found themselves on either side of a vast, unbridgeable cultural divide. Our show seemed more relevant than ever.

Perhaps that's why the army of people involved in shepherding *The Prom* from premise to Broadway show are so passionate about it. We are all desperately in need of hope. We all feel Emma's pain when she realizes that the whole town has conspired against her, we all cry when Barry dances with joy in his motel room after being told he is finally going to prom, and we all struggle with Mrs. Greene as she tries to see her daughter for who she is instead of who she wants her to be. The cast, the crew, everyone around the production table, we're all a mess after every run-through, because the show is filled with painfully relatable truths. In the end, *The Prom* is about how a small, rickety bridge is built in Edgewater, Indiana, between two sides of the culture wars. We hope that those who see *The Prom,* and those who listen to the recording, will laugh and cry and get inspired to build something of their own.

—Bob Martin

The following are excerpts from an interview conducted by cast member Josh Lamon with the creative team of Bob Martin, Chad Beguelin, and Matthew Sklar during a launch event for *The Prom* in New York City.

JOSH LAMON: From your perspective as a lyricist, as co-book writer, what has the show been like going through the changes from day one around the table, to the labs and Atlanta, to now?

CHAD BEGUELIN: It's changed so much. I think the biggest change, I mean, we're constantly tweaking it and working on it, but the world sort of changed. We were thinking that the world has gotten so much more accepting and wondering if this was as relevant, and then the election happened, and it suddenly became so important and so relevant. All of these things we thought we were past—suddenly the show took on this new level of immediacy. I couldn't predict that would happen. It's been a great journey and having this great cast has been so much fun for all of us to write for. It's been great.

We were really concentrating on this last pass of the script and the score to make sure that we didn't show the other side to be completely caricatures. We wanted to make sure that everyone was dealt with fairly—these people just had different beliefs and they had to work through them throughout the show.

JOSH LAMON: One of my favorite things about *The Prom* is that it is hilarious but also serious. We are talking about an actual story that happened.

BOB MARTIN: Several actually. It's based on several incidents that happened and continue to happen across this wonderful country.

JOSH LAMON: What was it like tackling the comedy versus the serious material?

BOB MARTIN: I like the combination of making potentially unpalatable truths easier to take when they're surrounded by people like you. You're the sugar that makes the medicine go down easily. I think what's really interesting about this show is that people cry, but it's an extremely funny show. As you can see there's a mixture of very broad comedy and the very grounded, serious story at the heart of it all. It was remarkable to have people come up to us after the show and be so moved. I had this woman come with her head down and confess that she was the mother depicted in the story, with tears in her eyes making this confession to us. I think it is a very moving show for that very reason.

JOSH LAMON: What was unique about this process for you?

MATTHEW SKLAR: Well, it's one of the first times I've ever really written something completely original from the ground up. Anything else I've ever written has had some kind of source material. So this was a great opportunity, and I just love working with these guys [Chad Beguelin and Bob Martin] and with Casey [Nicholaw]. I think we all bring out the best in each other. The story is just so moving. Once we started outlining the story, seeing where it was going, and figuring out where the songs would go, it felt like both sides complemented each other—the comedy and the dramatic aspect of it. It's been a joy to work on.